Michael Wood is a freelance journalist and proofreader living in Newcastle. As a journalist he covered many crime stories throughout Sheffield, gaining first-hand knowledge of police procedure. He also reviews books for CrimeSquad, a website dedicated to crime fiction.

www.michaelwoodbooks.co.uk

X x.com/MichaelHWood
facebook.com/MichaelWoodBooks
instagram.com/MichaelWoodBooks
BB bookbub.com/authors/MichaelWood

Also by Michael Wood

DCI Matilda Darke series
For Reasons Unknown
Outside Looking In
A Room Full of Killers
The Hangman's Hold
The Murder House
Stolen Children
Time Is Running Out
Survivor's Guilt
The Lost Children
Silent Victim
Below Ground
Last One Left Alive
Worse Than Murder

Dr Olivia Winter series
The Mind of a Murderer
The Devil's Code

Standalones
The Seventh Victim
Vengeance is Mine
Chapter One

DCI Matilda Darke short stories
The Fallen
Victim of Innocence
Making of a Murderer

WORSE THAN MURDER

MICHAEL WOOD

One More Chapter
a division of HarperCollins*Publishers*
1 London Bridge Street
London SE1 9GF
www.harpercollins.co.uk
HarperCollins*Publishers*
Macken House, 39/40 Mayor Street Upper,
Dublin 1, D01 C9W8, Ireland

This paperback edition 2025

1

First published in Great Britain in ebook format
by HarperCollins*Publishers* 2025

Copyright © Michael Wood 2025
Michael Wood asserts the moral right to
be identified as the author of this work

A catalogue record of this book
is available from the British Library

ISBN: 978-0-00-861880-3

This novel is entirely a work of fiction. The names, characters and incidents portrayed in it are the work of the author's imagination. Any resemblance to actual persons, living or dead, events or localities is entirely coincidental.

Printed and bound in the UK using 100% Renewable Electricity
by CPI Group (UK) Ltd

All rights reserved. No part of this publication may be reproduced, stored in a retrieval system, or transmitted, in any form or by any means, electronic, mechanical, photocopying, recording or otherwise, without the prior permission of the publishers.

Without limiting the exclusive rights of any author, contributor or the publisher of this publication, any unauthorised use of this publication to train generative artificial intelligence (AI) technologies is expressly prohibited. HarperCollins also exercise their rights under Article 4(3) of the Digital Single Market Directive 2019/790 and expressly reserve this publication from the text and data mining exception.

To Andrew Barrett
CSI supremo and crime writer extraordinaire.

Tuesday 11 August 1992
High Chapel, Cumbria

Alison Pemberton opened her eyes. It took a while for them to adjust from the darkness to the brilliance of the August sunshine. She'd been leaning against a tree, head down, eyes closed, counting, listening for the sounds of her sisters running away to hide. She heard the giggles and the swish of the long grass, but they were soon replaced by silence. She looked around her and saw nothing. Normally, she would be scared to be on her own, but this was a game, and games were fun.

'Coming. Ready or not,' she called out.

Alison, dressed in pink shorts and a white top, white-blonde hair pulled back into bunches, skipped over the knee-high grass.

In the last game, it had been Alison's turn to hide, and she'd hidden behind the prickly bush that scratched her legs. She headed for there now, hoping to find one, or maybe both, of her sisters crouched behind it. They weren't there.

She turned around as a warm breeze picked up. The grass swayed, but there was no other movement. Her sisters had hidden well.

They weren't behind the dead tree. They weren't under the overhanging bush. They weren't lying down in the dried-up stream, and they weren't hiding in their makeshift den.

Alison frowned, but she wasn't overly worried. She could still see her back garden and her house from here. If she didn't find them, she would just go home and tell their mum. Celia was so good at hide-and-seek though. She will have taken Jennifer's hand and run off to the best hiding place.

Alison stood stock-still and looked around her. Celia might be good at hiding, but she was terrible at staying quiet. She'd be struggling to hold in her laughter, and the urge to jump up and shout 'BOO!' to make her scream would be too much for her to hold in. All Alison had to do was stand and watch and wait and listen.

There was no sound. Even the wind had stopped.

Alison stood in the centre of the field and turned in a circle, looking for any sign of her sisters.

She heard something. It sounded like a car door slamming closed.

Alison wasn't allowed to go to the road on her own without either her mum or dad, but she went anyway. She ran to the edge of the field, up the slight incline and picked her way through the bushes. She stepped out onto the smoothness of the road, looked right, and saw nothing, looked left, and saw a car driving away.

In the back, her sisters, Celia and Jennifer, were looking at her out of the window. Jennifer waved.

Alison waved back.

It must be game over, she thought.

Alison watched as the car disappeared out of sight before scrambling back through the bushes, down the incline and back into the field. She didn't give her sisters a second thought as she picked up her sausage dog on a string and began playing on her own.

'Come on, Stanley, be a good boy,' she said to the dog.

Her stomach growled and she wondered how long it would be before her mum called her in for something to eat.

Thursday 17 June 2021
High Chapel, Cumbria

As PC Alison Pemberton enters the briefing room at High Chapel Police Station, a cheer explodes. Everyone rises to their feet and applauds. Alison stands in the doorway and blushes.

Inspector Gill Forsyth walks over to her and puts her arm around Alison's shoulders. She guides her to the front of the room to face the entirety of the police station – all eight of them.

'Ladies and gentlemen,' Gill begins. 'We have in our midst a true hero, a remarkable and selfless individual who, on Tuesday evening, while off duty, came to the aid of a man in great distress.'

A ripple of laughter runs around the room. Alison shakes her head in embarrassment.

Gill continues. 'Putting the lives of innocent bystanders before her own, PC Pemberton leapt into action and took control of what could have been a most dangerous and savage situation. I want you all to look at PC Pemberton with pride and hold her up as the true icon and role model she is. Congratulations, PC Pemberton.'

More applause rings out.

'You're all sods and I hate you,' Alison says once they finish mocking her.

'Fortunately,' Gill says. 'Thanks to the wonders of modern technology, there was a bystander on hand to capture PC Pemberton's heroics and post a photo all over social media. And, this morning, I received a delivery from the printers.'

Gill turns Alison around to face the incident board. There, in all its Technicolour glory, is a huge glossy print of Alison frog-marching a naked man down the High Street, one hand squeezing his arm, the other covering his private parts with her beanie hat.

Alison's embarrassment shoots through the roof. She puts her head down and struggles to hide her laughter.

'No prizes for guessing what the station's Christmas card will look like this year,' Gill says.

'I'm so making a calendar of this,' PC Guthrie says.

'We should have it put on a T-shirt,' someone else calls out.

'Good idea. You can put a photo on anything these days – socks, duvet covers, scarves, anything.'

Alison turns around and faces the room. She finds her composure from somewhere.

'I know you all expect me to be embarrassed,' she says. 'But I'm not,' she lies. 'I was simply doing my duty, and I'd do the same again should the occasion arise. And, fingers crossed, it will arise again at the weekend as we're having drinks together on Saturday.'

Everyone in the room cheers as Alison makes her way to her desk. The best way to get over an embarrassing situation is to own it.

'Are you really going out with him on Saturday,' PC Lydia Marsh asks her quietly.

'Of course, I'm not, Lydia, bloody hell.' Alison rolls her eyes.

'I wouldn't blame you. He's got a good body on him.'

'Why would I want to go out with a drunk who streaks through the whole town? I mean, where's the surprise now?' She winks.

'Okay, everyone, that's enough,' Gill says, bringing the room back to order. 'Can we return to some normality and get some work done now, please?'

High Chapel Police Station is not a busy one. It isn't the centre of a thriving metropolis. They're not struggling under the weight of a lawless community, though drug crime seems to be on the increase. Any major incidents are coordinated with several patches around the county, the largest being the central hub at Kendal. High Chapel is merely a focal point for the local community, particularly in the summer months during the tourist season.

'Now, the Met Office has issued a yellow weather warning for Saturday afternoon going into the early hours of Sunday morning. There's a storm coming, and they've aptly named her Storm Gill. As you know, storms are relentless, unpredictable bitches who can often be violent and deadly. You can understand why they've named this one Gill,' Gill says with a mock-severe expression. 'However, this one seems to be unseasonably strong, so we need to be prepared. All leave is cancelled from Friday onwards. The local farming community is out in force delivering sandbags to shops, restaurants, and hotels. We shall be helping wherever possible. What I want you all to be doing between now and when the storm hits is to get out there and reassure our local residents and the tourists visiting the area. Guthrie and Marsh, I want you two to pop along to the school and say everything right to stop the kids from worrying, and make sure everything is prepared for it to be used as an evacuation centre should it come to that. Dixon, James and Stokes, I want you walking the streets, popping into the local shops and seeing if they need anything. Daniels and Pemberton, I want you two to have a drive out to the farms and make sure everyone is on standby should the village flood. Before you go out, I need a word with you both. Hop to it, everyone.'

Everyone files out of the room while Daniels and Pemberton remain in their seats, waiting until the room clears.

It's another stifling hot day, and the fans are whirring away. Everyone has their fingers crossed the storm will take the edge off the temperatures.

'We've had a call from Nature's Diner,' Gill says. 'There's been another attempted break-in. You have to pass there to get to Peak Farm.'

'Another one? What is that, the third?' Sergeant Claire Daniels asks.

'The fourth, actually. Each time, they've never been able to gain access to the restaurant, but they've caused damage trying. This time, it would seem, a window was broken around the back. Now, I don't need to remind you who the owners of Nature's Diner are, or who their son is.'

'No,' Claire says.

Alison shakes her head. 'I've met Carl a few times. He's a lovely lad. Quiet.'

'He's bound to be.'

'It's not going to be related, though, is it?' Claire asks. 'I mean, it was years ago.'

'The people who kidnapped Carl were never caught,' Gill says. 'The couple who bought him are now in prison, but we don't know if they ever met the kidnappers or how much of them Carl saw. It is possible they could be coming back to try and silence the boy, or to frighten the family. Now, I've spoken to Philip and Sally Meagan, and they've increased their security. The whole place is covered with CCTV cameras and a panic button has been installed that goes straight to Kendal should anything happen. I want you two to reassure the Meagans we're doing everything we can to keep them safe. Take a forensic kit out with you and dust for prints, if you think it's required. If you suspect anything, give me a call, and I'll get someone senior from Kendal out there.'

'Yes, ma'am,' Claire says.

Alison and Claire stand up and begin putting on their jackets, ready to leave.

'Joking aside, Alison, I'm very proud of your actions on Tuesday night,' Gill says.

'Thank you, ma'am.'

'Lucas Brierley was drunk, he'd taken goodness knows what, and he has a history of violent behaviour. If you hadn't intervened, and he'd managed to get home to his wife, who knows what could have happened? Well done.'

It isn't often Gill Forsyth gives out praise and it's clear she isn't comfortable doing so. However, the words were meant, Alison can see that. Gill turns and walks quickly out of the incident room, sensible shoes clacking on the tiles.

'Wow,' Claire says, astonished. 'I thought she was going to hug you, for a moment.'

'Now, that would have been awkward.'

'While it's just the two of us,' Claire says, a dirty grin on her face and lowering her voice. 'When you were walking Lucas to your car on Tuesday night and you had your hand around his whatsits, did you cop a feel?'

'Claire!'

'I'm only asking. Was it a handful, or… you know.'

'I'm not talking about this with you,' Alison says, picking up her hat and heading for the door.

'Looking at that picture, your hand does look pretty full,' Claire says, following her.

Worse Than Murder

'Aren't you supposed to be engaged?'
'Yes. I'm engaged, not dead.'
'And also two months pregnant.'
'It doesn't stop me looking.'
'Claire, the guy is a drunk.'
'He's also very fit.'
'You disgust me. Come on.'

On 25 March 2015, two men broke into the detached house of Philip and Sally Meagan in an affluent area of Sheffield, South Yorkshire. Philip and Sally were away for the evening, attending an award ceremony in Leeds. Seven-year-old Carl was being looked after by Philip's mother, Annabel. The two men bludgeoned Annabel to death and kidnapped Carl. Days later, a ransom demand for a quarter of a million pounds was made for Carl's safe return. The exchange was to be made on 28 March at Graves Park at nine o'clock at night.

The investigation was led by Detective Chief Inspector Matilda Darke. On the day of the ransom drop, Matilda's husband died. He'd been suffering with an aggressive brain tumour. She had kept his illness private, and told nobody about his death. She returned to work as if everything was normal, clearly in denial.

Nine o'clock came and went. There was no sign of the kidnappers. Matilda's phone rang, piercing the silence of the night with its shrill call. She answered and the kidnappers asked, angrily, where she was.

Suffering with a grief she couldn't comprehend, Matilda's mind was not on the task at hand. There were two main car parks to Graves Park. One was at the Meadowhead entrance close to the tennis courts and bowling green; the other was at Hemsworth Road near the animal farm. The kidnappers were waiting next to the animal farm while Matilda was parked close to the tennis courts. Believing it to be a set-up, the kidnappers fled, taking Carl with them. Matilda was ordered to take time away from work and Carl disappeared without trace.

In 2019, a neighbour saw a child playing in the garden of a house in Gothenburg, Sweden. Knowing his neighbours had no children, and therefore no grandchildren, he made discreet enquiries only to be told there was no child at the house. When he saw the child again, he contacted police. The couple, unable to have children, had bought the young Carl from illegal traffickers and were raising him as their own. Carl was taken by the police to be reunited with his parents.

Finally, in October 2019, after four years and seven months, Carl returned home to Sheffield.

The Meagan family decided to leave the Steel City for a fresh start. Less than a year later, they sold the family home and the chain of restaurants that had consumed their time, and moved to the Lake Distract to start life afresh. Instead of building a large empire, they decided to scale back their business and bought a single restaurant in a picturesque part of the country. Philip and Sally's aim was to give Carl the best upbringing they could provide.

Now, it seems someone has a vendetta against the Meagans, as their lakeside restaurant, which they live above, has been targeted four times in as many weeks. Whoever is doing this has not managed to gain entry to the restaurant, nothing has been stolen and no damage has been done, as such. If it wasn't for who the owners of the restaurant are, police might not be taking as much interest in the case.

However, despite six years passing since Carl was taken, his kidnappers, the murderers of his grandmother, are still out there, and Carl, despite not being able to give much of a description of the two men, is the only witness.

Claire and Alison are often paired together, which they love. They've been best friends since the dawn of time and joined the police together. Claire is itching to climb the promotional ladder. She has dreams of becoming a chief constable, wearing power suits and being a complete bitch, whereas Alison has allowed her past to absorb her and is trailing behind her friend.

Claire is in her mid-thirties and petrified of turning forty, despite it being five years away. She's engaged to Geraint Turner who is a government official overseeing the decommissioning of the Sellafield nuclear site on the coast of Cumbria. Their wedding is planned for next summer, when, hopefully, she will have her figure back from having their unplanned baby. When she isn't working, she and Geraint can often be found in the hills of Cumbria walking miles and posting disgustingly happy selfies on Instagram. Despite the sometimes grim nature of the job, Claire nearly always has a cheerful smile on her face.

Alison, at thirty-four, is single and lives alone in the house she's grown up in. Her mother and stepfather live just around the corner on their farm. Alison had wanted to be a police officer since she was young. The urge to discover what happened to her sisters, and her dad, was too much to ignore, and it had bled into her soul and consumed her. The job isn't about promotion for Alison. She doesn't want to break the glass ceiling, scale new heights and be the youngest police commissioner in the country. All she wants to do is use the skills she has learned to find out the secret that has been plaguing her family for thirty years. It's what keeps her awake every night and gives her the constant air of darkness shrouding her.

They pull up in the marked police car outside Nature's Diner. It's an old building, dating back to the 1930s when it was originally a schoolhouse, later a convalescent home for injured soldiers during the Second World War, then a schoolhouse again, before it closed down in the 1960s. A property developer bought it in the 1970s and made it a family home. Unfortunately, the high price demanded made it virtually unsellable and it was left empty until the early 1980s when it was turned into a restaurant. Under the guise of various themes, it didn't last long and eventually closed, seemingly for good, in 1990. Then, the Meagan family came along in 2019 and saw the potential to turn it into an exclusive organic restaurant to tap into the tourist market.

Their timing hadn't been great. As they were due to open, the world was plunged into lockdown due to the Covid-19 pandemic. They turned their restaurant into a takeaway business until they were able to open their doors to an eager public desperate to return to some degree of normality, sample food not cooked by themselves and see what the latest incarnation of the restaurant had to offer.

When Nature's Diner finally opened in late 2020, it was an overnight success. Excellent food, comfortable surroundings, stunning views from picture windows, and the rumour of the celebrated owners, had kept the restaurant fully booked for months.

Claire and Alison make their way up the wooden steps and knock on the glass door of the restaurant. They peer inside as they wait. The place is in darkness. It's only early, and the restaurant doesn't open until lunchtime.

'I hope this storm cools the temperatures a bit,' Claire says. 'This uniform isn't made for a heatwave.' She adjusts herself. 'I had to wring my bra out last night.'

Alison pulls a face. 'Really?'

'Yes. I get very sweaty under my boobs. My greatest asset is my biggest flaw,' she says, giving her cleavage a squeeze.

Alison stifles a laugh. 'I love how ladylike you are,' she says, mockingly.

'How can you be ladylike in this bloody uniform? Mind you,' she begins, a dirty smirk appearing on her face, 'The other night, me and Geraint—'

'Oh, look, someone's here, thank goodness,' Alison interrupts, relieved at being saved from another graphic conversation about Claire and Geraint's sex life.

A figure emerges from behind the bar and comes over to the door. Philip Meagan is a tall, slim man. He wears his thinning hair cut short, is clean-shaven, and walks with a straight back and the large strides of a confident man. He smiles when he sees the two women in uniform, and this lights up his face, giving him a friendly, approachable look.

He unlocks the door. 'Good morning. Come on in,' he says with that warm smile.

'Mr Meagan. I'm Sergeant Daniels from High Chapel Police Station. This is PC Pemberton. We're here about the attempted break-in.'

'Yes. Well, it wasn't a break-in as such. They didn't actually gain entry, but they did crack a window in the utility area. Would you like to come through?'

'Sure.'

Philip leads the way with Claire following and Alison bringing up the rear. They walk among the tables towards the kitchen. Alison looks out of the huge picture window at the expansive view of Lake Windermere. It is beautiful scenery.

'We understand you have excellent security, Mr Meagan,' Claire says.

'Philip, please. Yes, the whole place is surrounded by CCTV and there's one above the door to the utility where the glass was broken. I've looked and it would seem that the angle of the camera was moved, somehow, before the attempted break-in.'

'They didn't appear in view of the camera before it was moved?'

'No. I'm guessing they used a pole or a large stick to move it, then sneaked in under the radar. I've ordered some cages from a security company to put around the cameras. These people always seem to think one step ahead, don't they?'

'I'm afraid so.'

They enter the utility area which is a large space, filled with industrial dishwashers and a walk-in fridge.

'Did the alarm sound when the glass was broken?' Claire asks as she kneels down to look closer at the broken window.

'It's a silent alarm. I received notification on my mobile and tablet. There's a sensor light in every room on this floor. The room would have lit up. Maybe that's what spooked him, and he ran off.'

'Do you have anything valuable on the premises, Mr Meagan?' Alison asks from further back in the room.

'All restaurant equipment is expensive. I'm not sure what the second-hand market is like for an industrial food mixer, but I'm sure it could be sold for a few quid to fund a drug habit.'

'Do you keep a lot of cash here?'

'No. All of our transactions are by card.'

'Alcohol?'

'Yes. We have a small range of wines and spirits, but we are hoping to extend that this year.'

'I think I read about that in the local paper. You've received planning permission to turn the basement into a wine cellar, haven't you?' Claire asks, standing to full height.

'Yes. It's just dead space down there and it would be perfect for a wine cellar. We could expand our range and do tasting events,' he says. His face shows his excitement for the new project.

'We'll get the forensic kit from the car and test the door handles either side for prints, but…' Claire says, trailing off.

'Thank you. I've got Warren coming out to replace the glass later, is that okay?'

'That's fine. You are doing everything right with regards to security. Hopefully, if they do try again, you'll have the cages up next time and we'll get a clearer picture of who is doing this. I'm just sorry you're having to go through it,' she says in her best placatory tone.

'Thank you,' he says, seemingly mollified. 'Can I get you both a tea or coffee?'

'I thought you'd never ask,' Claire says with a smile. 'As soon as you opened the front door, I got a whiff of coffee, and it set me off. I'd love a double-shot Americano with just a splash of oat milk and half a spoon of brown sugar.'

'No problem. Would you like anything?' he asks Alison.

'I'll have a tea, please.'

'Any milk preference?'

'I'm not as pretentious as Claire. Good old cow's milk is fine.'

Back in the main part of the restaurant, Philip begins making the drinks while Claire and Alison go out to the car for the forensic kit.

'Do you do private parties?' Claire asks on returning.

'Occasionally.'

'Would it be cheeky if I asked for a special price for my wedding next year?'

'Yes, it would be bloody cheeky,' Alison says. 'You can't use your position for personal gain. It's called corruption.'

Claire's face drops as the realisation dawns. 'Oh my God, it is, isn't it? I'm so sorry,' she says to Philip.

He struggles to hide his laughter.

'It's fine,' he says. 'I'm sure we can do you a good deal, simply as a local, and not as a police officer.'

'I… Thank you. I… I'll just…' Claire says, reddening with embarrassing and running back into the utility room, while Alison turns away to stifle a laugh.

'Mr Meagan,' Alison says, stepping up to the bar.

'Philip,' he reminds her.

'Sorry. Philip. When did the first attempted break-in occur?'

'The first one was about three weeks ago, maybe four, now,' he says, setting the hot drinks down on the counter.

'Did anything strange, unusual, or different to the norm, happen around that time to attract attention?'

Philip pauses for a moment. 'No. Not that I can think of.'

'I see.'

'Although,' he begins. 'We have a friend staying with us at the moment. She arrived just before the first attempt.'

'Could this be connected with her?'

Philip struggles to find the correct words to use. He opens and closes his mouth a few times before saying, 'It's complicated.'

'I don't understand,' Alison frowns. 'Who's your friend?'

'She's called Matilda. Matilda Darke. Detective Chief Inspector Matilda Darke from South Yorkshire Police. She's sort of… in hiding.'

In 2017, I ran the Sheffield Half Marathon. It was... well, let's just say it was an experience and one I have no intention of ever repeating. However, it's strange how life events can force you to change your mind about things. I've never been one for exercise. I eat fairly healthily apart from the odd bag of Maltesers, maybe a Crunchie every now and then and a couple of Snickers, and I'll not mention my alcohol intake. But apart from that, I'm pretty sure I'm in reasonably good health. Mentally though, I'm well and truly fucked and I've found the only things that stop me from overthinking and going completely insane are running and swimming. I even borrowed a bike yesterday and went for a cycle around the lake. I could enter the 2024 Olympics as a triathlete at this rate.

Shit. My eyes have blurred. Here come the tears.

Distraction. Distraction. I need a distraction.

I wonder what I'll be having for tea tonight? I fancy a big juicy steak. I hope Philip has one going spare I can nab. Maybe with a crispy jacket potato and some salad. Lovely.

Two months ago, I received an anonymous email from someone claiming to have committed five perfect murders. I've been a police officer for more than twenty years, a detective for more than fifteen. I know there's no such thing as the perfect murder. There was something about this that felt different, though. I don't know if it was the wording or what, but I had to look further into the claims. It turns out, whoever was doing this was right. He'd defeated me.

The first victim, twenty-year-old university student Liam Walsh suffered with depression and anxiety. He wanted to kill himself but didn't want to die alone. He accessed the dark web and posted a message on a suicide message board looking for someone to enter into a suicide pact with him. The killer was waiting online and groomed Liam. At the top of the Art's Tower in Sheffield, one of the city's tallest buildings, the killer revealed his true identity and pushed Liam to his death. Liam had left behind a suicide note for his mother and the coroner accepted this to be true. Liam's death was registered as suicide.

Twenty-year-old Josie Pettifer was the second victim. The killer ingratiated himself into her life and they developed a relationship, which, unbeknown to Josie, was completely one-sided. Josie suffered with many allergies, one of which was a peanut allergy. While preparing a meal, Josie's faux boyfriend laced her salmon with peanut oil. She had a massive anaphylactic shock, and the killer simply sat back and watched her die. Her death was recorded as a tragic accident.

Victim number three was eighty-six-year-old Audrey Wildgoose. She had recently been diagnosed with dementia and was being looked after by kindly neighbours until a place could be found for her at a nursing home. One morning, a neighbour visited to find the back door wide open. Audrey was later found in a nearby park. All signs pointed to her dying from exposure. If it wasn't for me receiving these emails from the killer claiming his victims, the coroner would have stated that Audrey had simply left the house one night, and in her confusion, had been unable to remember the way back home.

There was a marked difference with the fourth victim. The previous three all had elements to their personalities a killer could take advantage of, and they'd all appeared, at one time or another, in the local newspaper, which is how we believed he was finding his victims. Natasha Klein was different.

Nineteen-year-old Natasha was a wannabe influencer – not a proper job, if you ask me. She lived her life by social media. How she appeared on the killer's radar, I couldn't work out. Maybe he'd been spying on her social media pages and become obsessed with her. Until I catch him, I won't know the truth. Natasha was listed as a missing person and her disappearance made headlines around the country. The tabloids love a beautiful teenager. A candlelight vigil in Sheffield city centre went viral for all the wrong reasons. It wasn't long after that I received another email telling me where he had left Natasha. I found her hidden in woodland. She had died from hypothermia and exposure. He'd simply left her there to die a slow and painful death.

Four victims down, one to go.

Why do I keep going over this in my head? I'm pushing myself. I'm literally killing myself every time I think about this. Why don't I just put myself out of my own misery by walking into the lake with a couple of rocks in each pocket?

The killer called me. He phoned me and told me that he'd been watching me. He knew all about my mum's recent money worries and the fact her gas fire wasn't working properly. He told me my mum was his final victim.

I couldn't get to her house fast enough. Looking back, I've no memory of the journey. I called my sister, Harriet. She told me she was just returning from a weekend away in Scotland with her new boyfriend. She had left her sons, beautiful Joseph and Nathan, with our mum. All three of them were in that house. We found them… dear God… we found them… they were dead. Joseph and Nathan, teenagers with their whole lives ahead of them. They were in bed and looked as if they were sleeping. Mum was clinging to life.

I shouldn't be thinking about any of this. That's why I go running. That's why I pound the uneven ground of the Cumbrian countryside, to put my body through so much pain that I focus on my aching joints and muscles and not the torment going through my mind. If only I could flick a switch and turn my brain off.

Four days after Nathan and Joseph's lifeless bodies were discovered, four days after Mum was rushed into hospital, four days since the last email from that bastard killer telling me his work was complete, and me and Harriet were sitting either side of our mum's bed in a private room at the Northern General Hospital. We'd hardly spoken. Harriet blamed me. Every time we made eye contact, I could see the hatred there. I don't blame her. I'd hate me, too. In fact, I do. I hate myself.

Dr Felicity Wilde walked into the room. Her face was ashen. I knew what she was going to say before she even opened her mouth. I remember the conversation word for word. It's on permanent repeat.

'I've had a meeting this morning with two consultants.' She was using a low, sympathetic tone. I wanted to slap her. 'We've looked at your mother's charts and condition and I'm afraid it doesn't look likely there will be any improvement. We've run all manner of tests, as you know, and there is no function in the brain whatsoever. It's only the machines she is currently hooked up to that are keeping her alive. We all agree that it would be in all of your best interests if we switched them off.'

"We all agree…" We? Who is the we? I haven't been asked. Harriet hasn't been asked. We're her daughters. Why not ask our opinions?

To say the relationship I had with my mother was fractious would be an understatement. She never liked my job. However, in recent years, especially since the death of my father, the ice had started to thaw. I genuinely did love my mum. I turned to look at her. She looked old. Her eyes were closed, her skin was dry and free of makeup, her hair was flecked with grey. She would have hated how she looked right then. If I was being honest, I'd known for days that Mum was gone, just by looking at her. There was no life emanating from her at all. I'd clung on to the merest hint of hope. Now, Dr Wilde was telling us that there was no hope.

I looked up and across the bed to Harriet. Tears were streaming down her face. I wanted to rush around and hold her tight and never let go, but I knew she wouldn't allow it.

'Is there nothing you can do?' Harriet asked.

It was a pointless question. I knew the doctors had done everything possible for Mum. They'd really gone above and beyond.

Dr Wilde shook her head. 'Your mum's brain was starved of oxygen for too long, I'm afraid.'

Harried grabbed for a tissue on the bedside table and loudly blew her nose. 'Mum wanted to be an organ donor…' she said, leaving the sentence open.

I knew this wouldn't be allowed to happen. Mum's death would be investigated as part of an ongoing murder case. There would be no chance of her organs being donated while that was carried out.

'Unfortunately,' Dr Wilde began. 'The amount of carbon monoxide your mum inhaled, added with the lack of oxygen, will have made the organs unusable for transplantation.'

Harriet cried more tears. Mum always wanted her death to have meaning, to have her organs live on in someone else. I thought that was very generous of her. Harriet always found it creepy but, faced with Mum's death, she seemed to have come round and found it comforting that Mum's heart could beat again in someone else's body. Not now, though.

'When?' Harriet began. 'When do we... you know?'

'There's no rush,' Dr Wilde said. 'Take time to say goodbye. Come and find me when you're ready.' She turned on her heel and left the room. She couldn't get out fast enough.

When we're ready? When can anyone ever be ready for killing their mother?

The atmosphere plunged as me and Harriet made eye contact.

'Mum always hated your job,' Harriet eventually said. Her voice was low and heavy with vitriol. I'd never seen her so full of venom.

'I know.'

'She dreaded getting the call saying you'd been killed or maimed in the line of duty.'

I nodded.

'In the past few years, things have happened to you that have hurt this family. You've been shot, kidnapped, knocked unconscious and driven into a reservoir. You've been stalked. Even on Christmas Day, someone came to your house and put a noose on the front door to taunt you. The signs were all there that one day something horrible, something devastating, was going to happen to your family. You could have stopped all of this horror from happening.' Harriet spoke slowly. She was struggling to keep hold of her dark emotion. I could see she was shaking with fear.

'Nothing I could have done—' I began.

'You are poison,' she interrupted.

I hated myself even more for doing this to Harriet. She looked drawn. She seemed to have aged twenty years in the past few days. She was barely recognisable as the confident, fun-loving single mother I admired.

'You're the angel of death. Everywhere you go, everyone you're in contact with either dies or has something shocking happen to them. You've killed my boys, Matilda. *You've* killed them.'

There was nothing I could say. I was already blaming myself.

Harriet sniffed hard. She tucked her knotted hair behind her ears and composed herself. 'Joseph and Nathan will be buried at Hutcliffe Wood next Tuesday at ten o'clock. I don't want you anywhere near there.'

'What? Harriet, they're my nephews.' I needed to say goodbye to them.

'You killed them,' she said again. Her harsh voice was a mere whisper, quivering with pent-up anger itching to escape.

'I had no idea…'

'I don't want to hear it,' she said, wiping away tears as they fell down her face in a torrent. 'I can't stop you coming to Mum's funeral, but I don't want you anywhere near me. I don't want you to look at me, or talk to me, ever again. As far as I'm concerned, I'm an only child.'

'Harriet.'

She stood up and headed for the door. 'I'm going outside for some air. We'll talk about what to do for Mum when I get back. But when this is all over, you and me are finished. I never want to see you again.'

'Harriet, wait,' I jumped up and grabbed her arm. That was a mistake.

She shook me off and spun round to face me. Her eyes were

wide. She looked as if she was about to lunge at me and gouge my eyes out.

'When Dad was shot, Mum begged and pleaded with you to leave the police force. She told you to think of what you were putting her through every time you went to work. You ignored her. This is the consequence of that. You killed my dad. You killed my sons. You killed my mum. And you've killed me.' She leaned in close, her face a mere inch from mine. I honestly thought she was going to hit me. I wish she had done. 'I *fucking* hate you,' she spat.

Harriet stormed out of the room, leaving me on my own.

I went back to the bed, sat down, and took my mother's hand in mine. 'I'm so sorry,' I said to her. I meant it but it sounded hollow. Harriet was right. I'd destroyed everything.

I don't know how I got through the next week. The day of my mum's funeral is a blur. I remember returning home to my house and I didn't know what to do. I poured myself a drink, a large vodka, and I wondered what was the point in carrying on anymore. I rummaged around in the messy drawer in the kitchen and found a few boxes of paracetamol. I managed to get together around twenty. Would that be enough? That's how bad it was. I wanted to die. I was prepared to kill myself.

I didn't, obviously. I think the thought of killing myself frightened me more than the act itself. I packed a bag and headed for the Lake District. I needed to leave Sheffield behind, confine it to the pages of history. Philip and Sally had reached out to me when the news of what had happened had broken. They offered me a place to go if I needed time away. That's what I needed. Time away.

I've been here a month now. I haven't spoken to them about

what happened yet, about a serial killer plaguing me, taunting me, destroying everything in my life, and they haven't asked, either. They know I'll open up when I want to, in my own time. They've learned, from when Carl returned home, that it's important to allow the one who is suffering to recover in their own time. They've been so good with Carl and his recovery. And now they're being good to me.

My life now consists of going out every day to run or swim in the lake. Sometimes more than once a day. Right now, I'm running. I run until my legs are numb and it feels like my lungs are about to explode, and when I get that feeling, I run harder. I need to feel the agony. I need to punish myself. Many times I have to stop in order to throw up beside a tree. Then, I'll give myself a few minutes to recover, swill my mouth out with the water bottle attached to my hip, then off I go again, running, running for my life, running away from myself.

Alison and Claire have been around the farms to check they are prepared and on standby should the forecast storm hit as hard as predicted. On their way back to High Chapel, with Claire driving, Alison digs out her phone and opens Google. The mention of DCI Matilda Darke by Philip Meagan has been niggling away at her mind for most of the day. She's heard of Matilda, obviously – she has made the news many times due to the high-profile investigations she's successfully led over the years – but Alison wants to know what has brought Matilda all the way to the Lake District. Has whatever was happening to her in Sheffield followed her to Cumbria?

'I mean, I like some of the old-fashioned names,' Claire says as she pulls up at a red light. 'For a boy, I quite like Harold and, if it's a girl, I'm torn between Maud and Ethel. But Geraint wants to name her after his grandmother, if we have a girl. She's a lovely woman, don't get me wrong, but I can't call my daughter Clementine. Are you even listening?'

'Sorry?' Alison looks up.

'Have you heard a word I've just said?'

'Yes.'

'Really? What was I talking about, then?'

'Erm, something about satsumas?'

Claire puts the car into gear and sets off. 'Oh God, I'm definitely vetoing Clementine. I don't want no daughter of mine coming home from school in tears because some little bitch has called her an easy peeler.'

'What are you talking about?'

'It doesn't matter. What's so important you're engrossed in your phone? You're glaring at it like naked pictures of Ryan Reynolds have just been leaked online.'

'You wish.'

'I do, actually,' she says, wistfully. 'I wish my Geraint looked like Ryan Reynolds.'

'Geraint is a very good-looking guy,' Alison says, without looking up from her phone.

'He is. But he's no Ryan Reynolds. When he grew that moustache during lockdown he looked more like Bert Reynolds. I still can't believe he left the house with it. We wouldn't be getting married if he'd kept it.' She turns to Alison to see her still scrutinising her phone. 'Are you going to tell me what you're looking at?'

'Philip Meagan said that DCI Matilda Darke from South Yorkshire Police was staying with them. She arrived just as the attempted break-ins began. I'm wondering if they're connected.'

'And how is Google going to help you with that?'

'There's an article here written last month for the *Guardian* by Danny Hanson. Apparently, there's a killer in South Yorkshire who's been taunting Matilda, sending her emails, telling her who and where his victims are. According to this, he did something to Matilda's mother's gas fire to make sure it leaked and killed her by carbon monoxide poisoning.'

'Bloody hell.'

'At the time, Matilda's two nephews were staying with her mother, and they died too.'

'But how do they know the killer purposely tampered with the fire? Couldn't it have been a genuine case of carbon monoxide poisoning?'

'No. The killer told Matilda what he'd done in an email.'

Claire creases up her face. She looks sceptical. 'But if Netflix has taught us anything, it's that serial killers are, by design, liars. How can we take what he said to be true? Maybe he's a fantasist. Maybe he found out they'd died in a genuine accident and wanted to claim it for himself.'

Alison looks up from her phone for the first time. 'Huh. I suppose that could be true. Maybe. Bit of a coincidence, though.'

'Either way, it's sad about her family. No wonder she's decided to have a break for a while. Now, do you want me to drop you off at home or are you coming back to the station?'

'Actually, could you drop me off at the stables? I want to visit my mum.'

'Sure.'

'What are your plans for this evening?'

'Quiz night at the Frog and Toad. It's a rollover. First prize is £150.'

'Wow. A life-changing amount.'

'If I don't come in tomorrow, you'll know I've won and am currently in Tahiti,' she smiles.

Claire turns a corner and pulls up outside the front gates to Alison's mum's home.

'Send me a postcard,' Alison says, climbing out of the car and closing the door behind her.

Alison lets herself into her mother's cottage. She makes her way along the dark and narrow hallway into the brightly lit kitchen.

Lynne is at the sink, washing vegetables dug from the garden. She's wearing her usual beige gardening trousers, that are filthy and have seen better days, and a cotton long-sleeve T-shirt with the sleeves rolled up. Her greying hair is tied back into a messy bun. Alison goes to the radio and turns down Kate Bush.

Lynne spins round quickly. Her sad, lined face lights up into a smile upon seeing her daughter. 'Oh, hello. I didn't expect to see you this evening.'

Alison puts her arm around her and kisses her on the cheek. 'I thought I'd pop in. You don't mind, do you?'

'Of course, I don't. You're always welcome here.'

'Where's Iain?'

'He's out checking the stables. Have you heard about the storm forecast?'

'Yes. We've got the local farmers on standby. They'll be doing the rounds with sandbags from Saturday afternoon. Any chance of a brew?'

She holds up her dirty hands. 'Could you help yourself?'

'Do you want one?'

'Please. I don't feel like I've stopped all day.'

'Been busy?'

'Hay delivery came. Two hours late. Wrong again, as usual. I spent over an hour on the phone only to be told their new computer system was having teething troubles. The vet came out to put poor Agides to sleep. Julie was inconsolable. Of course, she was left to me to comfort. By the time her Brian came to pick her up, it's three o'clock and I've hardly done any of what I had planned for the day.'

'Poor Julie. She loved that horse.'

'She did. But twenty-seven is a good age and he had a good life.'

'Oh, how was the meal last night?' Alison asks, suddenly remembering.

'It was delicious,' Lynne answers, her eyes almost rolling into the back of her head. 'That has to be the best Chinese restaurant in the whole of the country.'

'Fifteen years married,' Alison says.

'I know,' Lynne replies, wistfully. 'Who'd have thought...' She stops herself and returns to scrubbing the vegetables.

Alison takes her mug to the small table, pulls out a chair and sits down. She looks around the busy kitchen and takes in the ornaments on the walls and windowsills, postcards stuck to the fridge with magnets. It's such a homely, comfortable place, but appearances are deceiving and there is always an element of sadness in the air.

'Are you all right, love?' Lynne asks, glancing at her over her shoulder.

'Yes. Fine.'

'You look very pensive.'

'I want to ask your advice on something.'

'Oh. Okay,' she says, rinsing her hands under the running tap and drying them on a tea towel. She comes over to the table and sits down. 'I'm all ears.'

'I'd like to ask you and Iain. It concerns you both.'

'This sounds serious. Should I be worried?' she asks, her face dropping.

'No. Well, it is serious, but it's nothing... I'm not ill or anything.'

'Oh, good,' Lynne reaches across and places a comforting hand on her daughter's. She looks around. 'Where did I put my mobile? I think I left it in the living room. I'll give Iain a ring and tell him to pop back. He'll be glad of a break in this heat.'

It's another ten minutes before Iain comes into the cottage via the back door. He spends a full minute wiping his wellington boots on the doormat. He enters the living room wearing combat trousers and a navy polo shirt which is past throwing out. There are so many holes in it, Alison wonders if he is ever confused which one to put his head through.

Iain has worked outdoors since the day he left school. He joined his dad running the family farm. Unfortunately, his father had hidden the truth about the costs of the farm and, when he died, Iain saw that he had spent his entire life in poverty. The farm wasn't working, and Iain had no intention of following in his father's footsteps. The animals were sold, and Iain turned the barns into stables and the land into a paddock. He made more money in a month renting out to horse-owners than his father had earned in a year. The success was bittersweet.

Iain is tall, well over six feet. He towers over Lynne. Their wedding photographs are a lesson in comedy. His face is ruddy, his hair permanently windswept and his shovel-sized hands are covered in cuts and callouses.

'Do you want a tea?' Lynne asks.

'No. I've just finished my flask.'

'How are the stables?'

'Fine. They should hold. I'm going over to Kendal tomorrow to get more groundsheets just in case we lose any tiles.'

Alison sits in the armchair and watches the play between her mother and stepfather. She misses her dad every day, but is glad her mother has moved on. What happened all those years ago was unbelievably sad and painful. She was only a small child at the time so had no comprehension of what her mother was going through, but she's pleased she has Iain for support. Alison remembers, fondly, fifteen years ago, when her mum and Iain sat her down and told her, with earnest expressions, that they planned to marry. They were worried how Alison would react to her mother marrying her uncle, her father's brother. They had been through such torment; she was over the moon that they had found happiness with each other.

'You wanted to talk to us,' Lynne says, turning to Alison.

She clears her throat. 'I did. I was called out to Nature's Diner this morning.'

'Oh, yes?' Lynne asks, sipping her tea.

'Yes. They've had another attempted break-in. The thing is, the Meagans have got a friend staying with them at the moment, and she's a police officer. A detective. She's taking some time off.'

She pauses and Lynne and Iain look at her with blank faces, waiting for her to continue.

'She's a DCI.'

More blank faces.

'I was thinking about maybe popping along to see her and having a chat.'

Iain frowns. 'What for? If you want promotion, wouldn't you be better off talking to Gill?'

'No. I'm not looking for promotion. Well, I am, obviously, but not right now. No, this detective, DCI Darke, she's worked on some really big cases over the years. I thought I might ask her about... Celia and Jennifer. And Dad,' she says, her voice quietening towards the end so as not to upset her mother and stepfather.

Silence fills the room. A clock on the mantelpiece chimes the top of the hour.

'Why do you think she'll be able to help? Why after all this time? Is there new evidence?' Lynne asks, her questions tripping over each other.

Iain reaches forward and places a hand on her shoulder.

'No. Not that I'm aware of. It's just… she has this amazing track record. She's a brilliant detective. She may be able to find something nobody else has.'

Lynne stands up and goes over to the armchair, perching herself on the arm. She takes her daughter's hand in her own and squeezes it comfortingly.

'Alison, sweetheart, do you really think it's wise getting someone else involved? I don't think your boss would be too pleased about it. She might think you're… what's the word?' she asks, looking to Iain.

'Usurping.'

'That's it. She might think you're usurping her, that you don't have any confidence in her as a detective.'

'Inspector Forsyth is a brilliant police officer, but she's never had a case like this before. Nobody has around here. This DCI Darke, she's worked on some really tricky stuff. I've been reading up on her.'

'Alison, why don't you talk to your boss first?' Iain suggests. 'See what she thinks. You don't want to step on her toes. You need to think of the future and promotion. It's not going to look good if you're seen as someone without respect for rank.'

'Iain's right.' Lynne reaches up and strokes Alison's hair behind her ear. 'You were too young to know what was going on back then, sweetheart. It was a difficult time. For all of us. I wish there could be some resolution to it, but we have to face facts that they might never be found.'

Alison swallows her emotion. 'And what about Dad? There have been sightings…' Her voice quivers.

Lynne steals a glance at Iain, then quickly back to her daughter. 'Alison, your dad was a very fragile man. He struggled with what happened to Celia and Jennifer. He couldn't… he refused to come to terms with it. It was all he could do to end the suffering.'

'I thought he loved me,' Alison says through her tears.

Lynne grips her hand tight. 'He did love you, Alison. He loved all of you. But when something tragic happens like that, when your whole life is turned upside down and you have no control over it, sometimes… sometimes you can't see the good for the bad.'

'I miss him,' she says, quietly.

Lynne pulls Alison into a tight hug. 'I know you do. I miss him, too.'

Lynne looks over to Iain. He nods at her and quietly leaves the room, giving mother and daughter some alone time.

It's another half an hour before Iain hears the front door close. He has finished washing the vegetables and is busy putting them away when Lynne walks into the kitchen.

'I wasn't expecting that conversation today,' Lynne says.

'Are you all right?'

'Yes. Fine. I look at Alison and I see her father looking back at me. She's got so many of his ways. Normally, I don't think anything of it, but there are times, like now, where it all comes flooding back.' She pulls out a chair at the table and sits down. 'How the hell did I get through those days?' she asks, putting her head in her hands.

Iain places a comforting arm around her shoulder. 'What did you tell her?'

'The same thing I've been telling her since she was old enough to understand. Her father sank into a depression, and he walked out into the lake. The thing is, she's always thought that, if her father had drowned, he would have been found by now. Because he hasn't been, she's got this niggling notion there is a remote possibility he could still be out there, living a new life somewhere. Those sightings haven't helped, either. People can be so cruel, can't they?'

'Surely Alison is sensible enough to know that he won't still be alive after all this time?'

'She is, but, well, you know what grief's like. It plays all kinds of tricks with your mind.'

'Who's this detective she said is staying at the restaurant?'

'DCI Darke, did she call her?'

'Do you think she'll go and see her?'

Lynne thinks for a long moment. 'I really don't know. Iain, I know we've talked about this before, but do you think we should tell Alison the truth?'

'We can't do that, Lynne,' Iain says. There is an edge to his voice. 'It would literally kill her.'

I walk into the living room and Sally and Philip spring apart like a couple of teenagers caught necking. They don't look at me and they've stopped talking. I know I've been the subject of conversation.

I've just had a long and scalding hot shower after my run. I'm in my dressing gown and I feel warm and cosy. It's a feeling that won't last for long.

The living room is huge. There is a massive picture window looking out over Lake Windermere. The sun is setting, and the sky is a burning red. It looks like a painting. You can't look out at this view and not take comfort. Being in the countryside has helped me enormously.

'Good shower?' Sally asks. She's tucked up on the end of the sofa. She's wearing a flowing summer dress in vibrant colours. She always looks immaculate. She says it's because she needs to look good for the customers, but she's one of those women who could wear a bin bag and look elegant. Even her feet are gorgeous, and, in my opinion, feet are the ugliest part of the body.

'Lovely. Thanks.' I sit down on the sofa opposite and look at them in turn. 'So, what's going on?'

'Nothing. Why do you ask?'

'You've both got guilty expressions.'

'No. We were just chatting,' Sally says, giving Philip a side-long glance.

'About me?'

'Erm...' Sally looks to Philip again, then back to me, then back to Philip. 'No. Well, not *not* about you.'

Oh dear. I've been waiting for this.

'Have I outstayed my welcome?'

'No. Absolutely not,' Philip says firmly.

'You haven't, Mat, honestly,' Sally agrees.

'It's just,' Philip begins. 'We had the police here earlier, while you were out running. They've taken prints around the utility door, but one of the PCs – can't remember her name – she asked if anything has changed since the first attempted break-in. The only thing that did was you arriving. Now, we've just been talking, and we can only see maybe three reasons behind the break-ins. One, that possibly you've been followed here. Two, Carl's kidnappers have come back for him. Three, it's totally random vandalism.'

'As far as I'm aware, nobody knows I'm here.'

I've noticed, lately, that my words sound slow and slurred, as if I'm drunk. I'm not. I sometimes think my body is too tired to even speak. I'm not sure if that's because I'm knackered from all this exercise or the grief is weighing me down.

'Mat.' Sally tucks her hair behind her ear. I've recognised this as her tell for being nervous. She does it with awkward customers, but she always manages to get the upper hand. 'How likely is it that they're coming back for Carl?'

'After all this time, I'd say very unlikely. Although...'

'Go on,' Sally prompts me.

'Carl's case is never closed. The cold case review unit looks at it every now and then. We still want to bring Annabel's murderer in. Maybe they've launched another investigation. Maybe they've been asking questions and they're getting close this time. Or, on the other hand… no.'

I really should think before I speak sometimes.

'What?' Philip asks.

'I don't want to scare you.'

'We're already scared.' Sally reaches over to Philip. He takes her hand.

'Put yourself in the shoes of the kidnappers for a moment. The type of people who kidnap a child for ransom and kill someone in the process are going to be involved in criminal activity of various kinds. Whatever they're up to, they're going to worry about people knowing who they are. Let's say, for example, one of them just happened to be here in the Lake District and saw Carl. They might worry he's going to recognise them and go to the police.'

'Jesus,' Sally says under her breath.

'So, you think one of the kidnappers has inadvertently found us?'

'I'm not saying that at all. It's just an option. But I don't believe it.'

'Why not?'

'Because he's tried to gain access to the restaurant four times and failed. He wouldn't have done that. And I don't believe he would try to kidnap Carl again. He'd…' I stop myself this time. I don't need to say it. We all know that, rather than risk being identified, the kidnapper would just kill Carl and do a runner. 'This has nothing to do with Carl,' I say, hoping to allay their fears.

Sally lets out a heavy breath. 'That's a relief.'

'It's just a random chancer wanting to steal a few bottles of vodka, then?' Philip asks.

'Or the serial killer has followed me here from Sheffield. I should probably leave. I don't want to put any of you in danger.'

'We don't want you to go,' Philip says. 'Carl loves you being here. We both enjoy you being here.'

Their kindness means so much to me. I can feel emotion rising inside me and tears pricking my eyes. Since when did I get so soppy over a few complimentary words?

'He killed my mum and nephews,' I say. 'I have no idea who he is. I don't know how long he's been watching me. I don't know if he's a random stranger with a fixation or if he's someone I know. I know nothing, and that scares me. I can't have any more people I know being put in danger.'

'We have CCTV all around this building, and a panic button,' Sally says. 'You're safe here and we want you to stay.'

I smile and nod. If I open my mouth, who knows what will come out.

'Besides,' Sally continues, 'We've got so many weapons in that kitchen should he get in here. He doesn't stand a chance against us.'

'She's right. Have you seen how Sally whips up an omelette? She's a nightmare with a whisk.'

Philip's attempt at humour lightens the mood a tad. I smile, but it hurts to do so.

I turn on the sofa and look out of the window. The view sprawls over the lake. The surrounding trees stand tall and lush and green, and they don't move an inch in the breezeless evening. It's like the world is holding its breath, waiting for me to decide what I'm going to do next.

I sigh and I can feel my body relaxing. I love it here. It's peaceful. It's the perfect place to recuperate. But there's an edge. Someone is out there; I can feel it. Right now, I'm not a detective, I'm a woman filled with a mixture of raw emotion –

grief and anger. If the killer shows his face and comes for me, I'm more than ready for him, and I'll kill him with my bare hands, if I have to, and fuck the consequences.

'Tea?' Sally asks.

'Please,' I smile.

When Lynne married Iain, the mortgage to the house she had lived in with her first husband, Jack, and the three girls, was more or less paid off. Lynne said that Alison would inherit it one day so she may as well take it on now and continue paying what was left of the mortgage while she moved in with Iain in the cottage overlooking the stables.

It was the house Alison was born in, the house she took her first steps in, the house she played in with her older sisters, where she sat on her dad's knee by the fire in the evenings while he read her a story. It was a house of happiness for the first five years of her life. After that, it was a house of pain, but it was one she couldn't leave. Despite it being decorated several times over the last thirty years, furniture changed, new carpets, new front door, it was still the home her parents had built, and she needed to hold onto those memories.

Alison had no idea of her part in the drama that surrounded her father's disappearance. On that fateful night, she had been plucked from a half-submerged car, wrapped in warm clothing, and taken to the safety of her home where she was put to bed. When she woke the next day, everything had changed yet again. She had no idea how or why.

Returning from her mother and stepfather's house, Alison closes the front door behind her and heads straight upstairs to strip off her uniform and have a cooling shower. The heat of the day intensified as it went on and she thinks of Claire as she unhooks her bra.

Going down the steep, creaking stairs, in a baggy T-shirt and loose shorts, Alison pours herself a glass of wine from the fridge and goes into the living room where she slumps on the sofa.

Looking around the small room, it is difficult to believe her mother and father planned to bring up three girls here. She has asked her mum on many occasions if they'd have moved once the girls had grown bigger and she had replied with a firm no. Her mother loved this cottage, the garden, the location. Some evenings, Alison would lie back on the sofa and close her eyes and imagine how three teenagers would have coped with the cramped space. She smiles as she pictures the rows about sharing a bedroom, one sister taking another sister's jacket or makeup without asking, her mother being the go-between, and her poor father with a constant headache in the middle of four bickering females.

She opens her eyes and sees she is the only one left in this house. Everything is a play in her head. When she recalls her actual teenage years, it is with a heavy heart. Anniversaries are always remembered – her sisters going missing, her father walking out into a swollen Lake Windermere. When Alison's birthday comes around, or Christmas, or Easter, they're tinged with sadness. They should be huge events with family gathered, not one person getting all the attention from a single parent and a step-parent with painted-on smiles. How can Christmas lunch be enjoyable with three empty places around the table? Exam results, passing her driving test, getting into the police force: all of these achievements were clouded by wondering what Celia and Jennifer would have been doing with their lives now.

Alison sits on the sofa and pulls out a leather-bound photo album from the shelf beneath the coffee table. She does this most nights when she's alone, which is often, too often. It's a thick and heavy album. Alison rests it on her lap and turns the pages. She smiles at the pictures of Celia and Jennifer in the same cot, wrapped in the same blanket, wearing matching baby-grows and hats. The identical twins balanced precariously on her father's knee with him beaming proudly to the camera. A similar set-up of her mother holding them both, looking tired but happy. A candid shot of her father pulling a face as he changes a nappy. A photo taken in this very back garden of her father on a blanket in the middle of the grass, two toddlers finding their feet, crawling all over him. The look on his face tells Alison he is loving every minute of it. Then, the photo Alison loves the most, the one of two girls dressed in their best clothing, sitting on the sofa, carefully cradling their new baby sister.

Alison wipes a tear away before it has a chance to fall. With every passing day, she remembers them less and less. She sometimes has to close her eyes tight and fights through her memories to the short time they spent together. She can't remember their voices or their laughter. She has no recollections of their touch and, when she enters their former bedrooms, she can't picture them there.

Even that day when they disappeared is fragmented. She doesn't know what a genuine memory is and what is what she's been told by her mother or read about in the many newspaper clippings she's saved. They were playing in the field behind the house. It was summer, the sky was a hazy blue, the sun was shining, the heat was intense, the grass was dry and hard to the touch as the three girls laughed and played. Then they were gone.

One question Alison has been asking herself for the last thirty years, the question everyone had been asking her at the time, was what the hell was the colour of the car?

She couldn't remember. Even now, she can't picture it. Sometimes it's red, sometimes blue, sometimes green, occasionally it is white or black or brown or beige. And, no, she didn't know what model it was. How many five-year-olds can tell the difference between a Fiat and a Peugeot?

Alison slams the album closed. She hates herself for being unable to remember. At first, she thought it was a game, that Celia and Jennifer were going to turn up in a few minutes and laugh, but as time slipped by, she knew they weren't coming back. Alison had gone back to the house, back to the garden, picked up her stuffed sausage dog on a string and began walking it around the garden, talking to it. How long was it before her mother came out of the house to ask where her sisters were? How long before she began to panic? How long before the police were called?

Alison looks up. Through tear-filled eyes, she sees a framed photograph on the mantlepiece of her sitting on her father's knee. It was taken not long before he walked to his watery grave. He's smiling, but the pain, the grief, the sadness, radiate from him. He has his arms threaded around his only surviving daughter, holding onto her tight. The five-year-old Alison has no idea what is going on and is smiling proudly to the camera. She is with her dad. He's her favourite person in the world. She's happy.

'I'm so sorry,' Alison says.

For nearly thirty years, Alison Pemberton has been told that all the tragedy that has befallen the family was born from one single act over which nobody had any control. Nobody could have foreseen that someone would kidnap Celia and Jennifer, that they would never be found, that her father, tormented and tortured by grief, would walk into a river during a storm and never be seen again. It was a snowball event. One tragedy after another. The only person to blame was the sick bastard who had stolen the twins in the first place. Alison certainly wasn't to blame.

It doesn't seem to matter what anyone tells her. Alison was the only person there on that day. There wasn't much a five-year-old could do, but if she'd have been paying more attention to the car, if she'd have tried to remember the colour of it, the make of it, any part of the registration number, if she'd done more than simply wave then go back to the garden to play with her toys, they might have been found. If so, her father wouldn't have drowned himself. He would still be alive today. Depression and sadness would not leech from her walls. Alison would be happy instead of faking it every single day of her life.

She grabs for her laptop and googles DCI Matilda Darke again.

For the next hour, Alison reads news story after news story about the cases Darke has investigated over the years. Matilda is an exemplary detective. She heads the Homicide and Major Crime Unit at South Yorkshire Police. She caught serial killer Steve Harrison. She arrested Stuart Mills, the killer of sex workers and the husband of one of her own team members. Jonathan Harkness got away with murdering his parents for more than twenty years, until Matilda reopened the case. Laurence Dodds jumped off a building rather than face arrest by Matilda and she was instrumental in cracking a historical child sex abuse ring that involved MPs, a chief constable, and high-profile businessmen. This is a detective who refuses to take no for an answer. Matilda Darke has faced murderers, rapists, serial killers and paedophiles, and she hasn't even flinched.

Alison has no idea what is going to happen, and she dreads how her mother will cope with the emotional upheaval of reliving everything again, but Matilda Darke is the woman she needs right now.

It doesn't take long for Philip Meagan to fall asleep. He works long hours in the restaurant and, by the time he falls into bed, he reads a couple of chapters of a Tom Wood, then reaches for the bookmark, turns over, and is snoring within seconds.

On the other side of the bed, Sally Meagan stays awake much longer. She's on her feet all day, too, sorting out the restaurant, mingling with customers, organising staff, and talking with suppliers, but when it comes to going straight to sleep, her mind is too switched on to allow her to simply close her eyes and drift away. She's sitting up, thin blanket pushed down, and looks at how many pages she has left of the latest Lynda La Plante. She's pretty sure she will finish it tonight. She snuggles down and begins reading. It isn't long before she's interrupted.

It's only a faint sound at first, but as it grows in its intensity, Sally can hear Matilda along the hallway struggling to muffle her cries. This happens most nights. Sally has no idea if Matilda is sitting up in bed, wide awake, crying for her dead family, or if she is crying in her sleep as her nightmares go over everything in minute detail.

Sally never tells her the following morning that she's heard her cry. She knows that Matilda will open up when she is ready. She wishes there was something she could do for her. All she can think of is popping into her bedroom and offering a placatory hug. That won't change the fact that evil has taken over Matilda's life. There are times when the raw emotions need to be allowed to play out. Once you hit rock bottom, that's when you need a good friend to help you back up. This is one of those times.

'I fucking hate you.'

I wake up with a start. My sister's words are always in my head. Every now and then, they're screamed at me and hit me like a freight train.

I struggle to sit up in the tangle of the cotton sheet. I'm dripping with perspiration and my pillow is wet with tears. Another nightmare. A repeat of the same horror I've been dreaming about for weeks. My family is dead. It's my fault. I may as well have butchered them with a knife.

I kick myself out of the sheet and place my bare feet on the carpet. It takes effort for me to lift myself off the bed and leave the room. I'm thirsty and hot. I'm hungry, too. Thank goodness I'm living above a restaurant where there are so many well-prepared goodies for me to gorge on for a midnight snack.

I push open the door to the kitchen. The cool tiled floor is heaven to my burning feet. There's already a small light on above the central island. Sitting there is thirteen-year-old Carl Meagan wearing a T-shirt and pyjama bottoms, sipping water from a glass. He looks up at me with heavy, tired eyes.

'Can't you sleep either?' I ask him.

He shakes his head. 'Too hot.'

'Same.'

'You do know you can't lie to me, don't you, Mat?'

I've got my head in the fridge, but I turn to look at him. There's a strong connection between the two of us, considering he's thirteen and I'm fort... a bit older. We've both been through so much torment. Often, we can spend hours in each other's company, not say a single word, yet we'll know what each other is thinking and feeling.

I know I shouldn't have burdened a teenager, but Carl is the only person I've opened up to about the events in Sheffield. On one of our walks with the dogs, we found a quiet spot by the lake, and I said one thing and, before you know it, it's all coming out and I can't stop.

In the fridge, I find a large piece of raspberry and almond frangipane tart. I grab two forks from the drawer and go over to sit beside Carl. I hadn't spotted the two golden Labradors at his feet. I should have known they would have followed him from his bedroom. They're his shadow. They never leave his side.

'I keep having the same dream,' I say, tossing him a fork. 'I run into my mum's house. She's dead. They're all dead, but they're talking to me, blaming me for killing them.' I pause while I put a forkful of tart in my mouth. I chew, but I find it hurts to swallow with the emotional lump stuck in my throat. 'They say some dark, horrible, hurtful things. And I agree with every single word they say.'

'You're blaming yourself.'

'Wouldn't you?'

He chews and swallows. 'Yes. But I'd know, deep down, that it wasn't my fault.'

I look up at him.

'You are not responsible for other people's actions.'

'I'm a detective. It's my job to catch killers.'

'Yes. But if you don't catch them and they go on to kill others, is that really your fault?'

'Yes.'

'Why?'

'Because I couldn't catch them.'

'What about the other members of your team? Christian and Sian. Do they blame themselves? Do the DCs and the PCs who do the house-to-house inquiries? Does your boss? Does every single member of South Yorkshire Police blame themselves?'

'I...'

'No, they don't,' Carl answers for me. 'The reason why they don't is because they're trying their hardest to catch the person responsible. And if they don't, they know there are many reasons why they didn't catch him this time. But they will. Eventually.'

'He killed my family,' I say, struggling to speak through the pent-up tears.

'I know. This one is personal. It's going to feel hard. But you've worked on serial killer cases before. They've killed others during the investigations while you've tried to catch them. You weren't responsible for those deaths and you're not responsible for the deaths of your mum and your nephews.'

'I wish I could believe that.'

'You will. But not for a while.'

I take a big piece of tart and chew it slowly while I think. I look over at Carl. He's below average height for his age, not even five foot tall, yet. His hair has lightened in the strong summer sun, but he seems relaxed in his home surroundings. There's still a pain in his eyes from time to time. He'll be sitting on the sofa, squashed between two dogs, watching a film, but you can see that he's somewhere else. I want to ask him where – back in his old house in Sheffield, watching his grandmother get killed? Trapped in the van the kidnappers had bundled him into? In a lonely bedroom in Sweden with a strange couple talking a language he can't understand? He's never spoken of what happened there. He's always said they looked after him. But how much is he suppressing?

'When did you get to be so wise?' I ask him.

'I wouldn't recommend it, obviously, but don't let anyone tell you getting kidnapped and sold to a childless couple doesn't make you grow up,' he says with a hint of a smile.

'You've missed out on a large part of your childhood.'

He shrugs. 'But look at what's happened in its place? Mum and Dad only have one restaurant now. They were building up an empire. I hardly saw them. It took me getting kidnapped for them to realise what was important. Do you think I would have gone on camping holidays with Dad if we were still living in Sheffield and I'd never been taken? I don't. I'm glad of the mum and dad I have right now.'

That's given me something to think about. My head sinks to my chest. It sometimes feels too heavy to hold up.

'I can't take anything positive from this,' I tell him.

'Of course, you can't. It's just happened. Everything is still hurting. You'll never get over what happened to your mum and your nephews. I still picture my gran in the living room, all that blood, but you learn to live with what you've got left. You can learn from what happened and adapt. It's what Mum and Dad did. They sold all the restaurants and moved here.'

'Maybe I should resign from the police force,' I say to myself more than to Carl.

'Would that make you happy?'

'I don't think anything will make me happy ever again.'

'Drama queen,' Carl says with a smile. 'Do you know what makes me happy right now?'

'What?'

'Three things. Right now, at this moment, three things are making me happy. My two dogs, and this really nice tart.'

'It is a very good tart.'

'You don't need to think about what's going to make you happy in five years' time, in ten years' time. It's wishing your life away. Just think about right now and the next five minutes. Right now, on this stool, talking to you with my dogs and this great pudding, I'm happy. I'll be happy when I go back to bed as I'll have my dogs with me. You build from that.'

'Bloody hell, Carl, you should give TED talks.'

'Would I get paid?' he asks, his eyes wide with anticipation.

'I've no idea.'

'Oh. I won't bother, then.' He jumps down from the island. 'I'm going back to bed. School in the morning.'

'Goodnight, Carl.'

'Goodnight,' he says over his shoulder as he and the dogs leave the room.

I think about what Carl's said. He's right. I know he's right. But it's not easy. Everything is too raw. I look down at what's left of the almond tart on the plate. I can't put what remains back in the fridge. I may as well finish it off and apologise to Philip in the morning.

So, what's making me happy right now? Right at this very moment in time, what is making me happy? Nothing springs to mind.

'I'm devoid of happiness,' I say out loud.

'No, you're not. You just think you are,' Carl calls out.

'I thought you were going back to bed?' I shout back.

'I am now. Goodnight.'

I have to smile to myself at that. I really am enjoying my time here with the Meagans. That's what's making me happy right now – their company.

'Thank you, Carl,' I say quietly to myself.

When Carl's at school, the two dogs usually have to wait impatiently for his return. Sally takes them out for an occasional run around the garden, but for a really long walk, they need to wait for their master to arrive home. Since I arrived, that's no longer a problem. Straight after breakfast and a shower, I clip on their leads, slip on my walking shoes and trek into the nearby woods with the Labradors trotting excitedly beside me.

I've no idea where I'm going. I'm glad to be out in the fresh air and wide-open space where I'm not surrounded by people and there is nobody to ask me if I'm feeling all right. Once we enter the darkness and coolness of the woods, I unclip their leads and let them run free. They never go far, and they keep stopping, turning back, making sure I'm still there behind them. I can certainly understand how some people prefer the company of dogs over humans. They don't judge. They live in the moment. One of the dogs brings a stick back and drops it at my feet. I pick it up and lob it as far as I can. Both charge off with excitement.

I should be more dog.

Here, in the Lake District, I'm away from the horrors of

what Sheffield now means to me. Here, I'm not a DCI with South Yorkshire Police, I'm simply a woman walking two dogs. I don't have a team of detectives looking to me for solutions to a demanding investigation. I'm not surrounded by murder and hatred, corruption and red tape. I'm free. For the first time in my working life, I'm finally free.

I miss my friends, of course. Scott and Donal are preparing for their wedding in August. I agreed to be Scott's best woman. I've no idea if I'll be back for it. I'm sure he'll find a replacement. I miss Sian and her family, and I feel bad about leaving her without a word. I miss Adele, too, but she's currently in Sierra Leone having already escaped the nightmare Sheffield represents to us both. Maybe I should have gone with her. Mum, Nathan and Joseph would still be alive if I had, and I'd still have a relationship with my sister.

Then there's Odell. He's the new pathologist who replaced Adele. We've been seeing each other over the past couple of months. I've no idea if we will last, if we will move in together or even get married, but for the time being, it's fun having a man in my life again. He ticks all the right boxes, apart from driving a Tesla with a personalised registration plate. Surely, it's cheaper to scratch 'wanker' on the bonnet.

I didn't tell Odell I was leaving, either. I didn't tell anyone. As I was packing, I turned off my mobile and left it on the coffee table in the living room. I locked the front door behind me and walked away. Well, I drove away. I took Adele's Porsche from the garage. It's not like she's using it.

I've cut myself off completely from my life in South Yorkshire, and, right now, I have no intention whatsoever of returning.

One of the dogs barks. I look down and there he is by my feet, looking at the stick he's waiting for me to throw. I pick it up. It's wet with dog slobber. I hurl it across the woods, and they charge after it. They're happy simply to be with me, amused by a simple stick.

I definitely need to be more dog.

I don't feel guilty about leaving without informing anyone of where I was going (maybe Sian, and Scott, and I could have sent a quick email to Adele). But I hope they understand that, after everything I've endured recently, not just mum and my nephews being killed, but all the dark murder investigations I've had weighing me down, that I need time away to process everything and work out where I go from here and what the future holds for me.

I follow the dogs through the woods and out into the open air of the countryside. It's another scorching day and I'm looking forward to going for a swim later to help me cool down and put my body through more punishment until my organs scream at me to stop. I do need that pain, though. I need to feel something other than grief. Grief is a massive energy sapper.

As much as I love torturing myself in the heatwave, I'm aware that dogs are not designed to withstand such temperatures for so long and, despite them loving charging after a stick for hours on end, it's in their best interests to return to the shade of the restaurant, a bowl of fresh water, and a well-earned Bonio.

'Come on then, you two, let's get you back.' I clip on their leads. They don't even try to stop me, and we walk slowly back through the woods for home.

There's a black Fiat Punto outside the front of Nature's Diner when I get back. The restaurant isn't open yet and Philip and Sally have gone out for the morning, after dropping Carl off at school, to pick up the supplies. Whoever the visitor is, it's nothing to do with me. I take the dogs round the back and enter the restaurant through the utility. I take off their leads and freshen up their water bowls. They're more than ready for a good, long drink. So am I.

There's a knock on the back door.

Through the glass, I can see a young woman with hair so blond it's almost white. She's wearing a short-sleeved shirt with police epaulettes. There's a forced smile on her face.

I open the door.

'Hello,' she begins after clearing her throat. 'I'm PC Pemberton. Alison. I was here yesterday talking to Philip about the attempted break-in.'

'Oh. Right. Well, Philip and Sally are both out at the moment. I can give them a message if—'

'No,' she interrupts. 'Sorry… You're… It's Matilda, isn't it?'

She's nervous. I'm sceptical.

'That's right.'

'Matilda Darke. As in DCI Matilda Darke.'

'Yes.' Now I'm suspicious.

'It's you I actually came to see. Would it be possible for me to have a chat with you? It's nothing to do with an investigation or anything. This is entirely personal.'

I take a deep breath. How do I say this without being insulting? 'No offence, but I don't know you. I've no interest in talking about anything personal to—'

'No,' she interrupts again. 'I'm sorry. I'm not coming across well, am I? It's not you I want to talk about. It's me. I need… I want… sorry. I…'

'Look, I've just been for a long walk with the dogs. It's baking and I'm sweating. I need a drink. Why don't you come in and let me freshen up while you find the words you want to use?'

I stand back and allow this nervous woman to enter. As she passes me, I get a whiff of deodorant and desperation.

I go over to the fridge and take out a bottle of water. I untwist the cap and drink half of it in a single gulp. I don't think I've drunk so much water as I have since I've been here. I've needed it to keep hydrated with all the exercise. My skin is certainly benefitting.

'Can I get you anything?'

'No. I'm fine, thank you.'

'Well, give me a few minutes and I'll be right with you. Don't mind the dogs, they're very friendly.'

I leave the room but steal a glance at this PC Pemberton over my shoulder as I do so. She has a worried expression firmly etched on her face. One that seems to have been there for a very long time.

I stand under the piercing hot needles of the shower when my sister's voice comes back to haunt me. Or to hurt me. I can't work out which.

'*I fucking hate you!*'

I agree with her. I fucking hate me, too. I close my eyes tight and try to silence my torment, the pain, the torture, the darkness. It's no good. I banish my sister's violent words and then I see my mum, lying in her hospital bed, the doctors turning off the machines, removing the tubes one by one.

'She's gone,' Dr Wilde says, sympathetically.

My mum is dead.

My legs won't hold me up any longer. I sink to my knees and press my hands against the shower tray. I open my mouth, and I let out a sound from the depths of my soul, a sound filled with agony. I'm crying. Water is mixed with tears, and they disappear down the plughole. I can't stop. It doesn't matter what I try to think about – Carl's kind words, the smiling faces of two happy Labradors, the warmth offered by Sally and Philip, that amazing almond and raspberry frangipane tart – I cannot stop the tears.

I don't remember how long I'm in the shower for. By the time I get downstairs, Alison has moved into the main part of the restaurant. She's sitting at one of the tables, gazing out at the view. The dogs are sprawled out, knackered, beside her. I'd hoped she'd have grown bored of waiting for me and gone home. No such luck.

I clear my throat to signify my presence.

'I never tire of this view,' Alison says. 'It's beautiful, isn't it?' Her voice is heavy, almost as heavy as mine. Another woman with a massive weight on her shoulders. I wonder what baggage she's carrying, and is it going to end up involving me? I bloody hope not.

'It is,' I say.

'You see everything that's going on in the world – wars, conflict, climate change, pandemics – you think of the horrors people do to each other, and it's difficult to believe that such natural beauty exists.'

I pull out a seat at the table and sit opposite this worried-looking PC. I guess her to be in her mid-thirties, but there's a sadness surrounding her that's aged her. She has dark circles beneath her eyes. I have a suspicious feeling this conversation is not going to be an easy one.

She looks at me and proffers a faint smile. It doesn't reach her eyes.

'I... erm... I notice the dogs have the same names on their nametags,' she says, clearly stalling.

'Yes. The older Woody was bought for Carl before he went missing. While he was in Sweden, the couple gave him a dog for company. He decided to name him Woody, too. When he came home, he brought his new dog with him.'

She smiles. This time, it's genuine. 'Doesn't it get confusing for them?'

'No. They never leave Carl's side when he's home from school. You shout for one dog, but they come as a pair.'

'That's sweet.'

I take a sip of my water. 'Have you found the words you want to use yet?'

She takes a deep breath and nods.

'I need your help. Your advice, really. I know why you're here. I know what happened to you back in Sheffield and that you're here to make sense of it all. The last thing you want is to deal with a huge murder investigation. I understand all that, I really do. However, I have nowhere else left to turn, and, I know this may sound selfish, but I'm using the resources which are at hand and, right now, that's you.'

I almost smile at her bluntness and honestly. I nod for her to continue.

'I'm the youngest of three children. I have two older sisters. Identical twins. When I was five years old, we were all out playing hide-and-seek. The next thing I remember is being completely on my own. I ran to the road nearby and I saw my sisters in the back of a car being driven away. I even waved at them.' Her voice begins to falter. 'It was the last I saw of them. It was the last anyone ever saw of them.'

'I'm sorry.'

'My dad was devastated. He took it really hard. He adored the twins. I mean, he loved all of us, but the twins were special.

They were twins, after all. A few months later, there was a storm. Dad had taken me to see my gran – his mum – and on the drive back home he... well, I don't know what happened. Mum found me asleep in the back of the car. We were parked right at the edge of the lake, the water rising rapidly. My dad was nowhere to be found. It's thought that he walked out into the lake and drowned himself.'

'Good grief.' And I thought I'd been through the shit.

'To say that my childhood was one of darkness and upset would be a massive understatement. I have no idea how my mother coped. I think she had some kind of breakdown. My Uncle Iain wasn't much help, either. I went to live with my Auntie Margaret and Uncle Colin in Tunstall for a while. It's not really something we talk about. Anyway, I wanted to be a police officer from a young age. I wanted to find answers. Unfortunately, I haven't been able to find any. I've no idea what happened to my sisters. Nobody does. And I don't know if my dad simply walked away or if he really is at the bottom of the lake. There have been sightings of him over the years, but... Mum thinks he's dead. Everyone thinks he's dead. I... I don't know what to think. It's the unknown that's eating away at me. How can there be nothing after thirty years?'

I take a deep breath. I know what's coming.

'I have a feeling I know the answer to this question, but what do you want from me?'

'I could spend an hour blowing smoke up your arse saying how brilliant you are as a detective. We both know your track record, so we know your history speaks for itself. I also know that, right now, you're grieving and you're angry. But there's a difference. You know what's happened to your family. I don't. I'm in limbo and have been for thirty years. Are my sisters dead or alive? If they are alive, are they together or have they been separated? Do they know who they are? Are they looking for me, too? Do they even remember they have another sister? It's the not knowing that's painful. It's the fact that there are so many variables that I can't get over. This is worse than murder. If they'd been killed, if we had bodies, I could grieve and visit their graves. I've got nothing.'

She looks down and composes herself. When she looks back up at me, her face has lost the redness of rage. 'Like you, I'm an excellent police officer, but I need help. I need *your* help. I'm not asking you to reopen an investigation. I know you don't have that power, and I know you won't, but I need a direction. I'm blinded as I'm too close to this. I need an outsider to tell me where to go next to find out what happened to my sisters and my dad. I will literally get on my knees and beg you for help, if that's what it takes.'

'You don't need to do that,' I say, sitting back and folding my arms across my chest.

'You're not going to help me, though, are you?'

I shake my head. 'I can't. I'm sorry. I really wish I could, but right now, I'm not in the best place to help anyone. Not even myself. That's why I'm here and not back in Sheffield.'

Alison struggles to hold back her tears. She's disappointed. 'Can I ask you for just one teeny tiny favour?'

'Go on.'

'When you get a spare five minutes, type Celia and Jennifer Pemberton into Google. Read the news stories. I'll not ask for your help again, but if there's anything, anything at all you can suggest I do to find out what happened, give me a call.' She reaches into the back pocket of her trousers and takes out a crumpled business card. She lays it on the table between us.

'I'm not expecting you to go all private detective on this. I just need a nudge in the right direction.'

'I'm not the best person to help you right now.'

'You are. You found Carl Meagan.'

'A neighbour found Carl.'

'Please.'

I look away.

Alison stands up. The dogs don't even move at the sound of the chair scraping across the tiled floor.

'I'll leave you to it. I hope you don't mind me at least coming here and trying.'

'No. I'd have probably done the same thing, if I were you. I'm just sorry I'm not in a position to help.'

She waits a beat, takes another breath and heads out of the restaurant through the main doors. She walks down the steps with her head down and slowly climbs into the car. As she's reversing out of the space, she looks up at me.

I turn away and look down at the dogs. 'Well, I think that answers a question I've been asking myself since I arrived. My days as a detective are over.'

I stay away from the bustle of the restaurant once the doors are open and the customers have arrived. They're here for a night out in a stunning location with fine wines, delicious food and a warm atmosphere. The last thing anyone wants to see is a miserable-looking woman sitting alone in the corner on the verge of tears. That would put anyone off their Steak au Poivre.

I'm in the living room, upstairs, with Carl and the dogs. The TV is on in the background but I'm not paying it any attention. Philip has passed on his love of classic British sitcoms to his son and he's currently working his way through *Only Fools and Horses*, having watched *One Foot in the Grave* and *Porridge* over the past month. While Carl has one eye on the screen, he's drawing up his plans for the basement on his tablet. He spent last weekend measuring up and put all the figures into an app he's downloaded which creates a scale model of the entire lower ground floor area. What Carl is doing now is using his creative skills to maximise the space and turn it into a money-making machine for his parents in the hope that, if they use any of his ideas, he can ask for a share of the profits. I love how his mind works.

I look at the TV. I've seen *Only Fools and Horses* many times over the years. James was a big fan. But, as much as I love the interplay between Del and Rodney, I'm not in the mood for comedy right now. I'm struggling to concentrate on much at all at present. My mind won't settle. I haven't finished a book in months, nor have I seen the end of any film.

'I think I'm going to have an early night,' I tell Carl, getting up from the sofa.

'It's not even nine o'clock yet.'

'I know, but I'm tired.' I'm not. I don't know what I am, but I feel the need to be alone.

'But Grandad's just died,' Carl says, pointing at the television.

'Carl, I've literally lost count of the number of times I've watched this.' I grab a handful of popcorn from the bowl on the coffee table as I pass him. 'You're going to love Uncle Albert, though.'

Despite my room being the smallest bedroom out of the four, it's large enough to comfortably fit a king-size bed and has an en suite shower room which is better than my own at home. The walls are decorated in a rich navy blue and the luxurious cream curtains are so heavy they have to be drawn using a rope pulley system. Fancy. I close the door behind me. In here, the sounds from the restaurant below are barely a whisper and I can hardly hear the sounds from Hooky Street in the living room. I'm surrounded by silence. The only noise comes from the horrors inside my head screaming for attention.

It's yet another stiflingly hot evening. I undress, throw back the cotton sheet and climb into the large firm-mattressed bed. The room is comfortable, cosy and welcoming. I have no idea how long I'll be staying here; they've all said I can stay as long as I like. I know, at some point, I'll have to return to reality, but it's up to me to decide where my reality lies, and, right now, it's not Sheffield.

Philip and Sally aren't big readers and I didn't think to bring any books with me from my massive collection at home. I found a well-thumbed PD James on a bookcase and started reading it last night. I managed two pages before I realised I hadn't absorbed a single word I'd read. Tonight, I don't even get to the bottom of one page.

'Sorry, Phyllis,' I say as I close the book and put it back on the bedside table.

I climb out of bed and leave the room. I pad, barefoot, across the corridor to the office three doors along. I've asked Sally if I can use their computer to access my emails, and on three occasions I've sat, staring at the login screen, and chickened out of typing in my password. Part of me wants to know what's going on back in Sheffield. Have they caught the bastard who killed my family yet? Has he claimed another victim? I expect there'll be plenty from Sian and Scott and Christan, asking, pleading with me, to get in touch. I'm not ready to do so yet, but I know if I read their emails, I'll grab the phone and dial. I can't let them see me like this.

This time, I don't click on the Outlook icon. I go straight to the Google homepage and type in Celia and Jennifer Pemberton.

Cumbria Today

Tuesday 11 August 1992 — 22p

BREAKING NEWS | BREAKING NEWS | BREAKING NEWS

TWINS MISSING

Twin girls have been reported missing in Dower Lane, High Chapel.

Celia and Jennifer Pemberton, both 7, were playing in the field behind their house with their younger sister, Alison, 5, when they were taken. Their mother, Lynne, alerted police.

Officers from Cumbria Police have been seen throughout the day around the village. DI Lionel Bell is leading the investigation and said in a statement: "It is imperative these girls are found quickly. We are asking everyone who is able to join the search."

There has been no word from the girls' parents, Lynne and Jack who were last seen entering the police station flanked by uniformed officers.

TV GUIDE (P16/17)   **BINGO (P23)**   **HOROSCOPE (P4)**

MICHAEL WOOD

WEDNESDAY 12 AUGUST, 1992 — *Cumbria Today*

SPECIALISED OFFICERS DRAFTED IN TO INTERVIEW PEMBERTON SISTER

By Tania Pritchard

Interviewing experts have been seen arriving at High Chapel Police station to interview only witness, Alison Pemberton, 5, over the disappearance of her twin sisters, Celia and Jennifer, 7, yesterday.

Alison was playing with her sisters when they were taken. Despite extensive searches by police and the local community throughout the night and today, there has been no sign of the missing twins.

Now, experts from Greater Manchester Police have arrived to interview the five-year-old in the hope of discovering what happened in the moments leading up to their disappearance.

DI Lionel Bell said: "This is an incredibly sensitive process. Alison is upset and missing her sisters. She is a young child and cannot understand the magnitude of the situation. We are taking time with the interview and allowing her to go at her own pace."

DI Bell refused to comment when asked if any arrests had been made, saying this is a developing investigation.

However, an official source told Cumbria Today that a man was taken in for questioning late last night.

All day police have been searching fields, farm land, barns, and outhouses.

High Chapel School, closed for the summer holidays, was opened for police interviews and teachers were seen comforting local children.

THURSDAY 13 AUGUST, 1992 — *Cumbria Today*

TEACHER INTERVIEWED FOR 12 HOURS

By Tania Pritchard

High Chapel Primary School teacher, Alex Costello, was interviewed by police for more than twelve hours yesterday over the disappearance of seven-year-old twins, Celia and Jennifer Pemberton.

Costello, 28, originally from Norfolk, has been teaching at High Chapel for two years. It is believed he doesn't teach any classes involving any of the Pemberton sisters.

Officers from High Chapel Police Station refused to comment on the interview.

Head, Flora West, said: "Mr Costello is a much respected member of staff. No action on his involvement in the new term will be taken until we have consulted with police."

However, calls are already coming into Cumbria Today from worried parents saying they don't feel comfortable sending their children back to school when it reopens in September.

DI Lionel Bell, leading the investigation, said they were pursuing many lines of enquiries.

FRIDAY 14 AUGUST, 1992 — Cumbria Today

PEMBERTON FAMILY AND FRIENDS INTERROGATED

By Tania Pritchard

The family of missing twins Celia and Jennifer Pemberton, along with close friends, have been interrogated by High Chapel Police.

Parents, Jack and Lynne, were seen entering the police station with grim faces where they remained for six hours. They refused to speak to journalists upon leaving.

Jack's brother, Iain, was also extensively questioned, as were close friends, Travis Montgomery and Clara Fisher.

In a brief interview outside the station, Iain Pemberton said: "I know the police are just doing their job but Jack and Lynne are going through hell right now. They don't need this."

'The police are totally clueless. They have no idea where Celia and Jennifer are.'
–Clara Fisher

Neighbour, Clara Fisher, said: "I've known Jack and Lynne for years. The questions I've been asked about them are horrific. I thought this was a safe and quiet community. I thought we all knew and respected each other. That's been ruined now. I'll never look at Lionel Bell the same way again after the accusations he was throwing around."

An officer on the team who asked not to be named said police are struggling to find a suspect and are worried the twins may never be found.

PARENTS DEMAND TEACHER TO BE FIRED

By Marcus Brett

Parents of children attending High Chapel Primary School have demanded the removal of teacher Alex Costello after he was interviewed for a second time in connection with the disappearance of twins Celia and Jennifer Pemberton.

Costello, 28, was released without charge on Monday evening with police stating they are now satisfied the teacher, originally from Norfolk, had nothing to do with the disappearance of the girls.

However, worried parents believe Mr Costello should be removed from the school and have called on headteacher, Flora West, to suspend him with immediate effect.

One parent, Sylvia Glover, said: "It is clear Alex's position at the school has become untenable. There is clearly something in his past that is suspicious and he should not be working with children."

Amy Moore, whose daughter is taught by Alex said: "My Rachel loved being in Alex's class but now she says she's worried about returning in September, and has asked if she can move schools."

Flora West said: "Alex Costello is on the rota to begin teaching again in September. The police are happy he is innocent, and so am I."

TUESDAY 18 AUGUST, 1992 *Cumbria Today*

MISSING PEMBERTON TWINS: ONE WEEK ON

By Tania Pritchard

It has been a week since seven-year-old twins Celia and Jennifer disappeared from the field behind their home in Dower Lane, High Chapel, and despite extensive searches, intensive and intrusive interviews, police are struggling to discover what happened.

In an exclusive interview with Cumbria Today, DI Lionel Bell, who has been leading the investigation since day one, told us the lack of information is baffling.

"I have worked on many cases over the years and there has always been a witness or a forensic clue to help steer the investigation. We literally have nothing."

Expert child interviewers have spoken to Alison, 5, who was with her sisters when they disappeared.

"Alison has been interviewed for hours on end. To her, it was a normal, happy summer's day. They were all enjoying the school holiday and the hot weather. She saw nobody. She heard nothing. Lynne and Jack Pemberton have also been thoroughly investigated which is the norm for cases such as this, as has everyone connected with the family. There is nothing to suggest any of them are suspects.

"My team is working around the clock, tirelessly, to bring this case to a conclusion. We will not stop until they are found. And I promise, we will find them." DI Bell stated.

As the investigation intensified, it seemed like the whole village of High Chapel was questioned. There was a photograph of a drawn-looking Jack and Lynne Pemberton leaving a police station in Kendal, holding hands, faces turned away from the media onslaught.

I skim-read the articles and hit print on every single one. I absorb information better when it's written down in front of me. I'm not a screen reader. There seemed to be very little for police to go on in the beginning. The only witness to the disappearance was five-year-old Alison and she couldn't tell them anything, despite clearly being interviewed on many occasions for long periods of time. All she remembered was seeing her sisters in the back of a car being driven away. There was no mention of the colour or make of the car, how many people were in the front, of even if the car was speeding or what direction it was travelling in.

I find the quote from Inspector Lionel Bell to be worrying. He said the police would not stop until the girls were found and promised he would find them. A direct quote, one he shouldn't have made, but clearly feeling he needed to reassure a panicked public they were doing everything they could. How did he feel after two weeks, a month, two months, a year, when the Pemberton twins still hadn't been found? I wonder where he is now. He's probably retired. The case will most likely have plagued him for the rest of his career. I bet, as he walked out of that station one last time, he felt as if he had unfinished business. There are some cases that refuse to let you go, and they nearly always involve children.

What became of the teacher, Alex Costello? Police said they were satisfied he had no involvement in the disappearance, but it required two intensive interrogations to reach that conclusion. Whatever they discovered hadn't been enough to sway the public as Google took me to a tiny article not worth printing which stated that Alex Costello had handed in his resignation and would not be returning to teach High Chapel primary pupils that September. There was no quote from headteacher Flora West, nor from Alex. However, there was a letter written by a member of the public that seemed to put an end to Alex's story.

MICHAEL WOOD

WE SHOULD BE ASHAMED OF OURSELVES

The last few weeks have been difficult for all of us in the wake of the disappearance of the Pemberton girls. My heart goes out to Jack and Lynne, and poor little Alison who had to witness her sisters being taken. One always hopes that in times of tragedy a community as close-knit as ours would band together. I am saddened that hasn't been the case with the public vilification of Alex Costello. A bright, kind, caring young man has not only been driven out of his job but also the village. Is this what we've become? There is no evidence whatsoever that Alex had any involvement in this appalling crime yet gossip and innuendo has run rife and he's been forced to leave for his own safety. I don't think life in High Chapel will ever be the same again.

**Lesley Saunders,
Attenborough Close, High Chapel**

With emotions running so high and accusations coming from every direction, it was no surprise that the investigation stalled before it could gain any traction.

A month on from the disappearance, Jack and Lynne Pemberton appeared on local television to keep the story in the public eye. I open another page and log on to YouTube, but I can't find any clip of the news item. It's probably been lost in the mists of time. There was a brief story in the local paper mentioning how worried the parents looked on television and how they pleaded for the safe return of their daughters, but that's all the reference to any televised appeals I could find.

After that, nothing. The next mention in the news was three months later when the village was hit by an autumn storm, and, once again, the Pemberton family found themselves back on the front pages as they were faced with further tragedy.

MICHAEL WOOD

Cumbria Today

Friday 27 November 1992 — 26p

MORE TRAGEDY FOR LOCAL FAMILY

JACK PEMBERTON MISSING AFTER STORM

WHOLE VILLAGE WITHOUT POWER

SCHOOL COULD BE CLOSED FOR WEEKS

JACK PEMBERTON, father of missing twins, Celia and Jennifer, has himself been reported missing following last night's violent storm. Jack, 36, was last seen by his mother around 3pm. His car was found partially submerged in the swollen lake with his daughter, Alison, 5, in the back.

It is believed he got into difficulty while driving home and succumbed to the rising flood water. *Cont. P2.*

STORM UPDATE: PAGES 2, 3, 4 & 5

WEEKEND TV GUIDE (P20-23) **WEEKEND SPORT FIXTURES (P40)**

'Bloody hell.'

If there was ever a family that appeared to have been visited by a plague of locusts, the Pembertons were it. Twin girls playing close to their home innocently, taken in broad daylight, and their father swept away by a surging lake while trying to protect his surviving daughter. How had Lynne managed to stop herself from going mad? In her darkest moments, what had stopped *her* from downing a bottle of vodka and a hundred paracetamol? Same as me, possibly: a tiny, minute trace of hope.

When I lost James, I thought my world had ended. The pain was too much. It was the strength of my mum and dad, Harriet, and my friends, that kept me afloat. Lynne, back in 1992, had only her five-year-old daughter, Alison, and she wouldn't have been much comfort. She was too young to comprehend the magnitude of what was going on around her. How had Lynne survived? How does a person come back from losing two of their children and their husband within the space of three months?

I had closure (horrible word). James was dead. He was buried. I have a grave I can go and visit. My mum and dad have graves I can lay flowers on and pay my respects. What does Lynne have? Bless her, Alison has grown up in the shadow of tragedy and horror. No wonder she's screaming for answers and clutching at any hint of a possibility to find the truth.

But then, the twist in the tale: had Jack Pemberton really died on the night of the storm?

> **MONDAY 11 JANUARY, 1993** — *Cumbria Today*
>
> # IS JACK PEMBERTON STILL ALIVE?
>
> **By Tania Pritchard**
>
> Over the past months, six reports have come into the Cumbria Today offices from people claiming to have seen missing local man, Jack Pemberton in the county.
>
> Mr Pemberton, 36, was last seen on November 27 last year during a storm when it is believed he got into difficulty driving home and was swept out into Lake Windermere. Despite extensive searches by police and experienced divers, a body has never been found.
>
> Jack Pemberton is the father of missing twins Celia and Jennifer, 7, who disappeared from their home in June last year.
>
> Susie Allinson, 43, of Lindon Road in Sedgwick said she knew the Pemberton family by sight only but was sure it was Jack she saw going into a Barclays Bank in Kendal.
>
> 'I had to do a double take,' she said. 'I've thought of the Pemberton family often over the past few months, more so over Christmas, bless them. When I saw Jack, I couldn't believe it. It took me a while to cross the road and I went into the bank but I couldn't see him anywhere. Hand on heart, it was Jack Pemberton.'
>
> Another witness, who didn't want to be named, also said she saw Jack Pemberton, also in Kendal, this time at a petrol station.
>
> There have been four further sightings of Jack including one close to High Chapel in which a tourist was taking a photograph of his daughters and captured a man in the background. Despite the blurred image, the likeness is uncanny.
>
> DI Lionel Bell from High Chapel Police Station said: 'We are aware of these sightings. However, all the evidence points to Jack Pemberton drowning in Lake Windermere. As sad as this is for the Pemberton family, we cannot alter the facts.'

Six sightings of Jack within two months are a significant number that Inspector Bell really shouldn't have ignored. Was Susie Allinson questioned thoroughly by police? Was CCTV at the bank checked to verify her claims? I wonder what Lynne has made of all this. It's given her hope, or maybe false hope, or maybe it's just stirred everything back up again. She can't rest, mourn, move on, while there are still so many unanswered questions.

On the tenth anniversary of the disappearance of the twins, the local paper ran several stories to keep the investigation alive and draw people's attention to the fact it was still unsolved. It seems to be the case that has defined the area, and the reporters were keen to capitalise on what made High Chapel stand out. There was a potted update, which I printed, an interview with Lynne, and, surprisingly, what appears to be the only interview I can find conducted with Alison.

MONDAY 12TH AUGUST, 2002 **CUMBRIA TODAY**

TEN YEARS ON: THE DAY MY SISTERS LEFT

By Tania Pritchard

Ten years ago yesterday, on a hot summer's day in a picturesque location in the Lake District, twin girls disappeared within sight of their home. The only witness was their younger sister, Alison, who was five at the time. Despite extensive searches and a decade of false leads and lost hope, there has been no sighting of Celia and Jennifer.

During the initial investigation, Alison was interviewed many times by specialised police officers yet she has never spoken to the media. Until now.

In a series of exclusive interviews with Cumbria Today, Alison Pemberton spoke candidly about that summer's day and the decade of despair she, and her family, have endured.

'I remember very little about that day,' Alison, now 14, said.

She is sitting with her mother, Lynne, in the home she was born in. It is modestly decorated and the walls are adorned with framed photographs of the three sisters, though only one has grown up.

'We were playing, as sisters do in the school summer holiday. It seems like one minute they were there and the next they'd gone. I didn't know how serious it was at first. I remember, that first night, going to bed, and not being able to sleep. My sisters weren't there. It felt strange.'

'Mum sat me down a few days later and told me they'd gone and she didn't know where and that I was the last person to see them and I would need to answer some important questions from the police. I was terrified. I couldn't tell them anything. That made Mum cry. It made me cry, too. I knew the weight on my shoulders was massive, but I just kept saying "I don't know" because I didn't.'

We paused as Alison became tearful. After a break, she continued. 'Three months later, my dad disappeared. It seemed like someone had it in for our family. Why were we suffering like this?'

A decade on and the Pemberton twins are still missing. Jack Pemberton is also missing and Lynne and Alison are clearly in pain. They're grieving, but they refuse to give up hope they'll eventually find answers to these tragic events that have plagued their lives.

TOMORROW: 'SEARCHING FOR MY SISTERS'

On the twentieth anniversary in 2012, there was less coverage in the local paper, and I can't find anything printed nationally. Next year will be the thirtieth anniversary, and I wonder if even the local press will bother writing anything.

Lynne, Alison and Iain will never forget. The anniversary will be a difficult day for them to get through, but they will remember whether it's 11 August, 11 January or 11 October. The key players in a tragedy never forget, despite everyone around them moving on. I speak from experience.

I google Lionel Bell. He interests me; or, rather, his silence interests me. How did the failure to find out what happened to the twins shape his career? Was it something he continued to return to, did it keep him awake at night like so many of mine have set up home in my head?

There is a raft of stories where Bell has played a key role in the local community, but nothing of the magnitude of the missing twins. On the announcement of his retirement, a story with the headline '**MISSING PEMBERTON TWINS WILL HAUNT BELL TO HIS GRAVE**' reveals how Lionel still thinks of the girls and how he hopes to provide an answer to Lynne, Alison and Iain. It ends with him praying there will be a solution in his lifetime, but the article lacks emotion. Is that Lionel washing his hands of the police force now he is leaving or is it sloppy writing by the journalist?

I've never trusted journalists. There's one in particular who I'd happily see chopped up and placed inside a woodchipper. I suppose I shouldn't tar all journalists with the same brush. I'm sure they're not all shysters like Danny fucking Hanson. There are probably plenty out there who are decent people. What's the collective noun for a group of journalists? A scum of journalists, probably.

I lean back in my chair and stretch. I'm getting stiff from sitting in one position for so long. I turn off the computer, pick up the reams of paper I've printed off and return to my bedroom where I climb into bed and begin to read through them all once again.

Something's wrong. Something doesn't sit well with me, and I'm not sure what.

In cases of this nature, the investigation always looks to the family of those who went missing. Jack and Lynne, and the rest of the family, had been extensively questioned by police at the time of Celia and Jennifer's disappearance. Why? Couldn't they provide an alibi? Their neighbour said police had asked intrusive and insensitive questions about the Pembertons. What had they been implying? Were Jack and Lynne suspects in their daughters' disappearance? If so, why wasn't Alison taken away from them for her own protection, even temporarily? Or was that the reason why she was sent to live with her aunt and uncle for a while?

If the girls were taken by a stranger – a passing paedophile, for example – then it was more than likely that after thirty years both girls were dead. They would have been dead long before now. They could have been taken, like Carl was, and sold to a couple unable to have children. Perhaps they were now living a life in blissful ignorance under different names. Were they still together or had they been split up? It sounded far-fetched but, in my experience, the truth is often stranger than fiction and anything is possible.

They obviously hadn't been kidnapped for ransom as no demand was made and the Pembertons weren't a rich family. Had there been a grudge against the Pembertons? Was the kidnap in revenge for something they'd done?

I had been hoping the local newspaper had run a photograph of Jack's car abandoned at the side of the lake. I'd like to see how submerged it was. Had Jack got into difficulty due to the storm and been swept away or had he deliberately walked out into the storm? In cases such as this, with missing children and a father showing signs of depression, it's entirely possible that Jack could no longer cope with how cruel life had become and wanted to end the suffering by taking his own life. It's a sad fact that people occasionally take others with them when the balance of their mind is disturbed. Jack loved his surviving daughter. But, if he wanted to die, if he thought he was going to be reunited with his twins, wouldn't he have taken Alison with him so they could all be together? The fact he abandoned her to an unknown fate in the storm left more questions than answers.

And there are those six sightings of him in the following two months. Have there been more since?

However, Jack could have used the storm as a stage to fake his own death. But why would he want to?

'Because he couldn't get over what he'd done,' I say out loud.

I feel a chill run down my back at that thought. It would have been welcome, given the heatwave, if it hadn't been such an horrific thought. Jack and Lynne were questioned at length. Difficult questions were asked about them to close friends and family members. The police obviously thought, at least for a while, the parents might have had something to do with the twins' disappearance.

Had the police investigation turned Jack and Lynne against each other? Many parents split up following the murder of a child. Had Lynne looked at Jack's relationship with his children and asked the question she hadn't wanted to know the answer to? Had Jack, racked with guilt, simply walked out into the swollen lake to end it all, or had he given everyone that impression and he was still alive somewhere?

If I'm asking all these questions after only half an hour scrolling through Google hits, surely Alison has been asking them herself for the past thirty years.

I rifle through the sheets I've printed off and look for a photograph of Jack Pemberton. He's leaving a police station, holding the hand of his wife. He looks drawn, shattered, but is he genuine or acting?

'Are you completely innocent in all this or did you abuse and kill your daughters? And, if you did, did you abuse Alison, too?' I ask him.

If only he could answer me.

The atmosphere at the breakfast table feels different, heavy, and for once it has nothing to do with my mood. I woke up and, instead of hot, blazing sunshine slicing through the curtains, I saw darkness and gloom. As I pulled them open, I saw clouds for the first time since my arrival. The sky is grey and getting darker all the time. The storm is approaching.

'Do you think we should close for tonight?' Philip asks. He's sitting at the round breakfast table in the family kitchen looking down at his iPad. 'We've had three cancellations already.'

Sally is also studying her tablet. 'According to the weather, the storm is due to hit early afternoon. I suppose we could put a message on social media, if it gets bad. Besides, surely people will use their common sense.'

That makes me laugh. After more than two decades in the police force, I've seen firsthand how little common sense the majority of people out there have.

I turn to look out of the window while nibbling on a piece of granary toast. The lake is still. Despite the heavy clouds, it is difficult to think that in a few hours a wild storm could be raging through the village. I was looking forward to a morning swim. I think I might give it a miss. I never understood wild swimmers before. You never know what's lurking beneath the waters to get tangled up in, but I've been enjoying having this part of the lake all to myself.

'Are we safe here?' I ask, turning back to the table. 'If as much rain falls as forecast, will we flood?'

'No. The restaurant is raised, so we should be fine unless anything biblical happens. The only thing likely to flood is the cellar, which, I suppose it could be good if some water did get in so then I'd know what needed to be done to make it water-tight before turning it into a wine cellar.'

Carl suddenly lets out a laugh.

'What's funny?' Sally asks.

'Nothing. I just find it funny how, when I bring my tablet to the table, I get told off, yet it's perfectly fine for you both to use yours.'

I busy myself with another slice of toast. It would be childish of me to laugh.

'It's work-related,' Philip says.

'So was mine. I had a maths test.'

Suitably chastised, both parents put down their tablets.

'How long have you been waiting to say that?' I ask Carl.

'The best part of a year,' he smirks.

'You've raised a smart cookie,' I say.

'Too smart, sometimes,' Philip says. 'I may have to give you my tax returns, see how smug you are then.'

'I don't think so. I'm not putting my fingerprints on your receipts. That would make me an accomplice, wouldn't it, Mat?'

Philip's face begins to blush.

'It certainly would.'

'He's learning a lot of bad habits from you since you arrived,' Sally says.

'You mean bad habits like the law?'

'Can we change the subject?' Philip asks, looking uncomfortable. 'I know we're only joking but I get nervous when it comes to all things tax related.'

'Is that the sign of a guilty conscience, Mat?' Carl asks me.

'Fine, Carl, you win. If you want to bring your tablet to the breakfast table in the future, you're more than welcome to. Now, let's move on, shall we?'

I smile as both Sally and Carl make fun of Philip who blushes at being made the butt of the joke. It feels warm and heartening to be around a happy family for a change. It's not long, though, until the darkness returns, and I realise I'll never have that again. Six months ago, I had a full table at Christmas. Now, three are dead, my sister hates me, and my best friend is in Africa.

I hear Carl and Sally talking, but I don't register what they're saying.

'Matilda? Matilda!'

'Sorry?' I ask, looking up. Carl has gone. When did that happen?

'Everything all right?'

'Yes. Fine. I was just… thinking about something. Listen, you don't happen to know of anyone round here who's lived here for a long time, do you?'

'May, one of our cleaners, she was born and bred here,' Philip says. 'Why?'

'I had a visitor yesterday, a police constable. Alison Pemberton.'

'She came about the attempted break-in the other day. Did she want me?'

'No. She came to ask me a favour. Apparently, when she was five, her twin sisters went missing. Never seen again. A few months later, her father couldn't cope and walked out into the lake. His body was never found. She asked if I could help her.'

'Are you going to?' Philip asks.

'I'm not sure. I don't really think I'm in a position to help anyone at the moment. I can't even help myself.'

'It might help you to have something to concentrate on,' Sally says as she begins to clear the table.

'Maybe. I just thought I'd feel out the story, see what the local gossip was.'

'How long ago did all this happen?' Sally asks.

'1992.'

'Talk to May,' Philip says. 'She's in her sixties so she's bound to remember it.'

'Poor girl,' Sally says, wistfully. 'Imagine living with not knowing what happened for thirty years. It doesn't bear thinking about, does it?' She places a hand on Philip's shoulder. She's clearly thinking of when Carl was kidnapped. He was missing for four years and that was a nightmare that seemed to be without end.

Sally leaves with the dirty dishes to take into the utility room where the dishwasher is, leaving me and Philip to finish our coffees.

'I didn't want to mention it with Carl at the table,' I begin. 'But have you looked at the CCTV cameras? Any attempts to break in last night?'

'No. All quiet. Speaking of last night, I had a phone call. I came to tell you about it, but Carl said you'd already gone to bed. Sian Robinson.'

'Oh?'

'She's been ringing and ringing you since you left Sheffield. She's tried everyone she could think of. Why haven't you been answering her calls? I thought she was a good friend.'

'She is. I didn't bring my phone with me. It's still at my house in Sheffield. Did you tell her I was here?'

'Yes. She was relieved to hear you're safe. She told me to tell you to ring her any time. She's worried about you.'

I don't say anything to that. There's nothing to say.

'She asked if she can ring me again; to check up on you. I told her that was fine. Look, Mat, I know you feel like you don't have anyone right now, but you do. Sian, Scott, Christian. Sian mentioned a Donal, and someone called Odell. They're all thinking of you. They're all worried about you. That's a lot of people to have in your corner. You're not as alone as you think.'

'And they're all police officers. Well, apart from Donal and Odell. I can't surround myself with police at the moment. It hurts. I keep thinking about all the people who would still be alive now if I hadn't joined the force. Faith. Rory and his fiancée Natasha. They'd have been married now, probably had kids, too. Ranjeet. He and Kesinka had just had a baby when he was killed. Chris.' I heard my voice break when I mentioned Chris's name. 'Valerie. My dad. My mum. My nephews. So many people have died because of me. I'm the biggest serial killer never to have been caught.'

'You're being far too hard on yourself.'

'Too many people have died for me not to be hard on myself.'

'So, what are you going to do for the rest of your life? I mean, you're welcome to stay here as long as you want, you know that, but are you really going to be happy spending every day just going out running and swimming and sitting around here with your thoughts?'

I take a deep breath. 'I was thinking that, if this storm hits as hard as predicted, I might pop outside and see if the wind will lift me up and transport me to another world.'

'Take a Woody to be your Tonto.'

'Toto,' I correct him.

'Joking aside,' Philip says, lowering his voice and learning forward. 'You wouldn't do that, would you? Just disappear.'

'Like Alison's father and sisters? I don't know. After James died, I hurt so much that I did think about getting in the car and driving away. Then I thought about what it would do to my mum and dad. That's what kept me in Sheffield. They're not here anymore. There's nobody to think about.'

'You've already run away, though. You've come here.'

'But people have found me. Maybe I didn't run far enough.'

Philip places a hand on top of mine. It's a sign of comfort, and Philip is a dear friend, but I want to pull my hand away and I don't know why.

'You have more people in your life to miss you than you think. Forget what they do for a job. If you were just a colleague, Sian wouldn't have been looking high and low for you. I'm sure Christian and Scott and the others feel the same. Then there's Adele in Sierra Leone, and there's me and Sally. And Carl loves you to bits. We'd all miss you, and I'm not just saying that because three of my waiting staff have decided not to come in this evening and I need someone to help peel the carrots.'

That makes me laugh.

'Half-circle, quarter slices or julienne?'

'You're learning,' he smiles. 'Fancy a job?'

'You may regret asking me that question.'

Me and Carl take the dogs on a long walk through the woods. It doesn't have the same openness and sense of freedom as when I was out with them yesterday. The sky is heavy and dark. The clouds are rolling in off the Irish sea and, for the first time in weeks, there's a breeze that's picking up strength by the hour. Without sounding melodramatic, it's a harbinger of doom.

We walk over uneven ground. The leafy canopy above gives the woodland a darker edge, particularly with the sun hidden by the clouds. It could almost be nighttime. The temperature is still hovering in the twenties, but it feels cooler. Icy fingers of uncertainty stroke the back of my neck, and it's not just fear of the impending storm. I have a dark feeling that something is happening right now. I'm just not sure what.

I keep thinking of the killer in Sheffield. If he hadn't emailed me and bragged about his crimes, he would have gotten away with them. He really is the embodiment of evil. My detective brain is kicking in and trying to figure out who he is and why he turned to murder. Was he born that way or did something happen to turn him into a killer? Try as I might, I can't fully let go of being a detective.

'What shall we do tonight when the storm hits?' Carl asks, bringing me out of my reverie. Thank goodness for Carl. 'I mean, if the power goes off, we won't have a TV to watch or anything.'

'Do you have any board games?'

'A few. I've hidden Monopoly, though. Dad gets really competitive with that one.'

'I used to like Operation. Me and my sister...' I stop myself. It's still too raw to think of me and Harriet in happier times, especially now she probably wishes I was dead.

'*I fucking hate you!*'

'I've got Dinosaur Operation,' Carl says.

'Really? How does that work?'

'You operate on a T-Rex.'

'Oh. Sounds fun. I think we should play that even if the power doesn't go out.'

We return to the restaurant at the same time as Sally pulls into the car park. She's been into the village to collect a few more provisions such as extra batteries for the torches and candles in the case of a power cut. Carl runs off to clean up the dogs while I attempt to make a coffee using the machine. I've been in so many coffee shops over the years, why didn't I pay attention to the baristas when they made my black Americano? Are all these buttons really necessary? The door from the kitchen is pushed open and the cleaner, May, breezes in with her caddy of cleaning supplies.

May is in her early sixties but doesn't have a single grey hair. It's dyed a dark blonde. She's wearing a long flowing shirt with the sleeves rolled up, and combat trousers with a duster sticking out of every pocket. A different cloth for a different job, I've heard her say. She's short, not much over five feet, trim, and always has a smile on her face.

'You're a braver woman than I am,' she says. 'I daren't go anywhere near that machine. It keeps hissing at me.'

'I'm beginning to wonder what's wrong with a kettle and a jar of instant.' I place a cup on a tray under a spout and press a button. Nothing happens. I press it again. Still nothing.

'It's like all these flavoured teas you can get nowadays,' May says. 'They all taste like scent to me. And, I'm sorry, but when I have a mug of tea, I want something I can dip my Digestives in.'

'I couldn't agree with you more,' I say as I give the Gaggia a dirty look. I decide to leave it until Philip comes back from wherever he's gone to. 'May, can I ask you a question about something?'

'Course you can,' she says, not stopping in her work. She goes over to the tables and begins clearing one of its place settings before vigorously polishing the smooth surface with a dry microfibre cloth.

'Philip tells me you've lived here all your life; I was wondering if you remembered the Pemberton twins going missing.'

May suddenly stops what she's doing. 'Oh, my goodness, that was a nightmare and a half. That poor family. And just when you thought it couldn't get any worse, the father went missing in that storm.'

'He got into difficulty driving home, didn't he?' I ask. I don't want May to think I know more than I do. It's better to let people think you know nothing.

'Yes. He'd been to see his mother, if memory serves me correctly. He had Alison in the back. We knew a storm was coming but I don't think any of us expected it to hit as hard as it did. He must have been taken by surprise with it. Bless him.

Fingers crossed we don't get a repeat today. I don't like the look of those clouds.'

'No,' I say, turning to look out of the window. Are they nimbostratus rolling in? Does it bloody matter? I turn back to May. 'Lynne Pemberton was lucky not to lose her other daughter, too.'

She nods. 'She didn't let that girl out of her sight for weeks afterwards. I mean, you wouldn't, would you?'

I go over to the table May has just cleaned, pull out a chair and sit down. 'What happened with the twins?'

'Nobody knows. They're out playing on a lovely summer's day, all three of them. Suddenly, two of them are gone, driven away. Never to be seen again.'

'No suspects?'

May pauses while she thinks. 'There was something about one of the teachers at the primary school. He'd changed his name when he was a teenager – can't remember why – police thought it was strange and latched onto him. Of course, he was innocent, but the damage had been done. He left soon afterwards. Poor man.'

'No-one else?'

'Not that I'm aware of. It really was as if they vanished off the face of the earth. I mean,' she looks around her to make sure no-one is listening and lowers her voice, 'When Carl was taken, there was a ransom, wasn't there? Not with the Pemberton twins.'

'Speaking as a detective, in a case like this, we look close to home for the perpetrators. Anything about Jack and Lynne?'

'No. I don't think… hang on,' she stops in her work again. A heavy frown appears on her forehead. 'I don't think either of them had alibis. Lynne was home alone. I mean, she was looking after the kiddies, but they were out. Jack… I don't know where he was, possibly out on the farm with Iain. That's another thing as well. Travis Montgomery.'

I remember the name from one of the news articles I'd printed off last night. 'Who's he?'

'He worked on the farm for a while. There was a rumour – now I'm only telling you this because of what I heard, I've no evidence of it myself – but there was a rumour that Travis and Lynne were carrying on.' She practically whispers those last two words.

'Carrying on as in having an affair?'

'I don't think it was a full-blown affair or anything, but there was talk, and you know what they say…' she says, leaving the comment hanging in the air.

'No smoke without fire,' I finish for her.

'Precisely.'

'Does Travis still live around here?'

'No. He wasn't local. He went back home not long after Jack went.'

That raises a few more questions. 'What did everyone in the village think happened to Celia and Jennifer?'

'Well, let's just say people held onto their kids a bit more closely after they went missing. Understandable, isn't it? Two pretty girls like that, it doesn't take a detective to twig on why they were taken. No offence.'

I smile. 'None taken. And Jack disappearing like he did, what did people make of that?'

'Jack was always a quiet man. He suffered with depression, had done since he was a child, according to Lynne. Something big like that happens, I suppose he's a ticking time bomb. You have to wonder what was going through his mind to leave Alison on the back seat of the car during a storm and walk out into the lake.'

'You think he deliberately drowned himself.'

'I do.'

'Yet, there have been sightings of him.'

'There have. I'm not sure what to make of those. They upset Lynne, that's for sure. I mean, she can't move on.'

'Are you close to Lynne?'

'Not as close as I used to be. We had kids the same age. She had the twins in the September. I had my Rupert in the December. I think she found it difficult to be around me straight afterwards.'

'Do you know what Lynne makes of all these sightings of Jack?'

She sighs. 'The same as us all, I suppose. If one person had seen him, you'd think it was a trick of the light or something, maybe even someone who looks a bit like him, but they kept on coming. You have to start believing them, don't you?' May pulls out a chair at the table she's cleaning and slumps into it. 'As I said, I've known Lynne for decades. I honestly don't know how she's coped. She's completely different to how she once was. I mean, it's going to change you, isn't it, everything she's been through, but she was always such a happy, confident woman. Before the girls went, she worked all hours as a midwife, she ran about this village helping anyone and everyone, a real backbone. Then, well, it was as if all the life had been torn from her. You look at her now and you can see she's a shadow of her former self. I hardly recognise her myself.'

'Lucky she has Iain.'

'Yes.'

'How long was it after Jack disappeared before she and Iain got together?'

May sucks in her lips as she thinks. 'Do you know, I've no idea. I never expected Iain to settle down. I know he doesn't look much now, but he was a very handsome man when he was younger. Tall, thick dark hair, broad shoulders. You saw him most weekends with a different woman on his arm. He seemed to get caught up in Lynne and Jack's tragedies and realised family was more important. He did a lot for Lynne after the twins went missing. When they announced they were getting married, it just seemed right. We were all happy for them. It was about time Lynne had some good luck for a change.'

I'm starting to get a headache. Is it so strange for Lynne to marry her brother-in-law following the disappearance of her husband? Was it love that brought them together or a shared grief? The more I think about it, the more I wonder if Jack's disappearance was through guilt rather than grief. If so, how much do Iain and Lynne know, and what are they keeping from Alison? Then there's the mysterious Travis Montgomery. Were he and Lynne having an affair? If so, why didn't she turn to him when Jack had gone and not Iain? Or did she shun Travis because she felt guilty for cheating on her husband?

There's that word guilt again. Maybe guilt has nothing to do with any of this. Maybe it's me feeling guilty about my actions leading to the deaths of my family and I'm trying to force it onto them so that I'll feel better.

'Or, perhaps I'm overthinking things.'

'What's that?' May asks.

'Oh, nothing. Just talking to myself.'

'First sign of madness.'

'Yes, that ship sailed a long time ago.'

May told me to pop along to the offices of the local newspaper, *Cumbria Today*, and speak to the editor, Tania Pritchard, who, apparently, came with her own dark past. I'm starting to wonder if anyone in this country is truly happy. According to May, Tania had planned on working for the local paper to learn her craft, then up sticks and move to the bright lights of a bustling metropolis where she'd be the first to attend any crime scene, desperate for the scoop on a pub brawl that had got out of hand, a domestic between husband and wife with a bloody ending, or the latest victim in a chilling serial killer investigation. She'd marry, obviously, but she wouldn't have kids, and when she retired, she and her husband, with their huge amount of disposable income, would spend their twilight years seeing the world while she wrote her scintillating memoirs.

Unfortunately, life had other ideas, and May told me the sad story of Tania Pritchard. She was the only child of Ruth and Willie Pritchard. Four months into working on the local rag, her father was killed in an eight-car pile-up on the M6. Ruth took his death hard and hit the bottle. Tania felt she couldn't leave while her mother was unstable, so she remained at home. Less than a year after the first anniversary of Willie's death, Ruth was diagnosed with MS and her decline was painful and slow. Tania's hopes for leaving Cumbria faded as she juggled working full-time on the newspaper and caring for her mother.

I open the door to the newspaper office, a former charity shop in the High Street, and look into the back office. I expect to see a hive of activity as reporters race to meet a deadline. What I actually see are five empty desks and a thin woman leaning over a laptop, her grey hair piled on top of her head in an untidy fashion, a vape sticking out of her mouth and a whirl of fake smoke with a smell of strawberries drifting around her. She must have heard me come in as she holds up a finger to tell me she'll be with me in a minute and carries on with her typing. I look around the room. It looks what it is – sad.

I suppose local media is dying a death. Most local newspapers are owned by larger organisations who are also struggling to keep afloat. Many have disappeared or merged in order to save money, and more and more pages are filled with advertisements than stories. The property sections disappeared when Rightmove and Zoopla came along. The personals were lost to Tinder and Grindr, and people find out about births, marriages and deaths by what people post on Facebook.

Eventually, she gets up from her chair and puts down her vape. She wipes crumbs off her bosom and smooths down her trousers as she comes to the front desk.

'Good morning. What can I do for you?' she asks. Her voice is gravelly, and she speaks with a thick local accent.

'I'm looking for Tania Pritchard.'

'You've found her.'

'I'm not local. I'm visiting for a while. I'm staying with the Meagan family who own Nature's Diner—'

'I know the Meagans,' she interrupts.

'I'm also a detective. I'm…'

'You're DCI Matilda Darke,' she says, her face suddenly lighting up. 'I wondered when I was going to clock eyes on you. Your stay has certainly got people talking.'

'Has it? Why?'

'Why? Seriously? You're the biggest piece of gossip our sleepy little village has had since the vicar's two poodles disappeared. Spoiler alert, they were found safe and well two days later.' She pauses to take a breath, and I can feel her eyeing me up and down. 'Now, some are wondering whether you're going to have brought the killer with you and if he's going to start picking us off one by one, or if you're here undercover to expose some kind of terrorist cell we didn't know we were part of,' she says with a wry smile. 'Oh, and I've had a call from one little old dear who thinks you might be a decoy. Don't ask me in what regard.'

Wow. I had no idea I'd been the focus of so much gossip.

'Well, I've never been undercover in my life. I'm pretty sure I haven't been followed by a killer and I'm no decoy. I can show you my driver's licence, if you like.'

'If I took every crackpot theory that came into this paper seriously, I'd contact the local water company and ask what they were putting into our supply.' Tania pushes some free copies of the paper to one side and lifts the flap in the desk. 'Come on through. You're the highest-ranking officer I've ever had in this building. I'm not having you standing there as if you're about to ask me to print a feature about a seventeen-year-old cat who's just died. Let's get the kettle on and you can tell me why you're here.'

Most of the journalists I've met over the years are of the

cut-throat variety who would climb over the dead body of their own mother to get a juicy story. I'm not getting those vibes from Tania, and I instantly warm to her as she leads me through into the main open-plan office. Tania pops into a small alcove and flicks on the kettle while I peruse a wall of framed first-page prints and maps of the local area.

'You'll see my byline a lot,' Tania says, coming back into the room. 'I write practically every single story.'

'You're the only journalist here?'

'The only full-time one. We've got three others. One's a trainee doing work experience, who I keep telling to choose a different career because he's bound to be jobless before he's thirty. One's the former editor who's an alcoholic and submits a story once every blue moon that I usually end up rewriting, and the final one is a mother of three who writes a regular feature on the life of a single mother in twenty-first-century Britain. She's the dullest woman I've ever met. I've told her to go out and get laid just to give her something new to write about, but she's not keen. She's discovered jam-making,' she says, pulling a face.

'So, you're the only one doing news?'

'News?' she says, as if the word is alien to her. 'I seem to remember a time when that word meant something.' The kettle boils and Tania trots into the back room to make the tea. She returns with two mugs on a tin tray with an unopened packet of Bourbons. 'There's no money in local news these days. I even have to buy my own tea and coffee. I tell you something, when I do eventually retire – if – this office will be empty. Even the sodding desk is mine from home.'

I pull out a chair and sit down. 'There doesn't seem to be many laughs in journalism these days.'

'It's all podcasts. There was a time when the ambition was to work for the BBC. Now, even their most experienced reporters are leaving to set up their own news podcasts. That's not going to catch on around here. So, what's the great Detective Chief Inspector Matilda Darke doing in our comatose village and is there a final stab at the big time in it for me?'

Tania's personality is infectious. I find myself wanting to open up a detective agency with her and for both of us to bring down the government. As she opens the Bourbons, I tell her about my visit from Alison Pemberton and the research I've done online.

'I know I shouldn't say this,' she begins with a mouthful of biscuit. 'But I milked that story for all it was worth. Not much happens around here. I knew at the time it was going to have a massive impact on the community, so I interviewed anyone and everyone I could get my hands on for their POV.'

'What do you think happened to Celia and Jennifer?'

'I think the father did it,' she says straight away.

'Jack? Why?'

'It's nearly always the father. Don't get me wrong, he put on a good act for the police and the media, but that whole getting swept away in the storm business, I didn't buy that for a minute.'

'You think he faked his death?'

Tania turns to her laptop and begins scrolling through as she talks. 'Back in the day, we were an important institution in the community, and we had a bigger staff number than we have now, though that's not difficult. We had someone covering sport, news, weather, events and features, the lot. We even had three full-time photographers. Anyway, the day after the storm, when we found out Jack Pemberton was missing, I was first out there. I had a shitty little camera with me, and I took a few snaps. They were useless. I can't take a good pic to save my life. Even now, with everything going on in an iPhone,

I can't get the focus right. Thank goodness for Photoshop – something else I've had to pay for myself. Here they are,' she says, finding what she's looking for. She angles the laptop so I can see the screen. 'These are the photos I took of Jack's car the morning after the storm. They're blurred so they were no good to print, but you can see what's there. Now, the water was nowhere near the car. If Jack had got out during the storm and it blew him about, there's no way it would have thrown him out into the lake. And why did he have to get out? The water wasn't anywhere close to the car. You can't tell on the photos, but you could see the tideline where the water was at its highest.'

'So, Jack's car didn't get into difficulty?'

'I'm no mechanic, but if it did, there's no reason for Jack to have gone near the water's edge.'

I frown as I glare at the three photographs on the screen. 'Do you have a magnifying glass?'

Tania produces one from her top drawer and hands it to me. 'It won't do you any good apart from give you a headache. Trust me, I speak from experience.'

She's right. I blink hard a few times but all I'm looking at is enlarged blurred pixels. 'Was the car locked or unlocked?'

'Unlocked. The driver's door wasn't fully closed either, I remember that.'

'Keys?'

'Still in the ignition.'

I shake my head.

'What are you thinking?' Tania asks.

'No parent, no matter how depressed, would leave their daughter in the back of the car with the door open and the key in the ignition, especially during a storm, especially when goodness knows what could happen to her. Given Jack's mental state at the time, he would go one of two ways.

He'd either protect her at all costs, or he'd take her with him.'

'And the fact that he did neither?'

I sigh. 'The six sightings of Jack—'

'There have been more than six,' Tania interrupts.

'Really?'

She turns back to her laptop. 'I used to put them in the paper at one point, but with no photographic evidence, there wasn't much to write about. Eventually, I stopped. Here we go.' She angles the laptop to me again to show a table she has made of the sightings. 'I stopped saving them after a while. I've got fourteen known sightings, but speak to Alison: she's got them all. She created a Facebook page where people could post their sightings.'

'Fourteen?'

'Mostly local. Though I think Alison had someone message her from Belfast once.'

'What do they say?'

'What you expect them to say. They've seen a bloke who stands out from the crowd, seems a bit nervy, that's what draws their attention to him, and he has a familiar look about him. By the time they've googled who he might be, he's disappeared.'

'And no photographic evidence?'

'No.'

'Is he listed as a missing person?'

'No. The local police believe he was swept out into the storm. Case closed.'

'What do you believe?'

'Can fourteen people be wrong?' Tania asks.

'Are the sightings still coming in?'

'You'd need to ask Alison about that. I haven't had one for a few years.'

'How well do you know the Pembertons?'

'Fairly well,' she says. 'When Jack and Iain were converting the farm into stables, they asked the paper to run a few features in the hope of generating publicity. They were very different, for brothers.'

'In what way?' I ask as I help myself to another biscuit. I can never resist a Bourbon.

'Iain was the confident, talkative one. Jack was always in the background. He couldn't make eye contact. Iain told me he suffered with depression. After Jack went missing, Iain turned to the drink. He told me in the local one night that, when they were kids, their father used to bully Jack.'

'Did he hit him?'

'I don't think so. Iain said that Jack was a quiet child. Iain was always out with a football, playing cricket in summer and rugby in winter, a proper lad, according to their father. Jack preferred to stay at home and draw or read. Their father didn't like that. He wanted his boys to grow up to be real men and real men weren't creative.'

'He sounds like a shit.'

'He was. There weren't many tears shed when Granville Pemberton died, despite how he went.'

I frown. 'How did he go?'

'He was working himself to death anyway, by all accounts. He was taking pills for his heart. The doctors assumed he had an attack of some kind and collapsed in the pigsty.'

I feel my frown deepen. 'I don't like where this is going. You said assumed.'

'There wasn't really much for a pathologist to examine. The pigs got to him before Jack and Iain could.'

'They ate him?'

'Not all of him. Parts of him.

I decide against another Bourbon. 'Oh my God!'

'You can see why the brothers were eager to convert the farm. They didn't want to be reminded of what happened. I tell you; it was a while before I ate bacon again.'

'What a way to go,' I say, giving a shudder.

'Strangely, it was Jack who took it the hardest.'

'I'm surprised they all stayed. If it had been me, I'd have sold up and moved on.'

'People around here either get out while they're still young or they stay here for life. Trust me, I know that only too well.'

I look at her and notice the hint of sadness in her eyes. Tania clearly wanted to have left High Chapel many years ago. She wasn't stuck here. She was trapped.

'If you suspected Jack was behind the disappearance,' I begin, taking the conversation back to topic. 'What did the other villagers think?'

'The majority focused on the tragedy. They couldn't do enough for Jack and Lynne. Iain sort of acted as a barrier, stopped the villagers from knocking on their door every five minutes with a cooked meal or a word of sympathy they didn't want to hear. I kept popping round, making a nuisance of myself. Eventually, it got too much for them, too. Iain started drinking more. Nothing anyone could do could help any of them.'

'And when the case went cold?'

'By then, Jack had disappeared too. A second tragedy. All the attention was on Lynne and Alison and making sure they were all right.'

'Who are the main players here apart from Lynne, Jack and Iain? Who else was involved? There was someone in the articles I read... Travis?'

'Travis Montgomery. Also known as Lady Chatterley's Lover.'

'Really?' I can feel my eyebrows disappear sky high. I should be on the stage with my acting skills.

Tania stifles a smile. 'No. I'm probably reading more into it than what was there. Travis was employed by Iain and Jack's father as a farm hand not long before Granville died. He stayed on for a while afterwards and helped with converting it into stables. There was rumour Travis and Lynne were having an affair.'

'Any truth in it?'

'It depends who you ask.'

'Where's Travis now?'

'No idea. He did a moonlight flit when the gossip started. He was only young. Mind you, he was a handsome young man: firm jawline, amazing cheekbones, dark floppy hair and his body was a bloody work of art.'

'It sounds like you had a bit of a crush yourself.'

'He was proper pin-up material. He could have made a calendar. Everyone lusted over him, but he was so shy with the attention, poor puppy.'

'He wasn't local?'

'No. He had a lovely Liverpudlian accent. Granville only employed him temporarily after his heart scare. He stayed on after he died to help out. Hang on a minute,' Tania suddenly sits upright and glares at me. 'My journalistic skills must be on the wane. I should have asked this right at the start: why are you asking all these questions about the Pembertons? What's going on?'

'Alison wants me to help. I did say I wouldn't get involved, but… I don't know, something isn't sitting right with what I've read so far.'

Tania's face softens. 'My heart really goes out to that lass. I've known her since she was little. She was there. She saw them get taken and there was nothing she could do about it. If you think about it, she's got all the answers locked away somewhere in her head and she can't find the key to access them. It must be torturous for her. So, what does your detective instinct tell you?'

It's a few long moments before I answer. 'I'm not sure. But Jack's disappearance and more than fourteen sightings of him, plus Travis doing a moonlight flit, are leading to more questions.'

'Who are you going to ask?'

'Lynne. Iain. Alison. You?'

'Me?'

'You were there at the time. You know all the key players.'

'If I help, will you let me write about it?'

'Something tells me I wouldn't be able to stop you.'

She rubs her hands together and grins. 'What's the first plan of action?'

'We need alibis for Lynne, Jack, Iain, and Travis for the time the twins went missing.'

'That's not going to be easy. Jack's possibly dead and I wouldn't even know where to begin looking for Travis.'

'But, surely, you'll have in your archives your interviews from the time. Maybe something is in there.'

'I'll have a look.'

'Celia and Jennifer's teacher at the time of their disappearance: male or female?'

Tania looks up to the ceiling as she thinks. 'Male.'

'Was he a suspect?'

'You're really testing my memory skills today. What was his name? Abbot? Anson? Ashton, that's it. Something Ashton. Damien Ashton. Wow. My memory is better than I thought,' she grins. 'I'm assuming he was interviewed by the police. Everyone was.'

'Is he still at the school?'

'No. He left for pastures new a long time back.' Tania turns the laptop back to her and hammers at the keyboard. 'Oh.'

'What?'

'In 2010, Damien Ashton was working at a school in Newcastle when he was forced to resign for having an affair with a sixteen-year-old boy.'

'Wow.'

She spins the laptop back around to me. There's a photo of a tall, plain-looking man in a navy suit and a sombre expression walking into a court building.

'Where is he now?'

'No idea. I can do some digging, if you like.'

'Thanks.' I turn to look out of the window and see that it's pitch-dark and a strong wind is blowing. 'I'd better be getting back before this storm breaks. You can ring me at the restaurant.'

'Will do. Can I ask you a personal question before you go?'

I nod.

'Why are you really here and not in Sheffield tearing the city apart looking for the person who killed your family?'

Normally, I wouldn't answer such a personal question like that from a journalist. The fact that I'm about to proves that I'm not my usual self.

'Because, the way I feel right now, I'm worried about what I might do when I catch him.'

BBC BREAKING NEWS: The Met Office has issued a rare red weather warning as Storm Gill hits Wales, Northern Ireland, Northwest England, and Southwest Scotland. Wind speeds of up to 95mph are forecast. 5,000 homes in Belfast are already without power.

I've never known rain like this. Eerily, the wind has dropped, but the rain is falling in sheets. It's like standing under a shower. As soon as it started, I had to go out and experience it. After a month of stifling heat, it's refreshing to feel the spray against my skin. I'm standing at the top of the steps to the restaurant, looking out over the car park and the lake beyond. All I can hear is the sound of rain hammering on the parched land. And that smell! There's a word for that smell released when rain hits parched earth – petrichor. Don't ask me how I know that. One of the many useless facts running around my mind.

'Matilda, you're getting soaked.'

I turn around and see Sally in the doorway. I look down and see I've stepped out further than I thought, and I am, indeed, getting wet. I didn't even realise. I should go back in, but there's something about the forcefulness of nature which is bewitching.

'I've got a really bad feeling about this storm,' Sally says as I go inside, and she closes and locks the door behind me.

Iain Pemberton slams the back door and enters the kitchen from the utility room. He's breathless, soaked, and windswept. Lynne resists the urge to laugh at the twig sticking out of his hair as she hands him a towel and takes his jacket and boots from him.

'You can always tell the people who've never been through a storm before. I've never seen someone so panicked. And they're higher up than we are.'

'Who's this? Not Shirley and Jim, surely?' He nods. 'That's not like them.'

'I think it's Shirley, really. She's worried about their new extension withstanding the winds. She never trusted that builder.'

'I didn't take to him much, either. There's no way those tiles were new. There's some soup left over, if you want it.'

'I'd love some. The wind's picked up again. It's really knocked the edge off the temperatures. It feels perishing out there.'

Lynne ladles soup from a pot on the stove into a bowl and takes it over to the table with a chunk of homemade bread. Iain sits down and tucks in. Lynne sits opposite him. She has a worried expression on her face.

'Iain,' she begins. 'I had a call from May earlier.'

'May?' he asks, blowing on his soup.

'Yes. Lives opposite the church. Dark-blonde hair. Her husband's a lollypop man.'

He nods. 'I know who you mean.'

'She was up at the restaurant cleaning this morning. She said that detective Alison was on about, DCI Darke, was asking about the twins and about Jack going missing.'

Iain swallows. 'Alison must have spoken to her, then.'

'I've looked her up, this Matilda Darke woman. She's a bloody good detective. Remember that serial killer who was killing all those sex workers in Sheffield a few years ago? She was the one who caught him. And that children's home sex scandal that we watched that programme about? That was her, too. If Alison's got her looking into this… Jesus Christ, Iain, what if she finds out about Jack?' she says, worrying at her fingernails as she spoke.

Iain sighs and places his spoon in the bowl, his appetite suddenly diminishing. 'We need to think about this. What—'

There's a flash of lightning followed, almost immediately, by a loud crack of thunder. Both of them turn to look out of the kitchen window. It's grown much darker in the last few minutes.

'I was thinking, maybe tomorrow, I might pop round to Nature's Diner and perhaps have a word with this Matilda Darke. If I tell her the truth – well, tell her what we told Alison – maybe she'll realise this is a family thing and back off. What do you think? Do you think that's a bad idea?'

Iain's face drops. 'Do you really want to involve someone else?'

'Well, no, but it's not looking as if we've got much choice. If this detective does start digging and she finds out… I don't want Alison finding out that way. And if she does… Iain, we've left it far too long for Alison to think we were protecting her when she was growing up.'

Reluctantly, Iain nods. 'I suppose, if you tell this detective all about Jack, it might stop her from interfering. If she's a mother herself, she might see it from your point of view, that you were just trying to protect your daughter.'

'I don't know if she is a mother. I couldn't find anything about her online. But she's good friends with Sally Meagan. She'll know all about protecting kids after what happened with her Carl.'

'Fair enough. We'll go first thing after breakfast.'

She thinks for a moment. 'Erm… I was thinking that it might be best if I go on my own, have a woman-to-woman chat.' She falls silent and begins to chew the inside of her mouth.

He looks up at her. 'You might be right. Are you sure you don't want me with you?'

She reaches across and places her hand on his. 'I'd love you with me, but it might be better this way.'

'I'll probably be busy, anyway, depending on how much damage this storm ends up doing.'

'Thirty years it's been,' Lynne says, a catch in her throat. 'Thirty years, I thought it was all in the past. Nothing can ever stay buried, can it?'

'I'm always here for you, Lynne, you know that. We're a team.'

'Thank you. It's all about protecting Alison, though.'

'And we will. Whatever it takes.'

She gives him a worried smile. 'Tea?'

'I could murder a cup.'

They take their mugs of tea into the living room. The lights flicker as a gust of wind whips around the house. Candles in holders and torches are already on the coffee table, waiting to be used should the power go out. A fire is lit, giving the room a warm glow.

'I can't believe I've had to light a fire in June,' Lynne says as she goes over to the window.

'The temperature's suddenly plummeted,' Iain says. 'It feels colder than it actually is.' He sits on the sofa and picks up his tablet. He logs onto the security system at the stables to make sure everything is as it should be.

Lynne peels back the curtains and looks out, watching the beginnings of the storm through the slats of the vertical blinds.

Heavy black clouds have rolled in from the Irish sea and turned what should have been a pleasant, early summer evening into the darkness of midwinter.

Lynne watches as the road is turned into a river, running downwards towards the school. She closes her eyes tightly shut and is transported back to that day in 1992 when Jack and Alison were out visiting his mother. She tries to think of the last conversation she had with Jack, and she can't. Alison has often asked her what the last thing they'd said to each other was; had Jack known how much he was loved by his family? Lynne can't give her the answer she wants to hear.

'Shit!' Iain exclaims. 'That bloody felt roofing has come off the end stable block. What did I tell you? I said this would happen. Remind me never to ask Warren to do anything ever again.'

'Has it all come off?' Lynne asks, moving away from the window.

'It's flapping about like mad. It won't hold for much longer,' he says, standing up and heading into the kitchen.

'Where are you going?'

'To do a bodge repair until the storm passes.'

'You're going out in this?' she asks, wide-eyed with fear.

'If the rainwater gets in, it will soak the hay, and any flying debris could spook the horses. It might even injure them. I can't risk it.'

'You can't go out in this, Iain. It's barely getting started and it's going to get much worse.'

'What else can I do?' he asks, raising his arms. 'Where are my waders?'

Lynne follows him into the utility room where he's putting on his waterproof coat and hat.

'I'll come with you.'

'No, you won't.'

'I can help.'

'I'm not having you going out in this.'

'We're partners, Iain. It's my problem as much as it is yours.'

'No. You need to stay here. Some of the owners will be ringing up asking how their horses are. They'll not be happy if the phone goes unanswered. They'll think something's happened.'

'No. They'll assume we're out looking after their horses. Let me come with you.'

Iain slips his feet into wellington boots and goes to his wife. He holds her firmly by the shoulders and kisses her on the forehead.

'I'll be fine. I'll be half an hour at the most.'

He opens the back door, and the storm hits him full in the face, causing him to recoil. He's only been back in the house for twenty minutes or so and already the wind has increased in strength. He pushes forward and pulls the door closed with a slam behind him.

Lynne stands, arms folded against her chest. The last major storm resulted in her losing her first husband. She couldn't stand it if she lost her second, too.

'You'd think it was midnight,' Alison Pemberton says as she looks out of the front passenger window of the police car.

Claire Daniels is driving, painfully slowly, blue lights flashing, as they make their way towards High Chapel Primary School. It's to be a place of safety should the village have to be evacuated. Unfortunately, a tree has fallen, blocking the road leading to the main entrance. A farmer with a tractor is on his way to move the tree, but the headteacher called the police to let them know of the incident.

'I hate driving in this,' Claire says. 'I can't see anything in front of me.'

The windscreen wipers are useless in such treacherous conditions.

'It's times like this I wish I had a safe job like a librarian or something,' Claire continues. 'I'd be indoors right now, sitting in front of the fire, duvet wrapped around me, reading a Jane Austen.'

'You've never read a Jane Austen a day in your life,' Alison laughs.

'I read *Wuthering Heights* at school.'

'That's Emily Bronte,' Alison corrects her.

'Same thing.'

'Philistine.'

'You've hardly got a PhD in English Classics. I've seen you reading *Bridgerton*.'

They turn a corner and Claire slams on the brakes as they almost collide with the felled tree.

'Shit,' Alison swears, as the seat belt pulls her back. 'That was close.'

'Too close,' Claire says, paling at the near miss, hands immediately going to protect her baby.

They both carefully climb out of the car, struggling against the elements. They can't put signs up to warn other road users as they'll just blow away. Hopefully, anyone brave, or stupid, enough to be out in weather like this will notice the flashing lights on the police car and slow down before they reach the bend.

'Who's coming to clear the tree away?' Claire shouts. 'We need to get access to the school if any of the houses in the lower half of the village need evacuating.'

'I don't know,' Alison screams back. 'Inspector Forsyth just said someone was on their way.'

'We can't...'

Claire stops as the sound of the flood siren begins. It's an eerie noise that chills the blood, reminiscent of the air raid sirens from the Second World War. The sirens are manually controlled from an incident room by trained duty officers who use forecasting information to decide whether the whole area needs to be informed of a possible impending natural disaster.

Alison and Claire freeze to the spot. The siren can only mean one thing: evacuations are about to begin.

'I don't like the sound of that,' I say.

We're all in the living room above the restaurant, watching the storm batter Lake Windermere and the surrounding countryside. The internet has cut off and the lights are flickering. Candles are on standby. We were all sitting in relative silence when the siren broke out.

'You'd think they'd come up with a different siren,' Sally says. 'You hear that, and you think we're at war.'

'It's the sound everyone knows means impending danger,' Philip says.

'I've never heard it before, not outside of a war film,' I say. It sounds different from hearing it on TV. It genuinely does send a chill down the spine.

'They did a practice run last year,' Sally says. She has to

raise her voice over the sound of the storm. 'Scared the life out of me and it was only a rehearsal.'

Philip moves up on the sofa next to her and wraps his arms around her shoulder, pulling her tight. I love how close this couple still is after everything they've been through.

Carl is sitting on the floor in front of the fire with both dogs. He's looking out of the window, watching the rain and flying debris lash against the glass.

'Are we—?' My question is interrupted by a loud crack of thunder that sounds as if the world is being torn apart.

I stand up and go over to the window. Lightning lights up the black sky as daggers of brilliant electric blue fork above the lake. It's an unsettling, yet beautiful, sight to witness. Triple-glazed glass is all that separates me from the onslaught of the storm. A masochistic part of me wishes I was out in this, to feel the full force of nature's wrath wrap around me. I've never heard thunder so loud. I place my hand flat against the glass and feel it vibrate with every rumble.

A flash of lightning hits a tree on the side of the lake. An orange finger of fire runs down its trunk and the tree almost explodes as it's torn in half.

'Jesus Christ!' I recoil.

Carl jumps up from the floor and runs over to the sofa to be with his parents. Both dogs bark at the thunder.

The wind intensifies and trees are almost bent double. Huge branches are torn from trunks, picked up and tossed around, landing with a splash in the lake. Another is thrown up and hits the window just beside where I'm standing. I jump back as if I've been hit. Behind me, Sally and Carl scream and the dogs are cowering behind the sofa. I look at the glass where the branch hit and see a small crack.

This is no longer a chance to marvel at the destruction of

nature. I'm standing in the path of violence, and I hate to say this but it feels amazing.

Lynne had been watching the live camera feed on her tablet since Iain left. When the power went out and the internet failed, she couldn't see him anymore. The last she saw of him was as he battled with the elements and struggled to repair the roof of the empty stable at the end of the block.

She goes around the living room lighting candles and turning on lantern torches. The fire is lit in the corner of the room, so she's able to keep warm, and the room looks cosy in the dim light, but outside, the storm is raging. She's never heard such a terrifying sound before in her life. Even the storm of '92 wasn't as bad as this.

She goes over to the window and pulls back the curtains. Trees are down in the middle of the road; rain is pouring down in sheets. Debris litters the ground, and a fence panel has smashed through the windscreen of Kitty Routledge's Volvo across the road.

Lynne's scared. She hates bad weather, storms in particular, for obvious reasons. She hates the fact she's alone. She hates that Iain is out in this and she's powerless to help. She hasn't heard from Alison since lunchtime. Where is she right now?

She grabs her phone from the coffee table and rings her daughter. It rings out until the voicemail kicks in. She wasn't planning on leaving a message but suddenly thinks that, if Alison sees a missed call from her mother, she'll likely panic and think something's happened.

'Alison, it's me,' Lynne begins. She's trying, but failing, to sound calm. 'I just want to make sure you're all right. I'm guessing you're very busy right now, but give me a call when you can. It'll be—'

Lynne screams and drops her phone as a tree comes crashing through her living room window.

Sally and Philip have taken Carl and the two dogs into Carl's bedroom at the rear of the building. It's sheltered by the woods and hopefully muffles the sound and danger of the storm. I remain in the living room, transfixed by the raging tempest. It's difficult to imagine that less than a day ago I was running in the midst of a heatwave beneath the brilliant blue sky. Now, that sky is angry and is unleashing hell upon the earth. The destructiveness inside of me is on the side of Mother Nature. Tear this planet apart. We're destroying it anyway, as well as each other.

Another tree falls and crashes onto the concrete car park. Fortunately, it's free of vehicles. The lights go out, plunging the room into darkness. I pick up a storm lamp from the windowsill and turn it on. I see myself reflected in the black mirror of the window. A flash of lightning lights up the scene. It hits a tree beside the lake which falls against another with such force they are both uprooted and fall into the water.

I've seen storms before, but nothing of this magnitude. It's electrifying and, after all these years of wondering why gawkers stand on the outskirts of a crime scene, I now know how they feel. Witnessing something dark and destructive is additive. Around me is total chaos, but I've never felt more alive as I watch the dance of a broken power cable spitting out blue sparks. I leave the living room and go out into the hallway. Everything in my head is screaming at me to remain indoors, but I defy all logic. I can hear my heart pounding in my ears. I throw open the front door and step out into the wildness of nature.

Lynne Pemberton is shattered. She hasn't been to sleep yet, and it's now getting light.

The storm raged until the early hours of the morning before it eventually began to die down. However, the damage had been done, not only to Lynne's house, but to the village as a whole. Lynne hasn't been out yet as she's still battling to save her own home.

After the tree had crashed through her living room window, and the initial panic and horror subsided, she set about covering all the furniture with any old duvet covers and blankets that she could find to protect them from the rain that was lashing into the room. She immediately called Alison, leaving a panicking voicemail, and Iain, where she screamed at him to return home.

There was nothing any of them could do until the tree, a mighty oak more than a hundred years old, was removed. Iain called Frank who has the next farm up and asked if he could come straight over. He'd been in the process of chopping the felled tree outside the school into manageable moveable pieces, but he came as soon as he could. By three o'clock, Iain was hammering up sheet board with Lynne,

Alison and Claire holding it in place. The only thing they could do then was wait until daylight and the electricity coming back on before a full survey of the damage could be done.

'I loved this carpet,' Lynne says as she squelches through the living room into the kitchen. 'I'm guessing it can't be saved.'

'We need to get it taken up and see if the floorboards beneath are damaged or soaked. They'll need to dry out before we can lay a new one.'

'What about my sofa?' she asks, looking longingly at it.

'We might be able to clean it. You did the right thing in pushing it out of the way and covering it,' he says, putting his arm around her shoulders.

'I know they're only things,' she says, emotions rising in her throat. 'They can easily be replaced, but... they're *our* things.'

'It could have been much worse. You could have been standing at the window when it crashed through. I could have lost you.'

'Don't say that,' she shudders.

'It's true.' Iain's phone vibrates in his back pocket. He pulls it out and looks at the text message. 'It's from Frank. He says the people from the electric board are here to try and restore power. Are you still planning on going over to see that detective?'

'What? Oh, yes. I'll go later. There's no rush. I'm guessing Alison will have too much to keep her busy over the next few days to worry about the past.'

She slumps into a wooden chair brought in from the kitchen.

'Are you all right?' Iain asks when he notices the angst on his wife's face.

'The last time there was a major storm here we were plunged into a nightmare. Now, it's happening all over again.'

Iain squats down to her level and wraps his arm around her, pulling her tightly into a hug. He rests her head against his chest and brushes her hair.

Neither of them says anything. They don't need to. They are both thinking the same thing. Their thirty-year secret is about to be blown wide open by an interfering DCI from Sheffield, and there is nothing they can do about it except wait for the fallout.

It's a much colder morning. A stiff breeze is blowing. The heatwave is over, and Philip, Sally and me are surveying the restaurant from the far side of the car park. There are a few missing roof tiles. A couple of trees have fallen which need to be removed before the restaurant can open later, but Nature's Diner seems to have been in favour this time around.

'Close call,' Philip says.

'It was scary there for a while. I don't know how those people in America cope with tornadoes,' Sally says with a shiver.

'Can I take the dogs into the woods?' Carl asks. It's obvious he wants to go and see how badly damaged the trees are. He can barely control his excitement.

'Yes, but be careful,' Sally says. 'Watch your step.'

'Excellent,' he grins.

'What happened to you last night?' Sally asks me. 'I heard the shower running when I got up to go to the toilet about four o'clock.'

'I went for a walk.'

'In the middle of a massive storm? You could have been

killed. What kind of a person goes out for a walk in weather like that?'

'I wanted to clear my head.'

'It would have been less risky with a bottle of vodka. Did it work?'

'I'm not sure.'

Philip moves away from us and tests the wooden steps to the restaurant to see if they need repairing.

Sally lowers her voice. 'I'm worried about you.' She rubs her hand on my arm. It's a comforting gesture, but I don't feel anything. 'You don't go out in weather like we had last night unless you're on some kind of suicide mission. You're not going to do anything stupid, are you?'

I think of Liam Walsh, the teenager at university struggling with his mental health. He wanted to die so much but he couldn't bring himself to take his own life on his own. He must have been going through so much anguish and hurt. I can certainly understand how he felt.

'I'm not going to kill myself,' I say, though even I'm not convinced by my words.

'You're killing yourself every time you go out running or swimming. You're putting your body through too much.'

'I'm screaming, Sally,' I say, turning to her. 'Inside, I'm screaming so loud that I can't hear anything else, and I don't know what to do to silence it. That's why I went out last night. I need to unleash all this pain.'

'What did you do last night?'

'I went down by the lake. I stood on the edge, and I cried. I shouted and screamed and cried until I was hoarse. Any other night, I'd have woken the whole village. The storm drowned out all the noise.'

'Do you feel better for it?'

I think for a moment. I look at her. I can't lie to Sally. 'No. Not at all.'

Carl heads off into the woods with both dogs, Philip and Sally continue to survey their restaurant, and I change into my wetsuit. The lake has been calm in the month I've been here. The wild winds of last night have died down but there's still a stiff breeze blowing. It'll be a change to push against the tide.

The water feels much colder, and I gasp as I submerge myself. I swim out a few meters doing a gentle breaststroke before turning over onto my back and looking up at the sky. Last night, it had been black and violent. This morning, it's blue and calm. In the woods, I can hear the echoing sound of dogs barking. The two Woodys are enjoying their adventure, jumping over felled trees, and picking up new sticks for Carl to throw. I smile to myself. I'm enjoying being here. I don't want my time here to end.

I roll back onto my front and swim further out. I love swimming in the lake. The water is so clear. Occasionally, when there's nobody else around, I feel like I'm in my own private oasis, my surroundings untouched by the negativities of the twenty-first century. Everything seems unspoiled and clean.

'Matilda!'

I hear my name being called. I turn and see Carl at the entrance to the woods, standing by a couple of felled trees. He waves and I wave back.

'I've found something.'

'What?' I call back, not hearing what he's saying.

'I said, I've found something,' he shouts louder.

I still can't hear him so swim quickly towards him.

'What did you say?' I ask, once I'm closer.

'I found that tree we saw get hit by lightning,' he says, his face dirty with soot. He's obviously touched the scorched bark. 'It's all black and in pieces. You can still smell the burning. It's so cool.'

One of the dogs jumps into the lake and swims out to join me. The other follows and swims around the trees, snatching away at the broken off twigs and branches.

'You look cold,' Carl says.

'It's a bit chillier than I expected it to be.'

'What's that?' He points to something entangled in the branches.

'Where?'

'There by Woody.'

I crane my neck to see where Carl is pointing. I swim over, both dogs joining me, getting in my way as I try to pull whatever it is free. It's a piece of plastic, rectangular in shape. I manage to free it, turn it over and wipe the smooth surface.

'It's a registration plate,' I say.

'Where did it come from?'

'I've no idea. E311 TVC,' I read it out. 'That's an old number. E-reg must be… I'm not sure…1990s, possibly.'

'Wow. That really is old.'

'It's not that old, Carl. I was born in… never mind,' I say, suddenly wondering if Carl would consider me ancient if he knew I was born in the 1970s.

'The storm wouldn't have blown that all the way out here, would it?' he asks.

I look around me. There are no cars around here. The woods are in the way of nearby streets. If a car registration plate had become detached somehow, there is no way it could have blown all the way out to the lake. There is only one place it could have come from, and that was from down beneath the surface of the water.

'Carl, take this,' I say. I swim to the edge and hand Carl the number plate.

'What are you going to do?'

'I'm going to have a look and see if I can see a car.'

'Oh, cool. You think there's one down there?'

'When it comes to the bottom of lakes and rivers, Carl, there are all manner of things down there. At the bottom of the River Don in Sheffield, police divers were searching for a missing man, and they found two abandoned ATM machines, a sawn-off shotgun used in a bank robbery in the 1980s, and a Sky satellite dish.'

'Was there any money in the machines?'

'No.'

'Shame. Did you find the missing man?'

'No. I believe he's still missing. Do you want to shout the dogs back? I don't want them trying to freedive to the bottom of the lake.'

'Sure.'

Carl shouts for both dogs. They ignore him until he plunges his hand into his pocket and pulls out a couple of small Bonio biscuits. They doggy-paddle to the edge and shake off the excess water before emptying his pockets of biscuits.

I swim away from the felled trees, take a deep breath, and dip below the surface. Despite the storm and trees crashing into the water disturbing the detritus beneath, it is still relatively clear, and I'm able to see further than the end of my nose. Unlike the filthy water of the River Don where it's not even safe to step into without wearing a full HAZMAT suit. Thinking about the level of pollution and the murky water makes me shudder. Compared to that, the water that makes up Lake Windermere is practically drinkable.

I surface, catch my breath, then go down again. I turn, look about me, and can't see anything resembling a vehicle. I swim down, left and right, but there's nothing there. Having never been diving before a day in my life, I'm not adept at holding my breath for long periods of time. I resurface.

'Have you found anything?' Carl shouts.

I turn to look at him and see I've drifted far out into the lake.

'Not yet,' I call, breathlessly.

'Maybe there's nothing down there. Maybe it was just the registration plate and the tree smashing into the water brought it up.'

'Maybe,' I say, though I think otherwise.

One final try. I take a huge breath and dip below the water. I swim down, open my eyes, and that's when I see it. A car. Judging by the amount of silt, mud and algae that's clinging to it, it has been down here for some time. As much as I want to get closer, to at least discover what colour the car is, my lungs won't allow it. I break the surface of the lake and gasp for air.

'Find anything?' Carl asks.

I nod. It's a while before I speak as I struggle to get my breath back. 'There's a car down there.'

'Excellent,' he calls out, his excited voice echoing around him.

Carefully, I swim back to the shore, using the felled trees to pull myself in. I'm knackered.

'Do you think this is a clue to a big murder mystery?' Carl asks, looking at the registration plate.

'I'd have thought you'd had enough of mysteries,' I say, dragging myself to my feet and wringing out my hair.

'Well, yes, they're scary when they happen to you, but when you're not directly involved, they're exciting.'

'Shall I tell you how exciting I think this will get?'

'Go on.' He looks up at me with wide eyes and a huge grin on his face, almost salivating.

'I think joyriders nicked a car and needed somewhere to get rid of it, so drove it into the lake.'

'Oh.'

'Sorry, Carl, no buried treasure, no bodies, and no serial killers. Sometimes police work is incredibly dull.'

We walk into the darkness of the woods. I turn to look back over my shoulder to where I picked the registration plate up from. I must have disturbed something when I jumped down into the water as another item bobs to the surface and becomes entangled in the twigs. I pause, momentarily, and squint to try to make out the object, but I can't. There's clearly a lot more beneath the surface that needs to be brought up.

I've never given any thought to entering a police station before. I work in one, so it's never registered that some people might be nervous about stepping inside one. I park around the corner from High Chapel Police Station in Adele's Porsche 911 and walk to the front entrance with the registration plate under my arm. I stand on the threshold and look up at the whitewashed building. A wave of fear sweeps over me. A police station no longer represents my career, a place of crime-fighting and law and order. I see a place of destruction. If I'd taken my mother's advice all those years ago and chosen a different career, so many people would still be alive today.

'Matilda?'

I hear my name being called and turn to see PC Alison Pemberton heading towards me. She's dressed in full uniform, which is smart and neat, but her hair is all over the place. She looks shattered.

'Hello,' I say and attempt a smile. Judging by the strange look on her face, my attempt has failed.

'What are you doing here? Are you looking for me?'

'I found something. I'm not sure if it's relevant to anything, but I thought I'd drop it in.' I hand her the registration plate.

Alison studies it. 'Wow. That's old. Come with me. I'll take you through.' She leads the way, pushing open the front door. 'I'm guessing your station is a tad more modern than our former post office.'

'Just a bit,' I say, taking in the high ceilings and ornate cornicing. This has character. South Yorkshire Police HQ has cork-tiled ceilings and damp patches.

Alison leads me through a warren of narrow corridors. She opens a door to an interview room and shows me in. I feel like I'm a witness to a crime.

'Can I get you a tea or anything?'

'I'm fine. Thanks.'

I've made a mistake coming here. I want to leave.

'Okay. I'll go and get some forms and I'll be right back.'

'Erm…' I begin. My throat is tight, my mouth dry.

'Yes?'

I clear my throat and swallow hard. 'I was speaking to Tania Pritchard. She told me there have been more than fourteen sightings of your father.'

She nods and looks around to see if she's being overheard. 'Twenty-six, at the last count.'

'Twenty-six?'

'The last one was in October last year. Someone emailed me a photo of a man standing on a hill overlooking High Chapel. It's blurred and you can't make out his face but… the build, the height…' She shrugs. 'I don't know.'

I think about this for a moment. Twenty-six sightings is a lot for a dead man.

'Did you show your mum the photo?'

'No. It upsets her.'

'What are your mum and Iain like?'

'What do you mean?'

'As a couple: what are they like, are they happy?'

Alison's face softens. 'I think so. I mean, I hope they are. They work well together. They've made the stables a thriving business. It's given them both something to concentrate on.' She thinks. 'They complement each other. They like the same films. Mum likes to sew and make her own clothes. Uncle Iain has his model aircraft he paints. They enjoy eating out. They're a normal middle-aged couple. Why are you asking about them?'

'Just interested,' I say.

'Does this mean you're helping me?' There's a hopeful look in her eyes.

'I... I don't know what I'm doing at the moment, Alison. It's certainly got me asking some questions.'

'Any I can help you with? Do you want me to bring over my list of sightings? I tell you what, I'll get the forms for this registration plate, and we can talk it over.' She leaves the interview room before I have a chance to say anything.

The door closes and I'm left alone. I look around at the crime prevention posters and warnings to people to look out for the signs of child abuse, illegal migrant workers, and people involved in a coercive relationship. I sigh. Twenty-first-century Britain is not a fun place to be, if any of these posters are a sign of the times.

I've been left alone in the small, stuffy room for almost fifteen minutes, and I haven't yet sat down. I pace around the table, looking out of the window through the dust-laden Venetian blinds at life in High Chapel trying to return to normal after the storm. I go to the other side of the room and look through the scratched plexiglass at the activity in the police station.

Uniformed officers are milling around, chatting, laughing, getting on with their work. I watch as two men, sitting next to each other, divvy up snacks bought from the local Co-op. I almost smile. I could be watching my own team. Sian and Scott having a playful row about who has taken all the Maltesers from Sian's snack drawer (usually me) and who has put something healthy and full of vitamins and protein in there (usually Scott to wind Sian up).

I feel a tightness in my chest. I step back from the window. The scene beyond becomes a blur. I'm in a police station, a place I have spent most of my life in, apart from home. I should feel normal here, yet I feel sick. The prickle of heat creeps up my back and it has nothing to do with the strengthening sun outside. I have to leave.

The registration plate is on the table. It has nothing to do with me. I'm simply a visitor to the area. Let them deal with it themselves. They don't need me.

I pull the door open and leave the room, heading for the front door at speed.

'Matilda.'

It sounds like Alison calling out to me, but I don't stop and don't look back. I have to get out of this building.

I sit behind the wheel of the Porsche and try to get my breath back, trying, but struggling, to remember the breathing exercises I was given by my therapist. Years ago, after James died, after Carl was taken, I struggled with panic attacks and often recited the names of British prime ministers to help calm me. It worked, but I don't want to go back to those dark days.

'Fuck it,' I say, starting the engine and reversing out of the small space. I'm heading for the restaurant when I catch sight of Tania Pritchard outside the office of *Cumbria Today* enjoying an illicit cigarette. I pull in.

When she sees me climb out of the Porsche, she drops it to the ground and stubs it out.

'Wow. Nice car.'

'If only it were mine.'

'Does the owner know you have it?'

'She doesn't actually, no,' I say.

Tania laughs then goes into the building. I follow.

'You survived the storm?' Tania asks.

'Just about.'

'My shed was catapulted into the neighbouring garden at three o'clock this morning. It scared the shit out of me. I didn't get a wink of sleep after that. On the plus side, I seem to have inherited someone's trampoline. I was going to call you later. I've found your alibis.'

'That was quick.'

'I'm not an award-losing journalist for nothing, you know.'

I pull out a chair and sit down.

'Lynne was at home alone, looking after the girls. She told police she was baking at the time. She went out to fetch them in for their lunch and that's when she noticed there was only Alison there. Jack and Iain were renovating the farm and, while Iain was working full-time, it wasn't bringing in enough money for Jack, so he was still working for Dudgeons. They were a parts manufacturer. They've long since gone. Iain was working alone on the stables. Now, this is where it gets interesting. Travis also said he was working at the stables and, at first, Iain confirmed that, but Iain was spotted at the hardware shop in the village so had to amend his statement. He'd left Travis at the stables on his own roughly around the time the children went missing.'

'So, Travis has no alibi?'

'No.'

'How have you remembered all this?'

'I still have all my original notes. I throw nothing away. I'm a hoarder. Fuck knows what I'm saving it all for. While I was looking for this lot, I found a file with all the scores from the bingo finals in 1993.'

'Riveting stuff.'

'You have no idea what life is like around here, Matilda. Orgies one night, cocaine parties the next, and the knit-and-natter events can get very raunchy.'

I smile. 'So, no alibi for Travis or Lynne.'

'You don't suspect the mother of kidnapping her own children, surely?' Tania asks, aghast.

'After twenty years in my job, you're no longer surprised by who does what to whom.'

'That's very sad.'

'Story of my life,' I add. 'Can you do some digging into Travis's background?'

'I can try, but the guy was a private man. He was so shy he hardly spoke.'

'He couldn't have been that shy if he was sleeping with Lynne.'

'I suppose not. I know he helped in the search for the Pemberton twins. I remember asking him for an interview, trying to get the inside story on how Jack and Lynne were coping. He gave nothing away. I saw him in the pub a few days later and bought him a pint, thinking beer will loosen his tongue. Nothing. He clammed up.'

'I read one of the articles online that mentioned Jack and Lynne being extensively questioned, along with Iain, Travis and a neighbour… can't remember her name.'

'Clara Fisher?'

'That's her.'

'She moved away not long after it all died down. She couldn't stand how everyone was turning against each other, suspecting everyone. She moved to somewhere in Portugal with her sister. She ended up marrying a man twenty years younger than her. Lucky cow.'

'My point is, everyone mentioned in the article made a comment, but Travis didn't. Despite his name being printed, he wasn't quoted.'

'Like I said, he gave nothing away. Every question put to him, about anything, was met with a monosyllabic answer.'

'There's a difference between being private and having something to hide.'

'You think he had a past?'

'We all have a past.'

'True. But how dark do you think his went?'

'That's what I'm hoping you're going to be able to tell me.'

'Leave it with me. Travis Montgomery is hardly John Smith, is it? There can't be many of them knocking about. By the way, I've tracked down the Pemberton twins' teacher, Damien Ashton. He no longer teaches, hardly a surprise, and he's back living in Cumbria at Seascale on the other side of Scafell Pike. I have his email address and his mobile number, if you're interested.'

'Wow. You're really good.' I'm impressed.

'I could amaze you with my journalistic skills, but he's put his entire life on social media. Between LinkedIn and Facebook, I'm pretty sure I could empty his bank account.'

'Pillock. I think he might be worth chatting to. Even if he isn't involved in their disappearance, he knew the girls so he might be able to give us some insight into how they were behaving at the time.'

Tania tears off a page of her notebook and hands it to me. She gives me a winning smile. 'I'm so glad you came here. I shall give thanks to St Francis de Sales, the patron saint of journalists, for bringing you to me.'

'Save your thanks for now. With my track record, I may end up destroying your village.'

'Now that would definitely make for a fun front-page lead.'

As I pull up outside Nature's Diner, Sally opens the door to the restaurant and comes running down the steps.

'Matilda, you've got a visitor,' she says.

'Really? Nobody knows I'm here.'

'It's Lynne Pemberton. Alison's mother.'

'What does she want with me?'

'I've no idea. I told her you weren't in, but she said it was urgent. She was pacing up and down out here for ages. It took all my powers of persuasion to get her to come inside. She seems very edgy. The power's just come back on so I'm going to make her a coffee. Do you want one?'

I look up at the restaurant and see the head of a woman sitting at a table in the window.

'As if you have to ask.'

We enter the restaurant, and Sally goes over to the coffee machine while I approach Lynne. From behind, I can see that she seems tense. Her shoulders are up beneath her ears; her hands, knitted together on the table, are squeezed hard, the knuckles almost white. Below the table, her left leg is jiggling. This is a nervous woman.

'I believe you're waiting for me. Matilda Darke,' I say as I approach.

Lynne turns and looks me up and down. 'Oh. You're Matilda Darke?'

'Yes.'

'I expected you to be taller. I don't know why.'

I pull out the chair opposite and sit down. 'I expected me to be taller, too. I'm guessing I'm too old for a growth spurt.'

Lynne gives a weak smile as Sally comes over with the coffees on a tray.

'Here we are,' she says with all the jollity she usually reserves for paying customers. 'Can I get you anything else?'

'No. I'm fine, thank you,' Lynne says, nervously.

'And for you?' Sally turns to me. 'Oh, sorry, I actually thought I was working then.' She slaps me playfully on the arm, laughs and walks away.

'I've never been in here before,' Lynne says, gazing at her surroundings. 'They've done it out nicely.'

'Yes.'

I take a sip of my coffee. Sally makes it exactly how I like it – black, and with an extra shot. The stronger the better. I can feel the caffeine kicking in with just one sip.

'You wanted to see me,' I say when Lynne doesn't make a move to begin the conversation.

'I did,' she says, taking a breath. 'I believe my daughter, Alison, has been to see you, asking for help.'

'She has.'

'I…' She hesitates. 'I don't want you to help her.'

'Oh?'

'I never told Alison fully what happened. She was too young at the time, but… I don't know, maybe I should have explained everything when she got older, but it was never the right time. Then, when she said she was joining the police, I thought… I'm not sure what I thought, but I didn't want it jeopardising her career,'

'Sorry, Lynne, you're not making any sense.'

She releases a heavy sigh and composes herself. She picks up her cup of coffee. 'This is good,' she smiles, nervously. 'Me and Iain don't eat out as much as we used to.'

'Iain's your husband?'

'Yes. Second husband. Are you married?'

'No. I was. I'm widowed.'

'I'm sorry.'

I used to feel great pain when I mentioned I was a widow or when I thought of James. Right now, I feel nothing. Is that due to the burgeoning romance with Odell Zimmerman back in Sheffield, or because I feel so numbed by recent events that all my emotions have completely shut down?

'As you know, I had twin girls before Alison was born,' Lynne begins. 'They were almost two when Alison came along. I was hoping for a boy. Jack, my husband, the girls' father, he wanted another girl. When the twins were seven and Alison five, they were out playing hide-and-seek. We lived in a cottage at the time, right on the edge of the village. There are fields behind it where all the kids used to play. According to Alison, the girls just disappeared. She saw them in the back of a car being driven away. She didn't think… well, she wouldn't at only five. But they were kidnapped. We never saw them again.

'We took it hard. We were bound to, weren't we? But me and Jack dealt with it in different ways. I had a bit of a breakdown at first. I was a mess. I sent Alison to live with my sister and her husband. After a while, I don't know, I seemed to just throw myself into work. I was a midwife then. I had to keep busy, you know? Jack, he went the other way. He was frightened of leaving the house in case we had a phone call or anything saying the girls had been found.'

She pauses. Her bottom lip is shaking with emotion and her face has paled as she takes herself back to a time that causes her great anguish.

'This is where things differ from what Alison believes happened.' Lynne lowers her voice and hitches her chair up to the table, as if worried about being overheard despite there being no-one else in the restaurant. 'I... we... no, *I* told Alison that, a few months later, she and her dad were coming back from visiting her grandmother – Jack's mum – on the day of a storm, that Jack had got into difficulty with the car and he was swept away by the swollen lake.'

A tear rolls down Lynne's cheek. She reaches for a napkin and wipes her eye.

'You don't have to tell me any of this, Lynne,' I say, despite itching to know everything.

'No. I do. I was... well, I wasn't getting over it – you don't get over something like that – but I was coming to terms with it. I was adapting. Jack, he wasn't. He was trapped in grief. He'd always suffered with depression. He was a complete contrast to his brother. Iain, my husband now, is Jack's brother. I suppose you think that's strange, don't you? Me marrying my brother-in-law. I don't know when things developed between us. We just grew closer as time went on.'

'It's not strange at all,' I say. I feel as if she needs to hear that.

Lynne takes a deep breath. 'Not long after the girls disappeared, something happened. I don't know what, Iain never told me, but he said he found something in the stables where they worked together, and they had a big argument, and

Jack admitted… I'm sorry,' she says when the emotion is too much for her to hold in any longer. She grabs for more napkins and blows her nose.

It's a while before she composes herself enough to be able to continue. 'It turned out that Jack had been abusing the twins. Sexually. He told Iain that he'd been watching the three of them that day, in the field, and he just… he took them. He couldn't help himself. He said something came over him and he… I don't know if he meant to kill them. I don't know what happened and, to be honest, I don't want to know.'

'Why didn't he take Alison?'

'I don't know.'

'What had he done with the bodies?'

'I don't know that either. Iain said that Jack couldn't remember. He said one minute he was watching them playing in the field, the next he was walking back to the farm. Hours had passed and he had no memory of what had happened.'

I nod. 'That is something that can happen. Jack's mind might have shut down in order to protect himself from what he'd done. I'm not justifying his actions at all, but it's possible he was trying to fight his urges but couldn't, and was struggling to admit what he'd done. Did you ever suspect Jack of—'

'No. Of course not,' Lynne interrupts, almost violent in her protest. She has another sip of her coffee, turns, and gazes out of the window for a while. She releases a heavy sigh before continuing. 'Iain told Jack to tell me. He said he couldn't. Iain gave him twenty-four hours. He said, if he didn't tell me, then he'd call the police and report him. Brother or no brother.'

'What happened after twenty-four hours?'

'He walked out into the lake before Iain had a chance to do anything.'

'You think he walked out into the lake purposefully?'

'It's the only explanation.'

'There have been sightings of Jack.'

'I'm aware. I don't know… I… I really don't know what to make of all those. He either killed himself or he walked away from his life. I'm only glad he left us,' she says, swiping away more tears.

'You said he went to visit his mother that day,' I say, after giving Lynne time to compose herself.

'Yes. She lived in the next village. She and his father divorced years earlier. Hardly surprising. I don't know how she put up with him for as long as she did. I wasn't a fan of Granville. He was a bully. Anyway, when we told her that Jack appeared to have taken his own life, she said that it felt like he was saying goodbye to her when he visited. She didn't last much longer after that. She'd always had a weak heart for as long as I'd known her. We didn't tell her anything about… about the abuse. We just said Jack was struggling with the girls being missing and that his depression had returned.'

I watch Lynne. Her face is a map of worry and confusion. 'Lynne,' I begin, my voice quiet, sensitive. 'Is it possible Jack abused Alison?'

Tears roll down her face. 'I've no idea,' she eventually says. 'Alison has never said anything. I've kept a close eye on her over the years, looking for signs of repressed memory or… I've read a lot about victims of abuse acting out in different ways to try and make sense of things or to punish themselves; I've not seen any of that in Alison. She's had a relatively normal life.'

'Did you and Iain ever tell the police about the abuse?'

She shakes her head. 'I wanted to. I wanted the police to tear the country apart looking for Celia and Jennifer. Many times, I stood outside that station, wanting to go in and tell them everything, but I kept thinking about Alison and what it would do to her if she found out. I didn't want her growing up with all that hanging over her head, wondering if her father had abused her too and she'd blocked it out. I thought it was best to leave everything as it was. Jack had killed himself. It's not like they could arrest him.'

'I can understand that, I really can. Alison is a credit to you. I've only met her a couple of times, but she seems like a strong, capable young woman. Who knows what path she would have gone down had she known the truth as a teenager.'

'I know.'

'You've had a lot to deal with on your own.'

'Iain has been a big help. He was strong for me, even though you could see he was struggling to understand what his brother had been capable of.' She pauses as she takes another drink of coffee. 'You can see why I don't want you helping Alison. After all this time, how would she take the news of her father…' She stops herself from mentioning the word abuse again. 'And how would she react to me for keeping it from her in the first place? It's all a mess, isn't it?'

'Alison isn't stupid, Lynne. She's constantly asking herself questions. What if one day she asks herself something that unlocks a memory?'

Lynne shrugs. 'I don't know. I think I can take whatever comes, but I'd rather not reveal it myself, if I don't have to. I've left a letter with my solicitor to give to Alison after I've died. It explains everything in minute detail. Hopefully, I've written it in a way where she won't hate me.'

'I'm sure she won't.'

'Promise me, you won't tell her.'

'I promise.'

'Thank you.' Lynne reaches across the table and places her hand on mine. 'I've been reading up about you. You're a good woman. I knew you'd understand.'

'Lynne, what can you tell me about…?' I stop. There's the

sound of a fleet of cars driving at speed into the restaurant car park. I turn to look out of the window and see a police car pull into the car park, followed by a police van with 'Crime Scene Investigation' written on the side.

What the hell have I done?

Sheffield, South Yorkshire

Detective Sergeant Sian Robinson had taken a few days off work. The demands of the job, as well as searching for Matilda Darke, had started to take their toll on her, so her interim boss, acting DCI Christian Brady, forced her into taking a few days annual leave to relax, put her feet up, and forget about work. That was easier said than done. They had a serial killer who had gone eerily quiet, a depleted workforce, and three new cases, one of which involved the murder of a six-year-old boy which Sian was finding particularly distressing. However, she hadn't argued with Christian when he told her to stay home for a few days. Her sleeping patterns were a mess, she hadn't had a decent meal in a week, and she was neglecting her children.

She spent the first day off in bed and loved every minute of it. When she was awake, she was watching endless quiz shows on television and being brought tea and sandwiches by her remaining two children living at home, Daniel and Gregory. The second day, she resumed her search into locating Matilda and found she'd sought sanctuary in the Lake District at Nature's Diner with Philip and Sally Meagan. She had no idea

Matilda was still in contact with them. Philip had told her that Matilda was fine, damaged, but functioning, and that he'd speak to her and get her to give her a ring. The fact Sian's phone had remained silent told her more than words ever could. Matilda was hurting, and she wanted to forget everything for a while. She could perfectly understand that, but experience told Sian that Matilda needed someone with her right now.

'Mum, you've got a Zoom call,' Daniel shouts from the living room.

Sian's in the kitchen chopping up fish to make a pie. There are potatoes boiling in a large saucepan. She's in the mood for comfort food. She and the boys are planning a movie marathon. Gregory has chosen *Rush* and *Le Mans '66*, while Daniel has opted for *Seven* and *Copycat*. Sian doubts there are going to be many laughs tonight, but it's quality time with her boys, and that's all that matters.

At the table in the living room, Sian's laptop is open. She sees who's calling and her heart lifts. The relief on her face is evident. She sits down and accepts the call.

Dr Adele Kean is Matilda's best friend. As a Home Office pathologist, she has worked with Matilda for many years and, following the death of her son Chris, she moved in with Matilda. Earlier this year, Adele's boyfriend had been unmasked as a killer. That, on top of still grieving for Chris, was too much and she decided she needed a clean break. She joined Doctors Without Borders and headed for Sierra Leone to help give medical aid when and where it was needed.

Sian is surprised by the change in Adele. She looks brighter and healthier than she's ever seen her. Her face is tanned, her hair is lighter and longer, she's thinner, and she has a glow of happiness about her.

'Adele,' Sian says. 'You look amazing.'

'Thank you. It's lovely to see you, Sian. Just to warn you, the internet isn't great out here, so if I disappear don't think I've hung up on you.'

'I won't.'

'Now, what's going on? I arrived back to the camp this morning and was told I've had about a dozen messages from you.'

'Where've you been?'

'There's a village in the middle of the Gola Rainforest National Park. It's completely cut off from civilisation and there are about a hundred people living there. It took us over a week on foot to get there. My goodness, Sian, you should have seen them. They have only the basic things in the world to survive on, but they're so... content. I helped deliver two babies. One was a girl, and the mother is calling her Adele. Honestly, I cried, Sian. I was crying buckets.'

As she talks, Adele's whole face lights up. She's doing good work and making a difference.

Sian tries to emulate Adele's happiness. She wants to share in her experience, but the lump in her throat won't allow it. All she feels at the moment is sadness.

Adele's face drops when she looks back at the screen and sees Sian's pained expression.

'Something's happened, hasn't it? Is it Matilda? Has she been killed?'

'No. Nothing like that. Matilda's... well, I've been told she's fine.'

'What do you mean you've been told? Where is she?'

'Adele, Penny's been killed,' Sian says, referring to

Matilda's mother. 'Joseph and Nathan, her nephews, they're dead, too. And Harriet won't have anything to do with her.'

The colour drains from Adele's face. She slaps a hand to her mouth to hold in her emotion. 'What happened?' she eventually asks.

Sian fills Adele in on the work of the serial killer who has been emailing Matilda, claiming to have committed the perfect murders. He was taunting his victims' families by sending them mock sympathy cards.

Adele is speechless. She doesn't move and Sian wonders if the internet connection has frozen.

'Where's Matilda, Sian?'

'It's taken me weeks to track her down. She didn't tell anyone she was going anywhere. It seems she went back to her house, packed a bag and disappeared. She didn't want anyone to trace her.'

'Have you tried the Meagans?'

Sian sighs. 'I did eventually. I didn't realise she was still in contact with them. That's where she is. I spoke to Philip. He said she's struggling. She goes out running every day, really putting her body through hell. She's punishing herself.'

'Jesus,' Adele utters.

'I told Philip to tell Matilda to give me a call, but she hasn't done. I'm guessing she doesn't want to speak to anyone. I can understand that, but she really shouldn't be on her own right now.'

'I should come back.'

'That's not why I called you. I thought you should know.'

'We've got a plane coming in tomorrow to take out a couple of people who need medical attention. I'll see if I can get on board. I'll go straight to the house, get my car, then go to the Lake District.'

'Matilda's got your car.'

'Cheeky cow. Sian, is there anything else I should know?'

'She's dating your replacement, Odell, but she's ignoring him, too.'

'This killer, who is he?'

'We don't know. He's gone quiet. We've nothing. DCI John Campbell, you know, Pat's son, he's been drafted in from Manchester to lead the investigation, but there's no evidence, no witnesses… It's like… well, we were wondering if he's gone quiet because Matilda's left.'

'Have you checked out Steve Harrison?'

'We have. It's not him this time. He's still licking his wounds after being scalded.'

'I'm coming home, Sian. I'll go straight to the Lake—' She freezes on the screen.

Sian guesses the connection has broken. She closes her laptop.

'Are you all right?' Daniel asks from the sofa.

She turns and looks at him. She didn't realise he was there.

'Have you been there the whole time?'

'You didn't say it was private.'

'No. Well, it wasn't. Adele's coming back home. She's going to go straight to the Lake District where Matilda's hiding.'

'Is she hiding?'

'Well, maybe not hiding, just… taking some time out.'

'Will Adele be able to convince her to come back to Sheffield?'

'I'm not sure. I hope so.'

'Me too. I really like Matilda,' Daniel says with a smile.

I can't move. I watch, frozen, glaring out of the restaurant window at the cavalcade of police vehicles parking haphazardly. An officer with inspector epaulettes steps out of the front passenger side of the leading car and heads straight for the steps. I watch her intently, not taking my eyes from her as she walks with confidence, head held high, shoulders back, firmly pushing the door open and breezing in.

Sally and Philip must have seen the commotion from the kitchens as they are waiting for her, a united front.

'Mr and Mrs Meagan, nice to see you again,' she says, a professional and courteous smile on her face. She holds out her hand and shakes both Sally's and Philip's. 'I was wondering if my team can use your car park while we investigate a discovery made in the woods by the lake's edge.'

She's not asking for permission to use their car park. It is merely good manners to explain why she's here. Her team are using the car park whether the Meagans like it or not.

'A discovery? What have you found?' Sally asks.

The inspector looks over her shoulder at me, then back to Sally. 'Your... *visitor*,' she says, emphasising my role as an outsider, 'found a registration plate floating in the debris of a fallen tree earlier this morning. As we investigated, we found other items which seem to have come to the surface. It's our estimation that the storm has dislodged something from the lakebed. We need to send a team of divers down for a closer inspection.'

I lean towards Lynne. 'Who is that?'

'Inspector Gill Forsyth. She's the main woman in charge at High Chapel.'

'Will we need to close?' Philip asks.

'There's no reason why you can't open as usual,' Gill says with a solicitous smile.

'Will your vehicles be gone by this evening? We will need the car park for our customers.'

'I'm afraid I can't say for certain. It all depends on what we find.'

'Well, would it be possible for your team to at least use the parking bays correctly rather than screaming to a halt wherever they like?'

I stifle a grin. It's unusual for me to be watching the beginnings of a police investigation from the outside. If I'd been in the inspector's position, I would have taken against Philip straight away for an aside like that. However, my head is firmly in the 'member of the public' camp, and I'm seeing the police as an intrusive force for the first time.

Go, Philip!

Gill inflates herself to her full height. 'I shall ask my team to park respectfully, yes.'

'Can we get you anything?' Sally asks. 'Teas or coffees?'

'No. Thank you. We're fine, for now.'

Gill turns on her heel and heads for the door, not before she steals a quick glance at me with a daggered stare.

I've not even met her, and she's pissed off at me. My reputation has clearly preceded me.

'I wonder what they've found,' Sally says. She reaches for Philip's hand.

'Where's Carl?' he asks. 'I don't want him seeing the police vehicles out front and panicking.'

'He's in his bedroom with the dogs.'

'I'll go and have a word with him.'

'Alison?' Lynne sees her daughter through the window, opening the boot of a marked police car, changing out of her sensible shoes and into a pair of wellington boots. She jumps up and runs out of the restaurant.

I watch as she flies down the stairs, calling her daughter's name. Alison looks up, her face pale with worry. She goes over to her mother, takes her by the elbow and leads her away from the scene, talking to her in what seems like hushed tones.

'What do you think they'll have found to have brought all this lot out?' Sally asks.

'You don't usually get this many police without there being a body.'

'From the storm? I haven't heard of anyone being missing.' Sally pulls her long cardigan tighter around her body and folds her arms. There's a look of worry on her face.

'I think this might go further back than last night. And judging by the fact that Lynne Pemberton appears to be inconsolable, I'd say they might have found her first husband.'

The police station at High Chapel is only a small one. It doesn't have a forensic team, a CID, a fraud squad, a drug squad, or a crime squad. There aren't even any holding cells or a custody suite. Any large-scale investigations are run from Kendal. Major incidents use officers from all three stations at Kendal, Barrow and Hunter Lane, often calling in those from

Lancaster Police Station who are a part of the British Transport Police.

At present, nobody knows what is lurking beneath the waters of Lake Windermere. Matilda Darke has presented them with a registration plate. Records show that a blue Vauxhall Astra 1.3 Merit Estate with the registration number E311 TVC was registered to Travis Montgomery. It was never reported lost or stolen, and the tax ran out in January 1993 and hasn't been renewed. Had Travis dumped it himself and later claimed the insurance money?

PCs Lydia Marsh and Katie Dixon were sent out to the site to have a look around. They immediately got on the phone to Inspector Forsyth and told her of their findings. Also tangled in the debris of the fallen trees was a child's-size shoe and a tarnished silver necklace which was lapping at the shore. As Travis had never been married and had no children, it was puzzling as to how these items and his car registration plate could be linked.

Gill stands on the edge of the lake with the items sealed in evidence bags. She has a dark feeling that there is something lurking at the bottom of the lake that will cause her many sleepless nights and a few thumping headaches.

'What do you want to do?' Sergeant Alan Stokes asks as he approaches. 'My brother-in-law goes diving on holiday. He's got all the gear. We can always ask him to go down and have a look.'

'No. If anything happens to him, it would come back to us. To me. We need a qualified commercial diver. Get on to the North West Police Underwater Search and Marine Unit. Tell them we've got a possible submerged car on the bed of the lake and to send a team out here to have a look. They'll have all the necessary equipment.'

'Right. And in the meantime?'

'In the meantime, we say nothing to anyone. There might not be anything down there.'

'But according to Alison, Matilda—'

'Matilda Darke is a grieving woman. Her family has been murdered and she's struggling to come to terms with what's happened to her. She's found a registration plate. Of course she's going to assume it's come from a car in the lake.'

'You think she's lying?'

'Not purposely, no.'

'How do you explain the other items?'

She turns to look at him. Her expression is tense. 'Just make the call to the underwater unit.'

Alan walks away, leaving Gill by herself. She looks over her shoulder to make sure nobody is close enough to hear her.

'Fucking Matilda Darke,' she seethes.

Reluctantly, I go below ground. I've been transfixed at the window of the restaurant, looking out at the car park as police officers gear up and head for the woods. It's strange to see a police investigation get under way and for me not to be playing a huge part in it. I feel like I'm on the outside looking in, and I don't like it. As relieved as I am not to have the weight of expectation and worry on my shoulders, I also feel sad about being a bystander. I have so much experience in this kind of work. I know exactly what to do when it comes to handing out tasks, putting a cordon in place, organising for a mobile incident room to be sent to the site, diving team, forensics on standby, neighbours to be talked to. I'm itching to get out there and take over. Yet, that part of my life is over with. I can't go through all that again. I've moved on. It's the sound of hammering from downstairs that drags me away from the window.

'Basements freak me out,' I say when I reach the bottom of the stone stairs and see Philip standing in the middle of the room, hands on hips, heavy frown on his forehead. There's no natural lighting in the basement and the only light is coming from the open door at the top of the stairs. It's dull and dank.

'Really? Why?'

'I'm not sure. It's probably got something to do with being kidnapped and locked in one.'

'That'll do it,' he says with a sparkle in his eyes.

'Did it leak?'

'Amazingly, no, it didn't.'

'That's good. So you can get on with renovating it into a wine cellar, then?'

'Hmm,' he muses.

'Problem?'

'No. Well… have you seen Carl's sketches on his tablet?'

'No.'

'When we first came down here months ago, I thought about this place just being a wine cellar, maybe have a few bistro tables down here for nibbles, things like that. Carl, and his creative mind, has drawn a picture of the restaurant, but he's taken out the whole of the back wall and replaced it with a huge picture window. It would show the entire lake from here. Can you imagine sitting down here having a meal or a glass of wine of an evening and seeing the sun set over the lake?'

I look at the back wall. In the poor lighting, all I see is darkness. 'That boy has quite the imagination.'

'I think it could work. This whole space is an L-shaped room. We could have the far side as the wine cellar, out of direct sunlight from the window, then the rest of the space could be a small, intimate dining experience.'

I look around me. I try my hardest, but I can't picture it. All I see is concrete and brick, and there's a smell of damp in the air.

'Wouldn't knocking out the wall weaken the roof at that end?'

'No. I've looked at the plans. There's a steel girder along the top. We might not even have to take out the whole wall, just a large square to fit in a huge window with toughened glass, you know, the kind they put in floors that you can walk on?'

'They've got a glass floor at the top of Blackpool Tower. James was jumping up and down on it. I wanted to vomit.'

'Not a fan of heights?'

'Not a fan of seeing all the way to the bottom.'

'Would you have a meal down here?'

'You might need to put in a few lights. I like to see what I'm eating.'

'Use your imagination, Mat. It could be so romantic,' he enthuses.

'I'll take your word for it.'

'Matilda, are you down there?' Sally shouts from above.

'Yes.'

'There's someone here to see you.'

I roll my eyes. Who the bloody hell wants me now? I head for the stairs. 'I'm coming up.'

I stop in my tracks when I see who my visitor is. The police inspector who, not half an hour ago, was shooting me a daggered look is standing in the doorway. Her face is unreadable, but her body language is oozing resentment.

'DCI Darke,' she says. It's an attempt at a greeting, but she almost spits my own name at me.

'Just Matilda,' I correct her.

She nods. 'Inspector Gillian Forsyth. Gill. Can we have a chat?'

I raise an eyebrow. A chat suggests a friendly exchange over a cup of tea and a Mr Kipling. Gill's pursed white lips and intense stare suggest she'd like to be throttling me right now.

'About?'

'You came into my station this morning with a registration plate you found.'

'That's right.'

'Yet you did a runner.'

'Again, correct.' I see no reason why I should lie.

'Any reason why?'

'Shall we sit down?' I point to the tables and chairs.

We head for the same table I had been sat at with Lynne, pull out the chairs and sit. I make a point of not looking out of the window at the police activity still going on in the car park.

'Judging by the daggered look you gave me when you first came in, I'm guessing you've looked me up.' Gill is about to say something, but I continue talking. 'I'm not here to take over. I'm not here to tread on any toes. I'm here simply because Sally and Philip invited me. I've been…' I pause and compose myself. 'I've suffered a family bereavement and I'm here to recover. It's as simple as that.'

Gill nods. Her face has softened. 'You're right. I have looked you up. I've read about what's happened to you over in Sheffield. I'm incredibly sorry for your loss. We got off to a bad start without even meeting each other, didn't we?' She tries to smile but it doesn't quite work. 'I heard about you coming here a couple of weeks ago. I'm afraid I let the gossip and mystery surrounding you cloud my judgment.'

'Mystery?'

'The infamous DCI Darke in the middle of a serial killer investigation suddenly ups and leaves her post to visit the Lake District. I understand you're grieving, but something was eating away at the back of my mind that you might be here to take over. We've had the threat of station closures and restructuring over our heads since before the pandemic.'

'I see. I'm here because I need a break. I've handled some disturbing cases in recent years, and it's taken its toll on me.'

'I understand. I'm sorry.'

'That's okay. So…?' I leave the question hanging. I want to know why Gill is here.

Gill clears her throat. 'I've been in the job for fifteen years and I've never left Cumbria apart from when I've gone on holiday. The most difficult case I've handled is when a child went missing three years ago and he turned up four hours later. Right now, I have a car at the bottom of the lake whose owner left here almost thirty years ago. Without my imagination running away from me, the only significant case going back that far is the disappearance of Celia and Jennifer Pemberton. If I call up Kendal and tell them I've no idea what to do, I'll be adding fuel to the fire that High Chapel can be closed down.'

'So, you want my help?'

Gill looks uncomfortable. 'I cannot begin to imagine what's going through your head right now. The last thing I want to do is upset you or interfere with you trying to come to terms with everything, but the people of High Chapel need this station to remain open. All I'm asking is for you to point me in the right direction.'

'I had a similar conversation with my chief constable back in Sheffield. We were facing huge budget cuts. I was asked to choose who on my team I should make redundant. Solving crimes shouldn't be about money. We're told throughout our training that, when we're the first on the scene of a crime, the number one priority is to preserve life. How can we continue to do that when we're told not to investigate certain crimes because they're not feasible?'

'You'll help me?'

I take a deep breath. I look out of the window. I watch as several uniformed police officers stand about waiting for… I have no idea what.

'Who did the car belong to?' I ask, reluctantly.

'Travis Montgomery. He lived here, briefly, in the early nineties.'

I nod. 'He was close to the Pemberton family, I believe.'

'You've heard about him, then. He worked with Iain and Jack when they were converting the farm into stables.'

'Does he have a criminal record?'

'No. There's nothing on the PNC, and he's not on the electoral register, either. It's like he doesn't exist. We've also found two items floating in the water. One is a child's shoe. The other is a necklace which looks like something a child might wear.'

'The Pemberton twins.'

'Possibly. I'm guessing when one of the trees crashed into the lake during the storm it disturbed something down there.'

'Maybe. Do you have an underwater unit?'

'Yes. The North West Underwater Search and Marine Unit. They cover a huge area stretching from Lancashire to North Wales. It'll be a couple of hours before they get here.'

'There's a search and rescue team called SRUK. It stands for Specialised Rescue UK. It's a private company. They're based in Birmingham. They help police forces all over the country when it comes to entering confined spaces. They have all the equipment and gear, and they'll know about protecting potential evidence. They run a twenty-four-hour service and can be here within hours. They'll bring the car up and take it to the nearest forensic-testing site for you.'

'Thank you,' Gill says. A look of genuine appreciation appears on her face.

'Just don't mention South Yorkshire Police to them when you call. I believe there was a bit of a hoo-hah when it came to paying their last bill.'

She sniggers. 'That sounds familiar.'

'Did Travis report his car stolen?'

'No.'

'Strange. There is one thing you might have to consider.'

'Go on.'

'Let's say that is Travis's car down there. Let's also say you find evidence linking it to Celia and Jennifer going missing. You'll need to consider Travis to be a suspect. You'll need to look at the original investigation and see why it wasn't picked up first time around. Two missing girls. A car that suddenly disappears. Why didn't anyone notice? The original investigating officer, DI Bell, is still alive?'

Gill swallows. She seems to struggle to find the words she wants to use. 'I'll… I'll look into it.'

I nod.

Gill stands up. She pushes her chair neatly under the table. 'People think I'm a ball-busting monster. I'm not. I'm doing an impossible job with impossible odds.'

I look up at her. 'No. You're doing an admirable job with complete tossers in charge who have no idea of the reality of life in twenty-first-century Britain. They may hold the purse strings, but don't let a title they lied, cheated and paid to get scare you. You have more knowledge and respect than they'll ever have.'

Gill holds out her hand. I don't know why I'm finding physical contact so difficult lately, even something as simple as a handshake. I reluctantly comply.

'Thank you,' Gill says.

'You're welcome.'

Gill leaves the restaurant. When she reaches the bottom of the steps, she turns back and looks up at me, gives me a wink and a nod of the head. I return the gesture.

'You almost sounded like a DCI then,' Sally says, entering the restaurant from the kitchen.

'Were you eavesdropping?'

'Of course. You miss the job, don't you?'

'No. Not in the slightest.'

'Can you smell that? I think Philip must have left something burning on the stove,' Sally says, sniffing dramatically.

'I can't smell anything.'

'Oh, no, wait. It's just your pants that are on fire,' Sally grins.

Sally leaves, chuckling to herself. I shake my head at her attempt at levity and turn back to the window and the police activity taking place right in front of me. I go to the bar, lean over, and grab the phone. I'd written the number of *Cumbria Today* on a Post-It which is crumpled when I fish it out of my pocket.

'Tania Pritchard, *Cumbria Today*, good afternoon,' Tania answers in what is clearly a faux posh telephone voice.

'Tania, it's Matilda. I'm calling you from the restaurant.'

'Oh, yes, so you are. I can see you.'

'Really?'

'Yes. I'm right outside. Turn to your left. Sorry, your right, and you'll see a shitty little Punto in baby-sick yellow.'

I turn and see the journalist standing next to her car. I smile and give a brief wave.

'I'd wave back but I don't want to draw attention,' Tania says. 'You never know where this is going to lead.'

'I've just had Inspector Forsyth here to see me.'

'Yes. I saw her leave. Was it nice to see her, to see her, nice?' she asks, referring to the famous catchphrase of entertainer Bruce Forsyth.

'I wouldn't go that far. She did tell me whose car it is at the bottom of the lake.'

'Travis Montgomery's.'

'You already knew?'

'I have my sources.'

'What was Travis's alibi again for when the Pemberton girls went missing?' I ask.

'He didn't have one. Did Gill tell you anything about how they found the car at the bottom of the lake?'

'A tree crashed into the lake last night during the storm. I was out swimming this morning. I found the registration plate and took it into the police station. Police came out and have found some items they believe belong to young children.'

'Jesus Christ! Celia and Jennifer are in that car?'

'We'll find out when it's brought up. How did you get on with trying to find Travis? Gill said he's not on the electoral register.'

'I can't find him anywhere. I've found a few Montgomerys in Liverpool. I'm going to do some phoning around. By the way, I was reading my notes about Jack Pemberton working at Dudgeons on the day of the twins' kidnapping and made a few calls to double-check. Dudgeons was closed down all that week due to industrial action.'

'Who was striking?'

'All the production staff.'

'Was Jack on the production line?'

'Yes.'

'Was there a picket line outside the factory?'

'Yes. But we don't know if he was there or not. Five hundred people were striking. Would they have noticed if he slipped away?'

'Possibly not,' I say. I look away across the car park and see Alison Pemberton walk towards the woods with her head down. I immediately feel sorry for the young PC. Whatever is discovered has the potential to destroy everything she believes in.

'Fancy a drive out to Seascale to talk to the teacher with an unhealthy interest in young boys?'

'It shows how sad my life has become that this will end up being the highlight of my day. I'll change my shoes and be right down.'

'Meet me at the top of the road. I'm already getting dirty looks from Brucie. I don't need to give her more reasons to hate me.'

'Nice to know police hating journalists isn't just a Sheffield thing. See you soon.'

'If, on your way out, a couple of muffins happen to fall into your bag, I'll help you dispose of the evidence.'

I end the call and smile. Tania is the refreshing change I need right now.

'Can I have a word?' PC Alison Pemberton asks as she approaches Inspector Forsyth at the edge of the lake. She looks worried. Her eyes are red from where she's rubbed tears away.

'Of course,' Gill replies. She steps to one side, so they'll have some privacy. She had been on the phone for the past hour updating her chief constable on developments. She was also waiting on a call back from the man in charge at SRUK about their ETA.

'I heard Cl… Sergeant Daniels talking, and she said there have been items found that belong to children. Do you think I could take them to show my mum? Do you think… could they belong to my sisters?' Her voice is filled with emotion. She's struggling to hold onto her professionalism.

'Alison, right now, all we have is a car at the bottom of the lake. We don't know what or if there is anything inside it.'

'The car belongs to Travis. He was very close to my family.'

'Alison…'

'But… the shoe and…'

'I will go and speak to your mum,' Gill says, softening her voice. 'Alison, I know you became a police officer so you could find out what happened to your father and sisters, but you can't allow that to jump to the front of your mind with every investigation. This could simply be an abandoned car.'

Alison nods. She looks away while she composes herself and swallows her tears.

'I want to help,' she eventually says.

'You will. Let's wait until we know what we're dealing with before we go any further. Get Callum to drive you back to the station. We've still got calls coming in from the storm. We'll take this one step at a time. Okay?'

'Thank you,' Alison says, trying to smile.

Gill watches her leave towards a marked car with her head down. She blows out her cheeks. She heads for Alan who's standing by his car, the boot open.

'Show me the items that came floating to the surface again,' Gill says.

Alan hands her the two evidence bags.

Gill takes them and scrutinises the shoe, in particular. 'What age girl would you say this shoe would fit?'

'Well, if Prince Charming was looking for his Cinderella, I'd say he'd be looking for a small girl about five, six, maybe seven.'

'And the necklace?'

'It's not a very long one, is it? Roughly the same age, possibly.'

'Do you know the story of Alison Pemberton's sisters?'

'We all do.'

She lowers her voice. 'What do you think?'.

'It would be a massive coincidence if they didn't belong to them.'

'My thoughts exactly. Would you like to come with me to show these items to Alison's mother?'

'Can I refuse?'

'You can, but you'll be doing the stranger danger talks to primary school kids every term until you retire.'

Lynne pulls up at the entrance to the stables almost at the same time as Inspector Gill Forsyth and her second-in-command, Sergeant Alan Stokes.

'Lynne, I've just been to your house looking for you. I saw the front window boarded up. Is everything all right?' Gill asks as she climbs out.

'What? Oh. Yes. A tree came through the window in the storm.'

'Is there much damage?'

'Only to the furniture. Did you want me for anything?' Lynne asks, leaning against her car, holding onto the open door for support.

'I need to talk to you. And Iain, if that's possible.'

'Is this about what you've found in the lake?'

'Is there somewhere we can go where we're a bit more private?' Gill asks, non-committal.

Lynne takes a breath. 'Of course.' She closes the car door. 'We can go into the office.'

She leads the way, opening the gate and asking Sergeant Stokes to close it properly behind him so the horses can't get out. She calls for Iain a few times before he shouts down to them from the far side of the roof.

'How's it looking?' Lynne looks up, shielding her eyes from the sun.

'Fine.'

'Can you come down for a moment? The police are here. They've found something.'

He leans further out and sees Forsyth and Stokes.

'Oh. Sure. I'll be right down.'

'We'll be in the office, is that all right?'

'Fine.'

Lynne takes them into the small room laughably called an office. A cheap pine desk with a laptop and a few files. The rest of the space is taken up by sacks of feed and hay. Lynne pushes them to one side while she finds a couple of chairs.

'Can I get you both a drink or something?'

'We're fine, thanks.'

'Take a seat.'

Iain comes in looking windswept, having been on the roof for most of the morning.

'Did the storm cause much damage?' Gill asks him.

'Not much. A few of the battens on the roof had come loose. All sorted now.'

'Horses okay?'

'They're fine. A little unsettled. Your Lauren has already been up this morning to check on Oliver.'

Gill gives a whisper of a smile. 'I sometimes wonder who she loves more: me or him. Erm, is this a good time for us to have a word?' she asks, looking towards Lynne who is already wiping her eyes with a tatty tissue.

'Yes. Fine.'

'Lynne,' Gill begins. 'As you know, a car has been discovered on the bed of the lake. We're waiting for a specialised recovery team to come up from Birmingham to help us pull it out. However, a couple of items have floated to the surface. We believe they're items belonging to a child. I was wondering if you'd look at them for me and let me know if you recognise them.' She talks in a delicate tone, hoping her soothing manner will make the horrifying situation less shocking. It doesn't work.

'What kind of items?' Lynne asks. She's sitting rigid on a

wooden chair, knees drawn together, fingers interlocked on her lap.

'There's a shoe and a piece of jewellery.'

'Do you think Celia and Jennifer are in the car?' Iain asks.

'We don't know if there is anyone in there at the moment. I'm keeping an open mind. However, the only local missing children we have on our records are your daughters.'

'Oh my God!' Lynne cries. She bows her head and seems to crumble in on herself.

Iain crouches down beside her and wraps his arms around her shoulders. 'It's all right, Lynne, it's all right,' he whispers to her. He holds her close and kisses her on the top of her head.

She nods and slowly sits back up. He hands her a fresh tissue from his pocket.

'Have they been there, in the lake, within spitting distance of my house, all this time?'

'We don't know anything at the moment, Lynne. Until we can get the car up, everything is guesswork.'

Lynne wipes her eyes with the sodden tissue. 'I understand.' She takes a deep breath. 'Can I see what you've found?'

Gill looks to Alan who brings the plastic evidence bags from behind his back. He hands them to Gill. She passes the one containing the shoe to Lynne first. Years of it being submerged in water has dulled the trainer. It's difficult to guess what its original colour had been. It's dirty and scuffed and the laces are missing, but it's clear what the item is.

Lynne holds it in shaking fingers. She turns it over, looks at the worn tread. Her facial expression doesn't change.

'I'm not sure,' she says. 'They had shoes like this, but... I'm not sure.'

'What shoes were they wearing on the day they went missing? They were playing in fields, weren't they?' Gill asks.

Lynne nods. 'I can't remember what shoes they were wearing. I know Celia was wearing pink shorts and a white T-shirt. Jennifer had on a purple short-sleeve shirt and a white skirt. I can't… I can't see their shoes. I'm so sorry.'

'Iain?' Gill asks him.

'I don't know. I didn't see them that morning so I couldn't say what they were wearing.'

Lynne closes her eyes tightly shut as she takes herself back to that day, thirty years ago. She feels sick. She opens her eyes and streams of tears roll down her cheeks. She hands the shoe back to Gill who swaps it for the second bag from Alan. When Lynne takes it, it looks empty. There doesn't seem to be anything in there. Right at the bottom is a small, tarnished silver chain. There are three tiny daisies linked together in the middle. Lynne runs her fingers gently over the flowers through the plastic.

'They both had one,' she eventually says. 'Their grandmother bought them one each for Christmas the year before they… They had an argument and one of the necklaces ended up losing two of its flowers. Of course, they blamed each other. I don't know who this one belongs to,' she says, squeezing the evidence bag tightly between her fingers and crying.

Iain leans down to her, kisses her on the top of her head again and makes soothing noises as he tells her everything is going to be all right. They're just words, though. They're meaningless. Nothing is going to be all right ever again.

'But the necklace definitely belongs to one of your daughters?' Gill asks.

It's a while before she receives confirmation. Lynne looks up. She seems to have aged a decade since Gill walked into the small office. She nods.

Gill allows the silence to grow. When nobody says anything

more, she continues. 'Lynne, looking back at the original investigation, it was thought your daughters were kidnapped and taken away from the area. If that's not the case, if your girls never left the area, it's possible you might have known the kidnapper. Is there anyone from that time who might have done something like this to your family?'

Lynne is holding on tightly to her husband. She's leaning into him for support. She can't do this on her own and is close to cracking completely. She squeezes his hand even tighter.

'We were just a normal family,' she says, barely audible between the tears.

Gill looks to Iain. He shakes his head.

'The car belonged to Travis Montgomery. You were close to him, yes?'

Lynne puts her head down. She wraps her arms tightly around her own body, hugging herself, protecting herself.

'It's Travis's car in the lake?' Iain asks. 'It's been there all this time?'

'It would appear so.'

'And the girls are in it?'

'We don't know that at present.'

'Travis worked with us on the farm,' Iain says. He leans back against the desk. His face is pale with shock. 'The land was in a mess. It needed digging over and levelling. He worked as hard as me and Jack.'

'I didn't know Travis all that well,' Gill says. 'What can you tell me about him?'

Iain shakes his head as he thinks. 'I... I don't know. He was a hard worker. He'd turn his hand to anything. He was quiet. He played guitar. Not very well,' he says with a faint laugh. 'He was just an ordinary, normal bloke.'

'Did he get on with Celia and Jennifer?' she asks, looking at Lynne.

Lynne slowly raises her head and makes eye contact with the inspector. 'He was in our house all the time,' she says. Her voice is soft, her words sound as if they're causing her pain. 'Granville employed him as casual, and he took the spare room here. Whenever Granville came over for a meal, he brought Travis with him. He helped cook. He…' Her words are lost to emotion.

The small office falls silent, yet the atmosphere is charged and heavy.

'We'll leave you to it for now. I promise I'll keep you informed every step of the way. However, please try to think back thirty years. Even if you remember something you don't think is important, it might be. Tell me anything and everything.' She proffers a sympathetic smile then ushers Alan out of the office.

'He helped with the search,' Lynne says.

Gill stops in the doorway and looks back. 'Sorry?'

'When the girls went missing. The whole village turned out to search for them.'

'I remember,' Gill says.

'Travis organised for a group of men to search the woods and walk up the peaks. Why… why would he…?'

There's nothing Gill can say. She opens and closes her mouth a few times, but the words won't come.

'Leave it with us, Lynne. I'll be in touch.'

She leaves the office quickly, as if eager to be away from grief and difficult questions.

Lynne and Iain are left alone in silence.

'I need to talk to Alison,' she says, suddenly jumping up.

'Not like this, Lynne,' he says, coaxing her back down into the chair. 'Have a few minutes on your own. Take some deep breaths and compose yourself. You don't want Alison seeing you like this.'

'It's all going to come out, isn't it?'

Iain doesn't say anything.

'What am I going to do, Iain? Alison will never forgive me when she finds out.'

According to the satnav, it should take one hour twenty-three minutes to get to Seascale. Tania Pritchard arrives just over the hour mark. She cares very little for the laws of the road and takes corners in fourth gear, speeds up when a green light changes to amber and overtakes slow-moving vehicles without a care for what's coming in the opposite direction.

'For someone who has a detective in the front passenger seat, you're very reckless with the highway code,' I say as I hold onto the handle above the door for dear life.

'I'm a very law-abiding person,' she says. 'But I think they've gone too far. I'm fine with the big stuff – don't commit murder, don't steal, don't take drugs, don't park in someone's designated parking space – but, once you start with laws and rules, people take them further until we get to a point we can't do anything without fear of being arrested. If I can get to my destination in one piece and not kill anyone, does it matter if I'm doing ninety on a dual carriageway?'

I find it difficult to think of a counter-argument.

Seascale is a small, picturesque village on the Irish Sea coast of Cumbria with a population of less than two thousand. It seems cooler here than inland where Nature's Diner is. As I step out of the Punto, and give thanks for surviving, I feel a chill.

According to Damien Ashton's LinkedIn profile, he works from home as a freelance copy editor. Tania found his address on the electoral register, and she parks outside his whitewashed cottage on the sea front. He has a stunning view from his front garden. For the first time in ages, I wonder if I should move. I live in a former farmhouse with massive rooms, tall ceilings, a formal dining room and its own library. There's only me there. I don't need all that. A quaint cottage would do me perfectly well. Something to think about.

As we walk up the short garden path, I see a man in a downstairs room, presumably the living room, turn and look at us. He answers the door before we can ring the bell.

Damien Ashton had been a good-looking man when he was a teacher at High Chapel Primary School in the early nineties. Now in his fifties, his once short dark hair is swept back, thinning and grey. His once smooth face is lined and gives him a tired, hangdog expression. As he smiles at us, his dull eyes wake up slightly, and reveal a hint of the younger, carefree man he used to be.

Tania introduces us both and asks if we can ask him a few questions about the disappearance of the Pemberton twins. It's usually me leading a conversation. I can't get used to deputising.

'Have there been any developments? Have they been found?' There's genuine concern in his voice.

'There has been a development,' Tania says.

Damien leads us into the house which has the aroma of freshly made coffee. He shows us into a tastefully decorated, yet untidy living room. There's a desk in the corner with two large monitors and a laptop.

'Let me just save what I'm working on,' he says, rushing over to his desk. 'Take a seat where you can find one. Sorry for the mess. I'm not a tidy worker, I'm afraid.'

'Do you live alone?' I ask as I look at the pictures on the walls. They're all landscapes and works of art. No photos of family members or friends.

'I do. Yes.'

'Are you married? Single?'

'I'm single,' he says, looking up from his computer as he shuts it down.

'By choice?' Tania asks, sitting down and making herself comfortable.

'Yes, actually.' He moves to the armchair and hitches up his skinny jeans as he sits. 'I don't function well as part of a couple.'

'Why is that?'

'You want to talk to me about Celia and Jennifer,' he says, avoiding Tania's question.

I go over to the sofa and sit down next to Tania. 'You remember their names?'

'Of course, I do. It was a massive news event. I was only twenty-four at the time. I hadn't been teaching long. It's strange: I remember thinking teaching was going to be fun, that teaching primary age kids was going to be this worthwhile job. Celia and Jennifer going missing sort of opened my eyes to the reality of adult life.'

'What does that mean?' Tania frowns.

'It was the first time I'd come face to face with evil.'

'Evil? That's a strong word,' I say. I've met evil. I've fought evil. I'm not sure if I've won or not. Right now, it doesn't seem so. Damien was Celia and Jennifer's teacher. He wasn't living with them. He wasn't personally connected to them enough to be close enough to experience evil firsthand.

'That's what it was. Someone took those girls. You don't have to be a detective to know that when two beautiful little girls go missing it's for... well, it's not going to have a happy ending when they're not found straight away, is it?' His fingers worry at the cuffs of his long-sleeve T-shirt.

'You thought they were beautiful?' I ask. I've seen photos of Celia and Jennifer, and they were beautiful. But should their teacher be thinking of his pupils that way?

'Well, yes. They were. They were always smiling, always clean and dressed nicely. They were lovely girls.'

'How were they in class? Any problems?'

'No. They were bright and attentive. They listened and did their work.'

'Did they have friends?'

'Yes. The whole class was friendly. There was no bullying.'

'None at all?'

'No. It was a fun group of children.'

'What about Lynne and Jack, the twins' parents? What did you think of them?'

'I... they seemed nice enough. They were interested in the girls when it came to projects and parents' evening, that kind of thing.'

I adjust myself on the sofa. It's not very comfortable. 'In the run up to Celia and Jennifer going missing, did you notice anything different about their behaviour?'

'In what way?'

'I don't know. Something that might stand out.'

Damien looks away and frowns as he thinks. 'I... No. I don't think so. Actually, yes. Jennifer fell down in the playground. She ran and tripped, nothing major, but she kept saying for a couple of weeks that her arm was hurting. I looked at it; I had basic first aid training and, when I pressed it, looking for a bruise, she cried out in pain. She'd only grazed it when she fell.'

'Was she bruised?' I ask.

'No. But she was clearly in pain.'

'Did you mention it to her parents?'

'No. School broke up for the summer holiday a couple of days later.'

'Where were you on the day the girls went missing?' Tania asks.

'I was on holiday in Cornwall.'

'Oh. Nice. On your own?'

'Yes.'

'Isn't that a bit odd?'

'I'm sorry?'

'A twenty-four-year-old going on holiday on his own? At that age I had loads of friends. We were always going away together.'

'Maybe I wasn't as confident as you were at that age,' Damien says, slightly acidic.

'On the day in question, 11 August,' I begin. 'Can you remember exactly what you were doing?'

'Am I a suspect?'

Tania opens her mouth to say something, but she has a confrontational style of questioning, and I think Damien needs a gentler hand. I jump in first.

'We're trying to establish where the main people in Jennifer and Celia's life were at the time they disappeared.'

'I've already said. I was in Cornwall.'

'On the day they disappeared, 11 August, can you remember *exactly* where you were?' I ask again, slowly.

'No. Can you remember where you were on 11 August 1992?'

'No. But I'm pretty sure I *would* remember, if I was a teacher and two pupils in my class went missing on that date. Do you remember where you were on Tuesday the eighth of January 2019?'

'No. Why?'

'I do. I was being shot. I'll always remember that day, just as I'd expect you to remember where you were when two of your pupils went missing.'

'Well, I'm sorry. I can't.'

'Why did you leave High Chapel Primary School?' I ask, changing the subject.

He shakes his head. 'It wasn't the same. There was always an atmosphere at the school after they disappeared. And after that business with Alex Costello and how everyone treated him, I felt people looked at each other differently.'

'I agree with you there,' Tania admits. 'The village changed that day. I don't think it's been the same since.'

'Where did you move to?'

'I got a job in Manchester teaching primary again, but I felt like I was seeing Celia and Jennifer everywhere. I moved again and changed to teaching older students.'

'You don't teach now, though,' Tania says.

He looks at her with hooded eyes. He knows where the conversation is going. 'No.'

'Why did you leave?'

'I think you know why.'

'Enlighten me,' Tania says, crossing her legs at the knee.

Damien sighs. He looks defeated. 'I was teaching sixth form in Newcastle. There was a boy there. We… we started seeing each other,' he says, almost embarrassed.

'How old were you?' Tania asks.

'I was thirty-one.'

'You were thirty-one and he was… what? Sixteen?'

'Yes. Look, I know I was stupid. I know I shouldn't have done anything, but I didn't force him to do anything he didn't want to do. I didn't groom him. The attraction was mutual.'

'But you were his teacher,' I say.

'I know. I know. There isn't a day goes by without I'm sorry for what I did, but we didn't actually sleep together. We... kissed, that's all. We went on dates. We enjoyed each other's company.'

I can see the hurt in his eyes. He seems genuinely sorry for abusing his position. He's paid the price by losing his job, his career.

'What do you think happened to Celia and Jennifer?'

'You're the detective, you tell me.'

'You know those involved, you tell me,' I fire back.

'I don't know. I honestly don't. But I seem to remember their younger sister, Alison, saying something about waving at them and they waved back? Something like that. That sounds like they were taken by someone they knew, or they wouldn't have been so relaxed, would they?'

'Does anyone come to mind?'

He shrugs. 'The father? I don't know.'

'Why the father?'

'It was just a guess. I really don't know. It's usually the father, though, isn't it?'

'The father. The uncle. The family friend. The neighbour. The trusted teacher,' Tania says.

'Me? You think I took them? That's ridic... why? Why would I do that? What's my motive?'

'You have an interest in people younger than you.'

'Oh, for fuck's... once. That happened once. And the person in question was a boy. I'm gay. I've always been gay. Why would I be interested in twin six-year-old girls? Are you one of those people who think all gay men are sexual predators or paedophiles? I thought we'd left the Dark Ages behind.'

I glare at Damien. I don't see a potential killer. I see a sad and lonely individual. We've asked him enough and I wrap up the interview. It's clear Tania wants to ask him more, but I fear it would end up in an argument. I thank him for his time, apologise for disturbing him while he's working, and even shake his hand on the doorstep. I'm not usually so pleasant.

It's not until we're travelling back to High Chapel at warp speed that Tania asks me what I think of Damien.

'He's living a very solitary life, isn't he?'

'Self-induced,' Tania says.

'Hmm,' It's all I can think of to say.

'What?'

'Nothing. Just thinking.'

'Is he a suspect?'

'No. Though, it's interesting what he said about Jennifer just before the school broke up for the summer holiday. She was clearly in pain. I wonder what happened to her.'

'You think she was beaten?'

'Someone had hurt her, and she hadn't told her teacher about it, which suggests to me it wasn't a simple accident and it involved someone close, someone who perhaps told her not to say anything to anyone.'

'A secret between Daddy and his special little girl?' Tania asks.

'That's what I'm thinking.'

'Where to from here?'

'I need to go for a run,' I'm feeling tense and claustrophobic.

'Do you think better when you're running?'

I don't answer that. I turn to look out of the window and watch a blurred landscape rush by. I don't think better when

I'm running. I run in order to silence the dark, disturbing, horrific, chilling thoughts that won't leave me the fuck alone. And now, on top of reliving my mum and nephews being killed, I've got the beautiful and smiling Celia and Jennifer setting up home in my mind, and the thoughts of the evil they witnessed in their final minutes.

I close my eyes and wish someone would invent something to return the brain to its factory settings.

There's something about running hard and far that I find addictive. My legs pound the rough terrain, I inhale sharply and blow out fiercely. My mind banishes the darkness as it concentrates on my breathing. I can understand why, after everything he'd been through, Forrest Gump just felt like running. There are times when I don't want to turn and head back to the restaurant. What would it be like if I never stopped?

But I always stop. Something clicks in my mind that tells me I've run far enough, and it's time to turn back. I hate that I give in to that voice every single time.

I slow down and take in the sight of the divers from the North West Police Underwater Search and Marine Unit suiting up. There's a boat in place ready to be sent out. Someone is rigging what looks like a torpedo on the back of the boat. Curiosity gets the better of me and I go for a closer look.

'Enjoy your run?'

I jump and turn around. Inspector Gill Forsyth has appeared out of nowhere.

'Yes, thank you.'

'I'm more of a hiker, myself,' she says. 'Every day off I

throw on the walking boots and the cargo trousers and I'm all over the hills.'

'Perfect location for it.'

'Yes. It helps clear the mind, too.'

I glare at her and wonder what she has going on in her life that requires her mind to be regularly cleansed.

'How's it going?'

'Painfully slowly.' She rolls her eyes. 'That thing on the back that looks as if it's about to be fired at an enemy submarine is a side-scan sonar. Apparently, it will take an image of a large area of the lake's floor and will be able to detect debris or anything else that may be down there. It uses a sonar device that emits fan-shaped pulses down towards the lakebed across a wide angle perpendicular to the path of the sensor through the water.'

'Is that expert knowledge you're imparting, or have you had a quick read on Wikipedia?'

'The guy with the ginger hair tying it on gave me a very long and detailed explanation.'

'I bet he's a riot at parties,' I say. 'How long will it take for them to find the car?'

'Well, we don't have an exact location of where it could be, only a rough estimate from where you said you were. They're going to start where the felled trees are and fan out. It could take a couple of hours.'

'Will they bring the car up, too?'

'No. They'll locate it and set down a marker. I've got the company in Birmingham you mentioned on standby.'

'Well, I'll leave you to it, then,' I say, turning and starting to head back to Nature's Diner.

'Matilda,' Gill calls after me. 'We've found a shoe and a necklace. I've shown them to Lynne Pemberton and she recognised the necklace as belonging to one of her daughters.'

'Oh God.'

'Why dump them where they lived? What's the point of that?'

'I don't know. Panic? Have you spoken to Lynne about their disappearance?'

'Not yet. I want to wait until we find out what, if anything, there is in the car.'

I nod. 'You need to speak to her. She has a lot to tell you that she hasn't told anyone before.'

'How do you know?' Gill frowns.

'Because she told me. But it's not my place to say anything.'

'She told you? How? Why? Do you know the family?'

'No.'

'Oh,' Gill says, looking slightly put out. She looks as if she wants to ask more but can't find the words.

I wait a few moments more, but the silence becomes awkward. I give Gill a cold smile before jogging off back to the restaurant.

After a shower, I join Carl and take the dogs into the woods. We don't go our usual route, as we would have had to pass the police activity. The storm has taken the edge off the temperature and there is a pleasant soft breeze blowing, but the sun is high in the sky, and it's hotter than it should be for the time of year. We walk in silence, pausing only to pick up a stick one of the Woodys brings for us to throw. I keep glancing over my shoulder. When we reach the optimum point, I find a felled tree to sit on and Carl joins me. From this vantage point, we can see out over the entire lake and view the police operation without being noticed.

The boat has gone out further than I remember swimming.

They're drifting slowly in an arc from the bank by the fallen trees, getting wider with each sweep. Surely, they should have found the car by now.

'Why does someone drive a car into a lake?' Carl asks.

'To destroy evidence of the fact they've stolen it. The driver might not have worn gloves so his fingerprints and loose hair may be all over it. Thirty years beneath the water will have destroyed all that.'

'Any other reason?'

'Insurance fraud. Maybe the owner of the car dumped it to claim the insurance money. Or perhaps the car was used in a crime like a burglary, or a bank robbery, and the criminal didn't want to be traced so dumped the car.'

'Would you hide a dead body in a car?'

'It's a good a place as any other.'

The dogs walk over to us, tongues lolling, panting loudly, and sit down beside us in the shade.

'They never found the van they took me in, did they?'

I look at him. I see the sadness in his face. Traumatic experiences never go away. They're always there. People merely learn to live with them. Occasionally, something happens to bring them back to the forefront of the mind. For the first time, Carl is witnessing firsthand a police investigation. Is he comparing it to what happened in the search for him?

'No,' I say. 'We looked everywhere for it. We never gave up. There's a cold case unit at South Yorkshire Police who routinely go through unsolved cases. They'll look at yours.'

'Do you think it's at the bottom of the River Don somewhere?'

'It's possible. It could have been resprayed and had its registration plates changed. It could have been burnt out. It could be hidden in a lock-up somewhere slowly rotting away.'

'Was this what it was like when I was missing? Were there police everywhere and looking in rivers?'

'No, Carl,' I say, putting her arm around him and pulling him close. 'The kidnappers asked for a ransom. It's completely different. You shouldn't be out here watching this. Come on, let's get back to the restaurant.' I stand up. The dogs notice movement and jump up, tails wagging. 'I bet I can guess your favourite dinosaur,' I say as we set off.

'I don't have one.'

'Everyone has a favourite dinosaur.'

'I don't. Do you?'

'Of course.'

'What is it?'

'Guess.'

'Tyrannosaurus?'

'No. Too obvious.'

'Triceratops?'

'Nope.'

'I don't know. Stegosaurus?'

'No.'

'I give up,' he sighs.

'Diplodocus.'

'Why?' he asks, looking at me with a frown.

'Why not? It was the size of four elephants. What's not to love about that?'

By the time we leave the woods and enter the clearing, we've worked out that Carl's favourite dinosaur is a Velociraptor, that the first *Jurassic Park* film is the best, Iron Man is the worst superhero because all he has is money, Hulk would definitely put up a good fight against Godzilla but would eventually lose, and *The Hobbit* is two films too long. We agree to disagree on who the best *Doctor Who* is. I opt for David Tennant; Carl prefers Matt Smith.

As we approach the restaurant, we see Philip out in the car park chatting to Gill Forsyth. He doesn't look happy. The car park is packed with police vehicles and there are very few places left for his customers to use. When Gill looks up and notices me, she holds a hand up to silence Philip and heads towards me. Judging by the pursed lips and the steam coming out of her ears, she does not have good news.

'Something's happened,' I guess.

'No. Quite the opposite actually. Nothing's happened.'

'What do you mean?'

'Three hours the underwater team searched in the area you said you saw the car. Back and forth they went. They even went out further just in case you were mistaken about the location.'

'And?'

'No car.'

'What?'

'No fucking car, Matilda.'

I decide to go for a walk. I knew I shouldn't have got involved in the investigation into the missing Pemberton twins. I knew their story would set up home in my already full mind and take root. Ever since I googled them and saw their innocent smiling faces looking out at me from the screen, I can't stop seeing them. Even though they were twins, they reminded me of me and Harriet when we were young girls, and those school photos we had where our mother had dressed us in near identical outfits because she thought we would look cute. The memory brings a lump to my throat. My sister is gone. She wants nothing more to do with me. I can understand why. My actions have led to the murder of her sons.

I fucking hate you.

'I fucking hate me, too,' I say under my breath.

And now, it seems, I'm bloody seeing things. There is no car at the bottom of the lake. But there is. I'm so sure I saw a car. Had I imagined it? Has finding a registration plate put pieces of a jigsaw together that don't belong together to reveal a picture that makes no sense? Am I losing my mind due to the heavy grief I'm suffering? If so, what next? Where do I go from here? Is there a chance of recovery?

'Matilda?'

I jump at the sound of my name and literally scream out loud.

'I'm so sorry, I didn't mean to startle you.'

I turn and see Alison Pemberton standing in the doorway of a picture-postcard cottage.

'No. That's fine. I was... I was miles away.'

'What are you doing round here?'

I look around me. I have no idea where I am. I'm walking in the middle of an unmarked road, flanked either side by mismatched stone-built cottages.

'I just thought I'd take a walk, discover more of the village,' I lie, unconvincingly. 'Do you live here?'

'Yes. This is home. I was actually born in the back bedroom. Never lived anywhere else,' she says with a smile. 'Do you want to come in?'

'Sure.'

I walk towards the house and up the small pathway. As I step closer to the cottage, I see it's not picture-perfect at all. The door surround is crumbling, the garden needs weeding, the windows need replacing and the chimney stack looks precarious. This house may hold memories for Alison, but they are all sad and dark and have leached into the building. When I step inside, I can feel the intensity of the emotion shroud me. I wonder if my own home back in Sheffield feels like this.

Alison closes the door and shows me into the living room off the small hallway. The ceilings are low, the walls painted dark, giving the room a cosy, yet claustrophobic feel. The furniture is clearly too big for the room. With no windows open and no air coming through, it's oppressive.

I sit down. 'You all lived here then? Two parents and three children?'

'Yes. A tight squeeze,' Alison says, sitting on the opposing armchair.

'It must be full of memories for you.'

'Not really,' she says, looking around her. 'I can't remember much. I was only five when my sisters were taken. I've got photographs but they're just pictures, aren't they? Sometimes it's like I'm looking at strangers.'

'Do you remember your dad much?' I ask, looking at the framed photo on the mantle.

'Bits,' she eventually says. 'I'm not sure what are real memories and what I've invented. He's my dad, I want to remember him as being a happy, loving man, but I know he was depressed. I know he had dark days. I sometimes picture him in this room smiling and laughing, but I don't think it's real. I think it's something I'm trying to convince myself of.'

'The sightings of your dad—'

'I've kept a record,' Alison interrupts. She jumps up and goes to an antique desk in the corner of the room. From the top drawer, she brings out a box file. 'I've kept all the newspaper clippings, and I've printed things I've found online about the investigation and missing people. Carl Meagan was missing for four years. He was found by a fluke, wasn't he? My mum keeps telling me I should forget about it, but it's not totally impossible that my dad is still out there, is it?'

'No. It's not,' I say, sceptically. I take the box file from her and open it. I bypass the newspaper cuttings and take out a plastic folder of all the sightings Alison had made a record of.

> Wednesday 18 November 1992   *Same clothes dad was wearing*
>
> Just over a month since dad went missing. A couple visiting the Lake District from Leicester were hiking and saw a man "lurking" around an abandoned farmhouse. Lee Frasier asked if he was ok and needed help. The man ran off. Lee and his girlfriend, Toni, thought nothing of it and carried on. Back home in Leicester, Toni couldn't stop thinking about the man and wondered if he might be someone who had wandered off. She rang High Chapel police but couldn't remember who she spoke to. She didn't find them helpful and called Cumbria Today. She described the man as being tall and slim. He was wearing thick walking trousers and boots and an oversized anorak she thought was dark blue. Louise Trainor at the paper said it sounded like dad and would look into it.
>
> *Toni looked at a newspaper archive in her local library at a photo of dad and said she was sure it was him. Police didn't go to search on the hills despite Louise telling them three times about Toni reporting it.*
>
> Sunday 29 November 1992
>
> Man broke into Wells' Bakery in Burneside. Bread and a few sandwiches stolen. Man was scared off by Derek Wells who lives above the shop. He described the man as tall and slim. He was wearing dirty clothes and a dark blue coat.
>
> Friday 4 December 1992
>
> Man found sleeping in High Chapel church. Rev Barney Flack tried to talk to him and offer help but he kept his distance, wouldn't look up at him and covered his face with the hood of his blue coat. Flack asked if his name was Jack and he did a runner. Flack reported it to police but nothing was found in the area. Story appeared in Cumbria Today. Nobody else reported seeing him.
>
> Tuesday 5 January 1993   **NO CCTV. WHY??**
>
> Susie Allinson from Lindon Road in Sedgwick saw a man walking into Barclays Bank in Kendal. He was the right height and build and had similar hair, but a bit longer and scraggly. He was wearing black walking shoes, jeans and a winter coat which could have been dark blue or black.
> Susie crossed the street and ran into the bank but it took her a while to cross the road and there was nobody in the bank who looked like dad.

I read the first page and put it back in the file.

'There are so many others, and they all say a similar thing. In the early days, he was wearing the same clothes Dad was on the day he disappeared. It's not a coincidence, is it? I mean, I know I want him to be alive and you're probably going to say something like I'm wishing this to happen, but it's not me who's made these sightings. These are real people who have no connection to us.'

'Why was there no CCTV at the bank?'

'I don't know. It was a long time ago, nobody can remember. There's another thing as well,' Alison says. She sits next to me on the sofa. She takes the file and begins spreading out the sheets of paper with all the recorded sightings of her father. 'Look at this: Christmas Eve 1995, he was spotted outside High Chapel. March 12, 1996, and over the page, March 12, 1997.'

'What's so special about March 12?'

'It's my birthday. He came back to the village to see me on my birthday.' She looks at me hopefully. She's willing me to agree with her.

'What about subsequent birthdays?'

Alison deflates. 'The sightings do become fewer and further between as time goes on, but the sightings are nearly always around the time something's happened. My first day as a police officer, he was spotted in the grounds of Gilpin Hotel. The day Mum and Uncle Iain got married, he was spotted in Storrs. There's a pattern.'

'What do you think happened to your dad?'

Alison sits back on the sofa. Her face softens. She swallows her emotion, and it's a while before she braves herself to talk. 'He was depressed. He couldn't cope with losing his girls, and he walked away. I can understand that. I only... I wish... I wish I'd been enough for him,' she cries.

I should put my arm around her. Alison needs a hug and I'm the only one here, but I'm the last person to be offering support right now. I hitch up closer to her. I put my left arm around her shoulders. Maybe to her it feels comforting. To me, it feels alien, and I don't know why.

'The fact he's been spotted around important events in your

life shows that you were enough for him, more than enough. He couldn't cope with what life had thrown at him and he needed to get away, but that didn't mean he stopped loving you. What happened was something neither of us can understand. It killed your dad. He couldn't cope with life, and he wanted to step away from that. I bet he would have loved to have taken you with him, but he knew the best place for you was with your mother.'

'You think he's still alive?'

I remove my arm. It feels plain awkward now.

'Twenty-six people can't be wrong, can they?'

She shakes her head. 'Why doesn't he make contact, then?'

'I don't know.' I shrug. 'Maybe he's ashamed.'

'What of?'

'Maybe he thinks he's failed at being a father for walking away. Maybe he's worried you'd hate him for leaving.'

'I'd never hate him.'

'He doesn't know that. And, as time has gone on, the hurt and the fear and the horror has mutated in his mind. He's been living with it all non-stop for almost thirty years. He doesn't need you to hate him, because he'll hate himself.'

I know exactly how he feels.

Alison makes us both a cup of tea. I look out of the kitchen window at the field at the back of the house.

'Was that where your sisters disappeared from?'

'Yes.'

Alison unlocks the back door, and we step out into the coolness of the evening air.

The ground is soft under foot after the deluge of rain in the storm. We go onto the field and take in the expanse of space.

'It's smaller than I remember it as a child,' Alison says.

'When we were kids, this seemed to stretch on forever. There weren't many children living here then. Celia and Jennifer, me and Claire, it was like this was our own private garden. Just for us.'

I turn back to the house. 'Your mum said she was baking. So, she would have been at the window looking out.'

'Yes. She could see us from there.'

'But she didn't notice anything was amiss until she shouted you in for your lunch,' I say, almost to myself. 'How long was it after your saw Celia and Jennifer in the back of the car before your mum called you in?'

Alison shakes her head. 'I've no idea. I don't think I had a concept of time back then.'

'But you played on your own?'

'Yes. I had this sausage dog on a string. I took him everywhere with me.'

'You were on your own for a while?'

Alison screws up her face as she thinks. 'I think so. I remember being hungry. I was asking for my dinner and Mum was in a flap about Celia and Jennifer.' She wipes a tear away. 'I didn't understand what all the fuss was about.'

I look across the field. 'Was there a gap in the hedgerow back then?'

'Yes. It's not there now. The hedges have overgrown, but there was a gap you could cut through to the road. Mum said we weren't allowed to go on our own because there's a blind corner. You can't always see cars coming from the right.'

'So, why did you go through the hedge?'

'I heard a car.'

'But you must have heard cars all the time while you were playing. What made you go through that particular time?'

Alison shakes her head. 'I don't know.'

'Did you hear anything else?'

'I'm not sure.'

'So, you went out onto the road. You looked left and right, and you saw the car driving away?'

'Yes.'

'Left or right?'

'Left.'

'You're sure? In the interview you gave with the specialised police officers, you said you couldn't remember which direction.'

She thinks again. 'No. It was left. I'm absolutely positive. I looked left and Jennifer and Celia were in the back of the car, and it was driving away as if towards the main village.'

'You waved?'

'Jennifer waved first. I waved back.'

'They weren't crying or anything?'

'No. They… they looked how they always did. Relaxed. Happy.'

I want to ask her about the colour and make of the car or if she saw someone in the front, but I know Alison had undergone extensive interviewing as a child to try to get her to remember and it hadn't worked. I also know that Alison will have spent the past twenty-nine years beating herself up to try to force herself to remember the colour of the car at least. Any memory now can't be trusted.

'When you were back in the house and your mum realised your sisters were missing, what did she do? Who did she call first?'

Alison sucks in her lips. She looks up as she searches her memory. 'She rang around a lot of people. I remember her being on the phone a lot.'

'Who was the first person to come to the house?'

'Uncle Iain.'

'Did he come alone?'

'No. Travis Montgomery came with him.'

'And your dad?'

Her face takes on a pained expression as she tries to remember. 'I... I don't know. He worked at Dudgeons, and they were on strike at the time. There was nobody in the office answering the phones and they didn't have mobiles back then. I don't think he came home until much later. By the time he did, the house was full of police.'

I don't say anything.

'I'm not stupid, you know,' Alison says, her voice much sterner. 'I know what you're thinking. I know what everyone else in the village is thinking, too. Dad took my sisters. He killed them for whatever reason and did a runner.' She turns on her heel and heads back into the cottage.

I follow.

'I'm not thinking that at all, Alison. I don't know your dad. I don't know your family. All I do know is that there are plenty of unanswered questions and the only person who I can ask them to is you.'

'Why me?' she asks, turning to face me. We're in the kitchen, standing beneath the dull strip-lighting. Alison's face is wet with tears.

'Because you were the only eyewitness to two tragic events. You were there when your sisters were taken, and you were there when your father disappeared. You know what happened.'

Alison slumps into a chair at the table. 'But I can't remember,' she says, her words almost lost to her tears. 'I've tried. I can't remember anything.'

'Because you don't want to.'

'Why wouldn't I want to?'

I leave the question unanswered. The reason why Alison can't remember is because she's afraid of the truth.

The sun is setting over the Lake District. After the violence of the storm last night, tonight is one of calm. The sky is clear except for a few whispers of cloud. As the sun lowers, the sky is lit up in a brilliant red. The patrons of Nature's Diner can't take their eyes from the view out of the sprawling picture windows.

Upstairs, I stand in the living room looking out over the lake. To the left, I can make out the shadowed figures of the North West Underwater Search and Marine Unit still at the scene, lit up by arc lights.

Glass of wine in hand, I take another long swig, as I watch the drama unfold. I had seen a car. I know it. I'd only seen it for a few seconds. All I had wanted to do was identify that something was there, then I came back up to the surface for air. But there is definitely a car on the bed of Lake Windermere. Definitely. Isn't there?

'My bloody shoes are killing me,' Sally says as she bursts into the living room. 'Where are my flats? I'm sure I left them… ah, here they are.' She sits down on the sofa and pulls off her heeled shoes. 'Nearly three hundred pounds these cost me. I've worn them four times and they've cut my feet to ribbons every single time. Phil will go mad when he finds out. I put them through the business.' She snorts a laugh. 'Are they still down there?'

I turn from the window. 'Sorry?'

'I asked if the police are still down there.'

'Yes. They've put on the arc lights now.'

'They must think something's there, or they'd have gone home by now, especially with the light fading.'

'Of course, there's something down there. It's a car. I know what I saw,' I say, almost snapping.

'I'm not doubting you, Mat.'

'No. I know. I'm sorry. It's just… I'm doubting myself. My head's all over the place at the moment. I keep trying to remember some of the exercises my therapist back in Sheffield told me about. My mind is blank. It's just fog in there.'

Sally stands up. New shoes on, she limps over to me and put her arms around me. I tense up. I hate myself for doing so. 'You can't expect to be thinking clearly at the moment. You're going through a massive trauma. I was the same when Carl went missing. Looking back, I can't remember a single thing of those early days. Did I eat? Did I sleep? Did I have a shower? Did I work? It's all a haze. You need time to come to terms with everything that's happened. And it's going to take longer than a few weeks in the countryside. Also, getting involved with whatever's going on out there isn't going to help you at all.'

'I know.'

'So, why are you standing by the window watching all the action?'

'Morbid curiosity.'

'Well, you're right with morbid. Look, why don't you come down to the restaurant? You can sit at the end of the bar, drink wine, eat olives and help me wind Phil up about the lack of parking spaces.'

'It's tempting.'

A car pulls into the car park. Sally leans forward and looks down to see who has arrived.

'Good grief, look at the state of her,' Sally sniggers. A party of four climb out of a silver Audi and head for the restaurant. 'I hope that fur's fake. Who wears a stole these days? Time to put on my fake smile and tell her she looks gorgeous. Are you coming to watch me play the role of the sycophant?'

'Maybe later.'

Sally kisses me on the cheek and heads for the door.

I look back out at the calm, black lake.

'There is a car.'

'Matilda, that Inspector Forsyth is downstairs to see you,' Sally says, popping her head around the door to the living room.

I'm on the sofa watching the blank television screen. I've lost all concept of time and have no idea how long I've been lying in complete silence. I crawl off, stand up, and feel the effects of two bottles of wine hit hard. I wobble. Dusk was setting when I last looked out of the window; now, it's pitch dark.

'Should I ask her to come back tomorrow?'

'No. I'm fine.'

I go over to the mantelpiece and look at my reflection in the mirror above it. I don't recognise myself. I look like death dug up. Still, it doesn't matter. I have nobody to impress with a neat hairstyle and perfect makeup. Let Gill Forsyth think what she likes.

'I've put her in the staffroom we use for storage,' Sally says as we make our way downstairs. 'I know we can hardly hide all the police cars in the car park, but I don't want our customers seeing police officers waltz in and out of the dining room.'

'I'm sorry for all this,' I say, my words slurring slightly.

'You're not to blame. It's just, why can't these things happen during regular office hours? Come into the restaurant when you've finished. I've opened a bottle of Sauvignon by mistake, and it needs drinking.'

'By mistake?'

'I was thirsty.' She winks.

I walk into the staffroom where there is a heavy aroma of onions and herbs. I want to sneeze.

Gill is standing by the window, sipping a glass of water.

'We've found the car,' Gill says.

I feel a massive weight lift from me. I was beginning to wonder if I *had* been seeing things.

'Where?'

'Where you said it was.'

'Why didn't they find it before?'

'Apparently, the side-scan sonar sends out soundwaves and they bounce off whatever is underwater. The car has been there for so long that it's thick in mud and algae and the sonar couldn't penetrate. They went back out with something called a Proton 4 Magnetometer which is a bit like a very strong metal detector, by all accounts. It located the car; they sent a diver down to check and that's when they found it.'

'Oh. Good. Nice to know I wasn't seeing things.' I try to sound playful and effect a giggle, but the alcohol on an empty stomach heightens how pissed I am.

'Indeed.'

'What happens now?'

'They've put down a marker. The light has gone. There's

nothing more we can do tonight. We'll have a scene guard overnight and Specialised Rescue UK will be out first thing tomorrow to bring the car up.'

'Right.'

'Thank you, Matilda,' Gill says, holding her hand out for me to shake.

I have to focus on her hand, but I manage to find it at the first attempt.

'You're welcome,' I say. Even though I'm half cut, I can recognise the look of a woman who has a bitter taste in her mouth. Thanking me was not something she was relishing.

Gill Forsyth makes her way down the steps of the restaurant, shivering in the coolness of the night. The sounds and sights of merriment fade into the background as she walks among the police vehicles and heads for her car. It has been a long day. She's tired, hungry, and needs a bath. At her car, she hears a noise and stops dead in her tracks. Turning around, she sees someone move quickly around the back of the restaurant. She opens the front passenger door, leans in, and takes out a torch. Flicking it on, she points the beam to the side of the building.

'Hello?' she calls out. 'Is there anyone there?'

There's no reply. A loud burst of laughter comes from the restaurant. She looks up and sees a scene of happiness as a young couple sitting at a table by the window both throw their heads back with huge smiles on their faces.

Gill steps closer to the building. She walks around the corner and points her torch into the woods beyond. There's nobody there. There had been. She would stake her pension on it. Someone had been watching her.

I walk downhill into the main village of High Chapel. There are many independent shops, which cater to the needs and wants of the tourists, and a few knick-knack and antique shops that I enjoy looking around. Unfortunately, the majority are closed following the effects of the storm. Heavy-laden sandbags litter the pavements and one particular shop, the unimaginatively titled High Chapel Antiques, has its door wide open and its owner, decked out in wellington boots but with full trademark 1960s makeup and hair whipped up into a beehive, is sweeping out dirty water with a rubber brush. She appears despondent. Wherever I look, the clean-up operation is in full force.

It's 21 June. Today is the first day of summer. Shopkeepers will be looking forward to a busy season as tourists flock to the area. After the disaster that was the summer season last year for trade, retailers are looking forward to a bumper summer this year. The last thing they need is to be flooded out.

I head back up the hill and push open the door to High Chapel Tearooms. Shops in the village may lack imagination when it comes to their names, but there's no mistaking what each of them offers.

The shop immediately makes me smile. It's warm and cosy. The scents of freshly baked cakes and brewing coffee fill the air and entice the taste buds. It's decorated in muted colours; chairs are comfortable and neatly laid out. The place is busy but there are a few seats still available. I go to the counter and survey the snacks. I order a large black Americano with an extra shot and opt for the Kenyan blend which, I'm told, is slightly stronger than the usual they sell. I take my time over choosing a pastry and eventually settle on a strawberry tart, though I may pop back for the carrot cake.

I chose a table in the corner of the room, sit down, and take a sheet of paper from my bag. It has been unfolded and refolded so many times it's almost coming apart. I don't need to read it. I can recite it almost word for word, but it's the reason I'm here.

While investigating the serial killings in Sheffield, the killer had taunted me by sending me emails. He was bragging about what he'd done, how he'd managed to evade capture, and how there was nothing I could do about it. There was no stopping him. Even after he'd killed my family, the taunts still came. When I returned home from my mother's funeral, an email had pinged on my phone. I read it and collapsed into tears. I printed everything off while I showered and changed before leaving the house, locking it up behind me, and running away.

> From: <qif9t58t8@gmail.com>
> Date: Monday, 1 January 1900 at 00:00
> To: Darke, Matilda <matilda.darke@southyorkshire.police.co.uk>
> Subject: Are we still playing?
>
> Hello Matilda,
> I saw you at your mother's funeral today. You looked very dramatic in your funereal wear. I watched, from a distance, as your friends and colleagues came up to you, shook your hand, rubbed your arm, kissed your cheek, and told you how much you were in their thoughts. Did you even hear a word that they said? I doubt it. You looked like you were elsewhere. I noticed you and your sister didn't interact. Is she blaming you for the deaths of her sons? I went to their funerals, too. I noticed you didn't.
>
> So, you're all alone in the world now, Mat. Your mother and father are both dead. Your nephews are dead and the one surviving relative, your sister, wants nothing to do with you. Your life has been ruined. Just like mine has. How does it feel? Does it hurt? Does it burn? It does, doesn't it? You feel like your heart is on fire, like your ribs are squeezing your lungs hard, making it difficult to breathe. You can't eat. You feel sick. You can't sleep despite being knackered. You're in absolute agony, aren't you? You want the pain to go away, but you don't know how it ever can. Welcome to my world, Matilda.
>
> I spoke to you at the funeral. I came up to you and told you how sorry I was. You looked at me. To be more accurate, you looked through me. I didn't take offence. It's perfectly understandable, you're grieving, even though all of this is of your own doing. But I leaned forward. I placed a comforting hand on your arm and told you I was sorry. It was a lie. I'm not in the least bit sorry. Now you know how it feels for your entire life to have been destroyed by someone else.
>
> So, what happens now, Mat? I've killed seven people. Where do we go from here?
>
> Here's a challenge for you, Mat. I promise, hand on heart, not to kill again, not to cause anymore suffering, until you return to work. The moment you resume your life we'll pick up where we left off. Take all the time you need. I can wait.
>
>
> Bye for now,
> The Steel City Slaughterer.

I wipe my eyes with a napkin. This is the real reason I can't return to Sheffield and my former life. There is no doubt in my mind that the man who has given himself such a pathetic nickname would remain true to his word and more lives would be lost. I can't cope with more deaths on my conscience. It would be the end of me. I've forwarded the email to the man who has taken over my role in the case, DCI John Campbell. He can deal with it. The ball's in his court. I'm having nothing to do with it.

I fold the email back up and place it in my bag. I take a sip of the cooling coffee and nibble on the strawberry tart but don't taste it. I close my eyes and take myself back to the day of my mum's funeral. Who had I spoken to? Who was there? The church had been packed. Mum knew a lot of people who wanted to say goodbye. Then there were my colleagues. Christian came with his wife. Scott and Donal. Sian and all four of her children. Finn and his wife. Tom and Zofia. My boss, Benjamin. I'm pretty sure his wife came with him but can't remember. Odell Zimmerman, Claire Alexander, Felix Lerego, all had come to pay their respects too; to show they were with me. I had huge support from so many people. But who was there under false pretences? Who had come up to me, laid a comforting hand on me, told me how sorry they were for my loss, while secretly revelling in the torment I was suffering?

I open my eyes. It's a futile exercise. Everyone was so sincere. On the other hand, I was so far removed from what was going on around me that I wouldn't have spotted a killer if he'd been wearing a T-shirt saying 'I murdered your mother'. It's torturous trying to remember the actions and words of everyone present. The only person I can see clearly in my mind is my sister shooting me daggered looks.

I fucking hate you!

'Are you all right?'

I look up and see an elderly man at the next table looking at me. He has a rugged, handsome face, and a warm smile. He reminds me of Sam Elliott, but without the moustache. My mum would have loved him.

'I'm fine.'

'Are you sure? You're crying.'

I bring a hand up to my eye. I look at my fingers. They're wet. I had no idea. 'Just… thinking about something.'

'Something sad?'

'Yes.'

'It's weighing you down.'

'It is, yes.' I don't want to get into a conversation with a random stranger. I finish my coffee and leave what's left of the strawberry tart. I've made a complete mess of it, anyway.

'You've heard the saying, what doesn't kill you makes you stronger?'

'Yes.'

'Make that your life's motto. I can see something bad has happened to you. It's etched on your face. But you've survived it. Let it make you stronger.'

That kind of makes sense and I offer him a placatory smile. 'I'm not sure I have survived this time, but thank you.' I stand up. It's time for me to leave before the tears come.

'You're the detective staying at Nature's Diner, aren't you?' he asks.

'Does everyone know everyone in High Chapel?'

'I'm afraid so,' he says with a smile which lights up his face. 'Matilda Darke, isn't it?'

'It is.'

'I read about you in the news. I'm sorry for your loss.'

'Thank you.' I put my bag on my shoulder and edge further away from the table.

'What doesn't kill you makes you stronger,' he calls out to me.

I look back but I don't say anything.

On returning to the restaurant, I find Philip outside with his back pressed against the wall, looking out over the lake. He's taking a photo of the view on his phone.

'What are you doing?'

He shows me the picture on his phone. 'Look at that.'

'What am I seeing?'

'The view.'

'Why do you need a photo of it when it's right there?'

'This is what the diners would see from the basement if we put a window in here,' he says, turning to the wall and showing me the square outline he's drawn onto the bricks.

'Are you trying to convince yourself?'

'I am, actually. I've had the estimate through for such a simple yet elaborate window. Who'd have thought a piece of plain glass would cost so much?'

'How much are we talking?'

'Five figures.'

'Wow.'

'Not low five figures, either.'

'Can you afford it?'

'I can, but would it add value to the business?' From his back pocket, Philip brings out a printed plan Carl has drawn up on his tablet. He unfolds it and hands it to me.

I take the sheet and I'm impressed by Carl's detailed design.

'It does look good. He's even put a terrace in front of the window so people could sit outside.'

'I know. Even I didn't think of that.'

'He's got a real eye.'

'An expensive eye.'

I look at Philip and see the hint of happiness on his face. 'What's your heart saying?'

'It's telling me to do it. I mean, imagine standing in the basement with a glass of Chateau Haut-Brion in one hand, a snack of some kind in the other, and looking out as the sun sets over the calm lake. Doesn't that sound like perfection to you?' He looks at me, his eyes wide with excitement.

'What's the snack?'

'Whatever you want.'

'A packet of pickled onion Monster Munch.'

'Now you're talking,' he laughs.

'Do you know something, Philip, fuck the cost, do it. I'll give you half. We'll do this together.'

'Seriously?'

'Absolutely. I've got money in the bank I'm not doing anything with. I've nobody to leave it to, so why not invest it in something I know will be a huge success. Put the window in. Build the terrace.'

He steps forward, gives me a hug and kisses me on the cheek. It doesn't feel weird, either. 'You know something, you should seriously consider moving out here.'

'You just want someone to peel the carrots you don't have to pay, don't you?'

'It would certainly increase the profit margin.'

I slap him playfully on the arm. We head to the main entrance of the restaurant.

'So, what's the next step?' I ask.

'Well, I've already been on to a builder in the village when I was thinking of simply converting the basement into a cellar. I called him again earlier. He's really busy at the moment, for obvious reasons, but he's going to pop round later in the week.'

'You'll miss the summer season.'

'True, but I can have a few run-throughs over the winter with the locals, test things out. I mean, even in the depths of winter that view is stunning.'

We reach the steps to the restaurant and see Sally struggling to open the door with a tray of takeaway hot drinks. Philip rushes up and holds the door open for her.

'Where are you going with those?'

'The search team have arrived to pull the car up from the bottom of the lake. I said I'd take them down some drinks.'

'Need a hand?' I ask.

'Yes please. This tray is overloaded.'

We head back into the restaurant, divide the drinks between two trays and set off together through the trees and to the lake.

'You were up and out early this morning.' Sally says as we walk extremely carefully so as not to drop any of the drinks.

'I thought I'd pop into the village, see if there was much damage from the storm.'

'Is there?'

'Yes. A lot of shops have been flooded out.'

'I might pop down later and see if I can help out. It's always good to get in with the locals.'

We turn a corner and see a row of navy-blue vans with bright yellow writing all over them: Specialised Rescue UK. The SRUK logo is everywhere. Next to the vehicles, members of the team are getting geared up to enter the water.

'Oh my God!' I say, stopping dead in my tracks.

'What is it?' Sally asks.

'The tall guy on the end.'

Sally strains to see. 'Well, he's got a nice bum, but I wouldn't say he was an oh-my-God type.'

'Don't you recognise him?'

'Should I?'

'Yes. That's Aaron Connolly. He was a DS on my team back in Sheffield.'

'High Chapel Police Station. PC Pemberton speaking. How may I help you?'

Alison sounds bored as she gives the greeting upon answering the phone. Until the car at the bottom of the lake has been retrieved and whatever is lurking inside has been identified, Alison has been confined to the station and manning the phones. She has a personal interest if her sisters are in that car. While everyone else is out at the lake helping with the search and retrieval, Alison is fielding calls from people mostly concerned about the aftermath of the storm. However, none of the calls are particularly taxing and she doesn't mind admitting that she is bored out of her skull.

'The power company are working hard to restore electricity supplies to all homes by the end of today, madam,' she says, not for the first time. 'If you are in need of anything, power has been restored to the primary school and they've opened the hall up to anyone wishing to have a hot meal or a tea or coffee.'

'I didn't know that. Thank you so much. I hope you didn't mind me calling the police for something that wasn't a criminal matter.'

'That's quite all right, madam. It's what we're here for. Take care.'

She ends the call and lets out a heavy sigh. In order to try and sound interested and patient, she's needed to wear a faux smile all morning. It's beginning to hurt.

'You look fed up,' Claire Daniels says as she comes into the main room.

'I am. I thought you were out at the lake.'

'I was, but I've got a sodding hole in my walking boots. Can I borrow yours?'

'Why not? It's not like I've got any use for them, is it?'

'Ooh, that sounded very bitchy.'

'It was meant to. Do you have any idea of the idiotic and mind-numbing conversations I've had this morning?'

'Looking at your face, I can hazard a guess. Bloody hell, what size are these? I can hardly get my feet in.'

'They're a four. Please don't stretch them with your big old clown feet.'

Claire jokingly gives her the finger. 'I saw that Matilda Darke woman out running yesterday. She's got a good figure on her for her age. Me and Geraint were reading about her online last night. She's got some balls, that woman.'

'I know,' Alison says, more to herself. She's hoping she has the balls to find out what happened to her sisters.

'She's rapidly becoming my hero. I may have to see if I can get a selfie with her,' Claire smiles.

'Slightly inappropriate.'

'I'm the queen of inappropriate.'

'So your Geraint tells me.'

'He better not have told you about Whitley Bay.'

The phone begins to ring before Alison can respond.

'High Chapel Police Station. PC Pemberton speaking. How can I help you?'

'I'll see you later,' Claire mouths as she dashes out of the station.

Alison listens and fakes interest for the caller asking why the tree lying across her front garden has yet to be removed.

High Chapel Police Station has never been a hustle-and-bustle station. There were never harassed-looking detectives with their sleeves rolled up bounding up and down corridors with a sense of urgency, screaming for an arrest warrant or an ETA on an armed response unit, but it has never been as quiet as it is right now with Alison Pemberton sitting on her own, feeling lost and useless. Even the phone has stopped ringing.

She stands up, goes over to one of the large windows, and looks out at the village through the slats of the Venetian blinds. Life is continuing as normal. The clean-up operation is well underway, and police officers are surplus to requirements at the moment. Returning to her desk, she takes a detour and passes that of Inspector Gillian Forsyth. She pauses and looks down at the neatly laid out paperwork. She reads the brief report of the operation yesterday detailing the location of a car at the bottom of the lake, the registration plate and the last known address of the owner, Travis Montgomery.

She looks around her, makes sure she's still alone, pulls out Gill's chair and sits down. She opens the folder and begins reading the contents. Travis's last known address was her grandfather's farm, now lived in by her mother and stepfather. There's no forwarding address for him. Where has he been living since 1992? Where has his post been going? Alison frowns as she flicks through yellowing paper from thirty years ago, statements given by Travis, her father, her mother, and Uncle Iain, giving details of where they were around the time the twins disappeared. At the back of the file, she finds another statement given by her mother. Why had she given two? She goes back to the first.

```
I spent most of the day in the kitchen baking. I'd done a couple of
loaves of bread and I kept looking at the clock as I wanted to get the
cake I was doing in the oven before I had to start thinking about lunch
for the girls. It was a hot day so I was just going to do them sandwiches
but I wanted the surfaces clear. By the time the cake was in the oven it
was almost one o'clock. That's when I went outside and shouted for them
but there was only Alison there.
```

Then she goes back to the second.

```
I lied. I wasn't baking. I had been baking but Travis came round. Iain
had gone out to get a part for the sink or something. He said he'd be an
hour or so. Travis came round and we went to bed for about half an hour,
maybe longer. I've been sleeping with Travis, on and off, for a few
months and we snatch whatever time together we can get. He left just
before one o'clock. That's when I called the girls in, but there was only
Alison there. I'm sorry I lied.
```

Both were signed by her mother. Alison recognises the signature.

She sits back, stunned by what she's read. Her mother lied in her original statement, given on August 11, 1992, the day her sisters went missing. Five days later, she amended her statement, admitting she was having an affair, cheating on her husband, on Alison's father, therefore giving Travis an alibi.

Alison feels sick. She knew her parents had problems. Her dad was depressed. He struggled to cope with day-to-day life. Sometimes it was an effort for him to get out of bed in the morning. She always imagined her mother as being strong and there for him whenever he needed her, but it turns out she had turned her back on him and was sleeping with a man ten years younger than her. How could she? How could she do that to her husband, to the family as a whole? She wonders if Iain knows.

Alison looks out into the reception area. The door's closed and there's nobody waiting to report anything. She acts quickly, just in case someone comes back unexpectedly, like Claire did to change her shoes. She runs to the photocopier to make copies and places the originals back in the file, hoping she's put them back in the same place, then returns to her desk.

She sits in silence, her mind going over the past thirty years, trying to understand her own mother. Why had she had an affair? She knew the relationship between her parents would have been strained because of her dad's mental illness, but imagine if he'd found out. Imagine how he would have reacted...

'Oh my God!' Alison says to herself. 'He did. He found out. That's why... Oh no, Dad, no, please don't say... you didn't kill them for revenge? No!'

She slumps onto her desk and cries.

Former Detective Sergeant Aaron Connolly left his role at South Yorkshire Police in 2019 following the shooting which killed so many of his colleagues. At the time, he was going through difficulties in his personal life. Married to Katrina, Aaron had had a brief affair with a woman connected to a murder investigation. Katrina agreed to give the marriage another go on the proviso Aaron left the force. He resigned straight away and they sold up and left Sheffield.

Unfortunately, the damage to their relationship had been done and Katrina could not get over the betrayal. They had been living in Birmingham for only three weeks before she told him the marriage was over. There was no going back. She moved out of their rented house that evening, returning temporarily to her parents' home in Bradford. They only saw each other one more time and that was before a solicitor when the finer details of their divorce were finalised. Outside, on the pavement, they shook hands, said goodbye, and went in opposite directions.

Aaron took a job with SRUK and travelled the country whenever they were called out. He volunteered for all the unpopular shifts and worked weekends, bank holidays,

Christmas and New Year. He was happy to give up the time people usually spent with loved ones to save him from being lonely. He soon rose up the ranks and was now director of the Birmingham branch of SRUK. There were two other sites in Glasgow and Devon with a fourth opening next year in Norfolk.

When I shout out Aaron's name, he turns around, and his serious face lights up upon seeing an old friend. As he approaches, the smile falls. No words are spoken, but it's obvious he's heard about what happened. He takes me in his arms and his embrace feels good. Surprisingly, I feel as if I could stay with my head against his chest for the rest of the day. It's comforting. When we eventually pull apart, I look up at him. He's a clear head taller than me. My vision is blurred with tears, but I can see he also has tears in his eyes.

'I'm so sorry,' he says.

'Thank you.'

He shakes his head. 'I couldn't believe it when I heard. Have you caught him?'

'Not yet. It appears he's gone to ground.'

'What are you doing out here in the Lake District?'

I shrug and swallow my emotion. 'Running away.'

His name is called. He turns back to see his team awaiting instructions.

'Can you give me five minutes?' he asks.

'Sure.'

I watch as he runs back to his team who are suiting up in diving gear. He seems to be in his element as he takes control and issues orders. He's put on weight since I last saw him, but on closer inspection I see that it's muscle. There's an air of freedom about him. He still has a demanding job. Now I think about it, searching underwater or in difficult to reach places could be stressful and challenging, even demoralising if they don't get the outcome they want, but Aaron seems happy in his work. It's evident in the camaraderie he has with his team, and the bounce in his walk.

'Don't you dive with them?' I ask when he returns.

'Not at the moment. I'm getting over a frozen shoulder. It'll be another few weeks before I'm allowed back in the water.'

'You seem to be enjoying your job.'

'I love it,' he says, a beaming smile on his face.

I hand him a coffee from the tray, and we go over to sit on the trunk of a felled tree. Aaron fills me in on everything that has happened since he left South Yorkshire Police. He's currently dating Emma Maguire and has been for the past six months. It's not serious. He has no intention to remarry. He realises he's not suited to a constrained life that the job and marriage brought. He likes that one day he could be working in Birmingham, the next in the Lake District, the one after in Cornwall. It's a wonderful life for him.

'You're happy,' I say. I'm tempted to ask him what that feeling is like, but I don't.

'I am,' he says without giving it any thought. 'How are you doing?'

'I won't lie to you, Aaron, I'm falling apart. I've no idea what to do next. I can't stay with the Meagans forever.'

'I heard you managed to reunite Carl with his family. How are they?'

'They're doing great. He's thirteen now. He's a bit quiet for a teenager, but it's understandable given what he's been through.'

'How long have you been hiding out here?'

'About a month.'

'When do you think you'll go back to Sheffield?'

'I don't know. I don't think I want to go back. Not to the job anyway.'

'Have you resigned?'

'No. I'm on compassionate leave. I've been told to take as long as I need.'

'Then, do that. Stay here. Go travelling. Have a holiday. Work for a charity for six months delivering aid to war-torn countries. Moping about here won't do you any good. You need to recharge your batteries. Refocus.'

I nod. He's right. 'I've tried to refocus. I go running and swimming every day. I'll have my ear pods in listening to early Stereophonics then, all of a sudden, I'm hit in the face with reality. My entire family is dead. They're dead because of me. I could have stopped it. It really is like hitting a brick wall. Until I can silence that, I can't move on.'

'Oh, Mat,' he says, putting his arm around me and rubbing my back. It's soothing. I like it.

I look out at the water as a lone diver begins to slowly walk out. 'Don't they go down in teams of two?'

'No. One diver goes down. Another stands on the side with the guide rope that's attached to the main diver. He's all togged up ready to go in if needed.'

'How long can he stay under with the oxygen tank on his back?'

'It's not oxygen. It's compressed air. And he's not using that to breathe through. That's for emergencies. Basically, what he's doing is going down to look at the car and see how best to bring it out. We're thinking of bringing in a crane and lifting it out by attaching cables to the axles. We just need to see what condition the car is in, if it's been down for as long as the local police suspect. Chassis are pretty tough so it should be able to be pulled out.'

I watch Aaron as he takes me through the role of SRUK.

'You're really settled, aren't you?'

He can't hide his smile. 'I am. I love this job. I always wanted to be a detective. I thought I was going to be one until I retired. It wasn't until I left that I realised how uptight and stressed I was. I feel so much freer doing this.'

'I'm really happy for you, Aaron.'

'Thank you. By the way, can you dive?'

'I've never done it. Why?'

'We're hiring.'

I let out a guttural laugh. 'I might be able to manage with diving, but I've seen your website. There's no way I'm going in abandoned mines and caves.' I shudder at the thought.

'Yes. You do need to be quite hardy in this job.'

We watch, me with acute interest, as the diving team recce the scene. Eventually, the lead diver breaks the surface of the water and gave a thumbs-up signal.

'That means we'll be able to attach the cables and lift the car out. I'll need to speak to the inspector about getting a crane in and a low-loader. What's she like, this Inspector Forsyth?'

'Prickly, but it's all an act.'

'Sounds familiar,' he says, nudging me playfully.

We stand up and Aaron hands me back the empty coffee cup.

'I'll try and come and see you later. I'm not sure how long all this is going to take us,' he says. 'Can I give you some advice?'

'Sure.'

'Do something to put the fear back in your life. Hand in your notice with South Yorkshire Police. Sell your house. Leave Sheffield and just go somewhere. Don't plan. Just go. You've run away to the Lake District, but it's still safe and comforting. You know the Meagans. You know they'll let you stay for as long as you want. In order to move on, you need to drastically change your life.'

I bite my bottom lip to stave off the emotions.

'You know I'm right,' Aaron says. He pulls me into another tight embrace and kisses me on the top of my head before releasing me and heading towards Inspector Forsyth.

'I know you are. If only it was that easy.'

I watch while Aaron and Gill speak. I can't hear what's said from this distance, and very little seems to be happening so I decide to return to the restaurant. My stomach is growling, anyway, and Philip has promised to cook the smoked salmon he's had hanging in the larder for a few days.

I walk through the trees, passing the myriad of police vehicles and SRUK vans, keeping my head down so as not to engage in eye contact with people who proffer faux sympathetic smiles. Rumour has got around that the infamous Matilda Darke is staying in the area and people seem to be interested in getting a glimpse at the car crash in human form.

'Can I have a word?'

Alison Pemberton is standing by a marked police car. She looks shocked by something.

'Sure.'

'Everybody is lying to me,' she says.

'I'm sorry?'

'They're all lying.'

'Who is?'

'Everyone.'

I can see she's struggling with her emotions. I take her by the elbow and lead her into the restaurant, up the stairs and into the living room.

'Start from the beginning and take your time. What have you found out?'

'My mum was having an affair,' she says through her tears. 'She gave a statement on the day Celia and Jennifer disappeared, and five days later she gave a completely different one.' She thrusts the photocopied pages to me.

I take them and read them through. 'My goodness. I'm guessing your mum has never spoken to you about this.'

'No. She knows… she knows how much I miss my dad. How could she do this to him, Matilda?'

'I'm not going to try and justify it, but your mum must have been very unhappy. It's not easy living with someone with depression, especially if you don't fully understand it. The early 1990s was a very different time. We didn't talk about mental illness as openly as we do now. And men certainly talked about it even less. Your dad will have hated how he was feeling. He wouldn't have talked to anyone, especially his wife. She might have seen him as cold and distant, and found solace elsewhere. Don't hate your mother, Alison.'

Alison grabs for a tissue on the coffee table. She blows her nose and wipes her eyes. It's a while before she speaks.

'Do you think Dad…' She pauses and composes herself. 'Do you think he killed my sisters as a sort of revenge for Mum and Travis being together?'

'No, I don't,' I say, almost immediately. 'If he had wanted to hurt your mother, he would have killed all three of you. You were all together on that day. There was no reason for him to leave you behind.'

She visibly relaxes. 'Thank you,' she squawks through her tears. 'All the way over here I've been thinking that…'

'I know. Alison, can I ask you a favour?'

She blows her nose again. 'Of course.'

'Take some time off. Take a step back from all this. I've got a feeling that you'll get some answers very soon, but you can't be a part of any of this. It will put all kinds of dark thoughts in your head, and you don't want that. Wait for the answers.'

'Are you sure you can get them?'

'I'm doing my best.'

Reluctantly, she nods. 'I looked Travis up. His last known address is the farm my mum lives in now. That was thirty years ago. What's he been doing for the last thirty years? Is he missing, too?'

'I think Tania said she was ringing around to try and find him. I'll give her a call. We'll find out what happened to him and what's going on.'

'I don't think I can handle it, if Dad killed them,' she says, the tears flowing once more.

I don't know what to say to that. Until the truth about her father could be revealed, Alison needed to grow much stronger, and quickly.

Tania thought tracking down someone called Travis Montgomery would be easy. It's not a common name. However, she called six Montgomerys within the Liverpool area, and none were related to a Travis or even knew someone by that name. She sucks hard on her vape, takes a sip of a cold cup of coffee, and unwraps a chocolate from a box of Roses she bought for herself. She dials the next number on her list and waits for the call to be answered.

'Hello?' an elderly male voice asks.

She takes a breath, ready for her spiel. 'Hello. My name is Tania Pritchard. I'm a journalist with *Cumbria Today*. I'm trying to track down Travis Montgomery. Does he live at this address?'

'You're calling about Travis?'

'Yes. Do you know him?'

'I'm his father.'

Tania's eyes light up. Halle-fucking-lujah, she mouths. 'Mr Montgomery, would it be possible for me to speak to Travis? If you don't want to give me his number, I understand. If I can give you mine...'

'Wait,' he interrupts. 'You're calling from Cumbria?'

'Yes. I live in a small village called High Chapel. Your son worked...'

'Yes. I know. He worked on the Pemberton's farm in 1992.'

'That's right.'

'Why are you calling for him?'

'He was working here around the time two young girls went missing. It's coming up to the thirtieth anniversary of their disappearance and I'm wanting to put something together,' she says, having worked on her excuse for tracking him down beforehand.

'But... I don't understand,' he says. 'Travis isn't here.'

'I see. Perhaps if I gave you my number you could pass it onto him.'

'No. Don't you know? Travis is a missing person. We haven't seen him since he left here in 1992.'

Tania's confused. She had checked with Claire Daniels before she started hunting down Travis Montgomery. Claire had informed her that his last known address was the farm in High Chapel. There is no mention of him being a missing person.

'Did you report him missing?' she asks.

'Of course we did,' he says, his voice taking on a severe tone. 'He was supposed to come home for Christmas 1992,' he begins before pausing to give a deep and raspy cough. 'He was working at a farm in High Chapel. The family, they'd suffered some bad luck, the two girls went missing in the summer. He phoned, told us what had happened, me and his mum, said he was staying on to help them out. Next thing, we get another call saying there'd been a big storm and the father, can't remember his name, had gone missing. He said he didn't feel as if he could leave them, but he'd visit at Christmas. He never turned up.'

'Did you phone the Pembertons?'

'We did. We were told that Travis had left the farm at the end of November. They said he felt he needed to move on.'

'And when did you report him missing?'

'It was between Christmas and New Year in 1992. My wife, Sylvia, Travis's mother, she was beside herself. He'd been gone for more than a month before the police started looking for him, but they had nothing to go on. There hasn't been a sighting or anything from that day to this.'

Tania can hear the sorrow and despair in his voice. 'I'm so sorry,' she says, genuinely meaning it. 'I'm not sure how to say this, Mr Montgomery, but I contacted the police before I started ringing round and they don't have Travis listed as a missing person.'

'Ah, well, no, they wouldn't. Travis was his middle name. He was called Julian, after me, but he hated it. Nobody ever called him Julian.'

'Right. So, he's listed as a missing person under his birth name of Julian Travis Montgomery?'

'Yes.'

'I'm going to need to do some digging, Mr Montgomery. Am I okay to get back to you at some point?'

'Of course. It's just… why have you called? Why are you looking for Travis? You mentioned about the two girls going missing. Have they been found?'

For the first time in her life, Tania is stumped for something to say.

'Are you still there?' he asks.

'Yes. I'm still here. Mr Montgomery, please, I promise I will get back in touch with you, but there's someone I need to see. Take care.'

She ends the call without waiting for him to say goodbye. She leans back in her chair and looks up at the ceiling, furrowing her brow as she tries to understand what everything means. Travis's car is missing, but not reported missing. It's then found at the bottom of the lake thirty years later with, potentially, two bodies in the back. And Travis himself is reported missing at the end of 1992.

'I wonder if he's in the car as well?' she asks herself.

Ordering a crane with a hydraulic arm and having a low-loader on standby is the easy part. The difficulty is getting the crane close enough to the edge of the lake in order for the divers to swim out to the submerged car and attach the cables to the axles. So Aaron told me when I took down a tray of coffees for him and his team at lunchtime. I decided not to wait and watch.

I'm in the living room, making notes on a pad, trying to work out how best to investigate Travis Montgomery without getting on the wrong side of Inspector Gill Forsyth. Everything I can think of could end up with Gill charging me with interfering with a criminal investigation.

I shrug. 'Fuck it! Who cares? It might be fun to be the one who is arrested for once.' I have to smile to myself when I picture it making the news. My boss would have a thousand fits. Is ACC Ridley still my boss? I still think of him as my boss so he must be. Does that mean I still think of myself as being a detective?

The door to the living room swings open.

'They're bringing the car up,' Carl shouts, before turning on his heel and running back out of the room.

I slam the laptop closed and follow. Of course I'm still a detective. What else can I be?

It's now dusk. The sun is setting over the horizon and the cloudless sky is lit up a brilliant red. Visibility isn't great, and arc lights have been erected. A crowd has gathered, too. Rumour has spread that a car beneath the water belongs to Travis Montgomery. Does the car contain the bodies of the young Pemberton twins? It seems the whole of High Chapel has turned out to see.

Me, Carl and the two dogs have joined the growing crowd by the side of the lake. I look for Aaron and spot him in a skin-tight diving suit in the shallows, guiding his team into position. I nod to Gill Forsyth as we accidentally make eye contact. She nods back, though her face is grim. I scan the crowd, and I see Alison Pemberton, now out of uniform, standing separate from her mother and stepfather, who look as if the weight of the world is pressing down on them. They're holding hands, supporting each other. I spot Tania Pritchard standing next to a uniformed sergeant I guess to be the Claire Daniels Tania has mentioned. We give each other a succinct smile. We don't want Gill thinking we've joined forces and are in league together, which I suppose we are, really. We had a long chat earlier where Tania told me about Travis being listed as a missing person. I wasn't expecting that. I'm now keen to know how many bodies might be in that car.

I look at all the other faces in the crowd, most I'm seeing for the first time. I wonder if one of them, perhaps hidden in the shadows of the nearby woods, is the mystery man Alison believes is her father. Surely, if he's been keeping an eye on things for the past thirty years, he'll want to be here to see this.

After a few false starts, the hydraulic arm of the crane begins to slowly rise. The slack cables tense and soon I can see movement below the surface of the clear waters of Lake Windermere. As the water breaks and the car becomes visible, I steal a glance across the crowd and look towards Alison. She's moved to her mother and has her arm around her, whispering soothing words to her. Lynne nods, raises a tissue to her eyes and wipes away her tears.

It's impossible to tell the colour of the Vauxhall Astra as it's covered with an amalgam of mud, silt and algae. Everything is hidden. Once it's fully out of the water, it's left to dangle in the air as water runs off it. When that's reduced to a trickle, the car is on the move again. Aaron and his team painstakingly oversee its removal to a nearby low-loader. In the background, Tania is taking photographs with something more professional than a smart phone. Once the car is in position and secured, it's covered with a tarpaulin to protect any forensic evidence from the elements and is slowly driven away.

'Are they going to look inside?' Carl asks.

'Not yet. It's potentially a crime scene. It needs to be looked at carefully in a clean environment.'

'Where are they taking it?'

'I'm not sure. They won't want to drive it too far, so somewhere nearby that's secure and sterile.'

'That's disappointing. I thought they were going to open the doors in front of us all.'

'Trust me, nobody wants to see a body that's potentially spent thirty years in the water.'

The crowd begins to disperse.

Two marked police cars follow the low-loader. Aaron stays behind and walks over to Gill. He's pointing out to the lake. His work isn't finished just yet, it seems.

I look over to Alison and signal for her to join me. She says something to her mother and hands her into the care of her stepfather as if she's an unexploded bomb, before heading over the uneven pebbles to me.

'Do your mother or stepfather recognise the car?' I ask her.

'They both say it's Travis's car.'

'How are things with you?'

She shrugs and, even in the dim light, I can see she's struggling with everything she's learned lately. 'I haven't said anything to them yet. When I think back to that time, I remember my mum doing a lot of crying. I don't want to upset her by having a blazing row.'

'That's a good idea.' I give her a sympathetic smile. It's difficult to know what to say when there are so many unanswered questions. 'Did Travis ever talk about his past to them?'

'I don't know. I didn't ask. Do you want me to question them?'

'No.' I'm quick to answer. I don't want Alison getting involved in this. She's too close to distance herself from the stark truth. 'Look, I'd like to talk to your mum and Iain. Will they talk to me?'

'Yes. I'm sure they will.'

'I'm not sure how much I'm going to be able to help. I very much doubt Gill will want me stepping on anyone's toes. But I'll do my best.'

'Thank you,' she says. 'Thank you so much.'

She looks pleased as she turns and leaves. I've given her hope. I only hope it's not false hope.

'I thought you weren't going to be a detective anymore,' Carl says.

'The problem is, I've been a police officer my whole life. I'm not qualified for anything else. I can't just not work. What else can I do?'

'You could go into partnership with Mum and Dad. Dad was saying last night how you know a lot about wines.'

'I know how to drink them, Carl. That's all. Come on, let's get back.'

We head for the woods, but I hear my name being called. I turn back to see Aaron running towards me.

'Did that go well?' I ask.

'Yes, it did. Very smoothly,' he says with a grin. 'The divers that went down to the car were wearing body cameras. I was watching from up here, and I still have my detective brain on occasionally. I've just been telling Inspector Forsyth. I believe the car was pushed into the lake rather than driven in.'

'What makes you think that?'

'The car was sitting on a shelf.'

'There's a shelf in the lake?' Carl interrupts.

'Oh,' I almost forgot Carl is next to me. 'Carl, this is former DS Aaron Connolly. He was on my team who helped look for you. Aaron, this is Carl.'

A smile spreads across Aaron's face. He holds out a hand for Carl to shake. 'It really is a pleasure to finally meet you, Carl.'

'Thank you,' he replies, slightly unsure how to respond. 'You said there was a shelf in the lake?'

'It's kind of like a big ledge before the lake drops even further below ground. Lake Windermere goes down to sixty-seven meters at its deepest point and there's a big drop-off just a few meters out from here. If the car had been driven in at speed, I think it would have gone completely off the shelf, sunk, and it may never have been discovered. The fact it was on the shelf makes me think it was pushed in only far enough to be hidden.'

'By someone who maybe doesn't know the lake too well.'

'Possibly. My team is going back in tomorrow to scan the bed of the lake to see if there's anything else down there that might have become detached from the car. I know I shouldn't, but I'll let you know if we find anything.'

'Thanks, Aaron. Where are you staying tonight?'

'We're booked into a hotel on the outskirts of the village.'

'Where did you take the car?'

'You're always switched on, aren't you?' He laughs.

'Always a detective. You said yourself your detective brain switched on.'

'True. It's gone to a warehouse about five miles away. It's a secure site Cumbria Police has used before for large-scale operations.'

I ask Carl to give me and Aaron a few minutes alone. He picks up a stick and throws it for the two Woodys to chase after, then he follows them. Standing to one side, I lower my voice.

'Are there bodies inside the car?'

'There's something in the back seat. Curiosity got the better of me. I smeared one of the windows and was able to get a high-powered torch on it. I'm just not sure what it is.'

'Bones?'

He nods. 'I think I saw a skull.'

'Anything in the driver's seat?'

'No.'

'Thanks, Aaron.'

'Are you going all Miss Marple on me?'

'Judging by the dirty looks Inspector Forsyth was shooting me during the recovery operation, I think I might be.'

I wink and walk away. I join Carl and we make our way through the woods back to the restaurant. All the way, I chew on my lip as I think. I have a lot of questions running around my mind and I guess I'm going to make a lot of people unhappy by asking them, but as I said to Carl earlier, all I know is how to be a detective, and I'm a bloody good one.

The majority of people who had gathered on the shore head for The Frog and Toad once the excitement of the car being lifted from the lake is over.

Sitting at a corner table, Alison and Claire are chatting. Alison is on her second vodka and tonic, Claire is disappointingly sipping at yet another apple juice. Several of the drinkers at the bar keep turning around to look at them.

'I feel like every pair of eyes in this room is watching me, waiting for me to burst into tears,' Alison says.

'The atmosphere isn't as lively as it usually is, is it?'

'No.'

'Even the hoo-hah about Kevin cheating on the quiz has died down. Ally, can I ask you a favour?'

'Of course you can.'

'I know it's only early. I mean, I'm not even showing yet,' she said, sticking out her flat-ish stomach. 'But I'm trying to get all the big things sorted before I end up being a big thing. I was wondering if you'd be godmother to whatever I've got growing inside me.'

Alison's face lights up. 'Oh, Claire, seriously?'

'Yes. You're my best friend.'

'I'd love to!' She reaches over and gives her a tight squeeze.

'Geraint's asking his brother to be godfather but we're going to write a will and I'm going to say I want you to be in overall charge of the little one's upbringing, should anything happen... you know.'

'Shouldn't you be thinking about cots and nappies rather than going all morbid thinking you're going to die before the child is old enough to look after itself?'

'Probably. I'm just... I'm really nervous about being a mum, Ally. There are times when I can't even look after myself. How am I going to cope with bringing a child up who is totally dependent on me?'

'You have nothing to worry about. You've got Geraint. You've got me. You're going to be a wonderful mum.'

'I hope so.'

'Want another drink?' Alison asked.

'Sure. Just an orange juice for me.'

Alison went to the bar and returned with two orange juices. She really wanted a double gin and tonic but decided to abstain in front of Claire. She didn't want to be seen to be indulging when Claire had to cut back.

'Claire, you remember Travis, don't you?'

'Of course.'

'What did you think of him?'

'I thought he was lovely. I remember having an argument with Celia about which one of us was going to marry him.'

'Really?'

'Yes. It even got to hair-pulling stage. In the end, we decided to share him. We'd each have him three days a week and he could have Sunday off,' she says with a smile at the memory. 'Bloody hell, can you imagine if something like that were possible?'

Alison takes a long sip of her drink. 'Do you think Travis took my sisters?' she asks, eventually.

'Oh, I don't know about that, Ally.'

'It's his car at the bottom of the lake. Look, Claire, if I tell you something, you have to promise not to tell anyone, not your mum, not Tania, and not Geraint.'

'I promise on my unborn baby,' she says, cradling her stomach.

'That's good enough for me.' Alison tells her about her mother's second police statement, admitting to an affair with Travis.

'Oh my God!' Claire says. 'No offence to your mum or anything, but her and Travis, that's... well, it's... I don't know. It just seems wrong.'

'Tell me about it.'

'Eww,' Claire shudders. 'How do you feel about it all?'

'I *was* angry. Then I spoke to Matilda. She reminded me that the early nineties were a different time. Things like depression weren't talked about as openly as they are now, particularly by men. Maybe Dad bottled everything up. Maybe he pushed Mum away.'

'It's possible. Where do you go from here?'

'Matilda is going to do some digging for me. She's going to speak to my mum and Iain. What I want to know is: why wasn't Travis's car reported as stolen? I've been thinking and going back to that time before Celia and Jennifer went missing. Whenever he had any spare time, Travis was always messing about with his car. It's been at the bottom of the lake for thirty years; it was there for three months before Travis left. Why did nobody notice?'

'Maybe they did.'

'Then why wasn't it reported stolen?'

'Maybe it was.'

'What are you talking about?' Alison asks, turning sharply to Claire.

'Who was in charge of the police here, back then?'

'Inspector Bell.'

'And what do we know about Inspector Bell since he left the police?'

The penny drops. 'We know that Inspector Bell isn't the upstanding, law-abiding police officer everyone thought he was.'

'Precisely. He took all that collection money, remember.'

'I should tell Matilda about that.'

'Well, good luck to Matilda trying to get anywhere near Lionel Bell. You know what Gill's like.'

'I do, but I also know how unstable Matilda Darke is right now. If Gill stops her trying to get to speak to her father, she's liable to smack her teeth in.'

A smile spreads across Claire's face. 'I would pay thousands to see that.'

For the first time since my arrival, I'm the first one up. Usually, I'm woken by the constant calls from Sally to Carl to get out of bed and dressed to get to school on time. This morning, I don't have a lie-in. I usually spend so long trying to get to sleep in the first place, and when I do, my sleep is disturbed by dark dreams. So, by the time it's morning, and actually time to get up, I'm physically shattered.

This morning, however, is different. I have a reason for getting out of bed. I have a task.

I pull up outside Lynne and Iain's house in the Porsche and look at the cottage. The after-effects of the storm are evident in the neighbourhood and Lynne is busy cleaning the inside of the new living room window as I walk up the path. We make eye contact and Lynne's face falls. She opens the door before I have a chance to knock.

'Good morning,' I say, proffering what I hope is a natural, friendly smile.

Lynne nods. 'I know Alison has spoken to you; asked you to look into what happened to her sisters, but...' She pauses and takes a breath. 'I've been told not to speak to you.'

'Oh?'

'Yes. I'm sorry.'

'Who by?'

Lynne looks down.

'Who is it?' Iain calls out as he comes from the kitchen into the hallway. 'Oh. Hello. You're Matilda Drake, aren't you?'

'Darke,' I correct him.

'Sorry. Yes.' He places a protective arm around his wife's shoulders. 'I'm afraid you've had a wasted journey. Inspector Forsyth has told us not to talk to you.'

'Has she? Did she give any reason?'

'Given that a car has been found and… the items found with it appear to point to the fact that Celia and Jennifer may be in there, Inspector Forsyth said it's an active investigation and any outside help might muddy the waters.'

'I can understand that,' I say, placating the couple, despite wanting to tell them that Gill's excuse is complete bollocks. 'However, I've spoken to Alison and she's really struggling with what's going on. She's placed her trust in me, and I like her. I'd really like to help.' I'm laying it on thick, but if it gets me over the threshold, I don't care.

'I don't… know,' Lynne hesitates.

She's weakening.

'If I could come in for five minutes. I promise I won't pry; I won't make waves. I only want to ask a few questions.'

'I really don't think…'

'It's just a couple of questions, Iain,' Lynne interrupts.

'But Inspector Forsyth…'

'Will never need to know,' I finish his sentence for him.

Lynne looks up at her husband with pleading eyes. Eventually he relents. Lynne stands to one side and allows me to enter.

'Thank you,' I say, as the door is closed behind me.

I'm shown into the kitchen. Lynne apologises for the state of the living room. The carpet has been taken up and is now in a mushy pile in the back garden. The sofa has been pushed to one side and is waiting to be professionally cleaned.

I sit at the small table while Lynne goes to the kettle and flicks it on.

'Did you buy any more teabags?' she asks.

'They're in the bag in the hall. I didn't get time to put them away.'

Lynne leaves the kitchen.

Iain leans over me. 'Please don't upset my wife,' he says, quietly.

'I'm not here to upset anyone.'

'She's been through a lot over the years.'

'I'm aware. I'm doing this for Alison.'

He nods and returns to his position by the sink as Lynne comes back into the kitchen, breaking the seal on a box of Yorkshire Tea bags.

Drinks made, Lynne sits opposite me. She looks nervous, as if she's worried about what I'm going to reveal.

'What can you tell me about Travis Montgomery?' I begin.

Lynne recoils. She looks to Iain. It's clear neither of them expects me to begin with Travis.

'He was a good man. He was very good to this family,' Lynne says.

'He worked with you and Jack on the farm, Alison was telling me.' I turn to Iain.

Iain nods. 'My father employed him as casual help. When he died, Travis stayed on. He helped us transform the whole site. We couldn't have done it without him.'

'What was he like?'

'He was a good bloke. Not afraid of hard work, and it *was* hard work, believe me. We were out in all weathers.'

'He wasn't local, was he?'

'No. He came up from…' He screws his face up as he thinks. 'I want to say Liverpool?'

'It was Liverpool,' Lynne confirms.

'You knew him well?' I ask Lynne.

Lynne glares at me. Tears fill her eyes. She remains deathly silent. It's clear she's struggling with something. 'We all knew him,' she says, her words loaded with emotion.

I glance between Lynne and Iain. I have a feeling I'm not going to get the full story with them both present. They're hiding things from each other. Or maybe they have a shared secret they're worried might accidentally be revealed.

'He left not long after Jack disappeared, didn't he?' I ask. 'Why was that? I thought he'd have been needed then more than ever.'

Iain looks uncomfortable. He moves away from his wife and rests against the worktop. 'He told me he needed to leave. The atmosphere was heavy. Understandable, considering, but Travis said he was struggling with it. He was sorry to leave us in the lurch, but he felt he had to go.'

'Did you ask him to stay?'

'Of course. The stables were still in their infancy. I needed all the help I could get. With Jack… well, with him going like that, I really needed Travis.'

'Yet he still decided to leave?'

Iain shrugs. 'He didn't owe us anything. He wasn't family, and he was only young. It was only supposed to be a temporary job for a few months. He'd already stayed longer than planned.'

'Did you have any contact with him after he'd gone?'

'No. This was in the days before mobile phones and social media. We thanked him for everything he'd done, didn't we?' He looks to Lynne.

'Yes. I cooked him a goodbye meal,' she smiles, though her face shows she's on the edge of tears. 'We were trying to be normal, but it was horrible.'

'Why was it horrible?'

'There should have been seven of us around that table,' Iain says. 'There were only three. None of us wanted to address what we were all thinking, but it was difficult to ignore.'

'Three? Where was Alison?' I ask.

'She was staying with my sister and brother-in-law for a while,' Lynne says.

I nod my understanding. 'Did you ever hear from Travis again?'

'No,' Lynne answers.

'Not until his father got in touch around Christmas,' Iain adds. 'He said he was missing, that he hadn't returned home. The police came up here from Liverpool for us to give a statement. We told them what we've just told you. He left, planning to go back home, and that's where we thought he'd gone. He gave no indication that he was going elsewhere.'

'He was only young, wasn't he?'

'Twenty-six,' Lynne quickly answers.

'Did he and Jack get on?'

'Yes. We all did,' Iain says. 'We worked closely together every single day. Travis lived in this house with me and Dad.'

'Did either of you ever suspect that he might have been involved in Celia and Jennifer's disappearance?'

'I told you what happened,' Lynne says, her voice quiet.

'I know you did. I'm just wondering, with Travis going missing not long after Jack, if they both might have...' I struggle with how to say this tactfully. 'Was it possible they were both involved in the twins' disappearance?'

Lynne's mouth falls open. 'What? No,' she says, the tears falling down her face. 'No. Not my girls. Please. Don't tell me they were both... no. Not that.'

'I really think you should leave,' Iain says, jumping to his wife's aid and putting his arms firmly around her shoulders. 'You're upsetting Lynne.'

'I'm sorry. I didn't mean to upset anyone. It's just... there are far too many loose ends here and, with Travis's car being at the bottom of the lake yet it not being reported stolen or missing, I find it odd that nobody has ever looked into this.'

'We were all busy... distracted,' Iain says. 'With the girls missing, we didn't know what day it was. We were all frantically searching everywhere to try and find them. Then... Jack told me... shit,' he says. 'I can't go through all this again.' He stands up and goes over to the kitchen sink, looking out of the window. 'My brother. He was my brother. I looked up to him. I wanted... why? How?'

I watch the both of them in silence as they fall apart, still struggling to understand the horror, thirty years later.

'The police investigation thirty years ago: looking back, do you think it was a thorough investigation? Do you think everything was done to find Celia and Jennifer?'

Lynne looks up at her. 'I... I don't know. I assume everything was done correctly.'

Iain turns back from the window. He wipes his eyes. 'The police turned this county upside down trying to find them. Inspector Bell worked round the clock.'

'What are you saying?' Lynne asks me.

'Right now, I'm not sure. But I'm finding myself asking more and more questions, and I don't know how to find the answers. This Inspector Bell, is he still alive?'

'Yes. He still lives in the village. He doesn't go out much,' Lynne says. 'You might want to speak to Gill about it first, though. I'm guessing he'll have told her all about it.'

'Why?'

'Well… Gill is Inspector Bell's daughter. I thought you knew.'

Did I hear that right? 'Gill is the daughter of Lionel Bell?'

'Yes. Sorry. I thought you'd have known. I don't know why, sorry,' Lynne says.

'I asked Gill about Lionel. I asked her if he was still alive, and I recommended she question him. She never said.'

'Ah. No. She wouldn't,' Iain says.

'Why not?'

'She's sort of ashamed.'

'In what way?'

'Of the way Lionel left the police force.'

'How did he leave?'

Iain retakes his seat next to Lynne. 'He was forced into taking early retirement. Back in the day, there was a much bigger police force here than there is now, and there were two inspectors: Lionel and Inspector Gideon Oliver. Gideon was diagnosed with stomach cancer. It tore through his entire body. Obviously, he had to give up work, but he couldn't afford not to work. The whole village had a big whip-round. We held all kinds of events to raise money for him. Unfortunately, Gideon died while we were raising it. Next thing, the money is discovered sitting there in Lionel's bank account. He was forced to retire. He's been a social pariah around here ever since.'

'That can't have been easy for Gill.'

'No. Why do you think she goes by her mother's maiden name?'

'But you said yourself, it's a small village. Everyone will know who her father is.'

'They do. But Gill is a good woman. They don't judge her by what her father did.'

Lynne has been silent while me and Iain have been talking about Gill and her father. She looks up and takes a deep, unsteady breath.

'Were Jack and Travis abusing my babies?' Her voice is heavily charged with dark emotion, but it's quiet, barely more than a whisper.

Iain tightens his hold on his wife.

'I really don't know, Lynne. The only people who can tell us that are both missing.'

'But... now the bodies have been found, they can do tests, can't they? Postmortems.'

'They've been under water possibly for thirty years. Any trace evidence will have long gone by now.'

'I'll never know the truth, will I?'

'We've got them back, Lynne,' Iain says, hugging her, resting his head on her shoulders. 'We've got them back. That's all that matters.'

'Iain's right.' I reach across and place a hand on top of hers. 'You can lay them to rest. You can have a place to go and talk to them.'

Lynne nods. She tries to smile, but it won't come.

I push my chair back and stand up. 'I should go. I'm sorry for upsetting you, but I've been in this job long enough to know that people can never fully rest until the truth is revealed, no matter how difficult it is to hear.'

'Sometimes the truth is better left buried,' Iain says.

'I don't agree. Lies hurt more than the truth. I speak from experience. I'll see myself out.'

I'm almost at the door when my name is called. I turn and see Lynne standing in the doorway to the kitchen.

'Promise me,' Lynne begins. 'Promise me you won't tell Alison any of this.'

'Alison is a very intelligent woman. If she asks me a question and I tell her I don't know, she's going to know it's a lie. I can't promise she won't find out, but I can promise that I will protect her as much as possible.'

I have to pass the restaurant to get to the offices of *Cumbria Today*, so I stop off. When I pull up outside the newspaper, Tania is parking in her spot directly opposite. I hold up a white box I've loaded with goodies.

'Ooh, excellent timing,' Tania says with a smile.

'You have information?'

'No. I've just been out buying tea bags,' she says holding up the box.

Teas made, me and Tania sit at one of the spare desks. The cardboard box has been pulled open to reveal slices of tart and cheesecake, and muffins. Tania's eyes are out on stalks as she tries to choose one.

'Between the cigarettes, the naughty calories and the bottle of wine I drink a night, I'm surprised I'm not dead already,' she says as she plumps for lemon and lime cheesecake with coconut shavings.

'You live alone?'

'Completely. I'm not even a crazy cat lady.' She scoops up a forkful of dessert and her eyes roll back. 'And with delicious things like this in the world, who needs men?'

I smile. I think of Odell. I'm being unfair to him. Our relationship had just been getting off the ground when I ran. I wonder if he's waiting for me or has decided to move on. I wouldn't blame him.

'You looked all sad there for a moment,' Tania says.

'Just thinking about things. What might have been.'

'I've had a few of those in my time. My mother was ill for years. I had to take care of her while working full-time. Suddenly, ten years go by and you haven't shifted, yet you're ten years older. When my mother died, I thought I'd be able to start living, maybe find myself a husband and settle down, but I wasn't a young twenty-something anymore. I'd also built a veneer around me. People think I'm hard as nails.'

'But you're not.'

'Nobody is. We're all the same. We all have emotions and feelings. People don't realise that. They judge you on what they see, and I'm a hard-faced feminist journalist who doesn't need a man in her life to be happy.'

'And in reality?'

'I don't *need* a man. That doesn't mean to say I don't want one. It's no fun spending your days alone in this shitty office and going home to a cold and empty house. Anyway, you didn't come here to listen to the sob story of my tragic life. I'm guessing you have information.'

I tell her all about Lynne changing her police statement and her affair with Travis.

'Lynne and Travis?' Tania's face takes on a look as if she's tasting something rancid. 'I'd heard rumours, but now that it's confirmed, it... I don't know. I find it a bit disgusting.'

'Why?'

'Because... well, I'm not being nasty to Lynne or anything, but she's not exactly a raving beauty, is she? Even thirty years ago she was no looker. And Travis, well, he could have been posing on the box of Calvin Klein underpants. Talk about a mismatched pair. I wonder who came on to who...' She ponders this for a moment then tries to shake the thought from her head. 'Actually, no, I don't want to know.' She shudders.

'Lynne and Iain seem suited.'

'Oh, yes. They're much more evenly matched. I'm pretty sure Lynne was seeing Iain first, then left him for Jack.'

'Really?'

'Yes. They weren't together long. When they were younger, Iain had a different woman every weekend. He was a very handsome bloke. Tall, rugged, manly, ooh...' She shivers again.

'It sounds like you fancied him yourself.'

'Not really. Just a filthy fantasy about being taken roughly in a barn by a sweaty manly farmer. I think I've been reading too many trashy romances. Either that or I need to stop scrolling through PornHub. It's strange, isn't it? You never know who you're going to end up with. Lynne and Iain dated for a few weeks, split up, Lynne married Iain's brother, then they end up together decades later. It was obviously meant to be.'

'Hmm.' I think about me and James. I'd thought we were meant to be, but I was robbed of him after less than ten years of marriage. It wasn't fair. Lynne had married who she assumed was her first love, but was she happy?

What does happiness fucking mean anyway?

'Do you think Iain knew about the affair between Lynne and Travis?' I ask. I really should stop my mind going off on a tangent.

'I'm not sure. Why?'

'Well, Lynne came to see me in the restaurant and told me all about Jack admitting to abusing the twins. I did tell you about that, didn't I?'

'Yes.'

'Sorry, my mind is all over the place at the moment. Anyway, I've just been to see Iain and Lynne, and Iain clearly knows she told me about the abuse, but she didn't mention she'd had an affair with Travis when that came up. I'm guessing Iain doesn't know about it.'

'It doesn't have anything to do with him though. She was married to Jack at the time. Not Iain. When you were married, did your husband know about all your exes?'

'Definitely not.'

'There you go, then,' Tania says, reaching for a chocolate caramel muffin.

'So, Lynne and Travis have an alibi for when the twins were taken. Jack doesn't. Iain does. I'd like to speak to Inspector Lionel Bell.'

'Why?'

'I get the feeling there's more going on with the original investigation than Lynne knows about. They mentioned something about Lionel stealing some money, yet I didn't see any of that mentioned when I was looking online the other night.'

'No. You wouldn't,' Tania says, a firmness in her voice.

'What do you mean?'

'I've known Lionel for as long as I can remember. I don't believe he did steal that money, so I refused to write about it.'

'What happened?'

'Gideon Oliver was the same rank as Lionel Bell. They worked well together. Gideon finds out he's got cancer and leaves work. The village turns out in force and raises thousands for him so he can pay his mortgage and bills. We did all sorts for him. Next thing, Gideon finds out that the cancer has spread like wildfire. He's dead within a week, bless him. He was only forty-one. Anyway, we'd raised all this money, and nobody knew what to do with it. I don't know how the rumour got out, but the whole village is talking about Lionel having it in his bank account.'

'Did he admit it?'

'Well, he admitted it was there because it was, but he was clueless to how it got there.'

'He would say that, though, wouldn't he?'

Tania composes herself. 'He turned up on my doorstep one night in floods of tears. He swore on his wife's life that he did not take that money. I believed him.'

'Yet he still resigned from the force.'

'He had no choice. Mud sticks, especially around here.'

'Who had the money in the first place, before it ended up in Lionel's bank account?'

'It was held in an account the newspaper opened to collect all the donations and everything we raised.'

'So, *you* had access to the bank account?'

'Not just me: anyone who worked on the paper. It was a bank book back in those days. We didn't have cards and PINs. Anyone could have accessed the money if they had the bank book. Look, Matilda, Lionel is a good man. I believed him. I still do.'

I nod. 'I think something is happening, here. I think this goes right back to when the twins went missing. For thirty years, someone has been trying to control this narrative to hide the truth; and with the car, and possibly the twins, being found, they're worried it's all going to come crashing down around them.'

'Who?'

'I'm not sure yet.'

'Who are your suspects?'

'Everyone living in this village old enough to commit murder back in 1992.'

'I hope you're not including me in that,' Tania says with a smile.

I don't say anything. I can't. But if there's one thing worse than a journalist printing gossip and innuendo, it's a journalist who refuses to.

Aaron Connolly and his team are back at Lake Windermere to continue the search. Now the car has been removed, their job is to comb the lakebed around where the car was situated to look for further evidence. A shoe and a piece of jewellery have risen to the surface following the storm which sent trees crashing into the water, disturbing what lay beneath. What else has left the confines of the car over the past thirty years?

Aaron stands on the shore. He's unable to enter the water but is dressed in a wetsuit and has a life jacket on standby in case any of his team get into difficulty and he's needed. He doubts that will happen. His team undertake regular training and are experts in their duties. Also, he checked the weather forecast and it's to remain fair throughout the day. Looking out onto the water, the merest of ripples appear on the surface in the gentle, warm breeze.

To comb the lakebed, SRUK use the Jack Stay set-up. Two buoys bob in the water, marking the area the car was located. Beneath them, anchors sit on the floor of the lake and a floating polypropylene line connects the two. A diver travels along the length of the line between the two anchors and scours the floor for any evidence or debris that could be useful for the police investigation. Whatever is found will be brought back to the surface, then the anchors are moved to another point along the lakebed. It is a laborious task.

'How long do you think it will take?' Inspector Forsyth asks.

She stands next to Aaron, wearing a zipped-up gilet, leggings, and wellington boots. Her arms are folded tightly across her chest.

'We'll be here all day,' Aaron answers without taking his eyes from his lead diver as he slowly walks out into the water.

'Right,' she says. 'I'll leave a couple of uniformed officers here in case you find anything that we need to know about straight away. I'll keep popping back, though. I gave you my direct number, didn't I?'

'You did.'

Gill doesn't make to move away. She clears her throat. 'I'm aware of your past with Detective Chief Inspector Matilda Darke. I'm guessing you were quite close at one point.'

Aaron doesn't say anything.

'This is my investigation,' Gill continues. 'If you find anything, you tell my officers and me only. Is that understood?'

He turns to look at her. 'Perfectly,' he says with a smile.

Ten miles away, in Kendal, a forensic warehouse owned by the Cumbria Constabulary is now home to the blue Vauxhall Astra 1.3 Merit Estate. It is high up on a raised platform as forensic officers in white scene-of-crime suits take photographs of the vehicle from every angle, including underneath. The seventeen-digit VIN number is found on the chassis and noted down. The registration number is recorded and matches the make and model of the car. The general condition of the bodywork is analysed to check for signs of damage. None are found, though nobody knows what's lying beneath the layers of mud stuck to it. Once it's washed off, the bodywork will need to be checked again. The locks on the doors and boot have been checked for signs of tampering. Again, none are found.

It's important to know if there are any specific reasons why the car ended up in the water in the first place. Had the vehicle been interfered with? Had a brake line been cut, either frayed through wear and tear or deliberately? Now the scene-of-crime team is satisfied, the exterior of the car has been covered, the platform is lowered and Crime Scene Manager, Louise Brocklebank, steps forward.

Louise is in charge of looking after the car and making sure everything is done correctly in the processing of any evidence. She has been in the background while photographs are taken, but now, as she approaches, she lifts up her protective hood and tucks in her shoulder-length blonde hair. She places a mask over her nose and mouth and pulls on a pair of latex gloves over the cuffs of the Tyvek sleeves.

Standing in the background is Sergeant Claire Daniels from High Chapel Police Station. She was asked by Inspector Forsyth to oversee the forensic investigation and report back any findings. Part of her thought this was a waste of time. The whole thing is being documented and recorded. However, for the sake of the Pembertons, she feels a need to be here.

'Are you ready, Brian?' Louise asks one of the CSIs who is behind her, camera held in front of him, recording over her shoulder.

'Yes. All good here,' he replies.

'Okay. I'm going to open the rear door.'

Claire steps forward to join them, yet maintains her distance.

The car is still covered in silt and algae, but most of it has dried overnight. She pulls the door hard before it opens. It wasn't locked. An arc light is brought forward, lighting up the interior.

After thirty years of being underwater, there is very little remaining of the inside of the car. The carpet and fabric seats have disintegrated, leaving only their metal frames and a layer of what can only be described as mulch on the floor.

On the rear seats is an amalgam of bones. Bodies left in water are difficult to analyse. Maceration of the skin begins within minutes in warm water, as in the case of deaths in bathtubs; but in cold water, like Lake Windermere, it is difficult to estimate a time frame. There are too many variables, such as the temperature of the water on the day the car went in and the condition of the water at the time. Exposed areas such as hands and face show the signs of immersion in water first and within a few days become wrinkled, pale, and sodden, the so-called 'washer woman's skin'. After several weeks in cold water, the thick keratin on hands and feet becomes detached and will peel off in a glove and stocking fashion. The hair and finger- and toenails begin to loosen around this time too. Areas of the body covered with clothing will take longer to break down and man-made fibres will protect the body longer than usual. Parts of the body not eaten by scavengers will simply slip off the bones and merge with the fabric of the seats or the carpet on the floor of the car. Either way, it will be lost over time. What remains is what Louise Brocklebank is now looking at, a collection of unidentifiable bones. How many bodies are here? It's difficult to tell by looking. They will need to be carefully transported to a postmortem suite and fitted together.

Louise stands to one side and allows the bones to be filmed

and photographed. It opens up the whole scene for Claire to see from where she's standing.

A feeling of sadness is heavy in Claire's heart, as she takes in the undeveloped bones. There are two skulls, both small, both obviously children. She hopes to God they were dead before they entered the water. If not, their final moments together will have been agony as they slowly suffocated or drowned. She looks down at the collection of phalanges that will have made up the fingers. She likes to think they were holding each other's hand for the last thirty years, together in life and death. She feels the swell of emotion rise up and she has to turn away. It's her imagination, as she's only two months' pregnant – she isn't even showing yet – but she's sure she can feel her baby inside her.

'Are you all right?' Brian asks her as she walks away, head down.

'Uh-huh,' she says, non-committal.

'Grim, isn't it.'

She doesn't answer. She can't. Grim doesn't cover it. What kind of a person could put two innocent children into the back of a car and leave them in a watery grave to disintegrate into nothingness? Not for the first time, she wonders whether bringing a child into a world where evil exists is the right thing to do.

By the time Specialised Rescue UK are finished, light is fading. It has been a successful day, and many items have been found on the floor of Lake Windermere. Some are random and could have been there for much longer than the car, others would need to be verified to see if they belonged to Celia and Jennifer Pemberton. It's times like this that Aaron is pleased to no longer be on the police force. Showing weathered personal items to a grieving mother is never going to be a pleasant task.

Throughout the day, Sally Meagan has been coming down from Nature's Diner with takeaway cups of tea and coffee for the recovery team. At lunchtime, she brought a selection of panini, and when she knew they were finishing she told all six of them to come to the restaurant once they'd packed everything away and they could have a meal on the house. Aaron had graciously told her it wasn't necessary, but Sally insisted and, once she saw Inspector Forsyth turn her back, quietly told Aaron that Matilda would like a word with him.

'We're very grateful for your hospitality, Mrs Meagan,' he'd said loudly enough for Gill to overhear. His acting skills left a lot to be desired, and Sally walked away rolling her eyes. No BAFTA nomination for Aaron this year.

Tania drives her Fiat Punto along End Lane. The atmosphere in the car is tense. I'm glaring out of the side window. There's a smattering of houses dotted about, each with a lengthy driveway and high privet hedges hiding them from the road. It's called End Lane simply because it's the final road of High Chapel. Turn left at the end and open countryside is revealed all the way to Kendal. Tania pulls up beside an oak tree.

'Which house does Lionel live in?' I ask, looking around, trying to get a glimpse of the properties hidden by nature.

'It's the very last one down there.' She points.

'Why have we parked here?'

'I don't want Lionel to see us arrive. We don't speak much now. In fact, Lionel doesn't speak to anyone much now, apart from his daughter and granddaughter. People around here have long memories, and according to them, he stole Gideon Oliver's money.'

'Haven't you tried to put them straight?'

'I believed Lionel,' she says, turning to me. 'I couldn't prove it, though. Neither could he. I believed him because I knew him.'

'But surely the people of High Chapel knew him, too.'

'Yes. But people are quick to condemn.'

'Why didn't you?'

'I... I just didn't, that's all,' she says, climbing out of the car.

I follow. The temperature is on the rise again. There is the merest hint of a breeze, but it doesn't alter the fact it's an intensely hot day. I dig out a pair of sunglasses from the pocket of my jeans and put them. Tania is already far up the road, heading for the final house of End Lane, a picturesque bungalow. I have to trot to catch up to her.

'You loved him, didn't you?' I ask.

'What?'

'Lionel. You fell in love with him.'

'That's ridiculous,' she says, without looking back.

'Why is it? You said, not an hour ago, that people see you as a hard-faced journalist but you're not, you have emotions the same as everyone else. Your words, Tania. There's nothing wrong with falling in love. Nobody is going to judge you. We all do it.'

Tania stops at the entrance to Lionel's driveway. When she turns, I see tears in her eyes.

'Yes. I loved him. I told him so, too. This was long after his Doreen had died.'

'What did he say?'

'He said he couldn't love me as he still loved his wife. I knew then there would be no future in it for us. I couldn't compete with a dead woman. We kept seeing each other. I think he saw me as a comfort shag while he was going through so much crap. I was punishing myself by allowing myself to fall deeper and deeper in love with him. Stupid, right?'

I place a comforting hand on Tania's arm. It feels strange to be offering someone comfort when I'm such a complete basket case. I quickly remove my hand.

'When you and I started out in our jobs, they were male-dominated, right?' Tania begins. 'We had to prove we were as good as the men, if not better. In order to do that, we poisoned ourselves, sacrificed our emotions. We didn't cry over a crime scene or a dark story, because we knew the men would laugh and tell us our hormones were getting in the way. Now look at us: we can't even comfort each other because we've forgotten how.'

She turns and heads up the drive, leaving me at the bottom, musing on her words.

She's right.

Lionel Bell's bungalow is neat and tidy. There's fragrances of furniture polish and air freshener.

'Nice to see you again, Lionel,' Tania says by way of a greeting.

He doesn't say anything back. He steps to one side and allows us to enter.

We stand in the hallway while Lionel closes the door. I look around me at the bright space. I take in the framed artwork on the walls, all landscapes, all local, and ones I recognise from my many runs through the hills and valleys. It's neutrally decorated in warm creams and beige, though the carpet is looking a tad threadbare.

Lionel is dressed in similar colours to his home. He's wearing beige chinos, a white polo shirt and a loose-fitting cream cardigan over the top. He leads us into the living room which is spacious and dominated by a huge picture window giving a view of the entire village.

'Wow,' I marvel.

'Sorry,' Tania jumps in. 'Lionel, this is Matilda…'

'I know. Nice to meet you again.'

I quickly turn to look at him. 'Again?' The penny drops. 'Oh, you're the man in the coffee shop.'

'That was me. How are you feeling now?'

I can't answer that. 'I'm... better, thanks.'

'You've met?' Tania asks.

'I was in the tearoom and looked over and there she was, bawling her eyes out. Understandable given what you've been through lately. I gave you some words of advice. I hope you're taking them on board.'

'I'm not sure. I'm trying to.'

'What did you say to her?' Tania asks him.

'I told her that what doesn't kill you makes you stronger.'

Tania quickly turns away and dabs her eyes.

'What?' I ask.

'That was what I told him when he was forced to quit the police force.'

'Did it make you stronger?' I ask him.

'It made me harder. I'm not sure if that's the same thing. Shall we sit down?'

We sit on a three-seat sofa. Lionel is about to sit on a matching armchair when he jumps back up.

'Tea? Coffee? I've got a bottle of wine open, and I think there's some gin somewhere. I assume neither of us are on duty,' he says with a smile.

'I'd love a coffee,' I say.

'Me too,' Tania echoes.

'Two coffees coming up.' He leaves the room for the kitchen.

I look around at the living room. More pictures on the walls, this time mostly photographs. I see one of a very young Gill Forsyth in uniform, back straight, head high, proud as punch on what, I assume, is her first day in the force. There are plenty of a young girl, starting as a baby and growing up into a beautiful young woman.

'That's Gill's daughter, Lauren,' Tania says, her voice low.

'Where's the father?'

'There isn't one.'

I raise an eyebrow.

'Lauren is the product of a turkey baster.'

'Oh.'

'Gill wanted a child but didn't want a husband.'

'What did Lionel make of that?'

'He didn't mind. He was there with her in the delivery room when she gave birth. He dotes on Lauren.'

I smile. 'I can see why you fell for him. You can tell he was a handsome man when he was younger. He's got a twinkle in his eye.'

Tania swallows hard and looks away.

'You still like him, don't you?'

'I haven't seen him for so long. I put a distance between us. I had to. Seeing him again, it's brought it all back.'

'I could have come here on my own.'

Tania quickly turns to look at me. 'And have you steal my man? I don't think so, bitch,' she says, playfully.

Using humour as a defence mechanism. That sounds familiar. I laugh anyway. It's a strange sound to my ears. It's been a long time since I let out a genuine laugh.

'What's funny?' Lionel asks, entering the room carrying a wooden tray with three mugs.

'Oh. Nothing. Just something Matilda said,' Tania says.

'What was that?'

'Nothing. It doesn't matter.' I clear my throat. 'Lionel, Alison Pemberton has asked me to help her find out what happened to her sisters. Do you mind if I ask you a few questions?'

'I'm not sure how much help I'll be able to be,' he says, taking his coffee from the tray and sitting in his armchair. 'Help yourself to milk and sugar. It was a long time ago and, although it was a massive event and not exactly something I'm going to forget, my mind isn't what it used to be.'

'Come off it, Lionel, you're as sharp as ever,' Tania says.

'It's been a while since we've met, Tania. Things change.'

Tania's smile falters. 'Are you all right?'

'What did you want to ask me?' Lionel turns to me, ignoring Tania's question.

I look from Lionel to Tania and back again. I can see there is unfinished business between the two of them. Tania is clearly still holding a flame for Lionel. Does he feel the same? Are they both living with a lifetime of regrets?

'Jack Pemberton. The sightings of him over the years. What do you think?'

'The odd sighting you can put down to someone having a likeness of Jack, but I know Alison has a file full of them. You can't argue with them, can you?'

'If he is still alive, why do you think he faked his own death?'

'There's only one explanation, isn't there? He killed his daughters.'

Everyone seems to be quick to condemn Jack as a guilty man. Nobody has suggested he might have faked his death simply because of his depression, because he couldn't cope with losing two of his children. Why are people so easily prepared to think the worst of others?

'Why would he do that?'

'Your guess is as good as mine.'

'I'm guessing you've heard about Travis Montgomery's car being found at the bottom of the lake.' He nods. 'It must have,

I assume, gone missing around the time the girls were taken yet was never reported missing.'

'Yes. No. You're right. No, it wasn't reported missing.'

'When the girls did go missing and suddenly there's Travis without a car, what did you think?'

Lionel blows out his cheeks. 'I don't recall, I'm sorry. I was very preoccupied with finding the girls. It was the biggest case I've ever had to deal with. I didn't give the car much thought.'

'But you knew it was missing?'

'No.'

'Did you know Travis has been listed as a missing person since December 1992?'

'Yes.'

Lionel isn't forthcoming with his answers, and I have the sneaky suspicion he's going to start playing the elderly card if I ask him something he doesn't like the sound of.

I study him. He's sitting, straight-backed in his armchair, feet planted firmly on the floor, hands wrapped around his coffee mug. His hands are holding it just a little too tightly for my liking. His knuckles are almost white.

I lean forward. 'Not long after Jack disappeared in the storm, you were forced to leave the police. It was believed you'd embezzled charity money. But you didn't, did you?'

Lionel steals a glance to Tania before turning back to me.

'No. I didn't.'

'But you couldn't prove it?'

'No.'

'Do you know who did put the money in your bank account?'

'No.'

Again, his answer came too quickly. He's lying.

'Who do you suspect it was?'

He takes a sharp breath and shakes his head. 'I really have no idea.'

Another lie.

Lionel looks, once again, to Tania.

From my point of view, I can only see the back of Tania's head as she's sitting on the edge of the sofa, mug in hand, looking to Lionel. Is she communicating with him, silently, via facial expressions, mouthing words to him, hoping I can't see what's going on?

'Did you know about the car at the bottom of the lake?' I ask.

'No. Of course, not,' he answers. This time, I believe him.

'Tania, did you?'

'What?' She turns to me sharply. 'No. Why would I?'

I take a deep breath. Inside, I'm screaming. I know I'm being lied to, but I don't know what they're lying about. I reach forward for my coffee cup and take a sip to delay asking my next question. I need my anger to simmer down. It's not easy though. My emotions are so close to the surface, it won't take much for them to be revealed. I feel sorry for whoever is in the vicinity when it happens.

The coffee tastes bitter in my mouth. I have no idea what brand of coffee Lionel uses, but it has nothing to do with that. It's the bile in my throat ruining my pleasure of taste.

'Lynne Pemberton came to see me the other day,' I begin. 'She told me that Jack admitted to Iain that he had abused Celia and Jennifer and murdered them. He'd had some kind of a black-out and couldn't remember what he'd done with the bodies.'

I watch Lionel as I say this. His facial expression doesn't change once. He already knows. I suspect Tania has told him. They may not have met in recent years, but I'm guessing they keep in touch over the phone.

'You don't look shocked,' I add.

'Are you shocked by anything you see, after all your time on the force?' he asks.

My mind goes back to when I walked into my mother's house and saw the bodies of my teenage nephews and my mum, dead.

'Of course.' My voice is quivering with emotion. 'I have to be shocked by what I see. That's how I know I'm still alive.' I lean forward and place my cup back on the tray. I stand up. 'I think I'm being lied to.'

'Who by?' Tania asks.

'You. Lionel. I don't know. Neither of you is reacting to the news that Jack sexually abused and murdered his daughters how you should be doing. Neither of you seems to care that Travis Montgomery is missing for whatever reason. And I think you did know about his car being missing, Lionel. You're both happy for all of these questions to go unanswered, and I don't know why.'

'Matilda…' Tania begins.

I don't allow her to interrupt. 'I think you know exactly who put that money in your bank account, Lionel. I think it was put there for you to be blackmailed for some reason. I think you know what's going on but you're too scared to say anything.' I turn to Tania. 'I'll find my own way back to the restaurant.'

Tania and Lionel remain in silence until the front door slams closed behind Matilda. From where Lionel is sitting on the armchair, he can see out onto the length of End Lane and watches as Matilda marches down the incline.

'I told you she was good,' Tania eventually says.

'You did. I didn't realise how good.'

'What are you going to do?'

'What I've been doing for the past thirty years. I'll endure.'

'You can tell me who put the money in your account. I won't judge you for keeping it secret.'

He bites his bottom lip and shakes his head.

'You're protecting Gill and Lauren; I can understand that. But with Matilda digging, you're not going to be able to keep this a secret for much longer, Lionel. She won't give up.'

'Could you leave, please, Tania?'

'What? Why?'

'I need to make a phone call.'

'Who to?'

'It doesn't matter.'

'Lionel, it does. You've gone pale. What's happening?'

'Look, Tania, please, just leave,' he says, raising his voice.

'What the hell have you got yourself mixed up in, Lionel? What exactly do you know about the Pemberton twins?'

'Tania, I've asked you nicely to leave. Don't make me get angry.'

Tania sits back and looks at her former lover. She suddenly realises she doesn't know who Lionel Bell is anymore.

I'm looking forward to joining Aaron and his team for a meal in Nature's Diner. It'll be the first time since I arrived in the Lake District where I'm eating a meal that isn't resting on my lap in the living room. After the meeting with Lionel and Tania, I walk back to the restaurant, the voices in my head trying to make sense of what I've witnessed. I change and go for a run. I'm still clueless about much of what is happening around me and I still have no idea who I can trust, but it calms me down. My emotions are settled, and as I stand under the intense heat from the shower, I can feel my body relax.

I know I shouldn't be getting involved in an investigation right now. My head is full of grief, horror and sorrow. What I don't need is other people's deceptions and manipulations playing tricks on me. I should leave. I should pack a bag and drive Adele's Porsche somewhere new. But when I close my eyes, I can see Alison Pemberton sitting opposite me in the restaurant, begging, pleading for help. That's my downfall. I need to help people. And if I can't help myself, I may as well help someone else.

After my shower, I wrap a towel around me and lie down on my bed. I close my eyes.

The next thing I know, there's a tap on the door. I sit up and notice the sun setting over the horizon.

'Yes?'

The door opens and Sally pops her head through the gap. 'Your guests are downstairs,' she smiles.

'What?'

'Aaron and his team.'

'Shit. Already?'

'It's eight o'clock.'

'What? Oh, bloody hell. I must have nodded off.' I jump off the bed and throw open the wardrobe. There's nothing in there. 'Shit. I was going to ask if I could borrow something to wear.'

'Come with me,' Sally says, holding out her hand.

It's been a long time since I've worn a dress. On the odd occasion I go out for a meal, whether it's with Adele or Scott and Donal, or even on a date with Odell, I dress casually in black trousers or fitted jeans. Sally grabs the perfect dress for me straight away. How she finds it among the millions of other dresses, I have no idea, but when she presents it to me, I know it's the one. I quickly change, ruffle my hair up in a messy style and apply a tiny bit of makeup to hide the puffiness of my eyes. As I look at myself in the mirror wearing a deep-red floor-length dress with thin straps and a low neck, I don't recognise myself. I hadn't realised how much my appearance has changed in the month since I arrived here. My figure is trimmer, firmer, my hair is longer, my skin is tanned. I smile at my reflection. This change in my appearance is most welcome.

'Bloody hell,' Aaron says, taken aback when I greet him. He

kisses me on both cheeks. 'You look...' he looks me up and down, 'stunning.'

'She does, doesn't she?' Sally says, standing behind me, beaming like a proud parent.

'I literally cannot remember the last time I dressed up for a meal,' I say, sitting down at the table. I'm surrounded by the six members of SRUK, all of whom are wearing thick utility trousers and polo shirts bearing the company's logo. 'I feel massively overdressed, but I don't give a toss,' I smile.

Conversation throughout the three courses focuses on the wide range of jobs SRUK are called out to. Aaron tells the story of searching Scafell Pike during a blizzard for two sisters who had gone out walking. It doesn't have a happy ending. He then tells of the massive team effort to locate an eight-year-old boy who had been playing on disused ground in North Yorkshire and had fallen down a poorly maintained closed mineshaft. Another story with an unhappy ending.

'I'm beginning to regret joining you all for dinner,' I say as I tuck into my raspberry mousse cake. 'Do any of your stories have endings that don't make me want to drown myself in the bath?'

'Scarlett, tell Matilda the story about your training on the Faultline in San Francisco.'

'Which one?' Scarlett asks. 'The one where I fell down the ravine and broke my ankle or the one where I slept with the instructor?'

'Ooh, can I have the one where you slept with the instructor? It sounds more fun.'

'It was great fun on the first night in my hotel room,' Scarlett says. She's sitting directly opposite me. She's small, possibly only just five feet tall. She has beautiful elfin features and shoulder-length chocolate-brown hair. 'The second night, he invited me back to his place. I couldn't get out of there fast enough.'

'Oh no. Why?'

'He had a mirror on his ceiling.'

'You're joking!'

'I wish I were. I didn't notice it at first. It was only when he asked if I'd go on top so he could watch that I looked up to see what he meant.'

'Bloody hell. Why would you want to watch yourself have sex? I don't even shower with the lights on.'

The whole table erupts into laughter.

Outside the restaurant, it's dark. Muted lighting on the car park. Philip hadn't wanted it to be bright and gaudy. He wanted his diners to enjoy the view, especially during the summer months when the sun set over the lake and lit the sky up a brilliant red. High-voltage light bulbs would ruin the atmosphere. In a car in the corner, in the shade of an oak tree, Inspector Gill Forsyth watches the restaurant. She sees Matilda, looking unsettlingly different in a figure-hugging dress, sitting with the six members of SRUK. They're relaxed, laughing, joking, having fun, swapping stories, enjoying themselves. She bites her bottom lip hard, chewing on the loose skin, seething with rage. Her father told her about Matilda and Tania's visit earlier. She expected Tania to be sticking her nose in where it wasn't wanted. She's a journalist after all, they were all reptiles, but she'd thought better of Matilda, especially after everything she's recently gone through. The grieving-woman act is clearly a ruse to worm her way in, and Gill had fallen for it. Rookie mistake. Watching her now, happy, drinking wine like she didn't have a care in the world, Gill decides it's time Matilda fucked off back to Sheffield. She's outstayed her welcome. She wants her gone.

After the dessert and coffees, me and Aaron excuse ourselves and go to a smaller table in the corner of the room where we can have a private chat.

'I called Scott last night,' he says, almost sheepishly.

'Did you tell him where I am?'

'He already knows.'

'Sian?'

He nods. 'He's worried about you. They all are.'

'I'm fine. Look at me in a designer dress and makeup.' I force a smile.

'He told me you've been seeing someone. Odell?'

'Yes.'

'According to Scott, he's waiting for you.'

I don't know how to react to that and feel a well of emotion rise up inside me. 'He might be in for a long wait.'

'You're not going back to Sheffield?'

'I don't know what I'm doing yet. Part of me wants to go back, find out who killed my family and tear them limb from limb. Another part wants never to set foot in Sheffield ever again.'

'I think we both know that you can't ever fully run away from your problems. They're always in here,' he says, tapping his head.

'Tell me about it. I keep going over everything. What did I miss? Could I have saved them, if I'd done something differently?' I take another sip of my coffee and look at Aaron over the top of the cup. 'What would you do, if you were me?'

'You're asking me for advice?' he asks, incredulously.

'I am.'

'Wow, you really are desperate.'

'You made a mistake. We all make them. But you were an excellent detective. I wouldn't have made you my sergeant, if I didn't think so. You're not in the force now. You're removed from it all. You don't have an ulterior motive for me to return to Sheffield. I'd like your impartial advice.'

'Okay.' He clears his throat. 'Based on what I know about you. Based on your drive and determination and never giving up on anything. If I were you, I'd take some time out here, like you are doing, then I'd go back to Sheffield and turn the city upside down looking for the fucker who killed my family. Then I'd hand in my notice and leave. The police force has taken up a great deal of your life. You've got the freedom and the funds to enjoy yourself. So, for once, be selfish and live.'

I feel a tear run down my face. I wipe it away. Aaron jumps up and runs around to me. He wraps his strong arms around my shoulders and pulls me close.

'He killed my mum, Aaron. He killed my nephews,' I cry.

'I know. I know. There's no getting over that. It will forever haunt you. But you can adapt, and you can only do that by catching the bastard who did it.'

'I know.'

'There's no rush, though. Take all the time you need.'

I nod. I sniff hard and wipe my eyes.

'I know I'm not on the force anymore but I'm only a phone call away. I will help out any way I can. And I know some excellent places to bury a body – should you need to,' he says, a twinkle in his eye.

I laugh.

'I shouldn't be here,' Claire Daniels says when Alison opens the door to her.

Claire had gone around to Alison's house. She hadn't even bothered knocking when she saw it in darkness. Instead, she drove to the stables and knocked on Iain and Lynne's door.

'So why are you here?' Alison asks.

'Because I want to burst into tears and you're my best friend.'

Alison pulls her into a hug. 'What's happened?'

Claire doesn't answer. She breathes in Alison's scent, holds tight onto her, and allows the tears to flow.

In the kitchen, Alison, Lynne and Iain, each with a glass of wine, and Claire with an orange juice, sit around the table while Claire tells them about the examination of the car in the warehouse.

'Inspector Forsyth told me not to say anything. She said it was need-to-know information, but I've known you all since I was a baby. You're all like family to me. I can't *not* tell you.'

Alison takes her hand in hers and squeezes hard.

'The thing is,' Claire continues. 'I don't think any of us have worked on a murder investigation before. I mean, there was that tourist a few years ago, but as he was from Southampton, the police down there took over the lion's share of the case. This is local. This involves people we know.'

'Claire,' Lynne begins, looking up at her through tear-filled eyes. 'What did they look like?'

Claire is struggling to maintain her emotions. 'They were just… it was just bones, Lynne.'

'Could you see what they were wearing?'

She shakes her head. 'Everything had disintegrated.'

'Will they be able to tell who they are?'

'They'll take DNA from the bones, Mum,' Alison says.

Claire sits back in her seat. Her hands go to her stomach.

'Claire, what's Inspector Forsyth saying about the investigation as a whole?' Iain asks. 'Do they think Travis was responsible?'

Lynne grabs for Iain's hand beneath the table.

'I don't know. We can't pull him in for questioning, can we? And it's going to be difficult asking people to try and remember if they saw him on the day of the disappearance. It was thirty years ago. Who's going to remember?'

'I don't think any of us will forget what we were doing on that day, at that exact time,' Alison says. There's a harshness to her voice. 'I'm sure you'll remember it second by second, won't you Mum?'

Lynne looks at her daughter. She swallows hard and nods. 'Of course. It's as clear as if it was yesterday.' She quickly looks away. 'I was in the kitchen making a lemon cake. You girls always hated me making lemon cake. You said it tasted funny. Your dad preferred lemon to chocolate.'

There's a whisper of a smile on her face. Alison is glaring at her, wondering where her mind is. She knows she's about to lie.

Lynne continues. 'I remember looking at the clock. It was just after one o'clock. I went out to call you all in for your lunch. There was only you there. You were playing with that sausage dog on a string. Do you remember that?' she asks, looking at her.

'Stanley.'

A smile of remembrance spreads across her face. 'Stanley. Yes. Stanley the sausage dog.'

Alison wipes a tear away. 'Were you on your own all morning, Mum?'

'Of course, I was. What makes you ask that?'

Alison doesn't reply but continues to stare at her mother.

Iain clears his throat loudly. 'It was Travis who told me.' Everyone turns to look at him. 'I was at the stables. We were having problems with the plumbing, and I had the sink off in the bathroom. Travis was shouting my name, really screaming it. I remember thinking then something was wrong. He came bursting in; said the girls had gone missing and would I help him organise a search party.'

'Travis asked you to organise a search party?' Alison asks. 'Why?'

'Why?' Iain looks at her with a frown. 'Because the girls were missing.'

'How did he know? Who told him?'

'I phoned the farmhouse,' Lynne says. 'Travis answered the phone.'

'Did he?'

'Yes. Alison, what is it? You've a very strange look on your face. Is something wrong?'

Alison takes another sip of wine. She shakes her head. 'I

don't understand why Travis immediately knew Celia and Jennifer were *missing*, though. We used to come up to the farmhouse all the time. Why didn't he ask if we were there, with you, Iain?'

Iain's eyes widen and dart from left to right as if he's trying to remember something he's forgotten.

'I... I... don't recall...' he says, slowly.

'Travis jumped to the conclusion they were missing. It makes no sense,' Alison says.

'It does, though, now, doesn't it?' Claire says. 'They were in Travis's car. Surely it's clear that he took them for... whatever reason.'

They all fall into silence. The atmosphere is oppressive. The only sound comes from a clock on the wall.

'I can't get my head around this,' Alison says. 'To think that Travis was responsible. He was always so good to us. He let us sit in the front seat of his car and pretend we were driving, do you remember?' Alison asks Claire.

'I do. I remember him showing me the gears. I know I was only about five, but I remembered it all. Clutch down, into first, find your biting point...' she says with a smile.

'It's difficult to imagine that same man being responsible for kidnapping Celia and Jennifer,' Alison says. 'There's no reasoning behind it.'

'Who knows why people do what they do?' Lynne says. She's looking away, down at the floor. Her voice is low. She's clearly uncomfortable, struggling with something. She's clutching Iain's hand firmly beneath the table. 'Excuse me.' She jumps up and runs out of the room, her hand over her mouth.

Iain, Alison and Claire sit in silence.

'Maybe I shouldn't have come over here this evening?' Claire asks.

'You're always welcome here, Claire, you know that,' Iain says. 'Only, it's bringing it all back, taking its toll on Lynne.'

'The truth is always difficult for some people to hear,' Alison says.

The silence intensifies.

I'm wired after all that coffee and alcohol. I take a warm shower to freshen up and go straight to bed with a gin and tonic from the bar. Sally has long since turned in and I can hear Philip moving around in the restaurant downstairs, cashing up and locking up. I pull the thin sheet over me and finish my drink. It's a warm and muggy night. I'm tempted to leave a window open a crack, but paranoia forces me to leave it shut. I turn over, snuggle down and close my eyes.

'Matilda. Matilda.'

I open my eyes. The room is pitch dark. Philip is standing over me. All I can see in the darkness is the whiteness of his eyes. They're wide and staring. Something is wrong.

'What is it? What's happened?' I can hear the panic in my voice.

He silences me with a hush. 'There's someone in the restaurant.'

'What?' I ask in a loud whisper, sitting up.

'I'd just finished in the bathroom. I was about to go to bed when I heard someone downstairs.'

'You're sure?'

'Positive.'

'Jesus.'

'I didn't want to wake Sally.'

'No.'

I throw the sheet back and swing my legs out of bed. I slip my slippers on and follow Philip out onto the landing. The single window on the far side doesn't have a blind or curtains. The full moon shines through. I see, for the first time, Philip is holding a shotgun.

'What the fuck is that?' My voice is still a whisper, but with a panicked force behind it.

'It's a gun.'

'I can see that. Since when did you have a gun?'

'Since my son was kidnapped. Since he was returned to me, and his kidnappers are still out there running free. Since we moved to the middle of nowhere and live in the woods. Do you really want to get into this now?'

'Are you licensed to have that?'

'Of course I bloody am. What do you take me for?'

'I can't believe you have a gun, and you didn't tell me.'

'Matilda, there is someone in my restaurant. Someone has broken in. Can we talk about this some other time?'

'Oh. Sure. Sorry,' I can't take my eyes from the gun. I hate guns, always have done.

The air around us is heavy with silence. Neither of us can hear a thing.

'Are you sure you heard something?' I ask.

'Yes. I don't know how they got in. Maybe they hid while I was locking up. But I heard someone walking around.'

'Okay. I believe you. Have you called the police?'

'You *are* the police.'

'Not at the moment, I'm not. Also, I'm in my nightie, and I've been drinking.'

A noise comes from downstairs. It sounds like someone has let go of a closing door and it has banged shut.

'You heard that?' Philip asks.

'Yes. I heard that.'

'At least we know it's not in my head.'

We edge down the stairs. Philip first, me pressed up close behind. We creep down in silence until we reach the bottom. We're outside the back entrance to the kitchen. Philip stretches to look through the round window in the door.

'What can you see?' I ask.

'Nothing.'

I shiver. 'I suddenly feel very vulnerable in this nightie.'

'Would you like me to wait while you run back to your room and change into army fatigues?'

'There's no need for sarcasm.'

'Sorry. I'm nervous. Carl does not need this right now.'

'No. I know.' I place a hand on his arm and can feel him shaking.

There's another sound. It comes from the main part of the restaurant. A chair is being moved.

'Give me the gun.'

'What? No. You're not licensed.'

'I'm not going to fire it.'

'What are you going to do with it?'

'I'll hit him with it.'

'I'm not letting you go in there on your own.'

'And I'm not letting you go in there with a loaded gun. Hand it over. Now. Come on.'

Reluctantly, he does. I break the gun and remove the cartridges, handing them back to Philip. 'Now, I'm tired and

I'm starting to get cold. I have no intention of spending the night listening for someone to nick a few bottles of scotch.'

I push open the kitchen door and walk, confidently, inside. Philip follows. There's nobody in here, and all the lights are off. I go to the opposite door which leads into the dining area and push it open. Light from the full moon filters through the half-closed vertical blinds.

I swing the barrel of the gun in front of me. I can't see anyone. From somewhere deep down, I latch onto a hint of bravado.

'Okay, whoever you are, we know you're here. We've called the police and I'm holding a loaded shotgun. You either get arrested or you get a bullet in your shoulder. Your choice.' I hardly recognise my own voice. I sound tough. If only I felt it.

A door to the corridor is pushed open. It slams against the wall and whoever is behind it, tall, dressed in dark clothing, comes charging out into the restaurant. He barrels into me, sending me flying to the floor. The gun is torn from my hands. I cry out in pain as my head hits the ground. Philip calls out. The man turns on his heel, points the gun to Philip and squeezes the trigger. Nothing happens. He swings the barrel towards him and hits him on the side of the head with it. The sound of metal on bone echoes around the empty restaurant. Philip falls to the floor. He's unconscious before he hits the ground. The intruder then drops the gun and legs it towards the exit.

I prop myself up on my elbow. My head is foggy, my vision blurred. I try to see whoever has broken in, try to find something that I can remember in the cold light of day.

'Jack!' I call out.

The figure pauses momentarily, before fleeing into the night.

Sheffield, South Yorkshire

Dr Adele Kean had been staying in an outpost close to Kangari Hills Forest Reserve. The plane that landed with fresh supplies had been unable to take her to Freetown International Airport, so she had paid for a local to drive her there in a Jeep with no suspension and no air conditioning. It took a little over five hours before she arrived, hot, sweating, shattered and aching. However, she had made a new friend in her driver, David Bangura, who had given her his life story and told her all about his wife, Aminata, who he clearly loved. She was pregnant with their first child and the smile he couldn't remove from his face showed how much he was looking forward to being a father. As Adele waved him goodbye, she hoped she would see David again at some point. He was a good man.

Adele had a five-hour wait at the airport before boarding a plane to take her to London Heathrow. She slept for the majority of the fourteen-hour flight, waking only to have something to eat, then again an hour before landing when she went into the bathroom to freshen up and change into clean clothing. She felt refreshed as she stepped onto British soil for what seemed like the first time in years, but was, in fact, only five months. She had seen a great deal during her time in Sierra Leone. She'd seen people living a life with the very basics of provisions, sometimes even less than that. The country had intermittent electricity supply, limited resources when it came to health care and education, but what she had seen among the people she came into contact with on a daily basis was gratitude and humility. She rarely saw anyone without a smile on their face (unless they were in great pain), and they made Adele feel very welcome when she went into their homes. They had little in the way of luxuries. They were living the simplest of lives, but together, in their family units, they were happy. Landing back in England during a time of massive consumerism, Adele almost felt sickened, as she witnessed the comparisons of poverty and riches. Sierra Leone was a fourteen-hour flight away. Compared to London, it may as well have been another planet.

From Heathrow, Adele made her way to St Pancras where she boarded a train to Sheffield. In less than two and a half hours, she would be back in the city she'd hoped never to return to. It had been her home for the last two decades, but it had also robbed her of her son, a close colleague and friend, and seen her come face to face with the evils people inflicted upon each other.

The train took Adele up the spine of the country. She sat back and stretched her legs. She looked out at the countryside and watched it blur past her. As she passed through towns and cities, she saw what was classed as depravation in England. In Sierra Leone, it would have been called luxury. She tried not to compare the two. She knew people in England were struggling with the cost-of-living crisis, but when she had seen people with literally nothing but the clothes they were wearing, it was hard not to want to tell people who at least had a roof over their heads, electricity, running water, smooth roads, a public transport service and free education and health care, to count themselves lucky.

She closed her eyes and tried to block out the sights of England. She thought of David Bangura and his wife Aminata and what their experience of bringing a child into the world would be like compared to an English couple with access to the NHS. She hoped Aminata would go full-term without any issues. She prayed the labour would go as smoothly as possible with no complications.

Adele steps off the train, dragging her wheeled suitcase behind her, and stands in the familiar surroundings of the train station. It's the early hours of Wednesday morning. She's knackered and is in desperate need of a shower, a cup of tea, and something covered in chocolate to eat. With heavy legs, she goes to the taxi rank and asks the driver to take her to Ringinglow. He tries to make small talk, asking Adele if she's been on holiday and is happy to be home. She gives him monosyllabic answers and soon the conversation runs dry. She's not being intentionally rude. She simply has no answers to give him.

Her home isn't easy to find, and Adele has to give him directions once they hit Ringinglow Road. They pull up outside the former farmhouse, and she can't take her eyes off it. Despite the darkness of the morning, she can see the house is unlived in and neglected. Weeds are growing through the broken tarmac and the windows are in urgent need of a good wash. She pays the driver, gives him a good tip, and drags her suitcase up to the front door. She hadn't taken her keys with her, but had sent a text to Scott who had put a spare set in a key safe attached to the side of the house. She taps in the four-digit code and retrieves the keys. They feel heavy in her hand.

Adele unlocks the front door and turns off the alarm with the fob on the keyring. She closes the door behind her and walks into the living room, flicking on the lights, wincing at the brightness.

'Welcome home,' she says to herself.

The room is cold. The fire hasn't been lit for some time and the air is stale. She slumps onto the chesterfield sofa. On the coffee table is Matilda's iPhone. She picks it up and tries to turn it on, but the battery is flat. Matilda must have been seriously in a state to leave her mobile behind. She thinks about Penny, Matilda's mother. She was a good woman, slightly nosy and a tad neurotic when it came to Matilda's job, but she was always up for a laugh and a long conversation, especially if alcohol was involved. Then there were her nephews, Nathan and Joseph, two teenagers making their way in the world. It was cruel the way some people felt they could kill simply for their own sick pleasures. How would they feel if someone wiped out their family?

Adele searches her pockets for her own mobile and scrolls through the contacts. She lands on Harriet's number. Should she call or send a text? What would she say? She decides against doing anything and continues scrolling until she lands on Sally Meagan's number. She's about to call, then thinks better of it. Sally might tell Matilda that Adele has phoned and is on her way. Matilda has left her mobile behind. She obviously doesn't want to be contacted. Would she run again?

Adele looks around her at the expansive space of the living room. She and Matilda have had many a fun night in here, drinking until the small hours, watching Marvel films and debating whether Thor was hotter with short hair or long hair.

Would those times ever return? She thinks about that question for a moment, and seriously doubts they ever will.

She pulls herself up from the sofa and staggers to the stairs. A long, hot shower, a change of clothes, a cup of tea and something to eat, then she'll book a hire car and plot a course for the Lake District.

I grab a tablecloth from the nearest table and stumble over to Philip. While I'm covering him to keep him warm and checking his airways to make sure there are no obstructions, Sally bursts into the restaurant, soon followed by Carl and the two dogs who immediately make a fuss. I shout to Sally to call for an ambulance, then I put Philip into the recovery position. I can feel a pair of eyes burning into me. I look up and there's Carl standing in the doorway. His face is ashen, his eyes wide and staring.

'It's happening again,' he says.

'It's not, Carl. It's not. I promise you,' I say as I cradle his father.

'You can't promise that.' A tear runs down his face, lit up by the moonlight.

'The ambulance is on its way,' Sally says, returning to the restaurant. 'I gave Inspector Forsyth a ring, too. She's coming straight over. Is he going to be all right?' Sally asks with a tearful voice, looking down at her husband.

'Sally, it might be best if Carl went upstairs.'

'I'm not going anywhere,' he says, defiantly.

I'm treated at the scene. I tell the paramedics I hadn't lost consciousness, and they believe me. Truth be told, I've no idea if I did lose consciousness. Philip is placed onto a stretcher complete with neck brace to keep him secure. He's then taken, by Air Ambulance, to Penrith Hospital. Sally and Carl go upstairs to change and follow in the car.

Gill Forsyth arrives at the same time as the ambulance. Her appearance looks softer out of uniform. Her hair is pulled back into an unruly ponytail, and she's quickly dressed in jeans and a jumper and battered North Face walking boots. With two uniformed officers dusting the doors and bar for prints as well as checking the floor for fibres and hairs, I take Gill upstairs and make us both a mug of tea. As much as I want alcohol, I decide against it following a bang on the head. See, I'm not totally reckless.

'What happened here tonight?' Gill asks once we're both seated in the living room.

I tell her as much as I can remember. Philip had been going to bed, the last one, as usual, when he heard a noise downstairs. Rather than wake Sally, he sought my help instead. He wanted to protect his wife and son as much as possible. Understandable.

'He has a gun. Do you know he has a gun?' I ask.

'Yes. It's registered and perfectly legal.'

'I hate guns,' I say, gripping the mug with both hands.

'I'm not a fan either.'

'I took it from him. I broke it and took the cartridges out. Whoever broke in, they grabbed it from me and aimed it at Philip. They pulled the trigger. They didn't even think twice about it. They just pointed it at him. They would have...'

'You saved his life,' Gill says.

'But did I put it in danger in the first place?'

'What do you mean?'

'These attempted break-ins only started when I arrived. Sally and Philip have put it down to chancers wanting to steal a few bottles of whisky. Tonight has shown how far whoever is doing this is prepared to go. They didn't know the gun wasn't loaded. They would have shot and killed Philip.'

'You think this serial killer who has been emailing you has followed you from Sheffield?'

'I… It looks like it.'

But then again, I can't help but think about the man pausing as I called out 'Jack'. Is Jack Pemberton still alive? Has he broken into the restaurant? If so, why? Does he want food and drink, or is there more to it than mere survival?

'Then why didn't he turn the gun on you?' Gill asks. 'You said it was you holding the gun, that the intruder snatched it from you and pushed you to the ground. Why didn't he try to shoot you then? He had the perfect opportunity.'

I think about that. I go through the incident in my head. Gill's right. Philip didn't shout out or anything. The intruder wasn't aware Philip was even there until he turned around and saw him blocking his escape. He could easily have shot me. So, why didn't he?

Gill takes a sip of her tea. 'Matilda, is it possible this could be about the Meagan family? Those who kidnapped Carl in 2015, could they be back to silence him?'

'I don't know. Carl wasn't able to give us a definite description of them when they took him. Years had passed from when he was kidnapped to when he returned. He'd been through a lot. It's understandable he couldn't describe them. The couple in Sweden bought Carl from a man and a woman. The woman has since been arrested. She turned out to be part of a huge illegal adoption scheme based in Germany. She refused to say anything and accepted the life sentence. She hasn't helped the police at all.'

'Let's say it *is* the kidnappers, coming back to silence Carl, why would they do that?' Gill asks. 'They've no way of knowing if Carl would even remember them.'

'Maybe their paths have crossed, somehow. One of the kidnappers could have seen Carl here in the Lake District, or elsewhere, and followed him home. When Carl first disappeared, it was a huge news story.'

'I remember.'

'If the kidnappers were ever found, they'd be arrested for not only kidnapping, but for murder, too. They killed Annabel, Carl's grandmother. They'd do anything they could to avoid being caught.'

'Including killing him?'

'Yes.'

'Jesus. It could be anyone, couldn't it?'

'All we know is that two men kidnapped Carl. We don't know anything about age, height, skin colour, accent, nothing. He could live in High Chapel, or the surrounding area, or maybe he was passing through and saw Carl from a distance. Or maybe he saw an advertisement for Nature's Diner and put two and two together.' I close my eyes as a wave of pain shoots through my head.

'Are you all right?'

'Yes. I think the pain relief might be starting to wear off.'

'Do you want me to get you anything?'

'No. I've got some Ibuprofen in my room.'

'You shouldn't be here on your own, not after a head injury. Would you like me to stay?'

'I'll be fine.'

'Why do I get the feeling that's your answer to every question?'

I look over to her and snort a laugh. 'Because it is.'

'No woman is an island, Matilda.'

There's a knock on the door. Gill looks up. 'Yes, Stokes, what is it?'

'This envelope was on the mat. It's addressed to Matilda Darke.'

I take the plain white envelope from him. All it has on the front is my name. Nothing else. 'It's been hand-delivered.' I tear it open and pull out a single sheet of A4 paper. It's old, yellowed with age. I cast my eyes left to right, from top to bottom, my mouth wide as I take in the contents.

'What is it?' Gill asks.

'I don't believe this.'

'What?'

'This is Travis Montgomery's statement from 1992 when he reported his car missing.'

'What?' Gill asks, incredulously. 'But it wasn't reported missing.'

'It clearly was. This is a typed statement taken by Inspector Lionel Bell and signed by Travis Montgomery in which he claims the car was stolen from outside the farmhouse.'

'What's the date?'

'August the eighth. Three days before Celia and Jennifer went missing.'

'Why send it to you?'

I don't say anything. I look at Gill. 'Why didn't you tell me Inspector Bell is your father?'

'Ah.'

'Are you embarrassed? Ashamed?'

'Of course, not.'

'Then why lie?'

'I... I didn't want him drawn into this. Not again.'

'Into what?'

'This!' she exclaims. 'This nightmare of the Pembertons. It almost killed my dad. He couldn't solve it, and he had an entire village looking at him for answers.'

'And the money placed into his bank account?'

'He did not steal that money,' she says, slowly.

'Are you talking as a daughter or a police inspector?'

'I know my dad. He's not a thief.'

'But someone made him into one, and I think I know why.' I hold up the statement. 'Someone clearly told your father to remove this statement from the records. They used the stolen money as a way to blackmail him into doing it. It didn't work as the news about the money got out anyway, but by then it was too late for your father to do anything. If he spoke up about the statement, he would have looked guilty for removing it in the first place.'

Gill's face bears an expression of sadness. She looks down. 'My dad did not take that money,' she says, though her words lack conviction now.

'There are only three people who could have sent this statement to me. One: your father. He's tired of having this hanging over his head and wants me to break the silence and expose the blackmailer who is very likely the killer of Celia and Jennifer. Two: Tania Pritchard. She's held a torch for your father since before your mother died. He could have given the statement to her, and she could have sent it anonymously to me so that I'll do the digging and the dirty work and have the population of High Chapel hate me when I expose a beloved member of this community as a killer. But I don't think it was either of them.'

'No?'

'No. I think it was you.'

Gill looks at me. 'Me? What makes you think it was me?'

'Firstly, because when I told you what was in this envelope, you didn't ask to look at it. That tells me you already know what it says. Secondly, you know I went to see your father today and you're trying to protect him from any awkward questions I might have. And three, there is no way this could have been left on the mat because the restaurant doesn't have a letterbox.'

'Doesn't it?'

'No.'

'Oh. I thought...' She seems to collapse in on herself. 'I'd make a terrible detective, wouldn't I?'

'Not terrible, but not great.' I sigh. 'I have a splitting headache, and I need a drink. Care to join me?'

'I don't usually drink scotch,' Gill says as she looks at the golden liquid in the glass. She takes a sniff and recoils.

'Neither do I.' I take a sip and wince. I wait as the alcohol burns my throat. It's a new sensation, and I like it. I take a longer drink. 'I think I could get used to this.'

Gill pulls a face after taking a mouthful. 'I don't think I could.'

'How long have you had the statement?' I ask.

Gill coughs. 'Too long. Years. Decades.'

'I'm right, aren't I? Travis reported his car stolen. The girls went missing. Your father was blackmailed to remove it from the file.'

Gill starts to cry. She stands up, goes over to the hallway door and closes it so we can't be overheard. She returns to the sofa.

'My dad *did* steal that money,' she says, her voice breaking. 'Mum had not long since died. She had no insurance. You don't think you're going to need it, when you're thirty.'

'How did she die?'

'She had a brain aneurysm. She went to bed one night, everything safe and normal, and didn't wake up the next morning.'

'I'm sorry.'

'With no second wage coming in, a funeral to pay for, mortgage, bills, food, and me, Dad couldn't cope. Gideon was dead. That money was just sitting there.'

'Who blackmailed your dad?'

'I don't know. He's never told me. I've asked him until I'm blue in the face and he's point-blank refused to name them.'

'Do you have an inkling?'

'No. I don't. I really don't. I know it's horrible for me to say, but I've tried to forget. I've hoped and prayed that the case would remain unsolved, at least while my dad is still alive. I know he won't be able to cope with it all coming out. Now the car has been found and the girls are in the back, I knew it wouldn't be possible to keep it a secret. I thought – and I'm so sorry for this – but I thought if you were the one to expose it, people might turn on you rather than me and my dad.'

'Thank you for that,' I say, flippantly. 'Well, I've got a serial killer in Sheffield after me; I suppose having an entire village wanting to lynch me on this side of the Pennines won't make any difference.'

'I'm sorry,' she says again. She wipes her eyes with the backs of her hands. 'What are you going to do?'

I remain silent while I think. 'Whatever your dad is wanting to protect you from is clearly still a threat thirty years after the event. That can only mean one thing – whoever took Celia and Jennifer is still out there. It wasn't Travis Montgomery. He was merely a scapegoat. The kidnapper is alive and well, keeping an eye on all of this and ready to strike when the truth is close to being revealed.'

'Jack Pemberton?' Gill asks.

'Who else?'

'So, he killed his daughters then faked his death to avoid capture. But why did Travis go missing?'

'Maybe Jack killed him. Maybe Jack really has been watching his family from a distance, keeping an eye on his daughter growing up. Maybe he saw Travis and Lynne together, didn't like it, so killed him.'

'Yet, he was fine with Lynne marrying his brother?' Gill asks.

'Clearly.'

'The question that springs to mind then is how do we find a man who doesn't want to be found?'

'We have to lure him out.'

'How do we do that?'

I think for a moment, but nothing comes to mind. My head is too heavy. 'I haven't a fucking clue, Gill.'

'Not running this morning?'

I turn to see Tania Pritchard approaching me. I'm standing by the edge of the lake. I'm wearing tracksuit bottoms and a thin hoodie. The coffee in my hand is untouched and now cold. I haven't slept since Philip woke me last night. I tried to, after Gill left at dawn, but my mind wouldn't settle.

'Not this morning.'

'Matilda, I want to apologise for yesterday. I know you think I'm hiding something from you, but I'm really not. Lionel has been sitting on a dark secret for thirty years. I know he knows more than he's told me, but he won't budge. At the end of the day, he knows I'm a cheap hack who'll sell my soul for a front-page lead.'

'You're not, though, are you?'

'No. I'm really not. Why do you think I've spent my entire career on a shitty local rag? If I was a super-bitch journalist, I'd be on the nationals, living in a penthouse apartment and shagging politicians on the sly.'

'Michael Gove, or Jacob Rees-Mogg?'

Tania stifles a smile. 'Eww. Do you mind? I'll bring my breakfast up. There are no sexy politicians, are there?'

'Certainly not in this country.'

'It's a strange state of affairs when you're watching the news, and you start wondering what Theresa May is like in bed.'

'Bloody hell, Tania, you've spent far too long on your own.'

'Tell me about it. Am I forgiven?' she asks, stepping closer.

'Of course, you are.'

'So, what happened here last night? Sally in the post office told Tara in the card shop who told Jean in the tearooms that an air ambulance left this place in the wee small hours.'

'Is that High Chapel's version of fibre broadband?'

'It is, actually.'

I fill her in on the events of last night, but don't tell her about Lionel really taking the charity money. I don't think Tania would cope with that.

'Jesus. Are you all right?'

'Apart from a massive headache, yes.'

'And Philip?'

'I haven't heard from Sally yet.'

'You really think it was Jack Pemberton who broke in?'

'I can't think of anyone else who it could be. It's not chancers after a few bottles of booze. Whoever it was aimed that gun at Philip and squeezed the trigger. They didn't know it wasn't loaded.'

'But even if it was Jack, why would he commit murder?'

'As a warning.'

'Who to?'

'Me? If he has been watching all this time, for thirty years, then he knows I'm here. He's seen me sticking my nose in and he's warning me off.'

'Bloody hell,' Tania says, concern in her voice. 'What are you going to do?'

'I've run away from Sheffield. I'm not going to run away from High Chapel, too.'

We both look out at the lake. It's calmer this morning, the sun sparkling on the surface of the water as it ripples onto the shore. The storm of last week is a mere memory.

'I was thinking last night,' Tania begins. 'Whoever took the girls, whether it was Jack on his own, or Jack and Travis, it's going to have been a sexual motive, isn't it?'

'That's the number one theory.'

'What I was thinking was, who else could Jack have abused? Did he only aim his advances towards the twins, or…?' She leaves the question unanswered.

I turn to her. 'Alison? Good grief. I suppose there will be other victims. He won't have stopped at the twins, they never do.'

'How do we find out for sure?'

'I don't know. We can't do anything before we have definite proof and that's not going to be easy to find. Alison is clearly struggling with her memory. I think she's trying too hard to remember, and that could lead to a false memory. I'm going to try and speak to Lynne and Iain again, but individually this time.'

'Why individually?'

'I got the feeling they both wanted to tell me something last time we chatted, but they wouldn't in front of each other.'

'They're keeping secrets from each other?'

'Of course they are. They're a married couple.'

Once Tania has gone, I return to the restaurant. It feels strange being in there on my own. The silence is palpable. I make myself a breakfast of two slices of toast and marmalade, then take a croissant and a strong coffee into the restaurant. I sit in the window and look out at the view. I try to enjoy it. I try to see the expanse of space as liberating and mind-opening. But even with a horizon stretching out far into the distance, I feel oppressed, hemmed in.

As soon as I see Sally's car turn into the car park, I jump up and run out to get news of Philip.

'He's fine,' she says.

The relief I feel is instant. 'Oh, thank goodness.'

Carl slowly climbs out of the front passenger seat. He looks drained. He comes over to me and hugs me. I hug him back. I know he's thirteen, a teenager, but there are times when I look at him and still see a lost little boy. I want to hug him forever.

'They're keeping him in for observation because he lost consciousness,' Sally continues. 'But he's had a scan and there's no damage at all. I always said he had such a thick skull. Now I've had it confirmed. How are you?'

'I'm fine.'

'You should have gone to the hospital too, you know.'

'Honestly, I'm okay. I think I was more surprised than anything. He didn't actually hit me.'

'What have the police said?'

'Very little. I couldn't give them much of a description. It was dark and it was over within seconds.'

We make our way back into the restaurant. Carl runs on ahead to see the barking dogs who have seriously missed him this morning.

'I think I'll keep the restaurant closed tonight,' Sally says. 'I'll ring round all the bookings later. I'm not in the mood right now.' She pulls out a chair at the nearest table and slumps into it. She looks shattered.

'That's understandable. Listen, Sally, I need to go out, but can you let me see the CCTV footage from the cameras when I get back?'

'Sure.'

'I think Inspector Forsyth will want to look at them, too.' I look over my shoulder to make sure Carl isn't in earshot. 'How's Carl?'

'We've had a few tears. I asked him if he wanted to go and see his therapist again, but he said he'd rather have a chat with you when you go on one of your walks.'

I smile. 'I'd like that.'

'What do you two talk about while you're out there?'

'Oh, you know, the usual. The state of the economy, who we think should win the Nobel Prize, whether Novak Djokovic really is the greatest tennis player of all time.'

'A wide range of subjects, then?'

'Oh, yes, we cover the lot.' I put my arm around Sally. 'And how are you?'

'Hungry. Tired. And I'm gasping for a cuppa. Why can nobody in a hospital ever make a decent cup of tea?'

'Come on, I'll make you both breakfast, and then I need to get going.'

'Anywhere nice?'

'That depends on how you feel about exposing a paedophile.'

'Funny you should say that, because that's number three on my bucket list.'

I feel different as I drive from the restaurant to the stables at the other end of High Chapel. I have a purpose. I have something to occupy my mind other than my own grief. Since 2010, I've been striving harder and harder with every case to make sure it's solved. Eleven years. Non-stop. It's taken its toll on my mental and physical health, and the murder of my family is the catalyst that's brought the walls tumbling down. I will recover, I know it, I just wonder what kind of Matilda Darke I'll be upon my return to Sheffield.

I drive along the winding, narrow roads of High Chapel in Adele's Porsche until I come to the stable car park. I slow down and find a space. I climb out of the car and am hit with the aroma of horse shit. I pull a face. It makes a change from smelling a decomposing body or the internal organs at a postmortem, but only just. It's another warm day. The sun is high in the sky, not a single cloud among the blue, and not a hint of a breeze either. I'm wearing cotton trousers and a light shirt, and despite the air conditioning in the car, it's still sticking to my back.

'Hello!' I call out as I enter the stable yard.

There's no reply. I look into the office through the open window, but there's nobody there. I walk along the stables and see a beautiful brown horse looking back at me.

'Hello,' I say in that playful, sickly voice people reserve for animals. The horse steps towards me, and I stroke him on the nose. 'You're a gorgeous fella, aren't you?' He nods his head as if in reply.

'He's called Odin.'

I quickly turn at the sound of the voice and see Iain Pemberton standing in front of me.

'Sorry, I didn't see you there. He's a lovely horse.'

'He's a Hackney. Four years old.'

'Is he yours?'

'No. I don't own any. I just look after them. Give them a home. Their owners come mostly at the weekends. I suppose I'm their foster carer,' he says with a smile.

'Iain, could I have a word with you?'

'I'm guessing you don't want to chat about horses?'

'It's not my specialist subject.'

'But murder is.'

'Unfortunately, yes.'

'I suppose it has to be someone's. We'll go into the office.'

He leads the way, his head down and shoulders slumped. I look back at Odin and brush his nose. He's a stunning-looking animal.

The office is small and cramped. The desk is hidden behind files and invoices. The shelves are packed with books and box files and in the corner is a small desk where a kettle and a couple of well-used cups stand, beneath which is a mini fridge containing milk and several bars of chocolate.

'All I seem to have done so far this morning is make tea,' Iain says as he flicks on the kettle. 'We had Inspector Forsyth round. She asked Lynne to identify a few more items found on the lakebed.'

'That can't have been easy. Was she able to identify them?'

'The majority, yes. I suppose that means the bones in the car belong to Celia and Jennifer.'

'It's more than likely, yes.'

'Milk and sugar?'

'Just milk, thanks.'

Iain hands me a Queen Elizabeth II Golden Jubilee mug while he takes an England football mug.

'What do you want to ask me?' He sits down in his comfortable, old high-backed chair, but he looks decidedly uncomfortable. I guess he would rather be mucking out the horses with his bare hands than talking about the horrors his brother got up to.

'Lynne came to see me at the restaurant last week. She said, after the girls originally disappeared, you found something belonging to Jack. You didn't tell her what it was, but it led you to believe Jack had harmed the twins in some way. Would you tell me what it was you found?'

It's a while before Iain begins. He blows out a breath, fiddles with the press studs on his gilet and flicks a piece of lint from his lapel.

'We'd not long finished converting the barns into stables. Everything had been delayed with Celia and Jennifer going missing. Jack seemed to have lost interest in the business, but I kept trying to get him to come up here. Even if he just sat in the office, it would at least get him out of the house. I came in here and he quickly hid something away. I didn't think anything of it at first. A couple of hours later, Jack was in the toilet, and… I don't know, something in my mind told me to look in his jacket. It was a magazine. It was foreign. It might have been German or Dutch, I've no idea. But the pictures…' Iain's bottom lip quivers, and he turns away.

'Take your time.'

'They were kids. Girls and boys. Some were naked, some

were half-naked. Some were on their own. Others…' He leans on the table and puts his hand in front of his mouth as if trying to stop a torrent of vomit. 'Men were doing things to them. I felt sick to my stomach. I feel sick now just thinking about it. I can… I can still picture them. In my head. I can't… I'm always seeing them.'

'You confronted Jack?'

'I heard the toilet flush. That must have brought me back from… I don't know… from wherever my mind had taken me. It was Jack's magazine. I'd seen him looking at it. But he was my brother. He was my little brother. How could he be looking at it when he had three girls of his own? It didn't make sense. He came back into the office. I turned to look at him and I just saw red. I threw the magazine at him. I can't remember what I said. I was asking him all sorts. Where did he get it from? Why? What did it mean? Who was he?'

'What did he say?'

'He didn't deny it.'

'Did you ask where he'd got it from?'

He nods. He takes a breath. 'He said it belonged to Travis and that he'd given it to him.'

'Travis Montgomery?'

'Yes. He said he found it…' Iain lowers his head and places his hands over his face.

'Iain.'

'I can't even bring myself to use the word he said,' he cries.

'What did he say, Iain?'

Iain reaches for a tissue and wipes his eyes. He blows his nose and tucks the tissue up the sleeve of his jumper.

'He said he found it stimulating.'

'Oh God.'

'I looked at him, and I realised I was looking at a stranger. I had no idea who he was anymore. I asked him how long he'd been interested in young children. He said for as long as he could remember. I asked him if he'd ever done anything about it. He said it wasn't until Travis arrived and he saw him... he...' Iain is clearly struggling to reveal the horrors of thirty years ago. It's completely understandable.

'Take your time, Iain,' I say, trying to offer him reassurance. He needs to get this out. He's been bottling it up for three decades.

'When Travis wasn't working on the farm, he was always tinkering around with his car. One day, Jack went out to look for him. The girls were all running around the garden. I think they had a few friends over, too. Jack found Travis in his car, watching them. He... Jesus. He was... pleasuring himself.'

'Oh my God.'

'The thing is, Jack...' Iain pauses. He swallows hard and it looks as if it hurts. 'Jack said that he understood how Travis felt. He said he felt relief that it wasn't just him who thought about... children in that way.'

I've heard some sick horror stories in my time, but this one is right up there with the most disturbing. It's suddenly very hot in here and I feel sick. I have so many questions racing around my mind, but I don't want to ask them as I really do not want to hear the answers. But I'm a detective. It's my job to ask these questions.

'What happened?' I ask. 'Jack and Travis. What happened next?'

'I've... no idea. Jack started crying. He broke down right in front of me. And I knew. I knew what he'd done.'

'Did he admit to killing Celia and Jennifer?'

'No. He said he must have done, but that he couldn't remember. He said he saw the twins, and Alison, playing in the field. He was watching them and smiling at how much fun they were having. Everything after that was a blank until he drove up to the house and saw the police there.'

'How much time had gone by from when he was watching them to getting back home?'

'He didn't know. I assumed it was hours.'

'And he had no memory?'

'None at all.'

'Did you believe him?'

'I didn't know what to believe.'

'Were Travis and Jack harming the twins together?'

'I… I don't know.' Iain looks as if he wants to vomit. 'I had so many questions I wanted to ask him, but at the same time I wanted to get as far away from him as possible.'

'That's understandable.'

'I told him he had to go the police. He said he couldn't as he wouldn't be able to tell them anything. I told him to at least tell Lynne. He refused. He said she was suffering, and he couldn't hurt her any more than she already was. I was so angry. I was fuming. I gave him an ultimatum. I said he had until the following day to either tell Lynne or go to the police, or I'd tell them myself.'

'What did he say to that?'

'He didn't. He walked away.'

'Was that the last time you saw him?'

Iain nods. 'The next day everyone was making a big fuss about the storm that was forecast. I was helping out on the farms and with sandbags. I called Lynne at lunchtime and asked to speak to Jack. She said he'd gone over to see Mum and had taken Alison with him. The next thing, it's pitch dark, the storm's blowing in and Jack's nowhere to be found. I went out to look for him. Mum had told me what time they'd left hers. I couldn't find him anywhere. I came back. Lynne refused to do nothing, so we went out again. That's when we found the car by the edge of the lake. Alison was asleep in the back.'

'What do you think happened?'

'I think he killed himself. He knew I wouldn't let it rest. He knew I'd either tell Lynne or I'd drag him to the police station. There was no other way out for him. Mum said later that she felt he was saying goodbye while he was there.'

'But why did he take Alison with him?'

'That was Lynne's idea. He said he was going over to see Mum and she said it would be a lovely surprise if she saw Alison. She hadn't seen her for a while.'

'And you never said anything about the day before, about finding Jack with the magazine and what he'd told you?'

'Lynne,' he says, his voice breaking. 'She knew that I knew more than I was letting on. Don't ask me how. She kept badgering me. I had to tell her.'

'What did she do?'

'She went apoplectic. I've never seen anyone like that before. I thought she was going to do some serious harm to herself. We spent hours talking, trying to work out what and why Jack had done what he'd done. Then, the topic turned to Alison, and we wondered if he'd ever… you know, touched her. Lynne knew how much Alison doted on her father. She didn't want her experiencing more heartache. We decided, together, with Jack gone, it wasn't in anyone's best interest to bring it all up, least of all with Alison.'

'But surely, Lynne wanted to find out where Celia and Jennifer were?'

'She did, but she said protecting Alison was more important.'

'When the twins disappeared, why did you give Travis an alibi? I've seen the two police statements. Lynne said she was on her own, baking in the kitchen. A few days later, she changed it and said she was sleeping with Travis. That wasn't true, was it?'

'No.'

'Then why lie? Why give Travis an alibi after everything he'd done?'

Iain takes a couple of deep breaths. The lines of worry and fear and hatred are etched on his face. He looked physically sick.

'You'd need to ask Lynne about that.'

'I'm asking you.'

'I'd rather Lynne tell you. It was her statement, after all.'

I nod. 'What happened with Travis? You didn't wave him off after a family meal, did you?'

'No. We lied to you. I'm sorry about that. After me and Lynne had decided what to do for the sake of Alison, I went round to see Travis. I told him I knew all about him and Jack, his past, and what they'd been up to. He said I had no proof. He was right. How I kept my hands from him, I've no idea. I wanted to… I wanted to smash his face in. I told him he was no longer welcome at the paddocks, or the house and I didn't want to see him again.'

'And he just left?'

'I might have been a bit more forceful. I threatened him. He had this grin on his face. He knew there was nothing I could do. I needed him to know that, if he stayed around here, I'd destroy him.'

'What happened?'

'I stood over him while he packed a bag. I drove him out of the village. We drove down the A591. I looked over at him and I decided I didn't want him in my car anymore. We'd driven far enough. I pulled over and told him to get out.'

'Where was this?'

'I don't know. It was the middle of the night, and to be

honest with you, I didn't give a fuck. I turned around and went back home.'

'Did he say where he was heading?'

'No. We didn't speak at all once we were in the car.'

'Did you…'

'Look, Matilda, I'm sorry, but I really don't care where Travis is or what happened to him. He came into our lives. My father gave him a job and a roof over his head, and he took advantage of that. He saw a happy, loving family, and he decided to destroy it for his own sick pleasure. My brother might have had…' Iain swallows hard. He's clearly struggling with who his brother really was, even after all this time. 'He might have had proclivities towards young children, but he never acted on it before Travis came along. He never showed… he changed once Travis arrived. Maybe Travis saw something in Jack and took advantage of it. He was an evil man and I'm glad he's missing. I just hope he suffered a long, violent and painful death. Now, if you don't have anything else to ask me, I've got horses that need mucking out.'

I don't move. I'm not finished.

'The sightings of Jack over the years. Did you think they might be real, that he might still be alive?'

'I don't know. I hope they're not. If I do ever see him again, I'll tear him apart with my bare hands.'

I look down at his huge, calloused hands and see they're balled up into fists, his knuckles white.

'The problem I have is with Jack's disappearance. At the time, he was struggling with all kinds of emotions. He'd killed his daughters. He was struggling with his sexual orientation towards young children, and he was about to be exposed. A man in that position would usually kill his last surviving child, and his wife, as well as himself, in order to protect them from the truth. Yet, he didn't do that. He walked away and made it look like he drowned. That takes planning and organisation. Someone in that state of mind doesn't have those skills.'

'I really wouldn't like to get into Jack's head on that last day. Despite all the horror he created and how much I physically hate him, he's still my brother. I can't begin to image how much he was suffering.'

'But if he cared about Alison as much as he claimed, why leave her in the back of the car on her own, in the middle of a storm, when who knows what could have happened to her? She could have died.'

'But she didn't.'

'Jack didn't know that.'

'Jack was obviously not in his right mind. He might not have even realised Alison was in the car with him. Maybe his mind told him to end it, and he listened. Look, the twins have been found. Lynne can finally lay them to rest. Surely, we can draw a line under this now. It's bad enough it's being brought back to light, but do we need to go over everything?'

'To get to the truth, yes.'

'We have the truth. Just because it's not on the front pages and everyone isn't talking about it, doesn't mean we don't know. Me and Lynne know what happened. That's the main thing.'

'Alison doesn't.'

'Alison doesn't need to know.'

'I think she does.'

'That's none of your business,' he says, sternly.

'No. But it is Alison's.'

'If you tell her, you'll kill her. She won't be able to cope with it.'

'If she'd been told the truth from the beginning, she wouldn't be in this situation.'

'You don't know what it was like thirty years ago. We were

protecting her. We still are. Look, you don't live here. You don't know what's going on in this community. You don't know this family. Don't stick your nose in where it doesn't belong.'

'Travis did report his car stolen. Three days before the twins disappeared. I…'

'Look, I'm sorry, but I'm really not interested in anything to do with Travis fucking Montgomery. He's done enough damage to this family. Now, I'm very busy. I've got two new horses coming today. I don't have time to indulge you in trying to occupy your mind against your own grief.'

Iain doesn't give me time to respond. He stands up and brushes past me, leaving the small office.

Is that what I'm doing?

Whenever I run, now, and I glance up at the hills that surround High Chapel, I see walkers and hikers in groups or walking their dogs. Occasionally, I'll see a lone walker in the distance and a part of me wonders if it's Jack Pemberton keeping sentry over the village.

I turn a corner to run along the edge of the lake and stop in my tracks when I see Lynne Pemberton up ahead by the water's edge. She's *too* close to the water's edge. As I approach her, slowly, I see that she's actually standing in the water and it's licking over her shoes as it sweeps into the shore.

I control my breathing. I've been running full pelt, and I'm knackered.

'Lynne,' I call out, quietly. She doesn't hear me. She remains motionless, looking out into the water that has hidden her daughters for thirty years.

'Lynne,' I try again, louder this time.

She snaps out of her reverie and turns to see who's calling her. There are tears streaming down her face. She gives me a pain-filled smile before turning back to the lake.

'I used to run,' she says. 'I didn't do it for long. I tried one of those spinning classes a few times. They almost killed me.'

I don't say anything. It's best to allow Lynne to lead the conversation. I'm glad I've finally got her on her own. She might spill something she doesn't want to reveal in front of her husband.

'It's a beautiful part of the country, isn't it?' she says. 'That's why tourists come here. The landscape is stunning. Untouched for centuries. Hikers. Wild swimmers. They love it. They come to the stables, and they all say how lucky I am to be surrounded by such beauty every single day. I always thought I was. I can't say that anymore. This lake. It isn't beautiful at all. It's been the home of my girls for thirty years and I never knew it. For thirty years, I've looked out at this view and breathed in the air, and it's calmed me when I've wanted to scream so loud I hoped my lungs would burst. It's cruel that what I thought was soothing was actually taunting me. My girls have been in this water all this time.'

I sit down and pull my knees up to my chest. I watch Lynne, see the pain etched on her face. I can feel the sadness and torment radiating from her. It's like looking in a mirror.

Lynne comes over to join me.

'Do you have kids?' she asks.

'No.'

'From when I was young, all I wanted was to grow up, get married, and have children. Not very modern, is it? I had so many dolls as a child. I called them my babies. I used to say I wanted to have hundreds of children.' She gives a pained smile at the memory. 'That's why I became a midwife. I just loved being around babies.'

'Why did you leave?'

'The stables,' she sighs. There's a bitterness to her voice. 'In the early days, there wasn't enough work to employ someone. Jack had gone. Iain needed someone to help him, someone who didn't need paying.'

'You could have gone back to midwifery once the stables were a success.'

She shrugs. 'Too much time had gone by. It's a strange concept; time. Sometimes you think it moves quickly and other times it seems to go slowly. Celia and Jennifer have been gone for thirty years. It seems like a lifetime. Me and Iain celebrated our fifteenth wedding anniversary last week. Fifteen years gone in a flash.'

'Did you do anything special?'

'There's a restaurant we go to a lot in Kendal. We just went there for a meal.'

'I know things are dark for you right now, Lynne, but you need to look at what you still have left. Iain clearly loves you. Alison is a credit to you. You have a lovely home and a thriving business.'

'Iain was my first love,' she said, wistfully, staring out into the lake. 'He was so handsome when he was young. All the girls wanted to go out with him. He chose me.'

'How did you end up marrying his brother?'

'Iain wasn't the settling-down type back then. I wanted to get married as soon as I was able to. Like I said, I wanted hundreds of kids.'

'How did you and Jack end up together?'

'There was something about Jack that... I don't know. I always felt he needed saving.'

'Saving?'

'He had a sadness around him. I didn't know it was depression at the time. I just saw this tall, handsome man who needed bringing out of his shell.'

'Didn't Iain mind you going out with his brother?'

'Me and Iain had long since split by then. Besides, Iain was working his way through the village,' she says with a laugh in her voice. 'For brothers, they were polar opposites. I mean, they looked alike, but talk about chalk and cheese.'

'And you ended up back with your first love.'

It's a while before Lynne speaks. 'I love Iain for helping me in those early days of the twins going missing, of Jack... he helped me. He saved me. He helped with Alison. He provided support and comfort when I needed it.'

'Didn't you want to have more children?'

'I'd have loved to,' she says, a warm smile spreading on her face. 'Iain can't have them, though.'

I clear my throat. 'In your police statement, you said you were having an affair with—'

'I didn't have an affair with Travis,' she interrupts.

'But you changed your statement.'

'Before the girls... before everything happened, I was a different woman. I loved my children with all my heart, but marriage to Jack was... difficult. He couldn't help it. It was his moods. They took over him. There were days when he wouldn't get out of bed, when he wouldn't talk to anyone. The atmosphere in that small cottage was unbearable. When the kids were at nursery and school, I'd go over and see Iain.' She looked at me. 'Like I said, they were opposites.'

'You were having an affair with Iain?'

She nods. 'Iain didn't want Jack to find out. *I* didn't want Jack to find out. Iain and Lionel – Inspector Bell – they were good friends. Iain told him that I was in bed with Travis at the time the girls went missing. Lionel said, if I went in and adjusted my statement, just me and him, nobody else would need to find out. I don't even think Travis knew about it. Lionel knew us. He took us at our word.'

I can feel the blood boiling inside me. That's not how a police investigation is supposed to be run. You don't take people at their word just because you know them. Lionel Bell had a conflict of interest. An outside unit should have been brought in to lead the investigation. Maybe, then, Celia and Jennifer wouldn't have been at the bottom of the lake for thirty years.

'But it means Travis doesn't have an alibi for the time the twins were taken,' I say.

'Jack did it. Jack confessed to Iain, then...'

'Then what?'

'I should go,' she says, quickly standing up.

I follow. 'Your husband confessed to abusing the twins. It's looking more than likely that Travis was involved, too. Do you think he abused only them? Do you think it started and stopped with Celia and Jennifer?'

Lynne stops and turns back to me. Her face is ashen. 'What? You think he... Oh my God!' She puts her head in her hands.

'Did you know?'

'Of course, I didn't.'

'Jennifer fell in school a couple of weeks before the summer holiday. She kept saying her arm was hurting her, but the fall only left a graze. That sounds like she had other injuries.'

'What? No. No. Why are you saying this?'

'Someone hurt her, Lynne. Someone forcibly grabbed her and hurt her.'

Her face is red. She's struggling to breathe through the tears.

'Everything changed when he came here.'

'Travis?'

'He wormed his way into our home, into our lives and he destroyed everything. I let him babysit my children. I bloody handed them to him.'

'Lynne, no, don't do this to yourself. You weren't to know. You couldn't have known.'

'So, did he and Jack realise they had this affinity for small children and together they...' She can't bring herself to say it.

'I've no idea what happened, Lynne. I don't think we should dwell on that. We can't do anything to change it. It might be for the best to focus on the positives.'

'Positives?' she asks, her head snapping up to look at me. 'I was married to a paedophile. I had three children to him. He and Travis did God knows what to my children and then he murdered two of them. Where are the positives, Matilda?'

I allow the silence to develop so Lynne can calm down. 'You've been searching for your daughters for thirty years. You've got them back. You can bury them. That's a positive. You'll have somewhere to go and talk to them.'

She inhales a deep and shaky breath. 'I... I suppose that's true.' She attempts a smile, but she looks to be in great emotional pain.

'Lynne, before Travis came along, did Jack ever display signs that he—'

She interrupts: 'No. Please. No. Don't do this to me.'

'Is it possible Travis could have manipulated Jack—'

'No!' Lynne screams. 'I don't want to hear this. I don't want to know. My daughters are dead. I've found them. I can bury them. I can finally move on.'

'You can't, though, can you? Your husband is still out there. He's still alive, isn't he?'

'I... No... I don't...'

'Has he been in contact with you? Have you spoken to him?'

'I have to go,' Lynne says. She turns and walks away at speed.

'Someone in Jack's position wouldn't have only killed himself. He'd have killed Alison and you to stop you discovering the truth, and there have been too many sightings for it to be a coincidence,' I call out, running after her.

'I don't *want* to know. I've got them back, that's all that matters. You've done enough. You need to leave right now before more damage is done.'

Lynne storms off. I don't follow. I look back out over the lake. Something has just happened here, and I don't know what. Whatever it is, I am sure I have answers to questions that have been bugging me for days. If only my head wasn't too fogged up for me to sort them out.

I make my way back to the restaurant and Sally hangs up the phone from cancelling another booking for tonight. She looks tired, bless her. She always has a smile and a bounce in her walk. It's gone. She's missing Philip.

'Tania's called for you. She's asked if you'll pop round to see her.' She hands me a Post-it note with Tania's address on it.

'Oh. Okay.'

'I thought I'd make us pizzas for tonight. What do you think?'

'It depends on the toppings.'

'Pineapple, green olives, anchovies,' she says. There's a smile in her eyes. The old Sally is still there.

'I'd arrest you for making a pizza like that.'

I drive Adele's Porsche to Tania's house. I can't park directly outside so have to use the pub car park and walk back. Tania's cottage is gorgeous. I don't recognise the weather-worn brickwork, but it's a building James would have loved. The chimney stack is centred and stands tall, reaching into the sky.

The roof looks bowed as if it's about to cave in at any moment, but it's all authentic. Period. It's a real house.

I knock on the pale blue door using the heavy iron knocker and marvel at the tiny leaded windows and the pitched roof of the open porch. I can almost picture the tiny rooms inside, the period details and the open fireplace, the cornicing and hardwood floor. I hope Tania isn't a gaudy decorator and hasn't thrown up flock wallpaper and Artexed ceilings.

Tania opens the door in a halo of cigarette smoke. She stubs out what's left on the door frame and tosses the tab end into a pot by the door. She smiles and beckons me to enter.

Through a small, dark hallway, I'm led into a large living room at the back of the house. I'm right about the open fireplace, but wrong about everything else. The room is a clutter of mess. Picture frames and overstocked bookcases adorn every wall. It's difficult to see what colour they've been painted. The carpet is an assault on the senses. A mess of gaudy colours, it would bring on a seizure if stared at for too long. There are two sofas, both far too big for the room, and they don't match. There's a fustiness in the air. A mixture of stale cigarette smoke, dust and old paper. It's claustrophobic.

'Have a seat,' Tania says, picking up a few files from the sofa and dumping them on the floor. 'I won't apologise for the mess. This is how I live. I know where everything is. Give me the name of any Thomas Hardy novel and I'll be able to get you several copies of it within a minute.'

'If only I knew the name of a Thomas Hardy novel.'

'Oh. Not a fan of the classics?'

'More of a contemporary reader.'

'I'm a huge Hardy fan,' she says, sitting down on the opposing sofa. 'I went on *Mastermind* in 2004. Reached the semi-finals.'

'Congratulations.'

'I sweated buckets in that leather chair. I can still remember the question that robbed me of a place in the final: what was Thomas Hardy's father's profession? How the bollocks am I supposed to know that? I read his books. I'm not writing his sodding biography. Bastards. It turns out he was a stonemason. I said he was a vicar.'

I smile. My eyes wander around the room and land on a framed photograph on the mantel. I think I recognise the people in it and go over to pick it up.

'Is that a young Alison Pemberton?'

'Yes. The girl next to her is Claire Daniels. They've been inseparable since little school.'

'How come you have this?'

'If you look in the background at the lanky woman with the awful hair, that's me.'

I lean in for a closer look. 'Oh, my goodness.'

'It was the nineties. I bet even you had embarrassing hair back then.'

'I believe I had a fringe. My favourite going-out jacket was pink with shoulder pads.'

'Bloody hell, shoulder pads. What were we thinking? Anyway, that was taken at an event on the lake the paper was sponsoring to get kids outdoors doing more active things. I shared a paddle boat with them. We fell in. I've got plenty of other photos of that day somewhere. I'll dig them out. I love looking down Memory Lane, don't you?'

'Sometimes,' I say, replacing the frame back on the mantel.

'Anyway, the reason I called is because there's been a new sighting of Jack Pemberton.'

'What? Where?'

'Right here in High Chapel.'

'Who told you?'

'A call came through on the main phone line for the newspaper.'

'What did they say?'

'They were walking their dog in the woods off End Lane, and they saw someone lurking behind a tree. They thought it was a hiker having a pee, but he was spending too long there for that. They walked closer and it was when their dog barked that he turned and looked directly at them, before running off in the opposite direction.'

'Description?'

'Tall, thin, dark walking trousers and dark anorak. Shaggy grey hair. Lined face. Spitting image of an old Jack Pemberton, according to the caller.'

'Who was the caller?'

'He said his name was John. It wasn't a great line. He talked with a stammer and, when I asked him for more details, he said something about not being able to hear me properly. To be fair, I couldn't hear him very well either. The call ended.'

'Did he call back?'

'No.'

'How long ago was this?'

'A couple of hours.'

'Long enough for him to have gone home and used a landline,' I say. 'Or pop into the newspaper office.'

'That's what I thought.'

'And why ring you and not the police?'

'Well, that's me being a nosy journalist. If you google Jack Pemberton sightings, one of the first hits is the extensive coverage on the newspaper's website and a link to report any sightings to yours truly. Alison has something similar on Facebook.'

'Do they often tell you who they are when they call with a sighting?'

'Usually. Most are tourists. The ones from further afield usually email in.'

I sit back and fold my arms. 'Are there many Johns in High Chapel?'

'Plenty.'

'Do they have dogs?'

'Most people have dogs around here.'

'You don't.'

'No. But then I'm a hard-faced journalist with no emotions.'

I smile. 'Who are you trying to kid?'

'So, is Jack Pemberton in High Chapel and is he going to make himself known?' Tania asks.

'Why would he? What's his motive? From the point of view of the police, he's a wanted murderer. Iain told me this morning he'd tear him apart if he ever saw him again. Lynne is hardly going to welcome him back with open arms. There's no reason for him to come back.'

'Unfinished business.'

'Such as?'

Tania blows out her cheeks. 'Maybe he wants to finally confess. Unburden himself.'

'Then just do it. Why hide? Look, I've been thinking, all this time I've thought of Jack being a serial abuser, that he was abusing his kids and went too far, killed them and did a runner. However, both Iain and Lynne, this morning, told me that Jack didn't show any signs of having tendencies towards young children until Travis came along. It's possible that young, good-looking Travis was a manipulator who saw something within Jack and brought it out of him.'

'So, let me get this clear in my head,' Tania says, a look of confusion on her face. 'Travis comes along, worms his way into the Pemberton family, sees a fellow paedophile in Jack and gets him to live out his fantasies on his daughters. Jack, disgusted, then kills his daughters and runs away.'

'Possibly.'

'Where does Travis's stolen car come into it?'

'My only guess is that he planned to abduct Celia and Jennifer, kill them, and use his car to hide their bodies. He said it was stolen to cover himself.'

'And what happened to Travis?'

I tell Tania Lynne lied about having an affair with Travis and Iain told me he literally drove Travis out of the village.

'I knew it,' Tania says, looking almost smug. 'No offence to Lynne or anything, but I didn't think Travis would go for someone like her. Why saddle himself with a married woman who had three kids?'

'When he could have had a sexy reporter with no ties.'

'Precisely. Although I did have a perm in the early nineties. Maybe that put him off. So, why is Travis missing, then? Is he dead?'

A thought springs to mind. 'Unless the sightings of Jack are really sightings of Travis. How old would he be now? Mid-fifties? If he's been living rough all this time, he's going to look older. He could look like how people might expect Jack to look and not everyone realised Travis was missing. To all intents and purposes, he left the village and returned home.'

'And Travis would have unfinished business as he's angry with Iain for driving him out in the first place,' Tania says. 'But why now, after thirty years? You know, I'd love to find out what really happened on the night of the storm all those years ago.'

'There is one person we can ask.'

'Who?'

'The person who was there. Alison.'

'Will she really remember, all this time later?'

'I'm not sure. But there is an interview technique we can try.'

I drive to the edge of Lake Windermere. I sit on the opposite side to where Travis's car was pulled out. It's quiet. The only sound comes from the birds in the trees and the ripple as the water laps the shore. It's calming, soothing and I can feel myself relaxing. The great outdoors is a tranquil place. In Sheffield, I go from home to the office and back again. I live right on the edge of the Peak District National Park but never take advantage of what it has to offer. That needs to change. I need fresh air and open space. It really does clear the mind. Sitting here, like this, taking in the beauty of nature, my mind is almost blank.

Almost. But not quite.

Would it be fair to interrogate Alison Pemberton? She was only five at the time her father disappeared. She wouldn't have had a clue what was going on while the storm was raging. Is it possible there is something locked away in her memory that can reveal the truth?

'I was told I'd find you here.'

I know that voice.

I don't move. I feel the emotion rise up inside me.

I know that voice.

It can't be. Can it?

Slowly, I stand up and turn around. I'm looking at a ghost standing by the Porsche.

'Adele?' I ask, softly, disbelievingly.

'Hello, Matilda.'

Oh my God, it's her. She's come back. I try to smile but the tears won't let me. I look at my best friend. I take in the change in her appearance. She's thinner. Her hair is longer. She's tanned. She's wearing a dress. She's a mirage, surely. She's in Sierra Leone.

'Is that… is it really you?'

'Sian called me. She told me everything that's happened. I'm so sorry.'

Adele walks slowly towards me. I'm pretty sure I'm dreaming. It's not until she puts her arms around me, pulls me to her and holds me tight that I know it's real. It's familiar. She's hugged me many times in the past. I know an Adele hug when I feel one. The familiarity causes my body to relax and releases the tears. Adele is crying, too. We both are. We can't stop.

We sit at the edge of the lake. Adele has her legs outstretched; her dress pulled up beyond her knees to catch the sun. I have my legs drawn up, hugging my knees.

'It's not like you to run away,' she says.

'If I'd stayed, who knows what I would have done.'

'I'm sorry I wasn't there for you.'

I shake my head. 'You've nothing to apologise for. You were looking after yourself as you've every right to do.'

'We've both been through the shit over the last few years, haven't we?'

'You could say that.'

'We should have stuck together, though. I shouldn't have left you behind.'

'He would still have killed my family.' There's a crack in my voice.

Adele scooches over and puts her arm around my shoulders once again. 'I still can't believe it. Poor Penny. And Nathan and Joseph. They were so young.'

We remain silent as we try to make sense of the enormity of their deaths. We can't. It's simply too incomprehensible.

'How's Harriet?' Adele eventually asks.

'I've no idea. She won't have anything to do with me. Not that I can blame her. I hate me, too.'

'You're not to blame.'

'I am. I should have left the force after the shooting.'

'And look at what would have happened, if you had. You saved Sian and her children from being killed by her husband. They would all be dead, if it wasn't for you. You are not to blame for the actions of others. The only person to blame is the man doing all this. Not you.' She speaks with force and conviction, and I almost believe her. 'Harriet hates you right now because she needs someone to hate and you're the closest. When the killer is caught, when she knows who really killed her boys, she'll come round. I promise.'

I take a deep breath. 'You know, sometimes I think I can fight. Sometimes I think I have the strength to tear Sheffield apart looking for the killer. Other times I struggle to find the drive to get out of bed in the morning.'

'You're grieving. It's natural to feel like that. Look, Matilda, you're not alone in this. I'm here with you. I'll be here for as long as you want me. And back in Sheffield, you've got so many people rooting for you. Christian, Sian, Scott, Donal, Finn, the incredibly sexy Odell. They're not just your colleagues, they're your friends and they care for you. Do you honestly think they're going to sit back and allow you to suffer like this? You say you don't have the strength to tear Sheffield apart, but they do. That's what they're doing right now. They're fighting for you.'

I stare out into the lake. I wish I was in the water, right in the middle, swimming, pushing hard against the tide, head in the water, blocking out everything around me.

'How's it going?' I don't want to know, but I do.

'The investigation? I don't know. I haven't spoken to Sian for a couple of days.'

'They haven't caught him.' It's not a question.

'Not that I'm aware of.'

'They won't, either.'

'Why not?'

'Because he's gone to ground. He's waiting until I get back, then he'll start up again.'

Adele frowns as she looks at me. 'Has he been in touch with you?'

'He emailed me on the day of Mum's funeral,' I say, quietly. 'That's why I ran. I needed to put some space between me and the investigation. I need to sort myself out.'

'Jesus Christ, Mat, why didn't you call me?'

'I couldn't reach you.'

'You could have left messages. I would have been on the first plane home.'

'To be honest with you, Adele, I didn't even know where I was half the time. When I walked into Mum's house and found her and the boys, I just... I don't know. I think my mind shut down. I have no memory of getting from her house to the hospital. I don't remember going home. I don't remember eating or sleeping or showering between then and the funeral. I seem to remember Sian being there a lot.'

'Are you still getting messages from the killer?'

'I don't know. Why do you think I left my phone at the house?'

Adele digs into her pocket and pulls out my iPhone. She hands it to me, but I don't take it from her. I want to hurl it into the lake. 'I've charged it for you.'

'I don't think I want to know.' As soon as I say those words, I hear Lynne Pemberton saying them not an hour ago. She said she didn't want to know what had happened all those years ago, yet I believe she needs to discover the truth. I suppose I do, too.

I take the phone from her and hold down the on button. The screen lights up and I see James's face smiling out at me. I quickly hand it back to Adele while it boots up.

'Shall we go back to the restaurant?' she asks.

'That's a good idea. I think I'm going to need one of Sally's strong coffees before I go through my phone.'

'She was telling me it was broken into last night. You and Philip were attacked by an intruder. Are you actively looking for trouble now?' Adele asks with a smile in her voice as we get up and dust ourselves down.

'It does seem to follow me, doesn't it?'

'There's more trouble coming your way, too.'

'What do you mean?'

'What the hell have you done to my car?' she asks. She walks around it, looking at the splatters of mud, the dulled body work, the dried rain drops, and the twigs stuck in the rear wiper.

'Ah. Well, you see, if I'd known you were coming, I'd have washed it.'

Adele opens the front passenger door and recoils in horror. 'Has a dog been in here?'

'Possibly more than one.'

'I expect a full valet within twenty-four hours,' she says, a twinkle in her eye.

We get into the car and close the doors. I put the key in the ignition. Before setting off, I turn to Adele.

'Thank you.'

'What for?'

'For coming back.'

'You didn't think I'd leave you to go through all this on your own, did you?'

'Are you staying?'

'Yes.'

'Permanently?'

She thinks for a moment. 'I'm not sure about that. However, I'll promise you one thing: wherever you go, I go. Got that?'

Why are my tears so quick to race to the surface? I bite my bottom lip hard to keep them at bay.

'Thank you.'

'You're welcome. Now, let's see how you've been treating my car while I've been away.'

I manage to distract Adele from going through my phone with me by taking her on a tour of the restaurant and telling her Carl's idea of the picture window in the basement and my idea to put money into the venture.

While we're making pizzas – all four of us choosing different toppings, Sally getting to grips with the pizza oven, Carl stealing toppings to give to the dogs, then the hassle with the triple-cooked chips – the conversation is light and there's even laughter in the air as Sally manages, perfectly, to cook each individual pizza, except for her own, which she drops on the floor. Her own fault for putting pineapple on it. We all donate slices from our own and she fills up on chips.

When I hear the sound of the *Coronation Street* theme tune coming from the TV, I make my excuses and say I'm off to shower and have an early night.

I stand by the window in my bedroom and look out over the lake and countryside. Darkness has fallen. The moonlight is dulled by the thin whisper of cloud sweeping in front of it. I hear the bedroom door open and turn back from the window.

Adele walks in. She looked exhausted. 'Bloody hell, that boy can talk. All evening he's been asking me about what it's like to be a pathologist. What's the most disturbing thing I've seen? How do I open a rib cage? Is the brain pink or grey? Which organ is the squishiest?' She flops down on the bed.

'That's a good question, actually. Which organ *is* the squishiest?' I ask as I climb into bed.

'I've no idea. I don't go around squishing them. In fact, the squishing of organs is greatly frowned upon.' She kicks off her sandals and sits up. 'So, are we Bert and Ernie, or Morecambe and Wise?'

There's no bedroom for Adele so she's having to share with me. We've done it before. It's not a problem.

'Adele, can I ask you a favour?'

'Sure.'

'Do you know any of the pathologists around here?'

'Erm, I'm not sure. Why?'

'I want to know the results of the postmortems on Celia and Jennifer Pemberton. I think there might be something surprising we haven't thought of yet.'

'Matilda, what are you doing?' Adele asks, sitting up.

'What do you mean?'

'You've left Sheffield. I can understand why: you need to sort yourself out. Yet, here you are, getting involved in the double murder of two girls. You're doing your job. You may as well send for Sian and Scott.'

'I can't forget. I'll never be able to forget what happened to my mum, to Nathan and Joseph. I can't undo it, either. I can sit here and mope and whine and cry, but nothing will alter the fact they're all dead and I was responsible—'

'Mat—' Adele tries to interrupt.

'No, let me finish. Everything that's happened has happened. There's no changing that. So, I need to find a way to move on, to continue living my life. I'm scarred, I know I am. I'm never going to be the Matilda I was a couple of months ago back in Sheffield, but I'm still me, and being a detective is all I know.'

'You're going to return to South Yorkshire Police, aren't you?'

'I'm taking Aaron's advice. He suggested I go back; I find the bastard who killed my family, then resign and do something else. I'm not saying that's what I'm going to do, but once I've tracked down the killer, I'll be able to close the door on all this and see what's left for me.'

'But you're not in a fit state to return to Sheffield, and your job, right now. And you won't be while you're running around the Lake District like you're Miss Marple.'

'I don't think she did much running.'

'Stop splitting hairs.'

'I have to occupy my mind.'

'Then do a cryptic crossword. There are other things to focus on than murder. Why do you always have to go dark?'

I smile. 'It is my surname.'

'Very funny,' she says, flippantly.

'This is all I know, Adele.'

'It doesn't need to be. I know you're no sparkling twenty-something, but you're young enough to start again.'

'Is that supposed to be a compliment?'

'You don't need to be a detective.'

'What shall I do? Open a sweet shop?'

'There are worse jobs.'

'Can you honestly see me standing behind a counter selling bloody mint humbugs and Dolly Mixture for the rest of my life?'

'No. Knowing you, you'd eat them all yourself and go bankrupt. Can I ask you a question?' Adele asks.

'You know you can.'

She reaches over and takes my hand, holding it firmly in

both of hers. 'Answer me honestly. When you find the person who killed your mother and nephews, are you going to kill him?'

I look at her. 'I haven't decided yet.'

'I'm really worried about you,' Adele says, a tear rolling down her face.

'Do you want to know the truth? I'm worried about me, too.'

I wake early. I open my eyes, look across, and see the sleeping face of Adele in front of me. It seems strange to be sharing a bed with someone again. It seems even stranger for that someone to be a woman. I lie back and try to return to sleep, but my mind is already at work. I decide to get up.

I make myself a mug of tea then pad through to the main part of the restaurant where I stand in front of the window and watch the sun rise over Lake Windermere. I could get used to a view of this magnitude.

'You're up early.'

I turn and see Carl standing in the doorway, a Labrador either side.

'So are you.'

'I like to take the dogs for a walk before school, if I can.'

'How are you feeling this morning?' Despite Carl's questioning of Adele about her job last night, he had fallen quiet whenever the break-ins and his father's injuries were mentioned.

He pulls out a chair and sits down. His smooth face is frowned with worry.

'Did you know, before I was kidnapped, Mum and Dad received a lot of silent phone calls?'

I don't answer him. I did know that.

'The kidnappers were obviously planning and preparing for their attack. Now, we've had these attempted break-ins. It's leading up to something, isn't it?'

I sit down opposite him. 'I'd be lying if I said I knew what was going on, but I can promise you one thing. After last time, your mum, your dad, and me, we're all on our guard. We will not let anything happen to you.'

A tear rolls down his face. He doesn't wipe it away. 'They killed my gran. They could kill any of you.'

I reach for his hand and squeeze it. 'I don't for one minute believe the kidnappers are back. If they were, they wouldn't have attempted this many sloppy break-ins. This is something completely different. I just don't know what it is yet. But I will.'

'I've got a bad feeling that it's going to end horribly.'

'Carl, right now, I'm the queen of doom-mongering. I cannot see the brightness in anything, and that's something I'm going to have to work on, but there are some things in my life that I am positive about and they are you and your mum and dad. You're a wonderful family and I love you all. I will fight to the death to keep you all safe. That's a promise.'

One of the Woodys barked.

'And I think he agrees with me too,' I smile.

This makes Carl laugh.

'Shall we take them out for a walk before they leave a puddle on your mum's clean floor?'

Carl nods. He stands up, comes over to me and wraps his arms around me.

'Thank you,' he says in my ear.

'What for?'

'For being here. For speaking the truth. For not treating me like a child.'

Carl's leaves the restaurant to fetch the dogs' leads. Naturally, they go with him. I turn to look back out of the window. Carl's words from yesterday ring in my eyes.

It's happening again.

I don't think it is. I don't know what's going on with the break-ins, but the attack on Philip, the fact he could have been killed had I not removed the cartridges from the gun, tell me that whoever is behind this is dangerous, and they won't stop until they get what they want.

After taking the dogs for a long walk with Carl, I'd worked up an appetite. I make myself scrambled eggs on toast. Sally has given me her access code to the CCTV cameras, so I look at the footage around the exterior of the restaurant. As I suspected, the intruder knew exactly what he was doing as he'd managed to find a blind spot at the rear so he wouldn't be seen as he reached up with a stick or pole and adjusted the camera's position away from the back door. Sneaky bastard. The sooner Philip upgrades the better.

I walk into the restaurant with my second black coffee of the morning to find Adele sitting at a table by the window. She's chipping away at half a grapefruit and drinking orange juice. I think she looks the picture of health until I notice the remnants of a bacon sandwich on a plate beside her.

I pull out the chair opposite and sit down. Sally has already taken Carl to school and is then going to pick Philip up from the hospital. The cleaners and restaurant staff have yet to arrive, so it's just us.

'Tell me what happens to bodies that have been in the water for thirty years.'

'I'm eating.' She pulls a face.

'Adele, I've known you to make dinner plans while draining a stomach of its contents. There's no way you're squeamish.'

'You know the effects of water on a body,' she says, putting her spoon down.

'I know, but what will the pathologist be looking for in Celia and Jennifer?'

'There'll be no organs to take samples from, no blood, no bodily fluids at all. All that is left is bone. If Celia and Jennifer were shot or stabbed, they might be able to tell where the bullet entered and left the body, or the trajectory of a knife if it hit bone. If they were beaten or suffered a blow to the head, there might be broken bones or a fractured skull. Anything else like suffocation, drugging or even if they were raped, is not going to be found.'

'Damn.'

'I've done a google search and I know who the pathologist is for this area. I've worked with him in the past. I'll pop along later to see him. But don't get your hopes up.'

'Thanks.'

A car pulls into a space outside the restaurant. We turn to look out of the window to see who the early morning visitor is.

'Who's that?' Adele asks.

'PC Alison Pemberton. Daughter of Jack. Sister of the missing twins.'

'Bloody hell. I bet she's going through the wringer right now.'

'Wouldn't you? I was going to pop round and talk to her later. I've got some very sensitive questions to ask.'

We make eye contact through the window. I signal to her and tell her I'll be right out.

'By the way,' Adele begins. 'If you're going out and you

pass a chemist, will you pop in and get some of those nasal strips that stop people snoring?'

'Why? You don't snore.'

'Precisely.'

'You've gone very bumptious since you got an all-over tan and found your waistline again.'

'I've always had a waist.'

'True. We all have a waist. It's just some of us hide it beneath a huge layer of bacon sandwiches.' I wink as I head for the door.

Adele picks up a crust of the sandwich she's left and throws it at me. We share a giggle before I leave. It's almost like old times. Almost.

'Good morning,' I trot down the wooden stairs of the restaurant. I'm trying to sound friendly and light-hearted. I want Alison to feel at ease and that she can trust me.

'Hi. How are you? I heard about the break-in.'

'I'm fine. Erm, look, Alison, I was going to call you later. Do you think we can have a chat?'

'Of course. What about?'

'Shall we go for a walk?'

'Okay.'

We set off for the woods. We're plunged into a shadowy world and the density of the woodland cuts off the sounds of the surrounding village, the canopy of trees in full leaf takes the edge off the morning sun. It's a couple of degrees cooler in here.

'I want to ask you about the night your father disappeared,' I begin.

'There isn't much to say.'

'Will you let me try something out on you?'

'Like what?' she asks with a suspicious frown.

We walk out of the woods and onto the shingle of the shore.

'This was where your father's car was parked when he disappeared, wasn't it?'

Alison nods.

'I'm guessing you were on that road up there and you came down to the water's edge through that narrow road over there.' I point.

'It's the only way down to the lake.'

'Let's sit down here,' I say once we're close to the middle where I roughly remember the car being from Tania's blurred photographs. 'I want you to close your eyes and think back to when you were in the car on the night of the storm. Don't think of anything else. Just concentrate on the sound of my voice and the questions I'm asking you.'

'Okay.'

'Take me through that day. You went to see your gran – and left early, right?'

'That's right. Mum said that Gran told her, because of the storm coming, we should leave after we'd had our lunch.'

'Do you remember that?'

'I...' The fight to search her memory is etched on her face. 'I remember being strapped in the back of the car and driving through the rain. It seemed dark, darker than it should have been for the time of day.'

'Did your dad speak to you?'

'I... I don't know. I... Do you know something, I don't think he did.'

'Did he usually?'

'He usually had the radio on. We used to sing along.' There's a hint of a smile on her face.

'But it wasn't on going home?'

'No. We didn't have it on going, either. Understandable, really. He'd lost interest in a lot of things since Celia and Jennifer disappeared.' Her face tenses. The smile has gone, replaced by worry and fear.

'The road at the top of the lake, here, was that your usual route home?'

'No. We had no reason to come this way.'

'Why did you?'

'I don't… I don't know.'

'Did you say anything when you noticed your dad taking a different route?'

'No. I was…' she stops.

'What?'

'I was tired. I wanted to go to sleep. It was night after all.'

'No, Alison, it wasn't. It was mid-afternoon. It was dark because of the storm.'

'That's right.'

'So, you weren't tired?'

'I was. I can remember. I couldn't keep my eyes open.'

'You're sure?'

'Yes. I remember when I was being lifted out of the car. I was so tired.'

'That would have been your mum.'

'No. It was a man.'

'A man?'

'Yes.'

'Are you sure?'

'I'm positive.'

'Your mum said she lifted you out of the car.'

'No. It was Uncle Iain. I opened my eyes. The rain was in my face. He was wet and cold, and he had on this big blue coat that smelled of horses.'

'Horses?' I ask, distracted for a second. I wish my mind

would focus on one thing at a time. 'Do you remember your dad getting out of the car at all?'

'No,' Alison replies, firmly.

'You don't remember driving down onto the shingle and up to the edge of the lake?'

'No.'

'But you remember leaving your gran's house, and driving along the road when it was dark, and then your Uncle Iain lifting you out in the rain?'

'Yes. He handed me to my mum.'

'What happened then?'

'I remember getting into bed. Mum gave me a hot Vimto. I used to love that as a child.'

I smile. My mum used to make me a hot Vimto when I was off school poorly. I can't stand the stuff now, hot or cold, but the smell always prompts a happy memory.

'Can I open my eyes now?'

'Yes.' There's something strange happening here. There is no reason why Alison should have such a gap in her memory, or why she seems to have been so tired after leaving her gran's house in the middle of the day. The first thing that comes to mind is that she'd been drugged. Had Jack given his daughter something to make her sleep so he could leave her in the car without her crying and calling him to come back?

'I haven't helped, have I?' Alison asks.

'I'm not sure. What can you tell me of the following morning? What time did you get up?'

'I don't know.'

'Did your mum tell you that your father was missing?'

'I think so, yes. She told me he'd gone away. He wasn't feeling well. That's what she told me for a while.'

'What did you do that day?'

'I really don't remember much at all. I'm sorry.'

'It's okay. Don't try and force a memory. That will only make things worse.'

'Tell me what you're thinking,' Alison says. 'I can tell by your face that your mind is racing at a hundred miles per hour.'

I take a breath. 'I'll be perfectly honest with you, Alison. You could be suffering with false memories, getting your dates and events mixed up, which is reasonable and understandable. However, at the back of my mind, I'm wondering whether you might have been drugged.'

'What?' she exclaims. Her voice echoes around the open space. 'Drugged. Why? Who by?'

'Possibly by your father but, given the number of sightings of him over the years, that makes no sense. On the other hand, I'm starting to think your father is being painted as having a bigger role in the disappearance of your sisters, and he's actually perfectly innocent in all this.' I suddenly forget Alison is there. It's as if I'm just thinking aloud. 'Jack suffered with depression. Back then, it was seen as a weakness. It's possible someone could have taken advantage of that and used him as a scapegoat.'

'The sightings of my dad. They might not be my dad, might they?' Alison asks, her voice cracking with tears.

I look at her. 'What makes you say that?'

'It's been thirty years. If whoever it is has been living rough all that time, his appearance will have changed beyond all recognition. Maybe people are seeing a homeless man and assuming it's my dad because he's never been found.'

'Is that what you're thinking now? That the sightings are false.'

'I don't know.'

She looks despondent. The hope is fading from her eyes.

'Who do you talk to about your past?'

'I talk to my mum sometimes. We can't talk about it for long. It upsets her. Iain is more receptive to ideas and theories. He listens to me.'

'Does he offer theories of his own?'

'Sometimes. He thinks the sightings might be of Dad. He's angry with him. Still. Even after all this time. If it's Dad, I'd love him to make contact, but I'm worried what Uncle Iain will do if he sees him. He hates Dad. I think…'

'Go on,' I prompt her when she stops.

'I think Iain believes Dad killed Celia and Jennifer.'

'Is that what you think, too?'

'If he did, there's only one clear motive, isn't there?' She looks at me with tears running down her face. 'He abused them and killed them to cover up what he was doing. My dad was a child abuser. And if that's true, I have to ask myself if he abused me, too. And I can't remember, Matilda. I can't remember anything.'

Alison collapses into me and I hold her tight. It's not the right time to tell her my theory that the mystery man might not be her father but could be Travis Montgomery. But then, I suppose it doesn't matter which one of them it is. If whoever it is was abusing the twins and possibly abused Alison, they've been lurking on the periphery all this time for a very dark reason which may come to light now that the girls have been found.

A dele Kean is not happy. Sitting behind the wheel of her Porsche 911, she looks around at the mess. The floor is littered with crumbs and dog hair. There are scuff marks on the front passenger seat and the steering wheel is sticky. There is also an underlying smell of something Adele can't quite put her finger on, but the screwed-up McDonald's paper bag in the side pocket of the door gives a hint of what it could be. She shakes her head. Matilda is definitely a changed woman. She was always so particular about her own car. The stress, anxiety, and depression she's currently going through are taking over her life. Everything else takes a back seat, including hygiene. She hopes this investigation into the Pemberton twins she's working on will help pull her out of her slump and show her that, despite her loss, life continues.

She reaches across to the glove box and pulls it open, hoping the packet of wet wipes she keeps inside are still there. As she reaches in, her hand touches Matilda's iPhone. She notices it still hasn't been looked through: all the notifications are still showing on the locked screen. Matilda must have hidden it in there on the way back to the restaurant yesterday.

'Sneaky cow,' Adele says to herself.

Steering wheel wiped, Adele sets off, leaving the restaurant and the Lake District behind her. She's heading for Royal Preston Hospital where the remains of Celia and Jennifer Pemberton have been taken. The postmortem has been carried out by Dr Boyd Hailstones, a man Adele has crossed paths with several times over the years. They've become good friends and often share research and information. During the Manchester Arena bombing in 2017, Adele and Boyd worked tirelessly together on all twenty-three victims.

Boyd is happy to see Adele when she breezes through the double doors to the post-mortem suite. They haven't met for more than three years and they have both changed dramatically in their appearances.

'You're thin,' she says, standing back and marvelling at the new, svelte Dr Hailstones.

'I had to do something,' he says in a thick Scottish burr, slapping a hand to his flat stomach. 'I caught Covid during the first wave. It completely floored me. I've had a complete lifestyle change. I still drink like a fish, obviously, but no more red meat and processed foods for me.'

'Good for you,' she beams.

'Look at you, though, you're tanned.'

'It'll soon fade.'

'I thought you were in Sierra Leone.'

'Personal circumstances have brought me back.'

'I read about DCI Darke in the news. How's she coping?'

'The jury's still out.'

'So, how come you're involved in this Pemberton case?'

Adele rolls her eyes. 'It's a long story, Boyd.'

'I've got all the time in the world. Come on through, I'll put the kettle on.'

Over a mug of tea, they swap life stories. Adele tells Boyd about her boyfriend being a serial killer, and he tells her about his new post in Newcastle starting early next year. Then they get down to the reason for Adele's visit.

Boyd opens a file on his computer and brings up the photographs of the skeletons of the two young girls side by side on the stainless-steel gurney. Their bones have been placed in order to form two full bodies. Having seen photographs of the girls when they were alive, it's sad to see them like this and think of their lives cut so horribly short.

'What can you tell me?' Adele asks, not taking her eyes from the screen.

'Very little.'

'I thought as much.'

'I can't tell you if they were sexually abused. I can't tell you if they were tied up or strangled or drowned or stabbed or shot. I can tell you they were healthy before they were killed and had excellent teeth. That's how we identified them, by the way. Celia had a filling on an upper molar. What I can tell you is that Celia Pemberton suffered blunt force trauma to the back of her head,' he says, selecting another file which shows a close-up image of her skull. There is a clear hole in the right parietal.

'She was hit on the head with something?'

'Possibly. Whatever was used was heavy enough to break the skull. A blow like this to a person who is alive would render them unconscious and in urgent need of medical assistance. Without that assistance, they wouldn't be alive for much longer.'

'What about Jennifer?'

'No blow to the head at all. Her bones are all intact. We're missing the phalanges of the toes on both, but that's common from a body left to the elements for thirty years.'

'Anything else you can tell me?'

'Yes, actually. Jennifer suffered a broken arm that didn't

heal correctly,' he says, pointing out a close-up of the right radius of her skeleton. 'I requested the medical records which nobody could find, unfortunately, but the coroner's office contacted the mother, and she said Jennifer never broke her arm. None of the girls did.'

'How long before she died did she break it?'

'A few months. Six at the most,' he muses. 'It's healed, but like I said, not properly.'

'She would have been in pain, though, surely?'

'Not necessarily. I broke three ribs while skiing a few years ago. It was months before I was x-rayed. I just thought I was bruised.'

'A girl with a broken bone and not taken to hospital sounds like evidence of a cover-up. How can a mother not notice?' Adele asks, speaking aloud more than seeking an answer from the doctor.

'Maybe she didn't want to notice,' Boyd says, a dark tone to his voice.

Adele shakes her head. 'I don't like people who turn a blind eye to abuse.'

'Me neither. In my experience, people who turn a blind eye do so for two reasons. One, they don't want to acknowledge it exists, or two, they're complicit in the abuse themselves.'

Adele suddenly feels very sick.

The restaurant is quiet. I stand in front of the Gaggia and I'm almost thinking about trying again to make myself a strong Americano when I hear the crunching of gravel outside. I recognise the sound of the whistling brakes and look out of the window to see Sally pulling into her usual space. From this angle, I can just about see that Philip is in the front passenger seat.

'How are you feeling?' I ask as I run down the steps to greet him. He looks fine; his normal self, dressed in jeans and a creased long-sleeve polo shirt. His eyes are droopy from lack of sleep and his thinning hair could do with a brush, but apart from that, he looks well.

'I'm okay,' he smiles. 'You?'

'I'm fine. Are you sure you're all right?'

'As I've told Sally every two minutes since leaving hospital, I'm absolutely fine.'

'The ward sister said he was the worst patient she's seen in her twenty-year career,' Sally adds.

'Let me guess: you were complaining about the food?'

Philip rolls his eyes. 'The toast was yellow and clock-cold. I've no idea what animal the meat I was given for lunch yesterday came from, but I don't think it was meant to be for human consumption.'

I pull a face. 'Eww.'

'By the way, I've ordered some new cameras for the restaurant. I never really wanted those cages up. They'd look too institutional. These ones are more sophisticated and can be hidden. Nobody will know they're there.'

'Shouldn't you have been resting?'

'That's what I was telling him,' Sally says scathingly, as she takes his overnight bag from the boot.

Philip makes his way up the steps to the restaurant.

'I've ordered them on a rush delivery. I want to find out who is trying to sabotage my restaurant,' he says.

I hold back from following, and look to Sally. 'Are you sure he's all right?'

'Oh, he's fine, physically. I'm just worried he's going to turn this place into Fort Knox. I'm expecting him to start interviewing for armed guards on the door any day now.'

'Has he thought about a metal detector in the doorway like they have at airports for customers to walk through?'

'I haven't lost my hearing, you know,' Philip calls out. 'Sarky mares.'

We follow him into the restaurant and find him at the coffee machine.

'Matilda, would you like a cup?'

'Silly question,' Sally mutters as she heads for the stairs to take Philip's bag up to the bedroom.

'Have the police said anything useful?' Philip asks.

I pull out a stool and sit at the bar which runs along the back wall of the restaurant.

'No. Typical. You know what police are like.'

'You do realise you are still one of them, when you've finished pulling them to bits?'

'My team excluded, obviously.' I'm still calling them my team, I notice. 'Anyway, forensics came out and did their usual thing. No prints were left behind. No footprints or tyre tracks outside. CCTV didn't reveal anything either.'

'Sally told me they'd been moved again. These new ones won't be easily tampered with,' he says as he passes me a cup of strong black coffee.

I inhale and feel myself instantly relax at the hit.

A thought enters my mind. I sit back and frown as I mull over what it could possibly mean. I look around me, taking in the door leading out into the car park, the door to the kitchen and stairs going to the flat above, and the door the intruder came out of the night before and attacked us both.

'What is it?' Philip asks.

'The burglar came through the back door, right?'

'Right.'

'He came in here and he came out of that door over there, when we entered this part of the restaurant, right?'

'Yes. So?'

'Well, to get this far, he had to pass the storage room where you keep your booze, the bar, here, where you've got those bottles of wine and whisky lined up, and the till where you keep the cash and card machines. He left all that and went through that door. Why?'

'I've no idea. He didn't hang around for me to ask him.'

'Apart from leading to the basement, what else is through that door?'

'Nothing.'

'So, only the stairs down into the cellar you're going to renovate?'

'Yes.'

'Huh.'

'What?'

'What else is down there apart from an empty room with damp?'

'Nothing. It's a shell of a room. And it doesn't have damp. It just smells like it does.'

'In that case, why did the intruder go down there? He didn't have a bag with him, so he wasn't planning on stealing anything. Why did he pass all this expensive stuff and go down into an empty room?'

Philip's eyes widen. 'Do you think he took something down there?'

'I'm not sure. It's possible.'

'Like what?'

'I don't know.'

'Something that would stop my renovations, that could possibly get me closed down?' He places his own cup on the bar and heads for the door to the basement.

'Where are you going?'

'To have a look. What if he's put a dead rat down there? Or worse, a live one. I don't want Carl going down there and finding it. I don't want bloody health and safety going down there.'

'Jesus!' I exclaim as I follow.

Philip leads the way, pushes open the door and begins to descend the stone steps. There's an underlying smell of damp, though it's possibly due to the fact this room hasn't been used much over the past couple of decades. There's no lighting so Philip pulls his phone out of his back pocket, turns on the torch and points it to the ground so we can see where we step.

At the bottom of the steps, he points the phone all around the floor. There is nothing there. A few plastic crates stacked in the corner, but no rotting rodents, nothing anyone from the health and safety department could object to should they wish to make a snap inspection.

I remain still at the bottom of the stairs. I'm not a fan of basements. I've developed claustrophobia since being kidnapped. I always need to be able to see a way out of a room and, as the cellar only has one exit, I remain where I can look up the stairs and see the door leading to daylight. My breathing has become shallow.

'I'm sure this place will look charming when it's finished,' I say, trying to make light of my mental battle.

Philip is walking around the vast space. 'I just... I can't understand why the intruder came down here when there's nothing here. There's nothing for him to take, and he left nothing.'

I draw in a deep, shaky breath. 'Is there any chance of some decent lighting down here?' I'd feel better if I could see the far wall, at least. The total darkness is making me feel more penned in than I really am.

'I've got one of the arc lights upstairs in the storage room. Will that do?'

'Yes.'

'I'll go up and—'

'I'll go,' I interrupt. I turn and scramble back up the stairs. I can't leave the basement fast enough.

I find the light with ease and also a long extension cable. I plug it in and bring it down with me. Immediately, the room is transformed as it's lit up with a brilliant white light. I feel instantly better and can breathe now I can fully see the dimensions of the room.

'It's bigger than I thought.'

'I know. It'll make a great wine-tasting space.'

Philip continues to talk, to share his vision, while I head for the back wall, the wall that Carl said will make a picture window overlooking the lake. I press the palm of my hand flat against the cold brick. I look up to the corner. My eye travels along the ceiling and down the other side.

'Have you had anyone down here?'

'Sorry?'

'Have you had any builders or anyone down here?'

'Not yet, no. I've spoken to Warren in the village. He was going to come down last week and measure it, but the storm has made him very busy with repairs. Why?'

'This is a false wall.'

'What?'

'This back wall is false.'

'What do you mean?'

'When you're building a wall, the bricks dovetail in the corners to add strength and stop them from falling over. These don't do that. Look.'

Philip looks up into the corner and spots the bricks sitting perfectly in a row.

'Oh yes. How do you know that?'

'My husband was an architect. He also very nearly knocked down our house when he was doing the renovations. I made sure I knew exactly what he was doing after that. Someone has built a wall in front of the original wall.'

'Why would they do that?'

'I've no idea.'

'You mean, behind there is a recess of some kind?'

'Possibly. I don't know how big it is. You'd need to measure the inside, then the outside, and you'd be able to calculate your discrepancy.'

'It can't be that big or I would have noticed before now.'

'True.'

'Why would anyone want to put up a false wall? I mean, what could be behind there?'

'I may have been in the police too long, because the first thing that came to my mind was a dead body.'

'The first thing I thought of was buried treasure.'

'Which makes you childish and me ghoulish.'

'Where do we go from here?' Philip asks after a long silence.

'Looking for a hammer and chisel.'

Iain Pemberton is a creature of habit. He has set times for doing set jobs. One of his regular jobs is popping along to the stables mid-evening to check the horses one final time. Alison uses this knowledge, waits until he's far enough way, so it doesn't look as if she's waiting for him to leave the house before approaching the front door and knocking.

'Oh, hello. I didn't expect you,' Lynne says, stepping back and allowing her daughter to enter.

Alison gives her mother a succinct smile. She has spent the day thinking about her past, her childhood, since talking to Matilda Darke, and everything she thought about she needed to have clarified by her mother. Is it possible she had been drugged on the night her father disappeared? If so, why? The only explanation she could come up with was that she'd been drugged so she could be sexually abused by someone. The only people she remembered seeing that day were her mother, father and grandmother. Had her father drugged and raped her? Had he hated himself for what he'd done to her, to her sisters, and then walked away, never to be seen again?

The sofa is back in the living room, the floorboards having dried out. There are various carpet swatches on the coffee table. Lynne explains that she's decided to have the entire ground floor redecorated and wants to have a radical change rather than stick to the safe variations of beige and cream that she's had in the past. Unfortunately, she and Iain can't yet come to a decision on a colour scheme.

'I get the feeling decorating the living room is going to have the same intensity of debate as the *Strictly* final,' she laughs. 'Is everything all right? You look… I don't know, you look like you're in pain,' she says, noticing her daughter's discomfort.

'I want to ask you something, Mum. It's not easy.'

'Oh,' is all Lynne can say. 'You can say anything to me, Alison, you know that.'

'I know. It's just… It's not a nice subject to talk about.'

'Is there something wrong? Is it work?'

'No. Mum, let me get there in my own time, please,' she says, struggling to find the words, and the tone.

'Sorry. Of course. You… go ahead.'

The atmosphere in the room plummets as Lynne sits on a knife edge, glaring at her daughter, taking in the pale face, the uncomfortable position, refusing to make eye contact with her mother, and the look as if she's about to be sick.

'I was talking to Matilda Darke this morning,' she begins. 'We spoke about Travis and Celia and Jennifer and, well, things have been uncovered that are shocking, to say the least. It's got me thinking and I've spent all day asking myself all kinds of questions, but I don't have the answers.' A tear falls which she quickly wipes away. 'I've been looking online, and it's possible to go through a traumatic event and not even remember it. I mean, I don't even remember the night Dad went missing, and I was there with him in the car—'

'You were only five, Alison,' Lynne interrupts.

'I know. But he was my dad. You and him were the most important people in my life. I relied on you. You'd think I'd remember the last time I saw him.' She wipes away more tears, reaches forward and whips a tissue out of the box on the coffee table.

'Alison, I've told you…'

'No, Mum, please, let me speak.'

'Okay.'

Alison takes a breath and composes herself. She looks up at her mother. 'Mum, was I sexually abused as a child?'

'Oh my God!' Lynne says. She starts to cry.

Alison leaps up and goes over to her. She sits on the arm of the chair and puts her arms around her, holding her tight.

'Mum, I don't mean to upset you with all this. It's just… if Celia and Jennifer were abused, was I abused, too? That's what I need to know, Mum.'

It's a while before Lynne speaks.

'Sweetheart,' she says, holding onto Alison's hands tightly. 'I've been asking myself the same things for the last thirty years. I always knew that, if Celia and Jennifer had been kidnapped, it was by someone who wanted to do them harm. I mean, why else would you take them? When you said Celia waved at you from the back of the car and was smiling, I knew that it had to have been someone they knew, someone I knew. Alison, I can't answer your questions. I don't know if you were abused. I pray to God that you weren't. I just… I just don't know.'

'I've remembered something,' Alison says. 'Well, I think I've remembered something. We left Gran's because of the storm, but when we left it was daylight. The next thing I remember is being picked up out of the car and it was pitch-dark.'

'It was early evening, but with the storm, it was as black as night,' Lynne says.

'But I was asleep. I never sleep in cars.'

Lynne shrugs.

'You always told me it was you who lifted me out of the car, but I remember a man in dripping waterproofs picking me up. Who was that?'

'I don't know, Alison,' Lynne says. She stands up and goes to the window. 'It was so long ago. I don't… I just remember seeing the car and jumping out of Iain's truck and running towards it. Maybe Iain picked you up and he handed you to me. I honestly can't remember. I was just so relieved you were all right.'

'What happened the next day?'

Lynne turns back from the window. 'What?'

'The next day? What happened? I have no memory of it.'

'We'd called the police as soon as we got you back home, but they were so busy with the storm. It wasn't until the next morning when someone came out to the house and a search began.'

'Where was I?'

'You… you were in bed.'

'All day?'

'Most of it.'

'Why?'

'You were tired. You'd been through an ordeal.'

'No, Mum, I hadn't. I was asleep in the back of the car. When I was picked up, I was half asleep. Then you put me to bed with a hot Vimto. I remember all that now. From my point of view, there was no ordeal. Why was I asleep for the following day?'

Lynne looks at her blankly.

'Mum, was I drugged?'

'What?'

'On the night of the storm, was I drugged? Did someone drug me and rape me?'

Lynne crumbles. She almost bends in two as emotions grip her like a vice. Alison runs to her and holds her in her arms.

'I'm so sorry, Mum, but I need to know what happened to me as a child,' she cries.

'I've told you everything I know, Alison,' Lynne screeches through her tears. 'I'm so sorry I wasn't able to protect you. Please forgive me.'

Alison holds her mother carefully. She hasn't received the words of comfort she had hoped for. She hasn't received the harsh, naked truth. In fact, she's left with more questions, and she doubts she'll ever get the answers to them. Despite her mother's clear distress, Alison has the dark feeling there is something that is being kept from her. Surely, the day after the storm, with Alison feeling tired, a doctor would have been called. Had one come out to the house and diagnosed signs that she'd been drugged and possibly raped? Just what is everyone hiding from her and how the hell is she going to find out the truth?

Philip Meagan knows that, if he begins tearing down a wall while his son is at school and misses all the excitement, his life won't be worth living. So, with tools bought from the local hardware shop, he waits until Carl is home before telling him of their plans for the evening once the restaurant is closed. Before Carl can even ask, Philip tells him, yes, he can stay up past his bedtime.

Like most Thursdays, business is slow in Nature's Diner, and Sally asks me and Adele to have dinner in the restaurant to give the illusion they're busy. A free meal is never to be refused so we accept and dress for the occasion. Sally comes to the rescue once again and furnishes us with evening wear from her vast collection. We're like two little girls playing dress-up with their mother's wardrobe.

We sit in the window of the restaurant. I'm wearing a figure-hugging dress with thin straps.

'I know inside you're probably a mess,' Adele says. 'But from the outside, you look so healthy. The outdoors obviously suits you.'

'Running and swimming seem to be the only things that

stop the screams in my head. I still cry but I can't tell what are tears and what's sweat pouring down my face.'

'I still can't believe it,' Adele says. 'Penny. Joseph and Nathan. How can someone do something like that? And for what?'

'To get at me.'

'But why? What have you done wrong that someone believes the answer is to kill…?' She can't bring herself to finish the question.

'If I knew the answer to that I'd know who'd done it.'

'How is the team getting on in finding the killer?'

I shrug.

'If you looked at your phone, you might find out.'

I turn away and look out of the window, so I can't see the look of disappointment on Adele's face.

'You can't keep running away, Mat.' She picks up her wine and takes a lengthy sip. 'Sian phoned me this afternoon.'

'Matilda!'

I whip my head around to see who's calling me, thankful of a distraction from a conversation I don't want to have. Tania Pritchard has breezed into the restaurant and is heading my way. She stops at a table to say hello to someone she knows.

'Gorgeous shade on your hair, Jean. Say hello to your Keith for me.'

She finally reaches our table.

'You're looking very posh. I almost didn't recognise you. Not interrupting anything, am I?' she asks, looking at Adele.

'No. This is Adele. The pathologist I was telling you about. Adele Kean, this is Tania Pritchard. The only journalist I've ever met who isn't a complete wanker.'

'I think that's the best introduction I've ever had,' Tania smiles. 'Hello Adele, nice to meet you.'

'And you.' Adele holds her hand out for Tania to shake.

'Better not. I had to change a tyre on my way over here. I'm all oily. I've just been to see Lynne and Iain. I spoke to Claire, and she told me about the results of the postmortems on Celia and Jennifer. Apparently, Jennifer had a broken bone in her arm not long before she died, and it hadn't healed properly. According to Lynne, she didn't know anything about it. How can a mother not notice that? If you ask me…'

'Tania, are you eating?' Sally calls out.

Tania pulls an agonised face, as if she's struggling to decide. 'I'm not sure. Is that butter chicken on the specials board?'

'Not tonight, sorry. We've got some beef medallions.'

'You've twisted my arm. Can you box me up a serving?'

'Will do.'

Tania turns back to the table. 'Have you had the butter chicken? My goodness. I don't know what they do to a chicken breast in that kitchen, but I bet it's illegal in some countries. Now, where was I?'

'Jennifer's broken bone,' I tell her.

'Oh, yes. Now, either Lynne knew her daughters were being abused and turned a blind eye, or she was part of it. What do you think?'

'I don't know. I can't read Lynne and Iain at all. They're both so closed.'

'Given everything they've been through over the years, you can understand that. I think Iain might know more than he's letting on, too. He hardly said a word when I went round. And he didn't offer me a drink. I don't think he wanted to leave me in the living room on my own with Lynne.'

'Why wouldn't he want you on your own with her?'

'I don't know. Maybe in case she said something to me he doesn't want me to know.'

'They're a strange couple. I can get my head around Lynne being in pain with her daughters being discovered so close to home, but she radiates a sadness that is deeply rooted. I think it goes back decades. If so, why did she get married to Iain?'

'For a final stab at happiness, maybe,' Tania said.

'It clearly didn't work.'

'She wasn't to know that.'

'But Lynne told me that Iain was her first love. Surely, you'd be happy marrying your first love after the horror you've been through.' I take a sip of wine. I haven't eaten yet, so I feel it making me lightheaded. 'I was thinking about this in the shower. Lynne told me Iain wasn't the settling-down type, so she went with Jack who obviously was. She also said she desperately wanted children, and that Iain can't have kids. I'm wondering if she actually dumped Iain for Jack, just so she could have a baby.'

'That's a bit sick, isn't it?' Adele asks. 'Dumping a bloke and going with his brother so you can have a child.'

I look over my shoulder to make sure I'm not being overheard and lower my voice. 'Lynne told me her revised statement to the police, where she said she was in bed with Travis, was wrong. She was actually sleeping with Iain. It's possible that she and Iain never split up in the first place and she went with Jack just to have a child.'

'You think they were a throuple?' Tania asks.

'Nothing so modern. Perhaps Jack didn't realise, while he was married to Lynne and seemingly living a blissfully happy life, she was still seeing Iain. It was the best of both worlds for all of them.'

'It's a bit incestuous, isn't it?' Adele pulls a face.

'Looking back,' Tania begins. 'Iain and Lynne were always more suited than Jack and Lynne. I remember being a couple of rows behind them in the pictures once – this is Iain and Lynne

I'm talking about – and they were paying Mel Gibson no attention whatsoever, if you know what I mean. Mind you, I was. I still go weak at the knees when I watch *Mad Max*. I've always been a sucker for a man in leather.'

Sally comes over with a white box and hands it to Tania, telling her to be careful as the plate inside is hot. Tania hands her a bank card. 'Slap that on your fancy card machine, Sal. I had another thought as well on my way over here,' she says, turning back to us. 'Oh, wait, it's gone. I knew I should have written it down. Oh, no, wait, I've remembered now. It's about the sightings of Jack. What if they are really sightings of Travis?'

'I thought that, too,' I admit.

'Oh. I thought I was being too clever for my own good with that one. Still, it's something else to give ourselves a sleepless night. Anyway, I'll let you enjoy your meal, and I'll report back in the morning, if I've managed to make any sense of anything. Nice to meet you,' she says to Adele. 'Bye, Mat.' She breezes through the restaurant, taking her bank card from Sally and waving goodbye to the people she knows.

'Does she always talk like she's about to run out of oxygen?' Adele asks.

'I think this is the first major story she's had in thirty years and she's remembering why she became a journalist in the first place.' I look out of the window and watch her walk at pace to her Punto. 'I feel sorry for her.'

'I was watching you while you were talking. You were back in full DCI mode for a while.'

'It's my job.'

'Still?'

I'm saved from answering that by Sally coming to the table with our meals. Mushroom risotto for Adele and Thai salmon cakes for me.

'There you go, ladies. Enjoy.'

We eat in silence for a while.

'As I was saying, I spoke to Sian,' Adele says. 'Everyone is worried about you. She's told me everyone has texted and emailed, and you haven't got back to them. Why are you avoiding them?'

'I'm not avoiding them. I've read my emails. I…'

'I'm not daft. You left your phone in my car.'

'Ah.'

'That's the first time you've ever lied to me.'

'I'm sorry. I'll be honest with you, I don't know what's going on in here right now,' I say, tapping my temple. 'I want to know what's going on, but I don't. I want to find out who killed my family, but I'm scared of what I'll do when I do. I'm trying to protect myself, yet at the same time I want to destroy myself. I've got too many conflicting emotions going on and I don't know how to address them.'

'Bloody hell, Mat,' Adele says, reaching across and placing a hand on top of mine. 'Why didn't you tell me any of this?'

'How can I tell you when I can't make sense of it myself? It's all chaos.'

We stare at each other in silence, neither of us knowing what to say next. I pick up my knife and fork and attack my salmon cakes. I'm not hungry, though.

'Who's Helen Walsh?' Adele asks.

Adele has obviously read my emails. I can't be mad at her. I'd have done the same if the tables were turned. I wish the table was turned; her risotto looks delicious.

'She's the mother of the first victim. It was believed her son, Liam, killed himself by jumping off a building. It turns out he was pushed.'

'Why is she emailing you so much?'

'I said I'd keep her informed of what's going on with the

investigation. Liam was all she had. She was struggling to come to terms with his suicide, so when I told her he'd been murdered, well…'

'The number of emails she's sending you is bordering on stalking.'

'She's grieving. She's angry. She's trying to make sense of the madness.'

'Sound familiar?' Adele raises a single eyebrow.

'I can't help her.'

'You can.'

'And what about me? Who's going to help me?' My tone is laced with dark emotion. There are tears in my voice.

'I am. Sian is. Then there's Christian, Scott, Finn, Donal, Odell. Sally and Philip and Carl. Don't sit there and tell me you're all alone, because you're not. You've got people around you to help, to support, people who love you who will come running the minute you snap your fingers. Who has this Helen Walsh got? She's got you. She's counting on you because you promised her.'

I'm fully crying now. I can't help it. I know I've got supportive people around me who will help, but for so long I've been the strong one. If people see my vulnerabilities, I'm worried they'll think less about me.

'Matilda, look at me.'

Reluctantly, I look up.

'Let me take you back to Sheffield.'

'I plan on going back.'

Adele visibly relaxes. 'Oh. Good. That's good. You're making the right decision.'

'I have one condition.'

'Go on.'

'We have to find out what happened to Celia and Jennifer Pemberton first.'

'It's been thirty years. You might never find out.'

'Then I'd better have my post redirected,' I say, turning my attention back to my salmon cakes.

P hilip closed Nature's Diner early. By ten o'clock there was only me and Adele left as customers. Sally came over and swiped up my plate just as I took the last mouthful of pistachio mousse cake. She even made a grab for my coffee cup before I batted her hand away.

'I've had a husband and a son badgering me every five minutes for the past six hours about knocking that sodding wall down. The sooner its done, the sooner I can go to bed and the sooner I get rid of this bloody headache.' She marches back towards the kitchen.

'What is it about men and knocking things down?' Adele asks.

'It makes them feel manly and masculine.'

'What makes women feel feminine, then?'

'Taking the hammer and chisel from the men and showing them how it's done,' I grin.

We go upstairs to change into clothes we're happy to see covered in dust. Something is niggling away in my brain. I grab Adele's mobile and hunt for Alison's number that I've scrawled down on a bit of paper. She answers almost straight away.

'Alison, sorry for calling so late.'

'It's fine,' she says. There are tears in her voice. She's been crying.

'Is everything all right?'

She sighs. 'Yes. I'm… I'm fine. What can I do for you?'

It's like I'm talking to a younger version of myself.

'I've been able to get the preliminary postmortem results on your sisters. They've managed to identify them through dental records. It seems Jennifer had a broken bone in her arm that didn't heal correctly. Your mother was asked, and she said she didn't know anything about your sister ever breaking a bone. I find that hard to believe unless it was covered up in some way. Is there…'

'Ah. I think I can fill in the gap there,' Alison said. 'It happened about a month or so before they disappeared. We were out playing one Sunday on the farm. There was an old coal bunker we were told never to go in. To mischievous children, that's like an invitation. So, obviously, we went in. Jennifer slipped and fell. She cracked her arm on the concrete floor. We all agreed not to say anything because we knew how much shit we'd be in. I didn't realise her arm was broken. I thought she'd just hurt it.'

'Right.'

'You thought she'd broken it while being abused or something?'

'It had crossed my mind.'

'We were adventurous when we were all together. We loved making up stories and going on imaginary hunts for treasure. Jennifer had such a…' She pauses as she composes herself. 'She was an excellent storyteller.'

I sit down on the edge of the bed. 'I'm so sorry for what you're going through, Alison.'

'It never goes away,' she says. 'I can be on a night out

celebrating a friend's birthday, and I'm laughing and having fun, and all of a sudden a voice in my head will ask me what Jennifer or Celia would be doing right now, if they were still alive, and it floors me.'

I don't know what to say. Alison is looking for answers, for reassurance, and I can't give them to her. I make some excuse about it being late and end the call.

There is no doubt in my mind I'll be able to find out what happened to Jennifer and Celia. I know I can solve this. I'm only worried about the effect it will have on Alison when she learns the truth.

By the time we descend the steps to the cellar, Philip, Sally, Carl and the two Labradors, are waiting for us. Carl, dressed in jeans and an oversized jumper and wearing safety glasses, has a huge smile on his face.

'About bloody time,' Carl says.

'Language!' Sally chastises.

'This feels like the unveiling of something. I'm expecting a Lord Mayor to come down the stairs to cut a ribbon,' Adele says.

'I'm nervous,' Sally says. 'I've seen *The Mummy*. I know what happens when you disturb something that's not meant to be disturbed.' Her eyes are constantly gazing about the room, looking for anything scurrying along the ground.

'Are you worried Philip is going to unleash thousands of years of bad luck and pestilence?' I ask.

'Considering everything we've all been through recently, including a sodding pandemic, I wouldn't be surprised.'

'Language!' Carl mocks. 'It might be the entrance to a secret underground tomb,' he says excitedly.

Sally shivers. 'I'm picturing those beetles in *The Mummy* that get inside your skin.'

'Really?' Adele asks. 'I'm picturing Kenneth Williams in *Carry On Screaming* howling "Frying tonight!"'

Sally laughs. 'I love that film.'

Philip exaggerates a cough. 'Is there any chance we can begin? I do plan on retiring in the next twenty years.'

'In this economy? You'll be lucky,' I fire back.

'Sorry, Phil. You begin. We'll stay back here and point out where you're going wrong.' Sally winks.

Philip shakes his head and rolls his eyes. He's seriously outnumbered. He unfolds a step ladder and places it in the corner of the room. He climbs up, hammer and chisel in hand, and begins chipping away at the cement between the bricks.

It's a slow process, but once he gets started passing the bricks down to me one by one, a large hole is soon revealed. He takes a torch from me, turns it on and looks inside.

'It only goes back a few metres. If that,' he says. He reaches inside. 'I can almost touch the back wall.'

'Can you see down to the floor?' I ask.

He leans inside and tries to look down. 'No. Not yet. I'll need to take more bricks out.'

'Why would you build another wall so close to the existing one?' Sally asks Adele from the back of the room.

'I don't know. Unless... is it possible it's a load-bearing wall? Could the structure be weak so that was built to hold up the ceiling?'

'And we're calmly taking it down while sitting beneath it ready to get crushed?' Sally asks, fear entering her voice.

'We're not exactly being sensible, are we?'

'When we bought the place, the surveyors said the structure was sound,' Philip reassures them.

'They didn't notice the false wall, though, did they?'

More bricks are removed and handed down to me. I hand them to Carl who is placing them, neatly, in the corner of the room. When the hole is large enough for Philip to lean fully into, he asks for the torch once again.

'Well? Anything?' I ask.

Philip looks back at his wife. 'Sal, maybe you should take Carl up.'

'Why?' she asks.

'No. I've been waiting for this all night. I want to see what's behind there. Is it anything valuable?'

Philip descends the steps, hands me the torch and tells me to take a look. Reluctantly, I do. On the top step, reaching up on tiptoe, I lean over and look into the black. I shine the torch down and look into the empty eyes of a leathered skull. I look up and down the small space and see a mummified body laid out on the ground.

'I knew she was going to be trouble the first time I heard she was in the area. You know what they're calling her online – the angel of death.'

Inspector Gill Forsyth is seething. She has received a call from Sally Meagan at Nature's Diner telling her a skeleton has been found in their basement. Gill has just sunk her third glass of Rioja and doesn't feel she should drive. She calls her sergeant, Alan Stokes, and asks him to come and pick her up. She knows he won't be happy about being called out, but he's a teetotal and has no choice.

'First the storm, then the girls in the lake, and now a bloody body in the cellar.'

'I hardly think she can be blamed for the storm,' Alan says.

'No. But I can blame her for bringing her bad karma to my doorstep. Why couldn't she have stayed in Sheffield where she belongs?'

Alan pulls into the restaurant car park and finds a space next to a marked police car and a CSI van.

'So, who do we reckon this body belongs to?' Alan asks as he climbs out of the car.

'I've no idea. But seeing as Matilda Darke is involved, it

could be anyone from Lord Lucan to Jack the Ripper. I'd even put money on it being Jesus,' Gill says as she makes her way to the steps of the restaurant.

We're sitting at different tables. Philip and Sally at one, Carl at another with the two dogs excitedly wagging their tails and, at the next table to him, me and Adele are sharing a bottle of wine. Gill enters the restaurant. Her eyes fall on me straight away and give me a dirty look.

'Mr Meagan, I don't know what to say. I'm incredibly sorry,' Gill says.

'Thank you.'

'Just to be clear, why were you hacking away at a solid brick wall late into the night?'

'To see what was behind it. I've already given a statement to one of your officers. It was Matilda who noticed it was a false wall.'

'I'm sure it was,' Gill says, an icy tone to her voice, as she looks over to me again.

'My husband was an architect,' I explain. 'I recognised the brickwork as not being that of an external wall.'

'You really are a mine of information,' Gill says. 'And you are?' she asks, turning her attention to Adele.

'Dr Adele Kean.'

'Oh, you're the one who's been pumping Dr Hailstones for information about the girls in the lake.'

'Dr Hailstones?' Carl laughs. 'What kind of a name is that?'

'It's Scottish,' I say.

'A fount of knowledge on the history of surnames, too, it would seem,' Gill says.

'Inspector, could you come downstairs for a moment,

please?' a man in a paper forensic suit asks from the doorway to the cellar.

Gill walks away, a bitter expression on her face.

'Aww, it's nice to see you've made a friend while you've been here,' Adele says, sarcastically.

The way to the cellar is lit up with brilliant white arc lights. At the top of the stairs, Gill changes into a forensic suit and walks down with a hand over her eyes to shadow them from the glare. In the windowless room of the basement, the light is more intrusive than usual.

A team of CSIs is gathering any evidence from the floor while a ladder has been placed against the back wall, half of which is lying in bricks on the floor. A head appears from the other side.

'Ah, Inspector Forsyth,' Crime Scene Manager Louise Brocklebank says, pulling herself up. 'Your new friend is certainly keeping us busy.'

'She's no friend of mine,' Gill hurriedly says. 'What have you found?'

'Another piece in your cold case jigsaw. There's a man back here fully clothed with a gaudy gold-plated watch and a wallet full of identification.'

'Go on.'

'All signs point to this being Jack Pemberton.'

'Jesus! So much for all those sightings over the years,' Gill says, squeezing the bridge of her nose. 'You're definitely sure it's him?'

'Not at all. You'll need DNA to confirm that. But there's a watch engraved with his name and a wallet with a credit card and driver's licence all bearing his name. I've requested a forensic pathologist to come out and take a look, but he's coming all the way from Manchester so it's going to be tomorrow before he gets here.'

'Can you tell how he died?'

'Not so far.'

'Was he dead before the wall was bricked up?'

'You're asking the wrong person.'

'Can you tell me anything?' Gill asks, her voice growing louder with frustration.

'Yes. I can tell you there is a body back here and all signs point to him being Jack Pemberton. That's all you're getting from me,' Brocklebank says, testily.

'Shit!' Gill spits.

'Brian, where are you with the camera?' Louise calls out from behind the brick wall.

'This flash is buggered. You're not going to get anything from this. I'm going to have to go back home to pick up a new one.'

'What's wrong?' Gill asks.

'I dropped my flash down the stairs,' Brian says, giving a 'oops' smile.

'I'm coming back up,' Louise calls out. 'I'm getting cramp here.'

'We'll have an officer posted outside. Tomorrow morning, we'll get a full team down here and a decent set of lights,' Gill says.

'My plans for tonight have been buggered up anyway. So much for date night,' Louise says, dusting herself down.

Gill turns to Alan. 'Call Claire. She was moaning earlier that Geraint is on nights and she's alone in the house. She can babysit the body. But tell her to keep her mouth shut. This goes no further.'

'Alison, sorry, did I wake you?' Claire asks. She's in her bedroom, mobile tucked into the crick of her neck while she changes from her pyjamas into her uniform.

'No. I was in the bath. What's up?'

'I've just had a call from Stokes. You'll never guess what's been found in the basement of Nature's Diner.'

Claire looks at her Apple Watch. It's three minutes past midnight. She's pleased she's not alone in the house. She hates Geraint working nights while she's stuck at home on her own, but right now, she wishes she was in bed rather than sitting in a parked car outside Nature's Diner keeping an eye on the place. Sally, very kindly, has given her a flask of coffee and a selection of cakes. Claire had hoped they'd see her through the night, but she scoffed the lot in under an hour and the coffee has almost gone, too. It's going to be a long night. Surely, she could have sat in the restaurant, rather than a cramped car?

She looks around at her surroundings, lit up brilliantly by the huge moon in the cloudless sky. It's peaceful, relaxing, inspiring, marred only by the fact that Claire is now desperately in need of a pee.

She climbs out of the car and looks around her. Philip pointed out where the CCTV cameras are, so she trots off into the woods to find a private spot behind a tree. She can't get there quickly enough.

Claire is a good five minutes, squatting in the woods. She walks back, guided by the light of the moon and stops dead at the police car. The driver's door is wide open. She knows for a fact she closed it, because she quietly clicked it into place so as not to wake anyone in the restaurant, particularly the cute dogs.

She looks around but there's nobody there. It's as quiet as the grave. She can hear her own heart beating in her chest. If someone approached the car, she would have heard them as they'd likely have broken a dried twig underfoot. She leans down into the car, picks up the radio and is about to call in when she'd grabbed from behind. A hand is placed over her mouth, and she's dragged out of the car. She tries to fight back, scrambling with the gloved hand, but it's no use. Her oxygen supply is being cut off. Her vision is blurring and she's struggling to breathe. Whoever has got hold of her is much stronger than she is. As Claire passes out, all she can think about is the damage being done to her unborn baby.

It's easy to break into the restaurant. The door leading into the kitchen is still damaged from the last attempt. The intruder walks, calmly, noiselessly, through the utility room, into the kitchen, up the steps into the restaurant, through the dining area, then down the stairs to the basement. The wall has half been taken down, revealing the true back of the building. On the floor are broken bricks, instruments the crime scene investigators have left behind and a set of ladders.

She places the ladder against the broken wall and ascends. Once at the top, she peers over and into the dark abyss below. Shining a torch from her jacket pocket, the body is revealed to her for the first time in almost thirty years. There is Jack Pemberton, looking up, as if pleading to be let out. He's mummified. His face is leathered and worn. He looks like a hideous Halloween figure, something from an old horror film. Their eyes lock. Real human eyes against hollowed dead ones.

From her backpack, she takes out a plastic petrol canister, unscrews the lid and pours it into the hole. From her pocket, she takes a box of matches, strikes one, and tosses it inside. She watches as the dry clothes catch fire. The flames lick high.

She jumps down from the ladder, runs into the restaurant and back the way she came in, out into the open night air.

I can't sleep. Nothing unusual there. I'm trying to think of something; to slot a piece into place, but I don't know which piece, or into which puzzle it's supposed to fit. It also doesn't help that the curtains haven't been closed properly and the sodding light from the moon is shining through the gap.

Adele is snoozing beside me, mouth agape, snoring gently. She was asleep within minutes of getting into bed. Lucky cow.

I get out of bed. I need darkness to be able to sleep. Maybe I should buy an eye mask. I peel back the curtains to look out at the clear night sky. I have never seen the moon so big before in my life. It's huge. I could almost reach out and touch it.

I'm about to close the curtain when something catches my eye. I look down and see a figure in dark clothing running from the side of the restaurant towards the woods. Before they enter, they stop and look back, and I get a full glimpse of their face.

'What the fu…?' My words are cut off by the sound of the smoke alarm.

I look around, take in Adele's sleeping form, and run out of the room. At the top of the stairs, I look down and see whispers of smoke gently float in from the restaurant below.

'Fuck!'

This makes no sense. Why? Why would she do this?

I run back into the bedroom and shake Adele hard awake while I'm hunting around for my jeans which I quickly put on and slip my feet into trainers.

'What?' Adele asks, grumpy. 'If you tell me I'm snoring, I'll…'

'The restaurant's on fire,' I say over her.

'What?' She's more alert now.

'There's a fire. We need to get out. Quickly, get dressed. I'll wake the others.'

I run along the corridor and bang on Sally and Philip's door. I open the door to Carl's bedroom and see he's already awake, sitting up, rubbing his eyes. I don't want to panic him, but the look on his face tells me he's heard the alarms. He knows something is wrong.

'Carl, sweetheart, get dressed as quickly as you can. We need to get out.'

'What? Why? What's…' he pauses and listens. 'Is there a fire?'

'Yes. You need…'

'Matilda?'

I turn and see Philip coming out of his bedroom, hastily putting on jogging bottoms.

'Philip, the restaurant is on fire. We need to leave now.'

He goes over to the stairs and looks down. He coughs as the smoke catches the back of his throat. 'Oh my God! Carl! Sally!'

'I've got Carl. Go and get Sally.'

Adele comes running out of the bedroom, mobile phone slapped to her ear. 'Fire,' she says, urgently. 'You've put my jeans on,' she says to me. I look down and see I'm wearing her indigo skinny jeans. 'Hello, yes, there's a fire at Nature's Diner in High Chapel. We're trapped inside. There's five of us and two dogs.'

I turn back to Carl. There are tears welling up in his eyes. 'We're going to die, aren't we?'

I bend down to his height and hold him by the shoulders. 'No. I promised you I wouldn't let that happen. I meant every word.'

'We can't survive fire. Nobody can.'

'I'm going to get us out. You trust me, don't you?' He nods. 'Good. Hold the dogs by their collars. Don't let them go. Keep them calm.'

'Carl!' Sally screams as she races out of the bedroom struggling to put on her trousers.

'It's all right. He's with me.'

Sally grabs him and holds him tightly to her chest. 'What are we going to do? How are we going to get out?'

'Is there any way we can drop down from up here?' I ask Philip. He shakes his head.

'The fire crew are on their way,' Adele says.

'There isn't a local fire brigade,' Sally says through her tears. 'It could take twenty minutes. We'll be dead by then.'

'Mum,' Carl whimpers, holding onto her tight.

'We're practically three floors up with the raised ground floor,' Philip says. 'We can't jump down.'

'Is there a ladder?'

'Yes. In the garage.'

'Okay. I'm going to go down, see if I can get out through the front of the restaurant. You all go to the other side of the building. I'll put the ladder up and you all climb down.'

'What about Woodys?' Carl cries.

I look back. I'd forgotten about the dogs, momentarily.

'I'm not leaving my dogs.'

'No. I'm not asking you to.'

I look at Philip. I see the worry in his eyes. I'm guessing he can see the same in mine.

'I'm coming with you,' he says.

'No!' Sally cries.

Adele takes charge. 'Sally, Carl, you two come with me. We'll go into the bedroom, close the door and put wet towels down at the bottom. That will give Matilda and Philip plenty of time to get outside and get a ladder.' She ushers them into the bedroom.

'How are we going to get the Woodys out?' Carl says, his voice lost to tears.

I don't hear Adele's reply.

Me and Philip are left on the landing that is rapidly filling with smoke. Philip pulls his sleeve over his hand and places it firmly around his mouth and nose.

He goes first, slowly edging down the stairs. I follow closely behind. As we descend, we can feel the heat becoming more intense. The noise of the flames cracking, destroying everything in their path is deafening. From below, glass breaks and small explosions break out.

'That'll be the alcohol exploding,' I shout. I can barely hear my own voice above the sound of destruction.

The door from the restaurant is blown off, landing at the bottom of the stairs. A cloud of acrid smoke and orange flame engulfs the hallway. We fall back against the stairs. We're only halfway down.

I feel something behind me. I hardly have chance to turn and look when I notice one of the dogs push past me in a panic and run down the stairs.

'Woody!' I call out.

The Labrador jumps over the burning door and heads for the kitchen.

'We should follow him,' I shout into Philip's ear. 'It's now or never.'

We run down the rest of the stairs, jump over the flames, and into the smoke-filled kitchen. I slam the door closed behind me. Woody is by the exit door, barking loudly to be let out.

'Where's the key?' I ask Philip.

'Upstairs on my bedside table.'

I cough. 'We need to break it down.'

'It's a security door. We should have turned right, gone through the utility.'

An explosion behind us rips off the door to the hallway. A brilliant burst of flames runs along the ceiling. Woody barks. We both scream in horror. I can almost smell my hair singeing.

'We're getting out of this fucking building, Phil.'

I grab a heavy food mixer from the stainless-steel island and hurl it at the window. It bounces right off and hits the floor.

'Fuck!' I scream.

Philip opens the cupboard beneath the sink. He pulls out a small fire extinguisher, handy for a small kitchen fire, but useless against a massive blaze. He jumps up onto the draining board and hammers the glass with the steel extinguisher. The glass splinters but doesn't break. He pauses to cough, slowly becoming overcome by the smoke. He tries again, smacking the extinguisher hard. Eventually, the glass breaks. He clears the rest of the window with the extinguisher, grabs a towel and places it over the rim before stepping to one side and telling me to jump out first.

I grab Woody, hurl him up onto the sink and shove him out of the window, following rapidly behind him. Then, Philip jumps down, extinguisher still in his hands, and we run towards the garage.

Upstairs, Sally is comforting Carl as he's in tears, gripping hold of the one Woody he had left. He didn't notice the other run down the stairs until it was too late. He begged and pleaded with his mother to let him go after him, but she refused.

Adele runs into the en suite, grabs as many towels as she can, soaks them in cold water from the shower and places them in front of the closed bedroom door. The room is cloudy with smoke, but they're still able to breathe. Just.

Adele goes over to the window and throws it open. She takes in great lungfuls of fresh, clean air and hopes Matilda and Philip have managed to get out. While at the bedroom door, all she could hear were the sounds of exploding bottles and the fire eating away at everything it touched. She looks down at the drop below and straight away dismisses jumping. It's too far. She strains, over the sounds of the fire below, to listen out for any sirens, but can't hear any. She turns back and looks at Carl and Sally, holding each other for support. She squats down beside them, wraps her arms around both of them, feels the cold wet nose of Woody on her arm, and closes her eyes.

Tania Pritchard can't sleep. Her mind is working overtime and won't switch off for some reason. She throws the sheets back and climbs out of bed. She thinks better while she's drawing on a cigarette. That's her reason for never giving up, anyway. She vapes, occasionally, but nothing beats the real thing. Vaping is like having vegan mayonnaise. It makes no sense.

She goes downstairs and picks up a packet of cigarettes from the coffee table, lights one and feels her entire body instantly relax as the nicotine hits.

Glancing to her right, she can see daylight through the thin curtains. She looks at her watch. Surely, it's too early for sunrise. She peels back the curtain and sees an orange glow in the distance. That's not the sun. That's fire. And the only thing she knows in that direction is Nature's Diner.

Stubbing out her fag, she takes the stairs two at a time and pulls off her nightie while scouring the floor looking for the clothes she discarded last night.

She runs to her shitty Punto, climbs in, turns on the engine and slams her foot down hard on the accelerator. This is where her erratic driving pays off.

Philip uses the fire extinguisher to smash the padlock on the garage. He pulls back the door and we run inside for the aluminium ladder. We grab it and run back to the restaurant, Woody following. Philip slows as he looks up and watches as his restaurant burns around him.

We prop the ladder against the end wall. It's too short and doesn't quite reach the open window to Philip and Sally's bedroom.

'Is this the longest ladder you've got?'

'Yes.'

'They're not going to be able to reach from there.'

'Shit.'

'Hold onto the bottom,' I say as I start to climb.

'What are you going to do?'

'Something incredibly stupid. Just make sure it's stable.'

'Shouldn't I go up?'

'I'm lighter than you.'

I call out for Adele as I make my way up the rickety ladder. It's strange how an emergency stops us thinking about our own personal problems. I should be cowering in a corner right now, rocking back and forth, crying like a baby at the prospect of losing more people I care about. I'm not. I've jumped straight into action to help them, to save them. This is my police training. It's engrained within me. I can't sit back and watch disaster unfold around me. I have to help.

'Adele!' I scream again as I reach the top of the ladder.

Adele pokes her head out of the window, looking relieved to see me.

'Are you all okay?' I ask.

'Carl's worried about Woody.'

'He's fine. He showed us the way out. He's down here.'

'Carl, did you hear that?' Adele turns back into the room.

Carl appears at the window and looks down. Woody, on the ground, barks and wags his tail as he sees Carl looking down at him.

'Adele, this is longest ladder we've got. It won't reach the window. You're going to have to back out and lower yourself down to the top rung. I'll guide you.'

'Shit,' she says.

'It's the only way out.'

There's a good five feet between the window ledge and the top of the ladder. Adele and Sally will just about reach if they're careful, but Carl is going to have to jump, and I haven't quite worked out how to get Woody out.

'Send Carl first,' I shout. I look down at Philip. He gives me the thumbs-up.

There's an explosion and one of the picture windows at the side of the restaurant is blown out, shaking the entire building. I hold onto the ladder tightly.

'It has to be now!' Philip screams.

'I'm not going,' Carl says. He steps back from the window and sits down on the floor beside the bed. Woody runs to him and curls up beside him.

'What?' Sally asks. 'Carl, sweetheart, I know it's scary, but Matilda will grab you and guide you down to the ladder.' She coughs. 'Your dad is waiting for you at the bottom.'

'I'm not leaving Woody.'

'He'll be right behind you,' she says.

'No. He won't,' he cries. 'He can't jump down to the top of the ladder and Matilda won't be able to catch him. He's not going to get out. I'm not leaving him.' He wraps his arms around Woody's neck and holds him close.

'Carl, I'm not losing you again,' Sally shouts. Her voice is shaking with terror. She's nervous but **trying** to sound forceful. 'You're going out of that window.'

'Woody looked after me in Sweden. He got me through it all. I'm not leaving him here to die.'

Adele grabs a curtain and yanks it off the pole. 'Carl, I'm pretty sure I can wrap this around Woody and lower him out of the window. It'll reach Matilda. She'll grab him and get him down. He'll be fine. I know it. But we have to move now.'

'He goes first.'

'No. You go,' Adele says, firmly. 'It'll give me a chance to make this secure.'

'Don't leave him to die,' he says, tears running down his face.

'I won't. I promise.'

Carl takes Woody's head in his hands. He kisses him on the nose and the frightened dog licks him back.

'I'll be right outside, Woody. I'll be waiting for you. I love you.'

Sally grabs Carl by the shoulders and pulls him away. 'Come on, Carl.'

There's a whoosh from the door. The wet towels have dried up and caught fire. The whole door is now ablaze.

'Jesus Christ!' Adele says. 'We've not got long.'

'What's taking so long?' I shout from the top of the ladder. I can't see into the bedroom from this low down.

'We're coming,' I hear Sally reply.

She appears at the window. She looks petrified. I know how she feels. She lifts Carl up. He wipes the tears from his face with the back of his hands and lowers himself out of the window.

'I'll see you soon, Woods,' he calls out.

I'm standing on the top rung. I don't feel secure. I risk a glance back and Philip is holding the ladder firmly at the bottom. I reach out for Carl, but I still can't get to him. There's a space of about a foot between my fingertips and his feet.

'Sally, you need to let him go,' I shout.

'Oh God!' she cries.

'Sally, let him go. Carl, I'll catch you.'

'Promise?' he calls out.

'Definitely.'

'I'm scared, Mat.'

'I know. I'm scared, too. But we can help each other not be scared. A few seconds and you'll be on the ground, safe and sound.'

'I can't do it, Mat. I can't let him go,' Sally cries.

'Sally, you have to. Trust me.'

'Mum, let me go,' Carl cries out.

'Shit,' she says.

Sally lets go.

Carl falls.

He screams and I grab hold of him firmly, perhaps too firmly. I practically slam him against the brick wall, and he screams again. He's going to have some scrapes and bruises, but I've caught him and he's out of a burning building. That's all that matters.

'I've got you. I've got you,' I repeat into his ear, soothing him. 'Lessen your grip slightly, Carl, you're strangling me.'

'Sorry.'

'Have you got him?' Sally calls.

'Yes. Fine. I'm going to pass him down to Philip. I'll be back up for you.'

'Sally, Woody isn't moving. He's gone under the bed, and he won't come out,' Adele says, trying, but failing, to coax him out.

Sally is emotionally exhausted. She wipes her eyes with her sleeves, squats to the floor beside Adele and looks under the bed. 'Come on out, sweetie,' she says in her best sickly-sweet voice. 'We're going outside. Do you want to see Carl? Carl?' His tail begins to wag. 'He knows who I'm talking about.'

'He's scared.'

'He's not the only one.'

'Who's next?' Matilda shouts from outside.

'Go. I'll deal with Woody,' Adele says.

'Are you sure?'

'Go!'

'Thank you,' Sally says, rubbing Adele's back.

Sally appears at the window. She's scanning the ground below and when she sees Philip and Carl, cuddling one of his dogs, she smiles with relief. He's made it. She looks up into the distance.

'I can see blue lights.'

'About fucking time,' I say. 'Sally, swing your legs out. I should be able to reach your feet and guide you to the top rung, but you may have to let go.'

'Shit. I bloody hate heights.'

'More than fire?'

'Good point.'

Sally lowers herself out of the upstairs window, holding onto the ledge by her fingertips.

I reach up and grab her ankles. 'Sally, if you let go, we're going to end up toppling back. You need to lower yourself down gently to me. Just a few inches, maybe not even that.'

'I can't.'

'You've literally no choice, Sally.'

'Fuck! Please don't drop me.'

'I'll try not to.'

'Okay. Letting go now.'

Sally lets go of the windowsill and I feel the full weight of her. She screams as her feet land on the top rung and she wraps her arms around my neck, like Carl did, only Sally has longer arms and a tighter grip and I'm pretty sure my eyes are going to pop out of my head.

'Jesus Christ, that was scary,' she says.

We're holding each other tightly, neither of us daring to move.

'Ease yourself down me then go carefully down the ladder.'

'You can do this, Mum!' Carl shouts.

Sally looks at me, tears in her eyes. 'Thank you,' she says as she painstakingly edges down the ladder.

I breathe a sigh of relief when I see Sally reach the ground and into Philip's arms. I turn back to the restaurant. The smoke coming out of the window is blacker and thicker than before. We can't have much longer left before it's too late.

'Adele, send Woody out next,' I shout.

There's no response.

Tania's Punto screeches to a halt at the side of the burning restaurant. She jumps out and looks up, mouth wide open. She hopes everyone inside has been able to get out safely. As she runs around the back, she stops when she sees the police car, driver's door open and a body on the ground beside it. Immediately, she recognises Claire Daniels and drops to her knees.

'Claire. Claire, it's me, Tania. Come on, sweetheart, wake up.'

Tania feels for a pulse, pressing her cold fingers hard against her neck. There's a faint pulse.

'Jesus. Come on, Claire, wake up. I don't know any bloody first aid.'

She carefully places Claire on the ground, leans into the police car and picks up the radio.

'Is there anyone there? This is Tania Pritchard. Sergeant Claire Daniels has been attacked and is unconscious. I have no idea what to do and Nature's Diner is on fire. You need to get an ambulance out here right now.'

'Tania, I don't know if you know me. I'm PC Guthrie. Callum. We know about the fire. There is a fire crew and ambulance on the way. I'm going to talk you through what to do with Claire. Okay?'

'Thank you, Callum. Thank you,' Tania says, relieved.

'Adele, the fire brigade is here!' I shout.

There's no reply.

'Matilda, come down. The fire brigade can take over,' Philip calls out.

'Adele? Adele!' I scream.

A ladder swings past me towards the open window. I see it rattling as a firefighter in full uniform runs up swiftly and confidently as if he's simply running upstairs at home.

'You need to go down, now,' he barks at me.

'My friend is in there. Adele. And a dog. Woody.'

'We'll get them out. Go back down, right now,' he orders me, severely.

I can't see his expression beneath the visor on his helmet, but I know when I'm being told off. Carefully, I lower myself down the ladder. Philip helps me on the last few rungs. I step back and look up as two firefighters disappear into the burning building.

All eyes are on the window. Nothing happens.

Eventually, there's movement and one of the firefighters swings his leg out of the window and onto the ladder. He has Adele over his shoulder. She doesn't look as if she's moving.

'Adele!' I scream.

She gives the thumbs-up sign.

I sigh. 'Thank God! I bet she's loving this. Dirty cow.'

Another firefighter follows, holding a terrified-looking Woody against him.

'It's Woody,' Carl screams.

The dog's tail wags, and the firefighter has to hold onto him tighter to stop him from jumping down.

I turn to see all three members of the Meagan family standing by a tree, arms wrapped around each other, grateful smiles on their faces. They may have lost everything in the fire – their home, their business, their belongings – but they have all survived. That is the only thing that matters.

I take a step back. I place my hands in the pockets of my jeans, feel something inside and pull out Adele's Porsche keys. I turn around and look into the woods. Why the hell had Lynne Pemberton been running into those woods seconds before the fire started? I run to the front of the building where Adele's car is parked.

'Where are you going?' Philip calls out.

I stop and turn back. 'I think I know what's been going on. When the police turn up, get them to come out to the Pembertons' house.'

'Why? Shouldn't you wait for them?'

'Probably. Just get everyone to the hospital and checked out. Make sure everyone is safe.'

'What about you?'

I shake my head. I don't give him my usual reply, that I'm fine, because I know I'm not. I can feel the well of tears rising up inside me and I don't know why. I head for the car.

I've changed a great deal in the last month. Nobody can go through such torment and not be changed. My tough exterior has hardened, despite the fact I'm crying more. I've become a contradiction and haven't been able to work out who I really am anymore. Now, I know, and I need to put the new Matilda Darke to the test. Tonight, I will either kill or be killed.

Lynne Pemberton is walking down the middle of Dower Lane, but she has no idea where she is. Her mind is blank. How did she get here? Where is she going?

'Mum?'

Alison had woken up and popped to the toilet. On her way back to bed, something caught her eye out of the window. She peeled back the curtain and saw the bright orange in the distance coming from Nature's Diner. She had run out of the house to go and see if she could help in any way, when she spotted her mother in the middle of the quiet road.

Lynne doesn't react. It's as if she hasn't heard her daughter or even seen her, despite the fact she's standing right next to her.

'Mum. Mum, what's wrong? What are you doing?'

Lynne continues to walk slowly, almost zombie-like.

'Mum, you're scaring me. What's happened?'

Lynne stops and turns to her as if seeing her for the first time. 'Alison?' Her voice is quiet.

'Mum, what are you doing out so late? You're shivering. What's going on?'

'I saw your dad.'

Alison recoils. 'What?'

'Your dad. I saw him. He looked almost the same as he did thirty years ago.'

'Mum, you're not making any sense. Why don't you come inside?'

'I don't know what to believe anymore, Alison. We killed him. We killed your dad. Yet, he's still there. He looked straight at me.'

'Mum, what do you mean, you killed him? You can't have killed him.' Alison grabs her mother, pulls her into a hug and coaxes her towards the cottage.

'I killed your dad, Alison. I killed him. And he's come back for me.'

I drive the Porsche at speed through the dark streets of High Chapel. There's no other traffic around. I saw Lynne Pemberton run away from the restaurant and into the woods. She turned back and watched as the flames took hold. Yet, from the look in her eyes, even from a distance, I could tell she wasn't in full control of what she was doing. It was then when everything seemed to fall into place.

Lynne and Iain recently celebrated their wedding anniversary and had gone to their favourite restaurant in Kendal, a good forty minutes' drive away, yet they had never been to Nature's Diner. Why? Clearly the answer is because they don't want to be in the same building as a body they placed in the cellar thirty years ago when the building was derelict. But there are other things, too. When I saw Lynne alone at the edge of the lake, she told me to go home, to leave High Chapel. I thought it was a threat, but now I see it was a warning. Lynne told me to leave before more damage could be done. Damage by whom? Lynne, herself? Iain?

Lynne and Iain had been in love when they were teenagers. He couldn't have children, and she yearned for them. She dumped him for his brother. How would that have made him feel? Angry? Bitter? Disappointed? Enraged? Murderous? He'd had to sit back and watch as Lynne and Jack created a perfect happy family unit while he remained at home with his father working on a farm that was haemorrhaging money. Yes, their affair had been rekindled, but it wasn't enough. Iain didn't want to sleep with Lynne when the opportunity arose behind Jack's back; he wanted something more. He wanted the oldest motive for murder: revenge.

I swing the car around the corner and slam on the brakes when I see Alison and Lynne standing in the middle of the road.

At the restaurant, two paramedics run towards Tania who is struggling to put Claire into the recovery position and keep her warm. They push her to one side and take over. They check Claire's airways and put a mask over her nose and mouth. There is nothing more for Tania to do. She runs around to the front of the restaurant, not taking her eyes from the burning building. She sees Matilda's friend, Adele, being placed on a stretcher and then into the back of an ambulance and the Meagan family receiving treatment with red blankets around their shoulders.

'What's happened? Are you all okay?' she asks.

'We're fine.'

'Claire Daniels has been attacked. The paramedics are with her now. Did you see anything?'

'We were asleep. We didn't know anything until the alarm woke us up,' Sally says.

'Matilda woke me up,' Philip adds.

Tania looks around her. 'Where *is* Matilda? Is she...?'

'She said something about going to see the Pembertons.'

'What? Now?'

'Yes.'

'Did she say why?'

'No,' Philip says. 'But judging by the look on her face, I think it's something big.'

'Jesus. I should go over there. If you see the police, tell them where I've gone.' Tania backs away and skirts around the fire engines to return to her Punto. 'Why do I get the feeling I'm about to do something completely stupid?' she asks herself.

'What's going on?' I ask, getting out of the car.

'I don't know,' Alison says, wiping away her tears. 'Mum said she saw Dad, but then she said she killed him, too. It's like she's in a trance or something. I don't know what to do.'

'Let's get her inside.'

Together, we both walk Lynne into Alison's cottage, into the living room, and sit her down on the sofa. Alison grabs a blanket from the back of the sofa and wraps it around her mum's shoulders. She's still shaking.

'Lynne, it's Matilda, can you hear me?' My voice is calm despite the rage I can feel coursing through my veins. Lynne could have killed an entire family tonight. Actions have consequences, and I'll not forget the look of horror on Carl's face as he lowered himself out of the window for as long as I live.

Lynne nods.

'I think I know what's going on, but you're going to have to tell me yourself. I saw you, just now, running away from Nature's Diner. You set it on fire, didn't you?'

'What?' Alison exclaims. 'No. She wouldn't. She—'

I silence her by raising my hand.

'Lynne, you went down into the cellar, didn't you? You saw the body behind the wall. You saw Jack.'

She nods. 'I don't know what I expected,' she begins. Her voice is barely above a whisper. 'After thirty years, I thought I'd be looking at a skeleton. I saw… I saw an actual body. He still had his hair. He was wearing his clothes. He was in the same position I'd left him in. How? How is that possible?'

'He was mummified. There was no air. You basically sealed him in a tomb.'

'Wait,' Alison says. 'Mum didn't kill my dad. She… didn't. She couldn't.'

'It was Iain who told you to set fire to the body, wasn't it?' I ask. 'It was Iain who told you that Jack had abused the twins and killed them. He said you should kill him to stop him abusing Alison. What happened? Did he kill Jack and tell you to help him hide the body?'

She nods.

'No,' Alison cries out, grabbing her mother's hand. 'I don't believe a word of this.'

'Everyone has said your mum changed after Celia and Jennifer disappeared and when your father supposedly walked out into the lake. It's understandable, but the change wasn't through grief. It was manufactured.'

'I don't know what you mean.'

'Do you ever go out with your mum, just the two of you?'

Alison frowns. 'Sometimes.'

'Answer me truthfully.'

It's a while before she speaks. 'No.'

'Why not? What about mother and daughter shopping trips? Nights out for a drink in the local pub, or to the cinema?'

'I... I don't... we...'

'Does she ever come over here to the cottage for a coffee and a chat?'

'No. I always go over to the stables.'

'Why?'

'What?'

'Why doesn't she come here on her own?'

'I... she's... she's busy with the paddocks and everything.'

'But you're not, though, are you?' I ask, turning back to Lynne. 'You're at home, alone for most of the day. You spend your time cleaning the house, making meals for Iain, making sure his clothes are washed and ironed and everything is perfect in the house for him.'

Tears are streaming down Lynne's face, but it's devoid of emotion. She can't speak. She nods.

'Why did you give up being a midwife?'

She shakes her head.

'Tell me, Lynne. Why did you give up your dream job?'

She opens her mouth to speak but a torrent of tears is released. 'Iain made me,' she cries.

'Oh God, Mum, what are you saying?'

'When you were young, Alison, just after Celia and Jennifer were taken, you were sent to stay with your aunt and uncle for a while. Your aunt is your mum's sister. Tell me, do they ever visit each other?'

Alison shakes her head slowly as reality begins to dawn.

'Why not?' I ask Lynne.

Lynne wipes her tears with the blanket. 'Iain says I don't need them. He says I only need him.'

I turn to Alison. 'For the past thirty years, your mother has been living in a coercive relationship. Iain has manufactured her entire life. He forced her to give up her work. He forced her to work on the paddocks when he needed her to, and he forced her to keep the house perfect for him. Whenever she goes out, he's with her. Always. I'm right, aren't I?'

Lynne nods. She turns to her daughter. 'I'm so sorry, Alison.'

'Why? Why didn't I see it?' Alison asks.

'Because you were too close. Because it happened so gradually and after such a massive tragedy over such a long period of time, that nobody noticed.'

'But… why? Why would he do that? He loves Mum.'

'He doesn't. There's a very fine line between love and hate. They're both extreme emotions and it doesn't take much for someone to switch between the two. I believe Iain did love your mum, years ago, when they were first together. But then Iain told Lynne that he couldn't have children. And all Lynne wanted was to be a mother. She dumped him for Jack, and he had to sit back and watch as they fell in love, got married, and had a family. A family that Iain believes should have been his.'

I allow a silence to descend. Alison is in shock as she looks back over the past thirty years and tries to fit all the pieces together. Lynne looks as if life has been drained from her.

'Iain hated Jack, didn't he, Lynne?' I ask.

She nods.

'Jack suffered with depression. It wasn't talked about as much in the nineties as it is now, and men certainly didn't talk about their feelings back then, especially sons of farmers, who are real proper masculine men. I'm guessing Jack will have told his father he felt sad at times, and I assume someone like Granville will have laughed and told him to pick himself up, stop being soft and be a man.' Lynne is nodding through all of this. 'And that made Jack feel worse. His depression, untreated, deepened and he isolated himself, took himself off to bed for days on end. That fuelled Iain's hatred even more. He was wondering what Jack had to be depressed about when he had a wife and kids, something he craved more than anything.'

'I didn't...' Lynne can hardly get her words out. She's shaking. She can't control her tears. 'I didn't want to... sleep with Iain...'

'Oh my God!' Alison cries. She increases her hold on her mother.

'It was New Year,' she continues. 'Jack was in bed. He had been, on and off, for most of Christmas. The girls were all in bed asleep. I was in the living room on my own. Ten o'clock on New Year's Eve, Iain came over with a bottle of sherry. I don't even like sherry. He kept filling my glass. I didn't know what was happening until it was too late to stop him.'

'And after that he forced you to keep sleeping with him or he'd tell Jack. And you went along with it, because you knew how fragile Jack was.'

She nods.

'Mum, I'm so sorry. I'm sorry I didn't see... I didn't notice...' Alison is crying into her mother's shoulder.

'Can I come in?'

We all look up to see Tania in the doorway.

'That Porsche is going to get stolen the way you've left it in the middle of the road,' she says, coming fully into the living room. 'I've just come from the restaurant. It's practically destroyed. Claire Daniels has been attacked. What's going on?' she asks, looking at everyone in turn.

'Claire?' Is she all right?' Alison asks, her eyes wide in disbelief.

Tania shakes her head. 'She's unconscious. Paramedics have taken her to hospital.'

'Who attacked her?' Alison asks.

'Iain,' Lynne says quietly. 'We were walking through the woods to the restaurant. We saw the police car parked around the back. He said he'd take care of it while I went into the cellar and set it on fire.' She talks with the expressionless tone of someone detached from the situation. 'I just went along with it. He said we needed to destroy the evidence. I didn't even question him. All those sightings over the years. I needed to confirm that we'd really put him there, that he really was dead.'

'Lynne, where is Iain now?' I ask her.

She shrugs. 'I don't know. Back home, I suppose.'

I jump to my feet.

'Where are you going?' Alison asks.

'To get answers to the questions I still have, and to put an end to thirty years of torment.'

'I'm coming with you,' she says.

'No. You need to stay with your mum.'

'No. I need to hear the answers for myself. I'm struggling to believe a single word of this. I need to hear it from him.'

I take Tania to one side while Alison settles her mother. 'Will you stay with Lynne?'

'Of course. But what's going on?'

'I'll explain it all to you later. Give us half an hour and then phone Gill Forsyth. Tell her to come to the stables.'

'Why? What are you going to do?'

'Iain has been lying and manipulating for thirty years. He's a master at it. He's not going to admit to anything we put to him. Looking at Lynne, I doubt she's going to be in any fit state to testify against him. I need to force him into doing something that he can be arrested for.'

'What?'

'Killing me.'

It's less than a five-minute walk from Alison's cottage to the farm where Iain and Lynne live. Me and Alison walk side by side in silence, the atmosphere surrounding us is fully charged. I have no idea of the questions I'm going to put to him or the response I'm going to get. Literally anything could happen in the course of the next half an hour, and I don't mind admitting I'm scared. I'm scared that I'm going to find out exactly what I'm capable of.

There's a smell of smoke in the air. As we turn the corner, I look back. I can just make out black smoke on the horizon, rising from the destruction of Nature's Diner. This has been a horror of a night. I shouldn't be here. I should phone Gill myself and get her to take over. I'm not a detective right now. I'm a woman. I'm a fucking angry woman, and that makes me incredibly dangerous.

We reach the house and I'm about to knock when Alison pulls out a set of keys from her pocket. She unlocks the door, pushes it open and steps inside. I follow. There's no turning back now.

'Lynne?' Iain asks, coming out of the kitchen. He stops,

mid-stride, when he sees who his visitors are. 'Oh. Where's Lynne? Have you seen Lynne?'

'Where do you expect her to be?' I ask.

'She should… I don't know. I woke up and she wasn't there. I came downstairs and she's nowhere to be found. I thought…'

'What? What did you think?'

'She might have gone out for a walk.'

'Have you tried looking for her?'

I look him up and down, take in the jeans, the walking boots and his jumper. I've no idea what time it is, but it's pitch-dark outside, and I know we should all be tucked up in bed and fast asleep right now.

'I was about to,' he says. 'I was getting worried.'

'I think we need to talk,' I say. I walk into the kitchen, pushing past him. Alison follows.

I'm worried about Alison. Her face is expressionless. She's withdrawn. She's a volcano and, any moment, she could erupt. I need to keep an eye on her.

I pull out a chair at the table and sit Alison down. I whisper to her to keep calm and let me take charge. I instruct Iain to take a seat while I remain standing.

'You want to know where Lynne is?' I ask. He nods. 'She's currently in Alison's house being looked after by Tania Pritchard. Alison found her walking in the middle of the road in a daze after setting fire to Nature's Diner.'

'What?' he asks, incredulously. 'Why would you say that? Alison, don't listen to a word this woman tells you. She's deranged.'

'Claire called Alison and told her a body had been found in the cellar. Alison told you and Lynne, and you knew that Jack had finally been unearthed after thirty years. Because that's where you put him after you killed him: in the cellar of a derelict building.'

'I killed him?'

'You did.'

'He's my brother. Why would I kill my own brother?'

'Because you hated him. He was living your life. He was married to the woman you loved, and he had the children you couldn't have. You hated him because he couldn't see how good his life was. His depression clouded all that. He struggled with his mental health, and you couldn't understand why, when he had a wife and three loving kids.'

'This is quite the fiction you're painting,' he says, a smile on his thin lips.

'Then Travis comes along. Young, fit, good-looking Travis who all the women in the village drool over. Suddenly, your status as the Don Juan of High Chapel has been usurped. And all this time, the cogs have been turning inside your mind, cooking up something dark and evil to hurt your brother and to get revenge on Lynne for throwing you over.'

'Surely this is slander. You're not telling me you believe all this?' Iain says, looking to Alison.

Alison stares back at him with steely darkness in her eyes. She sits still, but she's seething.

'Travis has nothing to do with any of this. He was a shy young man who couldn't understand all the attention he was getting. Something else you hated. You wanted the attention, and it had waned. So you put together a plan so dark, so evil, that could get you everything you wanted.'

'I think you should stop right there, Matilda. I'm starting to feel embarrassed for you.'

'A few days before the twins went missing, you stole Travis's car. You hid it somewhere out of sight. Then, on that day, you popped into the hardware shop to buy something you probably didn't need, but it got you seen by the villagers. You took the twins and drove them away, but you didn't kill them right away. You went back to the cottage, and you forced Lynne to go to bed with you.'

'Forced her?' he says, almost laughing. 'You're adding rape into this now, are you? Anything else? How about terrorism, or perhaps regicide?'

'Lynne is your alibi. Later, when everyone is out looking for the twins, you slip away, you murder them, and you drive Travis's car into the lake.'

'I was very busy that day, wasn't I?' he says.

'You killed them,' Alison says. She wipes a tear away quickly. She doesn't want Iain to see her crying. 'You killed my sisters.'

'Of course I didn't kill them, Alison. She's making it up. She's deluded. She's full of grief and hormones, and it's affecting her brain. I'd feel sorry for you, if it wasn't for the fact you're accusing me of double murder.'

'I'm accusing you of a lot more than that,' I say, folding my arms across my chest.

I'm now surer of myself than I've been in a long time. Iain's attempts to discredit me are laughable. I didn't want Alison to come with me, but I'm glad she's here. Had we been alone, I think I would be lying on the floor right now in a pool of my own blood. He'd have killed me, hidden my body and said I was crazy with grief and had run away, probably to kill myself. But Alison is my witness. He can't kill us both.

'A couple of months go by,' I continue. 'Jack, naturally, is struggling. But Lynne, resourceful, dependable Lynne, is adapting. She's even thinking of going back to work. You can't have that, can you? So you come up with another despicable plan. You tell Lynne you've seen Jack reading a magazine featuring child pornography and that he admitted to abusing the twins and killing them. You put on a wonderful act. She believed you. I believed you when you repeated it to me the other day, but looking back, it was just a little too perfect. Your anger was spot on. It's a speech you'd rehearsed so many times, to sound believable to Lynne, that it was too good.

'So, you tell Lynne that Jack is a paedophile and a murderer and there's still little Alison alive who Jack might turn his attentions to next. You need to get rid of him. You kill him. You make Lynne an accessory and you bury him in the cellar of a derelict building. And as for Travis: well, Travis was an insurance policy just in case questions were asked of you.'

'Are you going to say I killed him as well?'

'I am, yes. I'm guessing you're not going to tell me where you buried him.'

'I can't. I didn't kill him. Bloody hell, Matilda, I think you should see someone. Your grief has turned you loopy,' he scoffs.

'Did you drug me?' Alison asks.

We both turn to look at her.

'On the night of the storm, did you drug me so I wouldn't remember?'

'No, Alison, of course I didn't drug you. Can't you see what she's trying to do? She's failed as a detective. She failed to save her own family, so she's trying to atone by coming up with this elaborate non-murder she can try and solve.'

I clear my throat. I hope Alison still believes me and doesn't start falling for her stepfather's lies. She needs to keep picturing her mother and the blank look of fear in her eyes.

'You've been posing as Jack all these years,' I say. 'The various sightings. It's been you all along. Any time Lynne has expressed a sign of independence, you've shown up as Jack to taunt her that he might not be dead after all or that's he's haunting her. You even showed up as Jack on Alison's birthdays and on the day she started in the force, to add to the authenticity of a loving father still out there, watching in the wings. It was you who called in with the new sighting the other day, wasn't it? A random member of the public called John. John, a variation of Jack. You've been laughing at everyone all these years.'

'I've had enough of this,' he says, standing up. 'I want you to leave, now. What you're saying is wrong. It's all lies and it's destructive.'

'Alison has been asking questions all these years. She's wanted to know the truth, and every time she's asked something you fear could muddy the waters, up pops Jack to mess with her head and turn her focus to her father being the killer, ashamed of what he's done.'

'Out! Now!' He grabs me by the shoulders and forcibly drags me into the hallway.

'Alison said she could smell horses on your clothes when you picked her up out of the car, all those years ago. I could smell horses on your clothes when you broke into Nature's Diner. I called out Jack's name, thinking it was him. You stopped. I bet you loved that.'

'You're a sick woman, Matilda. You need help.'

I'm not sure exactly what happens next. There's a bang. Iain's grip on me slackens and I fall against the wall. Iain drops to the floor. I turn and there's Alison with the toaster in her hands.

Iain is dazed. He tries to sit up and puts a hand to his head where Alison hit him.

'You bastard!' she spits. 'You complete and utter bastard!'

'Alison, don't believe her lies,' he says as he struggles to lift himself up from the floor.

'They're not lies,' I say. 'The problem is, Iain, you've told them so many times over the past thirty years that you actually believe them yourself. You really think your brother was a paedophile and a murderer, when in reality he was a good man who loved his family but was struggling with his mental health.'

Iain slowly gets back to his feet. He presses a hand to his head and winces at the pain. 'Jack was weak and pathetic. He didn't deserve Lynne, and he didn't deserve Celia and Jennifer. You're right, Alison, I did drug you when you were five. Do you know what else I did while you were drugged and asleep?'

'No!' I scream. 'Alison, don't listen to this. This is a lie. He didn't do anything to you. He only wants to hurt you.'

'I fucked you, Alison. I put you to bed and I got in next to you.'

'No!' Alison cries.

'He's lying. He didn't do anything.' I turn to Iain. 'You've hurt this family enough. You don't need to do any more damage.'

Iain lunges forward. He grabs me and pulls me out of the way. He takes Alison by the shoulders and slams her up against the back wall. I can see he's whispering something in her ear. He's smirking, grinning, enjoying himself while Alison buckles and collapses.

I have to stop him. I have to stop him telling more lies and inflicting more damage.

I grab the frying pan from the cooker and swing it at his head. He falls, bangs his head on the table as he drops.

'Alison, listen to me,' I begin, taking hold of Alison and pulling her to her feet. 'Don't listen to a word he just said. He wants to hurt you. Don't let him. Go. Leave. Go back to the cottage. Tell Tania to call Gill. She needs to come now.' I push Alison to the back door and pull it open.

'Please,' she pleads with me, tears rolling down her cheeks. 'Please don't tell me he...'

'He didn't. I know he didn't. Go and get help. Now. Run!'

I slam the door and turn back to see Iain getting to his feet.

'I have never wanted to kill someone as much as I want to kill you right now,' I tell him. I can feel the anger rising up inside me. I hope Gill gets here quickly.

Iain smiles at me. 'You're right. You're absolutely right. I did hate Jack. I hated Lynne even more for dumping me for that pathetic excuse for a man. I hated Travis for having women offer themselves to him when he was too shy to accept it. I did steal his car. He reported it to the police, but I knew Lionel had taken that money raised for Gideon, so I told him to remove the statement or I'd tell the whole village.'

'You still told them, though.'

'Of course. I had to discredit him so that anything he might say would be seen as a lie, and it worked. He's kept his mouth shut for thirty years. Good old Lionel.' He winks.

'Why did you take only Celia and Jennifer? Alison was with them on that day. Why didn't you take her, too?'

'If you take everything away from someone, they have nothing left to live for. Like you right now, Matilda,' he says, calm and concise. 'But leave them something, just one thing – in this case, Alison – and you can see the pain and torment painted on their faces. I saw it in Jack. He really was on the cusp of suicide after Celia and Jennifer disappeared, but he was sticking around for Alison. He loved her so much. But it wasn't him I wanted to hurt. It was Lynne. She was the only woman I ever said 'I love you' to. And she said it back. I thought she was the one. Then I told her I couldn't have children. Within a week, we'd split up. How can you do that to someone? And then, to rub salt in the wound, she turned to my brother. What kind of a woman does that? She had to suffer, I mean, really fucking suffer.

'It turned out Lynne was stronger than I thought. She was

even planning on going back to work. So, I had to come up with something else. I told her I'd caught Jack wanking over a kiddie-porn mag. I convinced her we had to kill him to save Alison. There was no way Lynne was going to lose another child, so she went along with it. She was there when I killed him. She brought him to the stables. She lured him in, and I struck the final blow.

'Lynne hit rock bottom then. Give her her due, it took some doing, but she finally hit the floor. Then, I was able to mould and shape her into the Lynne I wanted her to be. She gave up her job at the hospital, she worked with me at the stables, and it wasn't long before we were sharing a bed. Job done.'

I can feel the rage boiling up inside me.

'You're evil,' I croak.

'I'm not. I'm really not. I'm what happens when you're cast aside, abandoned and used. I was fine to go out with for a few months and have fun, but as soon as I said I couldn't have kids, I was dumped like my feelings didn't matter. I was fine to work on the farm and do the drudge work. Jack was allowed to get a job and bring in a steady income, because he had a wife and three kids to support. And when things became too much, Dad brings in outside help in the form of young, good-looking Travis fucking Montgomery who every slag in the village swooned over. Once again, I'm in the background. You can only take the hurt, the pain and the torment for so long until you snap.'

He grabs me by the throat and slams me against the fridge. I can feel his rough, calloused hands around my neck, and he squeezes. He squeezes hard, and I can see the murder in his eyes.

I bring my knee up and kick him in the crotch. He screams out in pain, releases his grip and bends double, hands between his legs. I grab for the frying pan and smack him over the head with it again to take him completely down.

'That's me snapping.'

I loom over him. He's dazed but still conscious.

'Right then, Iain, it's about time you learned what happens when you fuck with the wrong woman.'

Iain opens his eyes.

He looks around him and sees that he's in the living room of his farmhouse. He hasn't been unconscious for long. He tries to move, but he can't. He's sitting on a kitchen chair, his hands tied behind him.

I walk in front of him. 'You're awake.'

'What do you think you're doing?' he asks. His voice is muffled. He lost a few teeth when I hit him with the frying pan.

'You're resisting arrest. I'm making sure you're nice and secure before Inspector Forsyth gets here.'

'Like she's going to do anything. She'll want to protect her father. And herself. I'm guessing he's confided in her what I told him. She's never liked me. I've seen the way she looks at me. Pure venom. When the police from Liverpool came round looking for Travis, I went over to see Lionel. I sat in his living room, and I told him that Merseyside Police would never find Travis because I'd buried him somewhere isolated and deep. Lionel didn't say a word. He couldn't. One: nobody would believe a man who'd stolen money from a dead man. And two: where was the evidence?'

I shake my head almost in disbelief. I've met some disturbed people in my time, but Iain Pemberton takes the biscuit.

'Jesus, you're sick, do you know that?'

'If I'm sick, then it's because my father, my brother, and Lynne made me sick.'

'Of course. You're blaming everyone else. I thought so. It's never your fault, is it? There's always someone else who's to blame.'

'Absolutely. Just like you're to blame for the murder of your mother and your nephews.'

That hurt.

'Just like you're to blame for the shooting back in 2019 that killed so many of your colleagues. And you're also to blame for what's about to happen next because you're so fucking shit at tying knots.'

Iain jumps to his feet and lunges for me again. He body slams me to the floor. With all his weight on top of me, I can't move. He grabs a handful of my hair and cracks my head hard on the floorboards.

I knee him between the legs again. It's all I've got. He cries out and I manage to push him off me. He rolls over and I jump on top of him. I sit on his chest and punch him hard in the face. He's laughing, grinning at me. I punch him harder and harder with everything I've got. I can see the skin breaking on my knuckles as I hit his teeth and cheek bones. It hurts, but I can't stop. The rage, the anger, the hatred, the pain I feel for that fucker who killed my family needs to be released.

I'm about to throw another punch when he catches my fist. He pulls me towards him and head-butts me.

I can hear a ringing in my ears. I'm dazed. My vision blurs. I stagger backwards and fall. I can feel a kick to my stomach, and another. I roll over. I try to protect my head, but the blows keep on coming. I roll onto my front, my other side, onto my back. I look up and I can see Iain, standing tall, looming over me. He raises his foot. He's going to stamp down hard onto my chest. I can see the underside of his boot coming towards me. He'll break my ribs. They'll pierce my lungs. I'll choke to death on my own blood.

No. That's not happening. I'm not having this fucker kill me. But he's stronger than me. I try to move back, but it's no good. I'm wedged up against a wall. I can't go any further. Then I see his foot race towards my face and everything goes black.

I open my eyes.

For a second I feel like I've been unconscious for days, but I look up and there's Iain, staggering to his feet, heading for the kitchen. From there, he'll escape through the back door and, if he gets to Lynne and Alison before the police turn up, who knows what'll happen?

I'm in pain. Every part of my body hurts. I can taste blood. I can see blood. My shirt is covered in it. I bring my hands up to my face. They're shaking. Adrenaline is charging through my body. I honestly don't know what I'm feeling right now.

Except I can't let him get away. I can't allow him to leave this house.

I struggle to get to my feet. I use the wall to help me up. I'm smearing it with blood from my hands. I've no idea if it's my blood or Iain's, and I don't care.

My head is pounding. My vision is blurred, and my legs want to give way with every step. I've no idea what's carrying me into the kitchen. Determination, probably. I can feel myself crying. I fall against the kitchen worktop. I close my eyes tightly shut and I can see my mum. She's lying in her bed at home. She's dead. I knew from the minute I entered her room that she was dead. I hear Harriet screaming from the spare room.

Nathan and Joseph. They were so young. They had their whole lives ahead of them.

Celia and Jennifer. *They* were so young. *They* had their whole lives ahead of them.

I grab something.

I turn.

Iain is at the door.

'Iain,' I call out.

He stops and looks at me.

I'm struggling for breath. The pain mixed with the tears is making it hard for me to breathe. I walk towards him.

I want to be sick. I want to bend over and vomit. But I refuse to let him win.

'You're forgetting one thing about me.'

'Really? What's that?'

'I'm a woman. And women never give in. Women always survive.'

With one push, I reach him. From behind my back, I bring out the knife I'd grabbed, and I plunge it into his stomach.

He falls back against the door and looks down in shock.

I pull it out.

He slaps his hand to the wound where the blood is escaping. He looks up at me.

I'm crying. And I can't stop.

I fucking hate you.

I stab him again.

Worse Than Murder

'I fucking hate you,' I scream.
And again.
'I. Fucking. Hate. You.'
And again.

I don't remember much after that.
　　I remember being on the floor of Lynne's kitchen, crying my eyes out, really bawling my head off. The knife is in my bloodied hands. Alison is holding me in her arms. She's telling me it's all over.

'I'm sorry,' I'm screaming. 'I'm so sorry.'

I repeat the same words over and over again.

'I'm so sorry I couldn't save you.'

'We need to get her to a hospital,' someone says.

'The ambulance is on its way.'

'What will happen to her?'

'I've no idea.'

'I can't get her to stop crying, Gill.'

'Just keep hold of her. The ambulance will be here soon. They might have to sedate her. She's in shock.'

'Matilda, it's Alison. I've got you. You're all right. You're safe. Everything's all right.'

'I'm sorry. I'm sorry. I'm sorry. I'm sorry. I'm sorry.'

I can feel Alison's arms around me.

I can feel Adele's arms around me.

I can feel my mum's arms around me.

I call round to Alison's cottage for the first time since that shocking night. It seems like an age has passed when I ring the bell. At the same time, it feels like it was only yesterday.

I'm in a great deal of pain, still. My ribs are bruised, and I have a broken wrist. My black eyes have faded, but my hands look like I've been sparring with a heavyweight boxer. And lost.

Alison opens the door. She smiles and beckons me to enter. Lynne has moved out of the farmhouse. It's up for sale – house, land, paddocks, the lot. She's moved in with her daughter, but it's only temporary as Alison has put her house on the market, too. A fresh start is required for these two amazing women as they try to rebuild their lives and discover who they both really are.

Lynne isn't here. She's struggling to come to terms with everything that has happened, the fact she wasn't living, merely existing, for thirty years in a coercive relationship. The man she thought she loved, the man who had saved her, had been lying, manipulating and manufacturing her entire life. She's struggling for answers and each answer leads to more questions. Today, she's in Kendal seeing her therapist. It's a long road to recovery, but she has determination. She'll get there in the end.

'Thank you for the flowers,' Alison says as she brings me a mug of tea.

'You're welcome.'

Yesterday had been Celia and Jennifer's funeral. As much as the whole village had wanted to turn out to say goodbye, Lynne and Alison wanted it to be private. As the twins were buried, at the graveside stood the surviving mother and daughter alongside Tania Pritchard, Lionel Bell and Claire Daniels, fully recovered and holding onto her stomach firmly. She still wasn't showing much, but she wanted to protect her unborn child more than anything.

'Tania told me it was a beautiful service.'

'It was. The sun shone. There wasn't a cloud in the sky or a hint of breeze. It was perfect.'

'How's Lynne doing?'

'She's getting there. Yesterday really helped. I'm worried the court case is going to draw it all out.'

Lynne is facing a charge of arson and endangering life. Her defence is coercive control and while she is on police bail rather than on remand, the thought of a lengthy court case and a jury deciding her fate isn't one she, or Alison, are coping particularly well with.

'And how are you?'

'Surprisingly, I'm doing okay. I think. My answer to that question changes depending on which day I'm asked,' she says with a weak smile. 'I've unlocked thirty years of pain and it's a relief.' She looks brighter, lighter, for the first time since I met her. Today is clearly a good day. 'How are you?'

'I'm getting there.' It's the most honest answer I can give. 'It hurts when I cough and sneeze still. And laugh. And breathe,' I smile. 'Tania tells me you're staying with the police.'

'Yes. For now. I'm going to see how it goes. We're looking at properties around Lancaster, maybe Preston. I've got so many friends here. I don't want to be too far away, but I think I want something more than High Chapel can offer. I'm going to take things slowly.'

'Good for you.'

'Inspector Forsyth was telling me there won't be any charges laid against you for what happened with Iain.'

'No. I've dodged a bullet there. Has Gill said anything about…?' I leave the question hanging.

'It's a slow process, obviously. It's taken him a while to recover from being stabbed five times, but he's admitted more or less everything,' Alison said, clearing her throat. 'He's got a solicitor and he's trying to blame diminished responsibility. I'm going to fight him all the way. Mum and Claire, too.'

'It's made you stronger, all this, hasn't it?'

'Tania told me that what doesn't kill you makes you stronger. I didn't always believe it. I think I do now.' She takes a sip of her tea. 'Matilda, about that night… when Gill and I came to the house and you…'

'Lost it,' I finish her sentence for her. 'I know exactly what happened. Gill practically broke her neck to give me all the details. I'm going to sort things out before I make any big life changes. I've learned that it's fine to run away, make a clean break of things, but you need to sort out your problems before you do so. I know a good therapist. He'll see me right.' I'm smiling so wide it hurts, and it has nothing to do with my bruises.

We sip our tea in silence.

From Alison's cottage, I go to End Lane where Lionel Bell is sitting in his armchair with his daughter, Gill, on the sofa next to him and Tania on the opposing armchair. I'm the last to arrive. I've no idea why I'm there, but something tells me I'm going to want to hear what Lionel has to say.

'I did steal that money,' he says, not looking at anyone, his gaze fixed firmly on the carpet.

Gill slaps a hand to her mouth, though I think she already knew about the money. Tania looks shocked, disappointed.

'I have no excuse. I could say it was a moment of weakness, but the fact is I needed it. It's as simple as that.'

I clear my throat. 'Iain knew, didn't he? He said he'd keep your secret if you removed Travis's statement about the missing car, which you did, yet he still leaked your secret. He discredited your reputation.'

Lionel nods. 'I couldn't prove Iain killed the twins, but I had my suspicions. If I'd told anyone, nobody would have believed me.'

'You could have told me, Dad,' Gill says. 'I would have helped you in any way I could.'

'No, you couldn't. I was protecting you, too.'

'What are you talking about?'

'Jason Marley.'

'Oh, God.' Gill visibly baulked at the mention of the name.

'Who's Jason Marley?' I ask.

Lionel looks at her daughter. Eventually, she nods, gives him the go-ahead to continue.

'Jason Marley was a bad lad. Always in trouble,' Lionel says. 'Gill here was going through her teenage rebellious stage and was following him around like a lap-dog. I tried to get her to see sense, but it seemed that, the more I objected, the more she carried on seeing him. He broke into a warehouse in Kendal one night, battered a security guard, put him in hospital. Gill was his alibi, saying he was with her all night. It was a lie, but there was nothing I could do to stop her. The charges against Jason were dropped. He got away with it.'

'So, what's that got to do with Iain?'

Gill looks at me. 'Iain saw me the night of the robbery. Jason had stood me up. I was angry. He was always standing me up. I went to sit by the lake with a bottle of WKD Blue to drown my sorrows. I didn't see Iain, but he clearly saw me.'

'Iain waited until the charges were dropped,' Lionel says. 'Then he walked into the station and told me Gill had lied for Marley.'

'I split up with Jason for good after that. I realised I was wasting my time. That's when I joined the police.'

'But Iain has constantly been dropping snide remarks ever since,' Lionel says. 'I couldn't say anything about it, or he would ruin her, too. I didn't mind him ruining me, but not Gill. She didn't deserve that.'

I turn to look at Tania. She's staring straight at Lionel, but she doesn't have the hard, embittered face of a newshound: she's looking at him with love and affection. Lionel has been living with pain and torment for thirty years. He's suffered in silence. Despite the fact he stole money from a dead man, he's more than made up for it by protecting his daughter under the cruel iron fist of an evil manipulator.

'Gill, can I have a word with you outside?' I ask her.

'Sure.'

We get up and leave. We walk down the steps and onto End Lane. The sun is high in the sky, not a cloud in sight. I turn and look to the sprawling view. This really is a beautiful village.

'What did you want to talk to me about?'

I glance over my shoulder into Lionel's living room, and I see him and Tania embracing. They pull apart and she kisses him softly on the lips.

'It's doesn't matter,' I say.

I'm not allowed to drive Adele's Porsche anymore. I'm banned. We drive to the pyre that used to be Nature's Diner. What meagre belongings that could be salvaged are in boxes and black bags and piled into the back of Philip's car. He looks up at the charred building.

'I don't feel anything,' he says to me as he turns his back on it. 'It's just bricks and mortar, isn't it?'

'I've always said home isn't a building,' Sally begins. 'It's the people inside it that make a home. When Carl was kidnapped, I realised then that the dream house we'd built wasn't what I wanted. I'd have been happy living in a tent for the rest of my life as long as I had Carl with me.'

Carl is running around the grounds with both Woodys, allowing them to shake off any excess energy and empty their bladders. They have a long journey ahead of them.

They're heading to Ireland where Sally's sister, Beth, lives. She called her the day after the fire, once her voice had returned from the effects of smoke inhalation, and asked if they could come and visit for a few weeks while they decided what to do next. The next day, Beth called back and told her she knew of a catering school in Wicklow that was up for sale.

It ran courses teaching adults the basic cookery skills. There was a house attached to the school and a couple of acres of land.

Sally was keen to buy without even looking at it. Philip was more pragmatic, but seemed excited by the idea. The only one not looking forward to moving to Ireland was Carl, but Sally had said he could have a third dog with all that space, if he wanted one. On the way to Ireland, they were stopping off at kennels to pick up a golden Labrador puppy Carl had chosen and wanted to call Woody.

'Three dogs called Woody. Really?' I ask.

'His happiness is paramount,' Philip says. 'I don't know how many thirteen-year-olds could have been through as much horror as he has and still be laughing and enjoying himself.'

We watch as Carl bounds around with the dogs.

'I'm so sorry this ended like it did,' I say, looking back at the charred remains of the restaurant.

'It wasn't your fault,' Philip says. 'Whether you'd come here or not, Iain would still have tried to stop the body being discovered. And if you hadn't been here, you wouldn't have taken the cartridges out of that gun, and I would be dead right now.'

Sally shivers. 'It doesn't bear thinking about, does it?'

'I can't believe how evil and manipulative he was, and for so long,' Adele says.

'He was full of hatred and loathing from a young age. He resented his brother for having everything he felt he should have had,' I say.

'Do you think they'll ever find Travis?' Philip asks.

'I doubt it. Iain has no reason to reveal the location of his body. It's his only trump card.'

'Bastard,' Philip says under his breath.

'You'll come to Ireland to see us, won't you?' Sally asks.

'Do you really want me to, after all this?'

'Of course.'

'You'd better come,' Carl chimes up.

I turn around to look at him. 'Once you're settled, let me know, and I'll come over.'

'You mean it?'

'Have I ever broken a promise I've made to you?'

'No.'

'There you go, then.'

'Come on, we'd better be heading off before we get caught up in all that traffic,' Philip says.

We all hug and say our goodbyes.

'I'm going to miss you so much,' Carl whispers in my ear as he wraps his arms around me.

'I'm going to miss you, too. Be good to your parents, however many dogs you end up getting. I'm at the end of the phone whenever you need me.'

He pushes himself out of my embrace. 'You could move to Ireland with us. Mum says your family is Irish. You could return to your roots.'

I smile. 'It's a good idea, Carl. I'll give it some thought. Go on, don't keep your mum and dad waiting.'

We wave them off, both with tears in our eyes.

'I'm going to miss them,' I say.

Adele puts her arm around me and squeezes me tight. 'They're a good family. We'll go and visit them very soon.'

'I'd like that.'

'In the meantime,' Adele says. She links arms with me, and we turn and walk away from the wreckage of the restaurant. 'What are you going to do next? As snug as it is in Tania's cluttered house, I think we're very close to outstaying our welcome.'

'Speaking of Tania.' I take my phone from my back pocket and open an email. 'She sent me a mock-up of the next edition of her paper.' I hand it to Adele.

WHAT TO DO IN CUMBRIA THIS SUMMER. PAGES 12 & 13

Cumbria Today

Thursday 8 July, 2021 — £1.10

HERO DETECTIVE SOLVES 30YR MURDER

SHOCKING TWIST IN MISSING PEMBERTON TWINS CASE

The infamous case of missing twins Celia and Jennifer Pemberton has plagued the sleepy village of High Chapel for almost thirty years. Now, it has finally been solved by DCI Matilda Darke from South Yorkshire Police. Her investigations have unearthed shocking police corruption, sexual abuse and coercive control by one of the village's most respected residents.

In an exclusive interview, Ms Darke, 42, gives us a step by step account of how she single-handedly solved a crime nobody else could.

Photo to Follow

DCI Matilda Darke

FULL SHOCKING STORY PAGES 3, 4, 5, 6

'Tania's asked me for a slutty photo.'

'Do you have a slutty photo?'

'I have one of me wearing a Sarah Lund sweater.'

'Ooh, chunky knitwear, very slutty. And what's this? Forty-two? Really?'

'You don't think I can get away with forty-two?'

She looks me up and down. 'You're going to need a lot of Vaseline on that camera lens.'

I snatch my phone back and pocket it. 'I'm not sure how Gill is going to take all this. I doubt Tania is going to mention her once in the article.'

'What's going to happen to Gill's father?'

'I'm not sure. He sat on the secret for thirty years that Iain blackmailed him into removing Travis's statement. Lionel's name was blackened throughout the village when it came out. If he had said Iain coerced him, nobody would have believed him.'

'Pemberton truly is an evil bastard. I can feel my blood boiling just thinking about him. Anyway.' Adele puts her arm through mine again. 'Let's confine Iain to the pages of history. Hopefully, he'll get a long sentence and he'll fade away a lonely and broken man.'

'Hope so.'

'And what are you going to do now? Are we heading back to Sheffield?'

I take a deep breath. I don't say anything.

'You need to find out the truth, Matilda. You need to discover who killed your family. That way, you can move on and rebuild your life.'

'I know.'

'So… what now?'

'A cup of coffee and a piece of chocolate cake,' I smile.

'And after the coffee and cake?'

'After the coffee and cake, I'll give Sian a ring and ask her to pop over to the house and put the heater on. I want it to be nice and warm for when we get back home.'

We head off into the village. There's a spring in my step. My mind is clear for the first time in a long while and I know exactly what I'm going to do next. I'm going back to Sheffield. I'm going to find the man who murdered my family.

And I'm going to kill him.

To be continued in
FIRST ONE TO DIE
Autumn 2026

Acknowledgments

Worse Than Murder is the thirteenth novel in the DCI Matilda Darke series and is being released ten years after the first. I sometimes have to take a step back and remind myself that writing is my full-time job. I genuinely feel lucky to be able to do this for a living and I'm incredibly grateful to so many people who have helped me along the way, not just for this book, but over the past ten years.

My agent, Jamie Cowen at Ampersand, is my champion. When times get tough, he's there in minutes to give me the guidance, confidence, and encouragement I need.

Everyone at my publisher, One More Chapter (HarperCollins), are superstars. Jennie Rothwell, in particular, works tirelessly on every single book and I am so proud and grateful that she works on mine. A huge thank you, as well, to Charlotte Ledger, Kara Daniel, Simon Fox and Lucy Bennett. I would also like to add a special thank you to all the previous editors on my Matilda Darke series – Kate Stephenson, Lucy Dauman, Finn Cotton and Bethan Morgan.

For this book, I had help from Peter Faulding at Specialist Group International (SGI) who imparted his knowledge on underwater search, rescue and retrieval. Thank you for taking time out of your busy schedule to answer my questions. Any errors within this book are all mine to fit the narrative of the story. His book *What Lies Beneath* is a must read.

Over the past ten years, I have built up a strong team of people who are always on hand to help me with the technical details of a crime thriller. I could not have written these books without the help of Philip Lumb, Simon Browes, Andy Barrett and "Mr Tidd". You are my Avengers.

Writing can be a lonely job. It helps to have people in the background to keep you sane. Well, as sane as you can be in this bonkers world. A huge thank you to my mum, Chris, Kevin, Jonas and Chris for their support and pitch-dark humour.

I also want to thank Trevor Wood and Barnaby Walter for the chats and the moans about anything and everything, and an apology to Scott Burdon for misspelling his name when I originally thanked him last time.

Finally, the book sellers, the librarians and the readers. I wouldn't have a job without any of you. Your support literally means the world to me.

Now, onto book fourteen. Spoiler: this one is going to hurt. Mwah-ha-ha.

The author and One More Chapter would like to thank everyone who contributed to the publication of this story...

Analytics
Imogen Wolstencroft

Audio
Fionnuala Barrett
Ciara Briggs

Contracts
Laura Amos
Inigo Vyvyan

Design
Lucy Bennett
Fiona Greenway
Liane Payne
Dean Russell

Digital Sales
Laura Daley
Lydia Grainge
Hannah Lismore

eCommerce
Laura Carpenter
Madeline ODonovan
Charlotte Stevens
Christina Storey
Jo Surman
Rachel Ward

Editorial
Kara Daniel
CJ Harter
Charlotte Ledger
Jennie Rothwell
Sofia Salazar Studer
Caroline Scott-Bowden
Helen Williams

Harper360
Emily Gerbner
Ariana Juarez
Jean Marie Kelly
emma sullivan
Sophia Wilhelm

International Sales
Peter Borcsok
Ruth Burrow
Bethan Moore
Colleen Simpson

Inventory
Sarah Callaghan
Kirsty Norman

Marketing & Publicity
Chloe Cummings
Grace Edwards
Katie Sadler

Operations
Melissa Okusanya
Hannah Stamp

Production
Denis Manson
Simon Moore
Francesca Tuzzeo

Rights
Ashton Mucha
Alisah Saghir
Zoe Shine
Aisling Smyth
Lucy Vanderbilt

Trade Marketing
Ben Hurd
Eleanor Slater

The HarperCollins Distribution Team

The HarperCollins Finance & Royalties Team

The HarperCollins Legal Team

The HarperCollins Technology Team

UK Sales
Isabel Coburn
Jay Cochrane
Sabina Lewis
Holly Martin
Harriet Williams
Leah Woods

And every other essential link in the chain from delivery drivers to booksellers to librarians and beyond!

One More Chapter is an award-winning global division of HarperCollins.

Subscribe to our newsletter to get our latest eBook deals and stay up to date with all our new releases!

signup.harpercollins.co.uk/
join/signup-omc

Meet the team at
www.onemorechapter.com

Follow us!

@onemorechapterhc

Do you write unputdownable fiction?
We love to hear from new voices.
Find out how to submit your novel at
www.onemorechapter.com/submissions